YOU'RE NOT DEAD

YOU'RE NOT DEAD

THE MIDNIGHT BOOKS
VOLUME 1

A NOVEL BY

GEOFF WARD

GARN PRESS

NEW YORK NY

Published by Garn Press, LLC
New York, NY
www.garnpress.com

Book and cover design by Benjamin J. Taylor
Cover artwork by Shelton Walsmith

Library of Congress Control Number: 2015952158

Publisher's Cataloging-in-Publication Data

Ward, Geoff, 1954-
    You're not dead / Geoff Ward.
       pages cm. – (The midnight books, vol. 1)
    ISBN: 978-1-942146-29-2 (pbk.)
    ISBN: 978-1-942146-28-5 (hardcover)
    ISBN: 978-1-942146-30-8 (e-book)
    1. Quests (Expeditions)—Fiction. 2. Time travel—
Fiction. 3. Magic—Fiction. 4. Black humor. 5. Fantasy
fiction.   I. Title. II. Series: The midnight books.
PR6123.A73 Y68 2015
823—dc23
                              2015952158

For Minnie

Contents

Prologue

- You can't come in. You're not dead.

- What the hell do you mean, I'm not dead? Look at me!

- That's a lethal head injury. I can see where you're coming from. But your name's not on the Guest List. And if your name's not on the list, one, you can't come in, and two, it means you're not dead. Dead's dead. You ain't.

- Gis a break, pal. What do I have to do, to get dead? Come on, if you've got the beans, spill. Or can I –

Something resembling a smile passed over what remained of his face, a broken gravestone briefly touched by moonlight. Suppressing his natural instincts, he placed his hands quite tenderly on the lapels of the tuxedo barring his way, realizing that for once that he was going to have to rely on wheedling and ingenuity, rather than violence.

- Can I have a second go? You know, get born, be a wean, grow up – live life to the full. Savour the moment, do all the things I used to enjoy – shotguns, bank jobs, grievous bodily harm? Maybe do them better, now I've had some practice?

- You're in transition. It happens. I can't say which way you're headed – sorry, that was an unfortunate choice

"

of…

- *Let us in, mate. We've been standing here for hours.*

The queue of dead people began to grow restive. A second tuxedo appeared from behind the gigantic iron door, yelling All right, all right! Natural causes form a second line! Unnatural, stay where you are!

The first doorman smiled absently, though his own dead eyes showed no emotion.

- Actually, he hasn't. Been standing here for hours. There's no time, down here. It's an illusion. He's stuck in his old ways of thinking.

- Spare me the philosophy, son. I want to see the manager. I *demand* to see the manager.

- On your own head be it. What remains of it. Sorry.

Tuxedo one winced and stepped aside. A curl of grey smoke that might just have been dry ice could be seen, as the huge black door to the Night Club swung slightly ajar.

Milestones

1

The College Librarian was sitting well back in his swivel chair, reflecting and tapping his teeth at intervals with the eraser-tipped end of a college-badged pencil. Sighing, he leaned forwards, and let the latter day stylus drop graphite first into a huge and ornate teacup. This strange receptacle served him not only as a pencil, but as pen, rubber band, small change and just about everything else bowl, after he had brought it back in triumph from a trip to Luxor, only to discover that boiled water made even the handle of the cup too hot to hold.

Around the lip ran a frieze, depicting many colourful and appropriate hieroglyphs, including an image of the Egyptian jackal-god of the dead, Anubis, who, in this instance at least, wore a cheerful expression suggestive of a can-do attitude. The Librarian searched in his breast pocket for a little red cloth which, having breathed on and steamed up the lenses, he applied to his glasses. He then got up and walked towards the whiteness of the faux-Japanese faux-window. This he did silently, a lifelong trait. Spendrift had at one time been viewed as a serious cricketing prospect, not that he himself took sport, at least team sports, all that seriously. The thickly Brylcreemed hair, unfashionable currently, perhaps always, bestowed on his head an ottery sleekness remarked on sometimes by others when not in his hearing. His office suits, tweed in winter and, as now, linen for summer, gave nothing away. The heavy black frames of the glasses allowed him to see out, none to see in.

Silently weighing alternatives, the Librarian stared for a while into the blankness of the blind. Moving more purposefully back to the desktop computer, he drummed his fingers in a brisk tattoo, and reached a decision regarding the email that lay open on his screen. The contents of this email concerned another email, which in turn concerned a book.

The book had a bit of a history. Published in 1895, anonymously, it was said to bring together a cornucopia of legends, spells and arcane lore originating in several European countries across a period spanning three centuries, newly translated into English for the cognoscenti. More than just a history of the occult, this was a book which, it was claimed, could literally teach its reader how to perform acts of serious Magic. To the Librarian, the several European countries-and-centuries stuff smacked of a rhetorical flourish. No: this exotic was the hothouse growth of a distinct time and a particular place. One where magicians, warlocks, hierophants of the Tarot and other self-proclaimed experts in the dark arts were springing up like toadstools. London. The London of the gas-lit and opiated 1890s, the decadent *fin-de-siècle*.

The book belonged, as fugitive sparkles of water belong to a wave, to the vogue for Oscar Wilde, whose career collapsed in scandal; to the circles that included his friend, Ernest Dowson, writer of verses as immaculate as his penchant for pubescent girls was not, so much a creature of the Nineties that he died on cue in 1900 at the age of thirty, as if unable to bear the bursting of his magical, tainted bubble; and to the time of Aubrey Beardsley's voluptuous satires in black ink, his Pans and fauns, impossibly curvaceous nymphs, and massively-endowed grotesques. Time of the *danse macabre* of masks and mimicry, transgression and theatricality; above all, the time of Magic. Two hundred copies of this resplendent, peacock volume had been printed – on vellum, with a Japanese rice-paper cover, virtually transparent, yet fashioned so as to contain incredibly intricate coloured threads, pulsing veins stitched in by hand.

Only a handful of copies, perhaps as few as two or three, survived their birth. The rest were destroyed in a cellar flood at the printers in the terrible winter of 1895, before the book could be delivered to the publisher. One of the survivors sat in the British Library, in the Reserved Section. Or at least it was supposed to. On the first occasion that John Spendrift had asked to see it, he who was now Librarian of Beltane College London, but at that stage an untenured history scholar of the late Victorian period, flustered and apologetic staff had been temporarily unable to locate the desired item. Two subsequent attempts to peruse the book were thwarted, one by an uncharacteristic attack of dizziness in the Tea Rooms, one by a power cut. Almost inevitably, the Library declared their copy of *Transmutations* mislaid, consigning the title after a decent interval to their Missing Presumed Lost file.

Of the two remaining copies of the fugitive volume, one was thought to have made it into the twentieth century, only to vanish from view along with its collector-owner, a voyager aboard the *Titanic*. Spendrift had begun to think in an amused way that his attempts to land this particular volume were doomed, and so had abandoned the quest. And, it had to be admitted that, although in itself extremely rare, this was hardly the only title of its *kind* from that period. Magic, along with sexual experiment, drugs and the paranormal, was pretty much the Nineties' norm.

Having duly succeeded in completing his PhD dissertation, John Spendrift had then duly failed to land a university lectureship. Sadly for him, these were the years of the freeze on university posts engineered by Mrs Thatcher, under whose spell Britain had fallen. Mrs Thatcher hated intellectuals. And coalminers. And, come to that, most other people, apart from Chilean dictators. Forlorn, Spendrift sank into the public sector, intent like many on keeping his head down. But once in that posture he became absorbed in what had, as it unfolded, become an unexpectedly rewarding career as a university librarian.

Nevertheless, the desire to one day get a sighting of the book still tugged at him, even after all these years. From time to time a new piece of the puzzle would float his way via a footnote, via some story in the press, or from the international hunter-gathering of librarians, a more intrepid tribe than Spendrift had assumed before winning admittance to their inner circle. The third copy was known to have passed through the hands of several notable owners. Moreover, it was said to be cursed.

The Earl of Montcalm, its first owner, lost his fortune, his wits and finally the will to live, after a fire destroyed the family seat, leaving him bereft of almost everything except the book, which he had locked in an octagonal tower in a secluded corner of the grounds. A grieving daughter kept this final memento of her father under glass.

Following her own swift demise it vanished, only to resurface in the hands of the Great Beast himself, Aleister Crowley, called by the *Daily Mail* the wickedest man in the world, who, it was rumoured, had put the book to practical use during rituals of unparalleled debauchery at his temple on the island of Cephalu. According to the memoirs of a disenchanted acolyte, Crowley came eventually to believe that the book 'went too far', and wished he had never acquired it, blaming his subsequent decline into poverty on an unlucky misinterpretation of certain formulae he had plucked from it.

Singed, and, it has to be said, rather unpleasantly stained, this copy had eventually found its way into the possession of latter day rock god Felix Manto. The guitarist singer-songwriter had perished in the later 1990s, trembling like a would-be suicide on the ledge of a new century, like the poet Dowson unable to contemplate the *fin* of his own particular *siècle*. A famously loud musician – indeed, the founding father of Nouveau Thrash – Manto had reverted by this point to a more pensive and blues-inflected style, particularly on his final album, *Trouble in Mind*. The lyrics of the last track, *Cry Like the Wind*, encoded sternly growled warnings on the subject of whiskey-headed women, women in general, birth in the Delta, death at the crossroads, and a certain occult treatise published in London in 1895 in a very limited edition with a fragile but intricate rice-paper cover - all of which the singer deemed likely to bring nothing but bad luck and trouble. Reviewers carped about rocking chairs, bourbon, and panned it. Inevitably, Manto's abrupt retirement following this final recording was blamed by his core admirers on the book, even more so his drowning in the icy waters of Loch Soutar, of whose surrounding estate he had only recently paid to become Laird, snared in his own lines while fishing for salmon by the fitful guidance of moonlight, high on crack.

But now the book was back. The only copy left in the world – and, to the amazement of this jaded Librarian, for sale. Miles Proctor, a young lecturer in English Literature at Beltane and a budding expert on the 1890s, had been about to delete as spam an email from something calling itself Redidivus Books of Fiddlers Court, London, but on idly opening it had found a genuine bookseller's catalogue of the older sort, listing soberly and for sale the contents of the late Mr Manto's library of gymnastically impossible pornography, grimoires, Teutonic woodcuts depicting (somewhat repetitively) the tortures of the damned, Crowleyan and other antiquarian fungi. One item stood out, even in this lurid treasure-trove.

As the asking price stood at about the same level as the entire annual library grant allocated to the English Department at Beltane College, Miles Proctor was pleading for financial assistance. John Spendrift had now decided he should have it. For one thing, what were Beltane's aspirations to be a leading research centre and not just a holding-tank for spotty undergraduates really worth, if, once in a while, the College couldn't splash out on a real find? Perhaps more importantly, the scholar in Spendrift that Margaret Thatcher had never quite succeeded in strangling wanted to read this book. Hold it, simply, after all this time. Proctor would get his wish. And Beltane would get the book.

2

Making his way from the Charing Cross tube, Miles Proctor had paced the length of Fiddlers Court twice before managing to locate the narrow doorway and discoloured brass plate on which he could just pick out the legend, Redidivus Books. It seemed strange that a bookshop in the heart of London should open only in the evening. And who, for heaven's sake, and in this day and age, in the heart of London, still had a bell-pull? Handling it gingerly, in expectation that the rope would either snap and fall around his shoulders like a dusty snake, or jerk him high into the air, the young man took a deep breath, and pulled.

Several minutes and a steep climb later, he was sitting opposite a balding and corpulent individual in late middle age, face the colour of putty, who, balancing his fingertips on pinstriped knees as if about to execute a virtuoso keyboard piece, leaned forward to impart unwelcome news.

- The book, I am sorry to say, indeed I am *ashamed* to say, is sold, sir.

- *Sold?* You said you would keep it for me. I'm buying on behalf of Beltane College.

- I know, sir. I am aware of the order of events from which, unfortunately, we have on this occasion, this *final* occasion, had to depart. Mr Winthrope, the owner of the business… The fact is, the rents have shot up since the early Nineties and are frankly crippling us. Mr Winthrope was on the point of selling up and retiring when we published that last catalogue, where you came across the item that the College is keen to acquire. But then, out of the blue, after your approach, he was offered…a startling sum, it is fair to say, enough to buy a little time and settle certain… The upshot is that Mr Winthrope, against our customary practice sir, *against the grain,* to tell you the truth, sold it.

-   Can I ask who the new buyer is?

The bookseller hesitated, then rose and moved to the window, seeming to look for an answer in London's maze of alleyways, tourist traps, rooftops and riverside rendezvous, that would never be beautiful but always be seductive, the finest old flame to those moth-minds drawn by mysteries.

-   I see no harm in your knowing. In any case, we have been overtaken by events. Mr Winthrope took a phone call from New York, from a bookseller called Mysteries of Gotham, on behalf of a private individual. You should know that Mr Winthrope is unwell. He has not been in the best of health for some years, but lately he has taken a turn for the worse, markedly for the worse, sir. We have this grace period to…tidy our affairs. But we are closing down. We are out of the game. And there will be an end to it.

The morose bookseller turned and looked Miles in the eye. Behind him the sallow light of early evening in the capital was beginning to fade into day's end. One long lank strand of hair had strayed; this he carefully pulled back across his balding pate in a doomed attempt to suggest full tonsorial coverage. As the light faded further he became a silhouette. Behind him in the city beyond the window, doors that had stood open would soon close, become tombs for the night. Others, locked enigmas hating sunshine, would open their jaws once this yellow light had died.

- We have not dealt with you fairly and squarely. So. It
  hardly matters now, to be frank, whether payment for
  the book comes in or not. If I were you, I might give
  Mysteries of Gotham a call. Flip, sir.

- I beg your pardon?

- Flip. Ask for Flip.

3

Impatient at the five-hour time lag, Miles telephoned from College the following afternoon. In the background he could distantly
catch the classic New York dissonance of jostling yellow cabs and
nasal East Coast accents, the sirens and sounds of a livelier life. He
asked for Flip.

- We surely do. You can have it, Professor, for the amount
  you would have paid if the original deal had gone
  through. The collector who wanted the book has just
  gone and died. I wouldn't want a rare item like that to
  get lost in the hands of lawyers and stuff to do with the
  estate. It might disappear, and never resurface. It needs
  a good home where it will be cherished by people who
  know what they're doing, what they've laid their hands
  on. Only thing is… Peggy, I told you, *not* over there, over
  there…sorry Professor Proctor. I don't want to mail it.
  I don't know if it was damaged in transit, or if the catalogue description was what you might term optimistic,
  but this item has lived a little. The spine's gotten kind of
  loose. I don't wanna be the one to open it right now. It
  might make things worse. *Very* rare book, though. Of
  course you know the history. Do you want to come over
  and get it? Do you have any reason to come to New York?

Get the book, Miles. Do it, for the College. That was all Spend-rift had said to him in response to the tale of woe from Fiddlers Court. And, *Yes*, thought Miles. Damn it. I have *every* reason to want to come to New York. The chief reason is that I am twenty nine years old, nearly thirty, and I have never visited the United States of America, let alone New York. His scholar's conscience (which dozed amiably for the most part, but which could spring into hyper-alertness when summoned by its master's self-interest) assured Miles that his annual research allowance remained largely unspent, and whispered to his inner ear reminders of items in the New York Public Library of huge interest to a scholar of the 1890s - not to mention the extensive holdings at Columbia and indeed New York University itself. Of course he would go. He *must* go. It would be wasteful not to.

On the way back to his flat, Miles dropped by a very different sort of bookshop, and purchased a Rough Guide to New York. Mysteries of Gotham, which he had pictured as some elegant brownstone gracing a tree-lined avenue on the Upper West Side, turned out to be located in the bohemian redoubt of Greenwich Village. And where was he going to bed down? The New York hotel tariffs made his eyes water. Riffling the deck of his Guide he found a reference to something called the Paramount, nearer Penn Station than the Village, but seemingly the only hostelry charging less than two hundred dollars a night. The name rang a bell. Miles had been regaled with anecdotes about this section of Midtown by his lugubrious Head of Department, Professor Transom, who, rolling his eyes, had intoned *Lead us not into Penn Station but deliver us from evil*, and announced, shaking his grey head in disbelief, that he had been forced to check out of the Paramount virtually on arrival some months earlier, on discovering that the place was full of, quote-unquote, pop musicians, creatures of the catwalk, and worse. Hoping for a glimpse or even a taste of worse, Miles dialled, purchased, packed, flew, and checked in.

4

The Paramount Hotel did not disappoint. It was the real thing – though quite what that thing really was, would be hard to say precisely. Once Miles' credentials had been given the once over by one of the smiling musclemen in identikit Armani who ran the show – another stood studiously placing dozens of single roses into tiny silver holders secreted in the walls of the atrium - he was assailed by a blizzard of colours. Trying to the eyes of the weary but excited traveller, the lobby sofas gave off acid green or yellow luminosity, their huge cushions alternately swelling and drooping, priapically engorged, vaguely extraterrestrial. Meanwhile the main staircase lunged dizzyingly upwards at strange angles as if trying to shake off the rest of the building, something out of a funfair or early German cinema. Helpfully, the weather forecast for the day appeared as tiny lettering in the tall mirrors that adorned each floor, but less helpfully, disappeared at once.

On inspecting his room, Miles finally located the TV at the head end of a mock-Egyptian sarcophagus, while every item of bathroom furnishing was, courtesy of designer Philippe Starck, sculpted so as to resemble a bucket. On first making use of the facilities Miles had to think quite hard, as if bumped forward to senility or returned at cartoon speed to a version of early childhood, about which part of his anatomy to bring into the proximity of which bucket, and for what precise purpose. In the immortal words of Felix Manto, *Didn't know where I was, not for one minute./ But I knew I was there.* The only disappointing thing was the view from the bedroom of a blank high wall inches from the glass, though even this fitted, on reflection. Because at the end of the day it was all a set, Miles thought to himself. A set with walk-in facsimiles, false fronts and cul-de-sacs. Smiling at the wall, he raised a brief toast in his mind. To me. To that suddenly friendly Librarian. To the Big Apple, not that any of the locals seem to use that phrase. Then he slept.

After baptism by full immersion in the cheerfully garish Paramount,

New York the morning after was, for all its carnival overload, pretty much as he had expected. Horns in cabs scolded, steam swore through grilles, while neon texted subliminal info-burns onto the retina. Beautiful young women in office attire bottomed off with sneakers hovered on the cusp of WALK/ DON'T WALK, tall coffees carried like hunting spears. Men wore funereal black, and smoked like it was still the 1950s. Chinese and Italian blurred into more recondite cuisines, failing to cut out something oddly chemical which, even above ground, Miles took to be essence of subway.

He felt a need to pull it all down into the lowest stratum of his lungs, as if what he was breathing and seeing was a perversely healthy way to zap any English, any residual timidities. He wanted to be cool, to be hip. His helicopter-view of his still young (just about young, anyway) self, was that he was, to cut his modestly short story shorter, not. Not cool. One of the Unhip. Already, on his first morning in New York, the ubiquitous mirrors of the Paramount had told him that his height, respectably over six feet, still located him in the gangling rather than the imposing category, and that dark glasses only made longer and straighter what was, though by no means an ugly nose, definitely a long, straight organ. Positively Pinocchioid. Salt and pepper hair he had in abundance, but silently hoped as he peered into each morning's mirror that the pepper would continue to win out.

Miles prayed for Manhattan to spare a little of its style, for him; a dash of its stardust, to save him from the sin of excessive fastidiousness. Just as testing to the personality in its subtle way as alcohol or hard drugs was the addiction, endemic in university life, to ever finer distinctions. He knew this. But Miles also knew that there were things he didn't know.

Big Apple. The golden apples of the sun. What was that other line. Yeats? The silver apples of the moon. The lunar apples flickered in Miles' consciousness, but were shrivelled to dust by full-on Manhattan, blaring to its own satisfaction that all apples of knowledge, of good and of evil, had been fully digested a long time ago and the pips spat out in this burg. So what did that leave? Maybe, even in its breath-taking vitality, this spit of land, stolen with beads from the Indians, was now just the carnival of commerce. It hadn't taken him long to realize just how effectively this slickest of cities slid those green slips of paper out of your wallet, their evergreen sameness of colour, be it a twenty, a ten, or one, somehow implying that a twenty pretty much was a one, right? Same dimensions. Back in Heathrow Airport, changing currency, Miles had paused, taking in the sheer whackiness of the One. Cornerstone of Western civilization, the dollar bill, featured a cyclopean eye floating and throwing out rays of light above a headless pyramid. What *was* all that about? George Washington shaking hands or tentacles with HP Lovecraft, somewhere down at the crossroads, in a Masonic lodge or on Mars.

But there remained, somewhere interior to this blizzard of noise, a concept of cool. It was there in the blank and hardened unread-ability with which New Yorkers themselves seemed to stare it all down and stay unmoved, a kind of zombie chic. Using it to gain strength. Not to be confused with the musclemen. More like the Velvet Underground era Lou Reed, all shades and poetic pallor, before he started to resemble a bug-eyed karate teacher berating a rheumatic class of seniors. A wall-like passivity. That was it – if you are staying in a movie set, become part of the set. Be your own wall, show a false front.

The false front glided south, past the sex shops, the theatres, the Church of Scientology, and the real churches where you picked your way around the bodies still in their sidewalk sleeping bags, preludes to ziploc. Avoiding contact, now, focussed on the hunt. But in New York City even the best contact avoidance strategies come messily unstuck. So when he realized that he was about to be accosted by a panhandler with grating voice and hygiene issues, Miles decided he couldn't be bothered to take evasive action, but accepted this as part of the price of admission, amiably letting himself be drawn into the harangue on which the curtain would come down only after hand had searched pocket to locate the dollar exit-fee. The man was weather-beaten. And beaten by *really* bad weather. African-American, sure, no surprises there. And some suggestion of, no Miles couldn't place it. Odd clothes, not just thrift store cast-offs, but something reminiscent…but whoops here we are. On stage. For one minute only, bringing a spittle-drenched harangue to a street corner near you.

-   *Ah'm a preese! A very high preese! You sail in me you have a hope that you don't have. You have no hope, do you, young gentleman? Gentlemen, my sister! All my sisters have come to me in the end, they do, they do come in the end, all my sisters get down to it, they get right down. But you, you are falling through a very blue sky if you think you can. I am a preese. Now fix it. Where you from?*

-   London. England.

-   *No, I am not that kind of a priest, I mean where you from. Left side, or the right?*

Miles thought he had now heard enough, but on reaching for some coins to drop into the crazily waving styrofoam cup, realized that the man had somehow already moved past him, almost it seemed, through him, and was hobbling jerkily away, peering awkwardly and wide-eyed over his shoulder at the younger man, clearly alarmed by something, seen or unseen. He also mouthed some final pieces of strangeness, but Miles, shaking his head, had turned off into a quieter side street before he felt he could piece together what it was the man had said. *You read with your hands, boy. We all read with our hands. Be careful what you handle.*

Well, that was weird. Mysteries of Gotham indeed, thought Miles, but put the encounter out of his mind in order to concentrate on negotiating the West Village and finding the bookshop. On the way he passed a hotel and, as its door was held open briefly by a laconic bellhop, glanced at the cracked black-and-white chess-board of the lobby floor, not knowing that shortly he would be perched unexpectedly at the late morning bar, downing bourbon, a drink he never drank, in a mixed state of mind. But first he had to locate Mysteries of Gotham, which he did without difficulty, and entered. No bell-pull this time, just the old-fashioned jingle of an independent bookstore, door comfortably loose in frame, glass a little loose in door.

Entering, he almost fell, missing the step down after his attention was drawn upwards by the giant latex spider, grinning and nodding in the currents of air he had briefly disturbed, the coffin beneath it on a gurney piled with books fictionalising, concerning, or in some cases written by, the living dead. In the surrounding shelves and alcoves there mingled promiscuously 1920s pulp horror magazines on the verge of disintegration, the indestructible, leather-bound ravings of Puritan witchfinders, seriously rare books alarmed in all senses, the most esoteric offended at finding themselves immobilised under glass and guarded by a poseable Edgar Allan Poe action figure. Crystal balls, skulls and the odd rubber hand served as bookends. Watched over by the smiling giant spider, Miles paused over an array of fortune-telling packs.

Here was the *Thoth Tarot*, designed by the Great Beast himself, Aleister Crowley. A lurid thing, but not without charm. Carefully, Miles plucked out cards at random – there was a beautiful but sickly Moon, decorated with a scarab beetle. Here the passionate Prince of Wands, atop his lion-drawn chariot, but there, demurely waiting, the Princess of Cups. Perhaps the Great Beast had an unexpectedly romantic streak. But then his attention was drawn by *The Faery Tarot*, on the backs of whose outsized cards winged maidens took off from the helipads of pond lilies, while gnarled elves delved in cryptic loam. As he dwelt on the charms of one intricately beautiful flying nymph, the eyes in her card seemed to widen and stare as if pricked out in emerald. How did they do that, he thought, head suddenly spinning as the eyes grew still wider, and he a little faint, but now the eyes were baleful meteors hovering over a tower struck by lightning where soldiers caught fire and then fell to stony death, as Miles himself started to capsize, and the wording on the box, as he saw in the instant before it clattered to the ground, was (what's happening to me, what's wrong with me?) *The Wrathful Tarot.* Miles, eyes and other parts of his sentient self swimming, fell heavily.

Every gleeful customer and staff member turned to look daggers at the new pariah, the klutz who'd dropped the fairies. As Miles crouched and pulled himself together, hunting for spilled cards to return to their tin box, an old lady smelling of cat pursed her lips, while hand-in-hand students glided, giggling, away. The Englishman in New York felt air conditioning chill the sweat on his brow, blamed tiredness and time-zones, and shuffled apologetically towards the towers of newly arrived books, and the flame-haired young vendor in the grey high priestess robe. Even to one peering in from the street and able to see only Miles' back, it would still have been obvious that what the oracle in crushed velvet had to say did not go down well.

- *Pasadena?* Isn't that in California? It can't be in Pasadena. I've come all the way from London to New York to collect this book personally. Let me speak to Flip.

- Flip isn't here today. He sends his apologies. Let me explain. When an old volume needs re-binding or needs some repair work on it, we always use the same firm. They used to work in a rented place two blocks away, but the rents shot up in the Nineties and they decided to move part of the business out to California. It's a drag, but they are absolutely the best, so we still use them. The book, your book, because I'm thinking of it as very much *your* book, believe me, was in with a small group of items, all occult-related…. which a certain buyer in LA took, sight unseen. But she didn't know about that one, it just got bundled in. It shouldn't even go to the binders. It has a history and needs to be just the way it is. It was an accident.… Peggy, how many times do I have to tell you!… Sorry, where were we. We've had staffing issues. We'll get it back for you. This is a one-off, we're happy to compensate. We know that book has to find its rightful home.

- So where is it now? On a plane, or in Pasadena?

- Ah, neither one. Not exactly.

The guardian of the Mysteries shifted from foot to foot, blasé about bicoastal detours, but evidently embarrassed about something else. She pulled her velvet robe tightly around her.

- We have an intern, an NYU intern, Becky Morrell. Just finished her PhD. She's driving the books over. There's some picking up and putting down of library acquisitions and other purchases, on the road. I believe she also has personal business to conduct. She said she'd fax but nothing's come through yet, which is…a bit weird. She may not be back in Manhattan for a while. I'm so sorry. If you want to chase the book we could definitely do some kind of deal on reimbursement.

She paused, conducted a quick visual sweep of Miles from north to south, and asked sweetly:

- Do you have any reason to go to the West Coast?

Miles' scholarly conscience released itself from its hammock with one perfectly executed back-flip, nodding furiously. *Yes*, thought Miles, I am twenty nine years old, which is very nearly thirty, dangerously close to forty, and I have never been to the West Coast of America. If what my head of department, the eminent medievalist Professor Transom tells me is true, Pasadena would put me in walking distance of the enviable scholarly resources of the Huntington

Library, the latter, as any schoolboy knows, only a short hop from the renowned Getty Collection. Thank you, Rapunzel, he thought secretly, suddenly relaxing and taking in the flame-coloured hair and other attributes. The name's Sybil, she thought back, reading his mind, and inclined her head, smiling.

Pulling out a College diary to get down some details, Miles was now parting with the Mysteries of Gotham on amiable terms. Reaching the door, he was even the recipient, or so he thought, of an absent smile from the old woman whose sense of bookstore decorum he had offended by dropping the tin box of cards, though now he could see that she had cataracts, and the balance in her smile between Go West Young Man and the depthless lacunae of extreme old age was impossible to weigh. But Miles had never been troubled by ambiguities. He was always one to hope for further, deeper mysteries. For some or for no reason the velvet guardian's phrase 'sight unseen' hung in a corner of his mind, spinning fast and casting dice or shadows.

To square things further with College as well as conscience, Miles retraced his steps and was soon standing in a hotel phone booth, fingering a pyramid of quarters while the barman poured him a coffee and a shot, and dialling half in celebration, half in apprehension, a Librarian who was five hours ahead of and some degrees Fahrenheit below his present location, but all he picked up was a pre-recorded message: *You have reached the extension of the College Librarian, John Spendrift. I will be in Cairo, attending the Annual International Conference of University Librarians until July 15th. Please leave a message when you hear the tone. And Miles, if this is you, just get that book. Do whatever it takes.*

5

Pasadena, California. Becky Morrell stood a full three inches over six feet. Very full. Wearing nothing but her endless black leather boots, she could crack that blonde mane like a whip, spurring the Beltane Lazarus to further, virtually magical endeavours. Unclothed or clothed, she could speak several languages, also speak in tongues, and play the steel-string guitar like one possessed. She lived on a tower, on a hill, on an island. She lived on vodka martinis, straight up with an olive. On the other hand and taken in the round she was a huskily low-voiced, heavy-lidded rose of Savannah, who knew little of life beyond a fantastically deep knowledge of literature of the 1890s and an even deeper desire to worship at Miles' feet. And kiss his toes. But in reality she was a dream-realtor, which of course accounted for the delay. Becky was terribly sorry. She had been showing a family of wraiths round a gingerbread condo, far away in the Land of Nod. You know how slow some people can be, making their minds up. Wraiths are worse; they have to find their minds first. But she had a confession to make. Dream-realtor was just a cover. She was in possession of The Book. Was in fact its cover. Was a grail withholding another grail, a charioteer through black night, the rarest of literary jewels meanwhile secure against theft and the weather, in her trunk. Her boot. She was an elephant goddess with a trunk, and also a boot. She did not exist. He had misheard the name. There was no book. No booty.

Miles groaned, turning over in his sleep at the Fuller Guest House. Dozing, he groaned again the day after, shaking his head over pointless papers in the library and thinking, I need coffee. Thinking, I know what I really came for, but it's not here. And she's not here, either. Working in the Ahmanson Room at the heart of the Huntington Library on rare manuscripts that would in other circumstances have more than claimed the whole of his attention, Miles had all the time in the world to worry about the no-show and no-faxes book stealer, Becky Morrell.

As Miles sat gazing hollow-eyed into space, Juanita the assistant librarian, whose main pleasure in life apparently revolved around moving his papers while he was at lunch, or failing to bring the right book, padded up from behind, tapped a shoulder to make him jump, put her right breast to his ear and breathed chewing gum.

- Call for you, hnnn? I'll put it through to Mr Stinson's extension.

Juanita ushered him into a shared office, the desk to the left almost bare, guarded by symmetrical Slav and Byzantine icons of the saints, mourning beneath closed blinds. By extreme contrast, the right hand desk was filled with snowstorm paperweights, a miniature xylophone and a clutter of stuffed toys such as hippos, giraffes and giant mice. He felt a mild surprise when it was the right hand phone that beeped.

By this time Miles had no particular expectation that the intern would phone, and he half-anticipated a voice from England. It came as a jolt therefore to hear not only Becky's voice for the first time, but to hear that, yes, she would be outside the Huntington in ten minutes' time, yes indeed, I promise, driving a magnolia Dodge Avenger, and that, best of all, yes, she had the book. He put the phone down feeling that plans always fall into place for those patient enough to wait, then retraced his steps with almost military confidence to the Ahmanson Room, and tidied his papers into an immaculate square while beaming pointedly at Juanita, who smiled thinly back.

Standing outside the Library, Miles thought, how is it that American cars can *glide*. British cars are sort of boxy, and have a kind of stop-start movement like a cough, but here they just glide. I'm not mad keen on cars in general, but. Just look at that. The Dodge Avenger drew up quietly and smoothly. Behind glass that bounced reflections of the nodding trees, Miles could make out the slightly formal, professional smile of a young woman who was about to present him with something unique. He could feel his heart beginning to beat faster. Then the window wound smoothly down, and the fist that shot out caught him smack on the nose and sent him reeling. The detached awareness that is often a side-effect of these unanticipated events assured him that only a fastened seat-belt and the awkward angle of the blow had saved him from a knockout punch.

- Oh crap, crap, I'm sorry, I thought you were my ex. He works here. I lost my glasses. Oh I am so sorry. Here, let me get you a tissue.

- Ffnaghh! Ffnaghh! *Ffnaghh!*

- Oh your poor nose. You know it's bleeding?

Becky Morrell stepped out of the car waving an aluminium car-box of Kleenex. Miles stepped sharply backward in case she intended to hit him with it. Becky shot both her hands into the air, as if to assure an invisible police officer that she was unarmed, then decided to press them to her sides, thinking it best in the circumstances to assume a bright and helpful posture.

- Professor Proctor? Becky Morrell.

The only response signalled respiratory blockage. In the adjoining and famous gardens of the Huntington Library, red and green birds sang.

- Would you like to see the book?

- Fug the bug! *Ffnaghh!*

Mouthing a silent Sor-ree, and stepping carefully and slowly around a gyroscopically rotating Miles, Becky opened the trunk and reached inside.

- Here.

And then it was as if all sound in the world had abruptly been turned off. Becky, the car, the breeze, the songs of the birds, the leaves on the Chinese elms and the whole world around the library were stilled in expectation. Miles forgot the insult to his proboscis sufficiently to take a slow and reverential look at what had been lifted from a candy-striped tote bag, then placed carefully in his hand, at an angle where any falling drops of blood and nasal mucus would not land on an open page, thereby diminishing the value of the whole. And this was, although profoundly unexpected, a rare find, indeed.

It was a first edition of the mother of all Westerns, *Riders of the Purple Sage* by Zane Grey. Its paper dust-jacket was only slightly chipped, and kept from further deterioration by a glassine wrapper of the kind favoured by serious booksellers.

-    You certainly did lose your glasses, didn't you. Fnagh.

-    Oh good grief. So where on *earth* did I….?

Becky began to search again through the contents of the trunk. Almost but not entirely beside himself, Miles couldn't help but observe the movements of a marvellously curvaceous female bottom, gently agitated in exciting, albeit contrasting, proportion to an otherwise lean and, as he had cause to know only too well, muscular frame. A number of fleeting thoughts passed through his consciousness, some to do with rare books, and others not. His nose had calmed, though his eyes still watered. Somewhere above, below or to one side of all this, the memory of a man who had in truth scared him a little, then moved away from him as if the man himself were scared, and the floating eye on a dollar bill, passed in fitful hieroglyphs of consciousness. He pulled a Kleenex tissue from the box, slowly folding and then applying it ceremoniously to his nose, a funny sort of crown or sign of passage, while beside him the rummaging continued.

6

The charm of suburbs such as Pasadena and San Marino lies in the unexpectedly harmonious combination of 1930s architecture and Pacific coast, Chinese or Japanese influenced gardens. What had been, back in the years of Art Deco, gas stations or cinemas, were now fancy restaurants and indie shops, some decorated with scrolling and figures from the early phases of the movie industry, often vaguely Greek or Egyptian. And the gardens are works of genius. Aided of course by the light.

There is no light in the world like Los Angeles light. Not just the myriad winking lights seen *en masse* from Mulholland Drive or one of the postcard views so familiar from Tinsel Town, but the ubiquitous soft dazzle, halo of light around light, light that softly leaks out to become a slowly fading but pearly, pearly mist of little sparks and hyphens. And the soft dazzle does this everywhere you look, around any old headlight, not just the oriental lanterns of seasoned stone which decorate the driveway here at Locust and Sepulveda, and which in the late afternoon were not yet shining, but soon would be, after a rapid and spectacularly pink-to-green setting of the sun.

The maid was in floods of tears, which didn't help. And it was fortunate that Becky knew some Spanish, so that between her, the maid, and the guys moving the boxed possessions of the deceased into hired trucks, it was all going as well as it was going to go, under the circumstances. The movers had blocked off the street, attracting the attention of a police officer or armed security guard, but he seemed OK with things now, lingering for no particular reason. Probably taken a shine to Miss Morrell. And who could blame him. Or was it the maid he liked the look of? You never knew. Miles knew that he was of no practical use in this situation, and stood some yards from the mellow sandstone house, with its gorgeous birds of paradise spiking furled colours into air, flanked by those flowers, common in Southern California but so exotic to British eyes, called angel's trumpets, but appearing to Miles more like swaying, silent bells. Good. We're getting somewhere. Becky has her notepad out.

Miles at this moment felt an unexpected and gentle pressure in his groin. Looking down he found his gaze met by that of an excited

Irish wolfhound with a nose that put his own to shame, and ears like curtains. *Seth*! Don't *do* that! The female jogger, in baseball cap and white tee, pink summer-sweater tied loosely round her waist, yanked hard on the permissively extended lead as she ran past, hauling the rangy animal away from its newfound zone of interest. More of a cat man, if push came to shove, or even if it didn't, Miles shifted his stance and watched, more comfortable for the loss of dog.

He was the first to see that what was going to happen was going to happen, and foresaw, more with spooked detachment than amusement, the dog-lead wind its way round the ankles of Man Number One, carrying a box of books out backwards from the driveway. The pink top then shook itself loose from the waist of Jogging Woman, who, instead of pausing to reel in the lead, fix the dog and free Man Number One, attempted to reach behind and downwards, to somehow do the impossible and retrieve her garment without breaking the momentum of her run. Rooted to the spot and his role as observer, Miles noticed that the potential for farce in this unfolding situation was rapidly draining away. His verdict was confirmed when the dog turned around, confused by its mistress's manoeuvre, thereby tightening its lead around the chinos of Man Number One who, falling, unnerved then knocked over the guard, who managed by accident to fire his weapon.

Time had done something. It had taken more time. Time had served itself, time and again, a straight ace. No, time had bent itself, trick-click in the head. Time rewound.

The charm of Southern California, as Miles was hardly the first to observe, lies in the quality of the light. Those first Spaniards, mistak-enly believing they had reached the earthly paradise, were actually quite right. There was nothing else on earth like the modulation into twilight seen from, say, the pier at Santa Monica, so fast you felt that the ancient sun had suddenly slipped a notch, that it really did move around the earth after all, but was falling right now, as fast as fireworks. Or the light along Huntington Beach after a shower, when the blue sky is cleaned, purified, and all good things made possible again. LA natives tended to identify the magic of light in their city with nightlife and cars, but to an observer such as Miles, inured to the more fickle and watery illumination of England, this round the clock miracle of changing light was something else again.

He looked over to see how things were progressing. Was that a maid, stepping out of the block? Yes. The maid was in floods of tears, which didn't help. The men moving the possessions of the deceased out into vehicles had blocked off the street, drawing the attention of a cop, who was haranguing them as Miles watched. But then again, no, going by the markings on his car, this was no cop. The majority of houses in this elegant suburb sported a garden sign carrying the legend Armed Patrol, or worse, Armed Response. This was Mr Armed Patroller. For heaven's sake, he thought, how much crime could there possibly be in this neighbourhood? The occasional Mexican gardener, tempted by an open Louis Vuitton handbag? A disabled scavenger who, for want of a decent healthcare system, was driven to purloin the choicer items of garbage? A serious accident involving a firearm was infinitely more likely than the restitution of justice by Mr Armed Patroller, wielding his gun.

Becky had her Filofax out. That was a good sign. Are we just possibly on the verge of knowing at long last where this book has got to. A woman jogged by, accompanied by a regal-looking – what is that breed called? Irish wolfhound – on an unnecessarily extended lead. Her pink top, tied around her waist but loosened by the run, was beginning to slip to the sidewalk. It fell.

- Excuse me, ma'am. Yours, I believe.

He had become so polite in such a short time in this country. Instinctively sensitive to class, ranks, types, the supposedly proper way to do things, and like many Brits irritated at himself on account of that very sensitivity, Miles still liked all the ma'am-ing and sir-ring. The British on their home turf were highly unlikely to be carrying a firearm, were even less likely to fire one, but would kick, elbow or swear anyone, even family – family most of all, probably - into a secondary position. By contrast, Americans were fastidiously polite up to that penultimate moment of lost bearings, after which all hell breaks loose. *Bang.* The lead had got caught around the ankles of Man Number One, busy with a box of books, just as Jogging Woman had turned to thank Miles for passing back her top. The box fell onto the sidewalk, but no real damage was done. Timing, thought Miles, idly. It's true what they say. It really is everything.

Time cracked for a second time. There's a first time for everything, in whose capacious underpass the other first times dawdle, shuffle around for a while, and then fade.

The light here is just extraordinary. Miles had been brought up first in the tropics, before his father was invalided out of the armed forces, and thereafter on the coast of Eastern Scotland, where the light can bestow an extraordinary clarity, as fascinating to the land-scape painters of Fife as the fiercer yet warmer glow of the tropics can be enchanting to just about anyone. He was visited by a sudden memory of his father, a gentle if taciturn man, absorbed in his early retirement in the stranger reaches of philosophy, standing holding Miles' hand, and gazing out to sea. That fine Fife light.

But the light in Southern California is something else. I know what it's going to do next. Now we're at the red phase. This will soften, then go to blue. Through these shades I'm wearing the light will be more polarized, richer with contrasts. Without them on, less striking but softer. Enchanting either way.

What's Becky doing? She's taking out her Filofax. Thank God, we're getting somewhere. No Mr Security Guard, she doesn't need you, her Spanish is good – you can tell by the way she hit it off with the maid. Adios to you too. Now who's here? Jogging lady. And, loosely connected to her person by one of those ridiculous leads – what do they call that breed? Wolfhound? No you don't, chum, you just keep focussed on that lolling tongue and looking like a hairy fool. That's right. I always thought I preferred cats. You just convinced me I was right. And lady, you're about to lose your pink top. That's right, pull it tight. And pull that dog in, too. Thank you, well done. I don't want any boxes spilling their books on the sidewalk, not these books. Not one book in particular. And right on cue, here comes that change in the light.

- You know the book's learning you. You think it's eluding you, but it's circling you, re-phrasing, working out exactly how it's going to get to you.

- Sorry Becky, I was watching the world go by. What did you say, again?

- I didn't say anything.

Becky, who had just walked over to speak to him, looked puzzled.

- I was thinking, though, that I *would* say to you, we have the address. I'm sorry this has taken so long. We can get out of here now. There's only one problem. The deceased got the book, on her last day alive – apparently she said, "great find folks, but too little, too late" – so there's no contest over ownership…

- I should hope not.

- So the book is yours. At the old price. It won't get sucked into the estate.

- That's all fine and dandy then. Isn't it?

- Well, not quite. The book's gone to the Valley, with some other stuff…

Miles' notion of regional American geography was still sufficiently vague for him to think the Valley meant, what, Laurel Canyon Boulevard or thereabouts? Thereabouts. Not as far as Disneyland, surely.

- The family home, Miles. In Death Valley.

Becky paused, and cleared her throat.

- Have you any other reason to want to travel to…

The scholar's conscience in Miles fell through a hole in the hammock of its comfort zone, and sat perfectly still, staring forwards. Pale. And quite without a comeback, for once.

7

Having set out from West LA to Barstow, which Miles reckoned was about the half way mark, sharing the driving and now getting on with his attractive, slapdash bookseller, he thought, well, I've come so far. No going back now.

Her driving was outrageous, not least because she couldn't see far without her glasses, which she was constantly losing – or thinking she'd lost, when they were hanging all the time on a lanyard round her neck – a fact which never dented her confidence when it came to foot on gas. He liked that confidence, which extended beyond the road. He liked her neck, too, taut with one little pulsing vein. Meanwhile the missing glasses would be resting on the emerging slope of her breasts, which he liked to look at even more, but in quick sidelong glances, not wishing to appear rude. She could hardly miss this, but was delighted by it, and thought he was a terrible driver, one of those ditherers who can cause a pile-up on the back of their own caution. Come on baby, she thought, you're getting us from A to B, not painting a watercolour. And what beautiful hands you have.

- Well let's see what the map says. Baker. You mean Baker, not Barstow. No, you mean both. Barstow then Baker.

\-   Then what? What's this guy doing…?

\-   I stayed there once. With my parents, ten years ago I guess. But for them it was still the 1960s. I was a non-communicating teen. And why wasn't I in school? Dad was assistant cameraman on a movie, *Return to Zabriskie Point*? One of your European art-house directors, not Rossellini…this wasn't exactly social realism…

\-   Canale? No, Antonioni. Michelangelo Antonioni.

\-   Yeah! You seen it?

\-   I saw the first *Zabriskie Point*. Didn't know there was a sequel. But yeah, I just know things. Retain them. I'm the king of trivia, a university lecturer in English Lit. Someone asked Maurice Foakes-Everight – he taught me, he's the doyen – had he read some book or other that had just come out. And Maurice said "Read it? I haven't even taught it yet." That's what it's like when you're…

\-   *Doyen*? Is that like in *The Godfather*? You a made man, a consigliere, no I'm just a *doyen*… Jeeze, Miles, where do you *find* these words?

\-   When they shoot in at an angle like that onto the freeway, are they allowed to do that? In Europe they'd have to give way. Well in England anyway…

\-   You're not in England. This is a free country. They come in at speed. They got rights, this is a democracy. And anyway, once we're out of Barstow and Baker, there isn't going to be any freeway.

\-   He cut me up! Bastard! *Why?*

\-   Oh, Miles.

8

For a while the scene unfolding outside the car window was comprehensible, a recognizable version of America. Although it might have driven you stir-crazy to live there, you *could* live there, for within a five minute drive, ten at most, you'd have the church, Wells Fargo, liquor store, gas station, Taco Bell, CVS Pharmacy. Nail parlor. Funeral parlor. Hell, you didn't even need to drive. You could walk, deemed thereby incurably insane, and soon be turned to road-kill by a midnight truck, lurching under the guidance of some dozing Baptist. Cut straight to the funeral parlor. The Lord is my Shepherd. Brother arriving from London too late for the ceremony, floppy-haired older brother, smuggest of the smug and on an upward curve at Deloitte & Touche. Philip was always, always the golden…

- *Miles!* Now do you want me to take over? You're tired. You need to keep in lane.

- Lane, shmane. This is a democracy. Actually, yes. Thank you.

He dozed for a while. Past Baker, signs of human habitation fell off sharply. Then the desert began, and Miles awoke.

The desert is profoundly quiet. So insistently quiet, that the couple hushed, and Miles found himself turning the dial on the car radio to Off, out of deference. And it rolled around and over them, the redness. Deep, dry, red waves. At sundown, such creatures as can manage to live in this place begin to stir. If you decide to take this trip, and if you step out of the car to dwell on the view, binoculars in hand, be sure to look downwards first. And do not put your hand anywhere you cannot see. Rattlesnake. Black widow. Admittedly, the danger of the former is a little overrated. Only about one in four of those deep bites ever turns out to be venomous, and, provided you keep the bitten hand or arm raised above the level of the heart

– while walking many miles to find a doctor – you should be OK. If the bite is on the leg or a nether region, then clearly you have a problem.

So the guidebook advises the wearing of full-length trousers, socks and stout shoes, even while walking in temperatures that exceed 100 degrees. The guidebook does not go on to add, do not be tempted to make love in the perfect dunes of white sand, which punctuate the red; that's strictly for the movies. The book assumes that you will in any case be reluctant to ditch either trousers or stout shoes, because of the spiders and snakes. By late spring, the rocks may be too hot to touch by mid-morning. In summer, this vast maw is strictly out of bounds, to all save those to whom the actively dangerous has become the only pleasure. The hottest place on the planet, with the highest atmospheric temperature ever recorded: 134 degrees. Nor should humans camp out, not at any time of year. At night the bobcat prowls, all thirty to forty pounds of him. He eats anything. Or at least he'll tear off a piece, and give it a go. Simply walking across the dunes incurs the subtlest and the greatest danger. Walking, you will not see the dunes warp and change behind you. And no matter what the month, getting lost means dying. This is unlikely to be what you came here to find out. And, by the bye, there are no phones here. Well hello, says the desert, you're pretty. Welcome to Death Valley.

The so-called badlands, though, are truly the good lands, if good means amazing rock formations. Though in reality there is no good or bad here. Zabriskie Point recalls nothing seen prior to this, stilling the mind by the force of its own wild insistence. Try to describe it afterwards, and the words will tumble, crack open, slide off a memory of the rock, and into silence. The cones and volumetrics of Cézanne, overlaid by the stripes of a zebra, bathed in red and blue light, then blown up to the size of the world's largest castle, repeated from all around the field of vision? This rock was here before zebras and Cézanne. And will be here when all animals and paintings are extinct, things never known. And the size: immeasurably itself, itself only. In Death Valley all comparisons have gone. Quite often, the third dimension itself disappears, and the vast rock rearing up in front of the panicked eye will turn perfectly flat. And here, at the centre of the badlands, is Badwater.

Badwater is the navel of Death Valley. It is also the lowest point in the Western hemisphere, and those giant letters, high on the mountainside, say 'Sea Level'. Is that mountain near or far? Impossible to tell. Perspective just mopped its brow, gave up the ghost, and trudged off to Nevada. Meanwhile the person walking effortfully towards you, glimpsed and then un-glimpsed through heat haze and mirages of water, is tiny. Then suddenly right in your face, gasping hot breath. What happened to the in-between of distance? Drained, like the gallon of water needed for drinking as an absolute minimum, each day. Here the floor of the desert is not rock, or sand, but first of all clay - then salt. Mile upon mile, of salt. Walking in Badwater for a mere half hour may or may not shrivel the souls of men, but it will devour the soles of shoes. That packed salt loves to eat rubber. Stand under the shower that night (if you can find one) for as long as you like. You may sleep that night secure in the knowledge that next morning you will still taste, and still taste of, salt.

Miles and Becky checked into the last pre-Badwater zone of civilization, the Vulcan's Forge Inn. And, God bless America, or Mars, wherever we are, they have a pool.

Under the stars, the only guests – at least the only humans out and about – they set down towels and sandals by the side of the 1930s pool, and dropped into water that issued from hot springs beneath the rock. Torches caused shadows to flicker on marble and sandstone, lifting the spirits and the gaze in tired eyes. What a great body she has, he thought, so rounded down below, but so strong, and her neck so long, as if she were craning always to see higher. And wild auburn hair, which he had learned well enough to see the flickers of copper there, moving and swaying everywhere on from the centre parting, down to her strong and level shoulders. A few dark red freckles on her back, her upper arms, her slightly turned up nose. Something growled in the parking lot. Full moon. And then she dropped like a stone, vanished, leaving bubbles at the surface and came up again, hair plastered down now, which made her mouth look even heavier, and her dark eyes darker with a mercury pinpoint in the artificial light. Miles plunged down too, in deference and play, came up, and they started to swim.

Proctor's breast stroke was the outcome of exacting, if somewhat militaristic training at private school, and he was rather proud of it. He knew that the swimmer should keep head barely raised above water, both to maintain the speed of the stroke, and to preclude excessive strain on the upper vertebrae. The kick should be as wide as possible, then turn into an arrow-straight propulsion, head now beneath the water, that builds on the power of the kick. Head up, for the briefest of breaths, then start the cycle again without a pause. After twenty consecutive lengths of this, he would feel smug in the knowledge that he had expended less effort and used fewer strokes, while covering more distance than anyone else in the pool, even if his sense of achievement was mitigated by a suspicion that the other more casual swimmers had just unwound, while he now felt tense from monitoring his own performance.

He started his breast stroke private school thing, hoping that Becky would gaze on his synchronization, and marvel. He started from one end, she from the other, and Miles could indeed catch the occasional sidelong glance, made easier by the fact that she kept her head out of the water all the time, just as he had been taught not to. There would be no candlelit dinner *à deux* out here in the desert, but this courtship by breast stroke under torchlight would do just as well. Suddenly, to his bafflement, she doubled her speed. His balletic head up for-the-briefest-of-breaths number was wrecked by the fact that, instead of gliding swan-like in the synergy of water music beneath the calm of desert stars, Becky was powering up and down in a wild if highly effective butterfly, shooting spray up his still slightly tender nose and threatening to deposit all the weight of water from the hot spring on to the desert. Then some tiny thing that needed to snap, snapped, and he thought, smiling inside and deep in his loins, whatever, whenever, however. Whatever you do is right. Teach me to care, and not to care. Teach me to fuck.

Or we learn, and teach us. Is this wise? I haven't even kissed you yet. It is wise, but when to kiss. O now we are. The meniscus from her butterfly see-sawing light, reflected by torches and moon as she leaned in a corner of the pool, Miles pressed her lightly. And Becky laughed in delight at the evidence, which she fingered briefly, up and down, that Miles' excitement was now manifest in ways that would be visually unacceptable if he stepped out of the pool – except to the bobcat, whose agenda was of a different sort. Then, strong as a great cat herself, Becky pulled herself up, rising to the poolside with a single move, her bottom on the edge, gazing down smiling at Miles, turning circles in the water with her toes, and, to settle herself a little more comfortably, spread her legs.

And, well, after all, in a swimming costume, what, he thought to himself, is there to see? Nothing. Yet how can a nothing, how can this flattish space, a couple of inches of Lycra from which the last drops of water are falling back into their source, how can it be so exciting. Conscious or unconscious of his mildly probing thought, she brought her legs together. And how can that be even more exciting. Before there was nothing to see, and now there's even less. She parted her legs again – but this isn't nothing, this is everything – then turned, bottom rising for a moment in the air. In there. The dark park, the rose, and the lane between. How far will she encourage me to wander, and play? What does she like to do? Does she know; do we know? Are we in our entirety, only what she and I have known in life, so far? Is that the point, that it is time once more to learn, but learn together? Bouncing slightly, Becky moved to where towels lay on li-los. Miles flipped on his back, lay for a long moment in his hammock of water, and caught a shooting star. Thank you. He moved to the side of the pool, thinking his state of excitation down for a moment, not that anyone was watching (though he still had an odd sense of being under observation – watching yourself watch yourself, Miles, now stop it) and climbed out. Becky was looking at towels, and bathrobes.

- Hey. His'n'hers. You know buddy, I can't remember which is whose.

Does it matter, now?

She laughed.

- No. Sure. I guess it won't matter, soon. Doesn't matter now.

And they padded back quickly, hand in hand in silence, to his, or to hers. There came one final growl from the dark lot.

9

Now it is early morning, and they are walking across Badwater salt in heat that is already hardly to be borne. Death Valley salt, mingling with the salt from their own bodies, runs down into their eyes and then across their lips like tears.

But there, in the distance, is the house. It shimmers, like a mirage inside another mirage. One of only two or three, built in the 1930s on the back of the new movie industry, winter vacation follies for stars and millionaires who tired, in the end, of so impractical and so deeply unnerving a location. The Vulcan's Forge, with its delightful swimming pool that draws on hot springs, went up at the same time. But the inn is located on the Barstow and Baker side of the desert. This must be the last house still standing. Totally, defiantly, in the wrong place. Miles could not judge the distance left to walk, but knew that he must by now be closing in on his book.

If truth be told, the desert had knocked it, all casually, from the altar it had occupied in his imagination. *This place says that books don't matter. An earthquake would not matter. Hit by the big one, the whole of Los Angeles could crash into the sea, and the plates under Badwater would just creak, and drop a little. Turn in their sleep. The badlands had seen stranger things, would do so again, and had no use for any of it. No reaction.* When the Romans came, saw, conquered and departed, Miles thought, when the British Empire first ruled the world, then sagged and burst like an old sack of guts - what changed, in this desert? *And this bookety book. Suppose every spell in it works. Suppose it allows you to travel in time, take a thousand lovers, pluck the last greenback from earth's final bank vault, and wave it, the flag of your own cult; how much meaning would all of that have, weighed against this? Meaning is specific to humans. Whatever happened in the next hours, this was journey's end. A bit of the desert had rubbed off on Miles.* He didn't care. *So, then, what is this scholar's quest really about?* The shimmer of an idea was beginning to form, in the back of his mind. But first Miles had to focus, if he wasn't going to pass out. *Let's just get to this house with Becky then back into our world, the human world, without burning up and flaring out.*

The house was of calm grey-yellow stone, with tall shutters to at least make a pretence of keeping out the heat. Somewhat pyramidal in shape. While they debated their next step, Becky tugged idly at a shutter, which gave up and came open like a broken, salty scab, allowing a partial view of a room in which a box of books and other belongings had been hurriedly dumped. One or two titles had fallen, lay at angles on the table.

-   That's it.

-   The book? Where?

-   On that table. What other book would have a cover like that.

Miles peered in. *OK. This is it. I'm not going back without it. I care* again. For the sake of this book I have crossed the salt desert. This whole thing has gone too far for the niceties to be observed.

- Stand back. I'm going to break the glass.

- Maybe you won't need to.

Becky swung the tall window open. Slow screech of a salt-rusted hinge. She made a be-my-guest gesture. No alarm sounded as he climbed in hesitantly, and started to cross the wooden flooring. Not that anyone would hear it, in the desert. The sudden cool focussed his thinking. He felt obliged to tiptoe, and a slight sense of desecration, not just of theft but a feeling of sacrilege, came and then went as he picked his way in silence, through alternating bars of light and shadow, to the table. The feeling now pushed to one side by a new sense of ownership. A sense of entitlement.

Knowing the risk he was taking, but needing to savour the moment, Miles, quite dangerously as it turned out, paused.

10

Eventually, he let his hand close on the book. Gently. In the words of Master Flip, this book had lived a little. Although he could feel that the spine was beginning to lose its grip, the hand-sewn pages clicked softly back into the spine's embrace, once more becoming, at least in Miles' hand, and in the phrase used by the antiquarian book dealer's trade, a good tight copy. There would be time to heal this, without causing further injury.

Books like owners. They know that they deteriorate with use, but view this as a necessary sacrifice. What book doesn't want to be read? A book can't read itself. How could it exert its powers, trapped under glass in a cabinet, or crammed upright at its sentry box in a university library, shoulder to shoulder with a thousand other volumes. Seldom read. Seldom handled, except occasionally by someone kind enough to blow the dust that gathers on its head. Irritating, that dust. Though a lot less irritating than the indignity of the blue stamp; Property of Beltane College, London. Then, worst of all, the gummed white paper, which totally gives the game away. Last taken out ten years ago. Ah. Nobody wants you, you're out of date. So when there's a cull, it's out to the lobby for you, and onto the portable, scarred shelves on the trundled, squeaking wheels. Five pounds. One. Then the skip.

Concerned individuals, the sort who peer at the world in sorrow through pince-nez, write on occasion to the local newspaper. Look what that vandal, the University Librarian, is doing. A first edition of the complete works of X, on sale for a measly Y. Yours in consternation, Colonel Z. But their affections are shallow in truth, both promiscuous and born of sentiment, spread thinly over books in general. It is the book itself that puts the highest value on itself. That wants a single owner. And mates for life, like the swan. But that always craves influence. New lives, changed readers. More vampire, perhaps, than swan. And so in a book there are always at least two books, extravert and introvert. But made of the same words.

As his hand closed on the book, all reverentially, all possessively, Miles was in no doubt as to whom this book belonged. As to who belonged to the book, well, that interesting question could wait to be unravelled. *Transmutations*. This was it, all right. Under the title, in flowing script adorned with playful dragons and serpents, *The Book of Magic, by Divers Hands*. Not just *a* book of magic. *The* book. Divers hands. He had always liked the old-fashioned phrase used to indicate a number of writers, picturing behind it an irrelevant image of a deep-sea diver, flippers undulating in green water, stretching a hand into the waving coral to pull up a ring from some wrecked Spanish galleon, or some human bone, cleaned by the ocean of the violence that first set it down there. Perhaps not such an irrelevant image, after all. We'll see. He stepped back towards the outside world. Walking the way he had come, back across the room, a slightly different person. The book grew warmer in his hand.

It couldn't possibly be carried. Not all the way back to the Inn, in this brutal heat and sunlight. The cover would fade. And while his palms were not sweating at this moment, as he inched his way through the last bars of darkness and light, preparing to climb the sill, they very soon would be.

- Becky?

But Becky Morrell had gone.

Miles shrouded the world's last remaining copy of *Transmutations* in a handkerchief, and slipped it gently into the thigh-side pocket of his combat long shorts, which he buttoned. He then made a slow circuit of the house, calling out her name. If Becky had set off to walk back the same way they had come, surely she would be visible. He peered into the heat-haze. Intermittently visible, at least. But why on earth would she have done that? Looking the other way, if she had climbed that dune, which she would certainly have had enough time to accomplish – (why did I hang around in there? Why didn't I just grab the bloody book and get the hell out?) – she could be just the other side, out of sight. Though distance is incredibly deceptive here, and the dunes shift, all the time. But again, why would she do that? You don't split up, walking in these parts. Heatstroke? She seemed OK, or as OK as you could be out here. Beautiful. Arousal flickered, slapped down by heat and her absence. He called again, more loudly. It isn't safe to walk alone.

Remember though, she knows this place. She had talked about stepping out alone by night or day, against advice, bored sitting around while her father was preparing Take Fifteen, or awaiting instruction from the perfectionist Italian film-maker. And this was the art world, people who had never really noticed that the 60s were over. On another planet themselves, parents were happy to shoo the kids off to initiate their own experiments. Becky had lost her virginity not so very far from here, and Miles had felt uncomfortable about the details, though pleased that she had told him, that she trusted him with stories of her life. She'll be OK, she's tough: tougher than me. He liked that. Back home, he taught. Here, he was learning. He had no doubts about Becky Morrell. None. She'll be OK. I hope. I can't lose you, not after last night.

Swigging from his plastic bottle water that had already begun to taste brackish, he set off back across the flat salt desert, caught in a dust-storm of pique, then bafflement and worry, then alarm, then (with some effort) trust and calmness, let's just get through this, triumph even, at moments, but then the fall back to annoyance. Plus, he realized, the beginning of a nagging swarm of questions about where, as a novelist of the same period as his trophy might have written, his affections were leading him. Though that's plain as a pikestaff and actually it goes wider than that, doesn't it chum. Do you want to teach Eng Lit all your life? Sweat ran down into his eyes. And if not, then what? Write it? Sell it? Or ditch it, for spilt tawny hair, straight shoulders, snub nose with freckles and a heavy, gorgeous mouth. Inside her mouth, running round her tongue, beneath her breasts, her scent, the signs and words, the signals out of the desert to the airport and the cities of new light.

11

A strawberry madman, exuding a vapour of sweat, heat-stress and impatience, he almost threw himself across the Front Desk. No, Miss Morrell had not checked out. Then he walked as if drunk down the steps, with their carefully spaced paper bags, each of which held, throughout the night, a lit wax lantern. In Death Valley it was important where you placed a hand, a foot. Then on to the single-story cabins, past giant cacti, and their dominating shadows. No response. Miles stood for a short while and pondered. He returned to his cabin and took a fast cold shower, groaning with relief. Then he packed, wrapping the book carefully in clothes, plumb in the centre of the case. This he locked. There came a faint scrabbling at the door of the cabin. The top half of frosted glass showed him that someone was there. He shot to the door and opened it.

Although it was the long black coat that first struck him as inappropriate outdoor wear for the desert, the coat was merely container to a three piece suit of heavy black wool. But this was no banker on vacation. The collarless shirt was grimy and threadbare. The snap-brim Fedora, while equally inappropriate, would at least keep the sun off as it hit the huge aviator sunglasses. This man looked like an undertaker after a heavy night. An unshaven seventy. Scar in a half-moon shape, up from lip to ear. A smaller female was making her way slowly up the steps behind, her own face veiled by shadow.

The man moved his head slowly from side to side. The special alertness of the blind was legible in his careful movements, as he moved his fingers on the bronze Braille panel next to the jamb. *Twenty seven. Not my number, not my number at all. My sincere apologies, we'll get out of your way.* Behind him, the second figure continued to advance, very much a step at a time. *Would ye have the time, by any chance? It's not generally an issue around here. In fact, I can tell the time from the heat and the way the light hits, so I don't need to know the time, thank you very much. You can keep your f... time. What I need to know is* their *time. They want us to check out, do they not, Meg?*

- *Aye, Ken. What a shame eh.*

So I dinnae care *what time it is, but I have a need to know what time it is. An unfulfilled need. One of many, hmm.* He paused, and inside the pause the hair on Miles' neck and arms rose up in tiny, vulnerable battalions. *You're alive, I hear you breathing.* Trying to progress beyond astonishment, Miles turned on the linguistic radar left in place by an upbringing in Fife. West coast? I think Glasgow. His radar wasn't quite working, today. This guy's whiny rasp could stop anything from working. His watch seemed to be coping, though. Just coming up to eleven o'clock, he replied brightly. And now if...

- *Englischer Schweinhund! Land's sakes, what's an Eng-*

lishman doing in Death Valley? Personally I don't mind Englishmen. Not sure I could eat a whole one, though.

Harsh laughter. Terminated by coughing.

- *I'm not fanatical about the air here, I have to say. It brings on my asthma. That makes me apathetic. And anxiety is a terrible thing. Do you not think so?*

He was now quite close to Miles, who stepped back as the man's long fingers gently tried the air around his face. The fingers stayed in the air, stroking it pensively. *Anxiety is the doorway to…what? To excitement, of course, sometimes, but only if it's somebody else's anxiety.* The fingers drooped, listless now. *Och well. Here's tae us, wha's like us? Damned few, an' they're all deid. Let's find our room, Meg, and that's us away. A doorway is a doorway is a doorway, to lead you who knows where. Am I right, Meg? Meg's my sister.*

- *Aye, Ken, you're not wrong. Everything in its own good time, eh.*

Something about her appearance, as she paused a few steps behind her alleged brother, caused Miles to look away at once. Who were these people? In these amazingly wrong clothes. A hundred and fifty or more years ago there would have been Scots prospectors, like the panhandler for gold whose horse wouldn't drink, down by the creek that led to the flats. It was he who tried the trickling water, the only water for miles around, tasted salt, and named that strange place Badwater. The name stuck. He went away. None of them really settled. But what were these two prospecting for?

It occurred to him that, had the man been sighted, Miles would have brought this pointless encounter to a close by now. He needed to move, to find Becky. Once again and, it seemed, for almost rhetorical effect, the man fingered the doorway to the cabin. *Number twenty seven.* It was thoughtful of the Inn to have placed Braille numbering by each keyhole. *No, that's not my number, not my number at all. I have to go looking with my hands, son. I read with my hands. And my ears. In my own defence, I will say this, what I have lost in sight I have gained in powers of hearing. More than gained. Praise be, I can hear like a bat.* The man rotated his cranium slowly, stretching his neck like someone performing warm-up exercises in the gym. Fat worms of muscle on the bull-neck wriggled. This drew Miles' attention to the neglected ear-rings of jet black hair curled round the outer gristle of a pair of long, very long organs of hearing, terminating at their north end in sharp points, that moved seemingly of their own volition to escape the Fedora. Almost as startling was that scar, that ran from the man's lip up to one pointed ear. Now he wanted, badly, suddenly very badly, to bring this to an end. Find Becky and get out of here.

He made to close the door, but a strong hand now prevented this. *No rubbishy sound in the desert. Is there now. No cars, no crappy conversation, nothing to say, just the song of my old pal the crow. And what is he saying? What is the burden of his melody. Death, death, and death. And jewellery. Jewellery and death, they do so go together, d'ye not think? Like catch-colt and coffin-cart, as they used to say in these parts. I love the smell of jewellery, the way it catches the scent of the woman, not just the man-made scent she puts on – I can sense a little heliotrope around this door, citrus, ooh thitrooth, with ground notes of vervain…* Accent shifting briefly to a toney Anglo-Scots, he sniffed the hot air like a hound. Then the rasp was back. *Of musk, yes, of both artificial and natural secretions. The latter for preference. Some quite salty to the taste. And of a vivid hue when shed profusely, if memory serves. But I'm holding you back, son. You just go next door, and finish what you started. I smell her there, waiting. A little perspiration, a little anxiety in the air, I dare say. Manacled. Wee hankie in her mouth. And if not, you'll soon see to that.* Miles, enraged, was also paralysed, chiefly by physical force but to a degree by the performance. He thought to himself, even in his fury, this is an actor. *Aye, son, there's an inevitable element of performance. It's inherent, in any act of communication. All the world's a stage, like your bletherin' English poet wrote. Or forced an actor to say, night after night. Some pressurised boy, in a girl's wee dress, some schoolboy Cleopatra. Sometimes we have to force people to speak, do we not, Meg? They generally oblige. It's a helpful world and everyone knows pain. But in all sincerity:* he jabbed his head forward like a desert snake, assuming for a moment the unctuous solicitude of an old-time game show host: *I really, really want you to know this.* Whisky breath and spittle covered Miles' face in an unwholesome veil. They were now locked in a strange embrace, the man's right arm bunched in hard on Miles' kidney, moulding his hips to his attacker's, the left preventing Miles from slamming the door. *All the world's a skein, but if you want to see that, really see that, you sighted box of tricks…there's a good book on the subject. I can recommend it to you. But you already have it in your possession. You already think you own it. I don't. I'd like to borrow it. I'd like you to read it to me. I'm not sure that my hands are those it craves. You can read to me when it's my bedtime. Oof!*

The man jerked, faking a blow from invisible hands. Then a further spasm. Perhaps not faking. *No, I don't think it wants me here at all. Jings, that one hit the spot. Another time perhaps.* The man roared, and jerked his head backwards. Miles prepared to hit him, though his hand moved only in slow motion, nothing but pins and needles. Then the visitor rallied, stage-whispering in the young man's ear. *The world's a skein alright, but to catch the systemic linkage, the underlying patterns, you do need a p-r-e-t-t-y high level of receptivity to tenuous connection. Know what I mean, eh? Of course you do, laddie. Be seeing you.* The man shrieked briefly. *Where's my dog, my wee jackal-guide? My white stick, my jewel-encrusted staff? I am shedding my last drops of dignity and for what? My* palanquin? *WHERE'S MAH FUCKING PALANQUIN?* The terrible visitor rolled his head around. Miles tried to yell in turn, tried to strike back, but failed. His new acquaintance fired a last spray of venom. *You need to get out more. Grow some points on those pink little ears. Pull him off me, Meg, I think I'm having an event. Oof, my encrusted staff...* The figure moved back, seemed to fade. Miles, abruptly free, could punch now with all the force at his command, a movement that only succeeded in propelling him outwards on to the clean and empty steps, where he tumbled, fell to a halt and at last looked up, alone and seeking to draw some kind of reassurance from the bright Californian day.

No, they were not aware of a blind septuagenarian Scotsman and his sister having passed through the hotel. No one had stayed here recently, apart from Miles and Becky, and a week ago the two men who had delivered the books to the shuttered house. One of them had required medical attention. Probably just the heat. Yes, they would send a security guard to double-check Miss Morrell's cabin, but they hardly saw any need, as she had settled the account for both cabins, and the bellhop who brought down her luggage to the car had seen her drive away. About a quarter of an hour ago. No, no message. Dorothy? Sorry, there was a message. 'Good Luck Miles.' That's all? That's all, folks. Miles felt something move beneath his finger as he pressed down on the front desk. One of Becky's business cards. Every word on it was familiar, but he had never expected to see them in combination. Rebecca Morrell, Antiquarian Book Specialist, Redidivus Books, Fiddlers Court, London.

12

The long journey back to London allowed Miles and the book to become better acquainted. He was in no rush, and having finally laid hands on *Transmutations*, at considerable and on-going cost of every sort except the one that impacts the wallet, he was going to take his time. The act of theft bothered him, but the mysteries of Becky's business card put settlement of that particular account on hold, for now. In the reaches of his conscience hung a bell-pull, one to which he knew he would return, in time. Time. Timing. The terrible old man had been hung up on time issues, unless that was just an opening gambit to get Miles to speak. Musing and dozing

on planes, in airport lounges, he kept going back in his mind to
the opening paragraph of the Book of Magic. Although he never
let the book travel any significant distance from the inside pocket
of his jacket, he had committed its opening to memory:

> *The error this treatise will set out to correct, hinges
> on the true relationship between Magic and Time.
> Even practitioners of the sixth and seventh levels,
> to whom an ambition to rise to the status of Adept
> is no mirage, allow themselves to be captured like
> the meanest slave, made to toil in a workhouse of
> futile and unnecessary labour. The fault is entirely
> theirs. To practise Magic is not to set going a process
> of startling change in the hebdomedary, the custom-
> ary world. Such is the province of those mounte-
> banks and professional deceivers – charming at best,
> clowns at worst - who lure the throng like moths into
> the circle of the lime-light, sawing the lady in half
> (one hopes, as preparation to restoring her person at
> all points!), plucking gay flowers or tame birds from
> the air, or more likely the sleeve.*

> *The quickness of the hand deceives the eye; the quick-
> ness of a word deceives the fool. In the latter case
> these mock-savants take questions from the cheap
> seats, causing the groundlings to marvel at facts re-
> garding their lives of which they had perfect prior
> awareness, the Magic, soi-disant, residing solely in
> their hearing this drivel from the mouth of a strang-
> er on a stage. The percipient, the true Magician, will
> take the exact reverse view.*

> *True Magic lies in the removal of all that's strange.
> The alteration brought about by the agency of Magic
> will be so swift as to erase from memory the state of
> affairs that preceded it. The act of Transmutational
> Magic, once having taken place, can, thereafter, nev-*

er not have occurred.

Miles was already very taken with the book. Even when period charm was discounted, it exercised a powerful tug. Beneath the flowery language of the Victorian Nineties lay a rich mulch of intrigue, spawning questions as to the motives burrowing behind the words. And that flowery style was really just a lure, a way to catch the mind of the new reader, buzzing with other things. Once you were caught, the book moved fast; as if time was tight. And with no concessions at all to the general public, let alone the literary intelligentsia. This was a how-to manual for trainee magicians – and only the bright ones, the potential Adepts, the Magical equivalent of fast-track graduate entrants at Deloitte's. But for all that, there was not a single practical action described, at least up to the point Miles had reached. He was not in any rush. He read the first chapter repeatedly, beguiled by the way that philosophical speculations around concepts such as time, memory and forgetfulness were whizzed along. The book had its own special clarity and rigour. It was just that the central tenet underpinning the book – that acts of Magical Transmutation are possible – was completely false.

Or was it? Within the last days he had seen a man who had just assaulted him fade into air. But then again, was that atrocious meeting more strange, in the overall scheme of things, than Zabriskie Point itself? What could be stranger than the badlands? And in fact (as he had now largely convinced himself) wasn't the multiplication of lost bearings in the desert, plus a touch of heatstroke, the likeliest explanation for what he had seen? Was seeing a man fade in front of you any different from a mirage? But the book talked of Magic as the loss of strangeness. But, but, but (Miles, get some sleep now, you're going round in circles) surely the scholarly interest of *Transmutations: The Book of Magic, by Divers Hands* lay in its singularity, its history, not its contents as a manual. This was no Victorian Methodist tract on how to get rich while salving your conscience.

But – and the thought struck him like a fist – was it a dream-version of exactly that. A Samuel Smiles tract for dreamers and aesthetes, too clever to be comfortable in the straitjacket of Methodism, but too fey and impractical to get out there and win? People like you, Miles? Get some sleep. Ask some more questions when you wake up tomorrow. Such as, why is it that although I have memorised the opening of the book, every time I look at it afresh I find I missed something, or got it slightly wrong. So I memorise it again, but always when I go back to reading it, I was wrong again, but can't now remember the exact wording of the version I memorised… And why are the chapters so short, with blank pages or half-pages at regular intervals? Was the reader – am I – supposed to *write* on them? Perish the thought. That's vandalism. Think what John Spendrift would say. And, God help me, what am I going to say to John Spendrift?

And then he couldn't sleep, though the lights on the 757 were now out, and most passengers snoring and shifting uncomfortably under blankets and blindfolds, or red-eyed and determined to make it to the dénouement of their Airport Exclusive, or formatted movie. What could he say to the Librarian? That he was sorry, but the pursuit of the book had ended in a wild goose chase? First it was the fault of Mysteries of Gotham, who should have kept the book for him, but instead let it be transported to California, in the trunk of a Dodge Avenger. Then the intern had misfiled it. He had chased it all the way to Death Valley, but there was no-one at the house, no-one knew anything, and the book was caught up in estate issues following the death of an elderly collector. That was a lie. But Miles felt that the book was now his, and he had no desire whatsoever to yield it up.

How, then, was he going to explain himself? Yes, he had the book. Technically, it was a free gift to the Special Collection in Beltane College Library, because he had not paid a dealer for it, but purloined the thing from the house of a deceased collector. What were the chances of keeping his lectureship? Doubtless more than reasonable, in the end, but there would be embarrassment and awkwardness, all round. Additionally, he needed privileged access to his book. And for quite some time. The idea of being parted from it even for the short period it would take the Library to catalogue it, was unbearable. Miles tried to picture a third possibility. Make out the cheque to Mysteries of Gotham, for the original amount. You're in the clear, Flip's happy, the Librarian's happy. The Librarian accepts that I've been through hell and high water on this one, and I get privileged access to the book for an agreed period, maybe even get to hang on to it, provided we all countersign a letter of agreement.

But then I would have to turn in my badge and gun, forfeit my detective's rights, the right to dig myself in deeper, to get to the truth, the real relationship between Redidivus and the Mysteries, between the missing Becky and her employer, or employers. He was angry with her, for doing something he did not understand. But Miles was often most attracted to things that were hard to understand – and anyway, he thought he might be falling, seriously falling, in love and into mystery, for the first time.

Someone To Watch Over Me

1

The Librarian of Beltane College sat well back in his swivel-chair and sighed, tapping lightly on his desk with a paper knife, a souvenir of the international conference of Librarians he had just attended, held for the first time in Cairo. The knife was engraved with a number of the more fanciful and alarming hieroglyphs from Egyptian mythology, including the jackal-god Anubis, whose snarl indicated an unambiguous readiness to rumble. On the other side of the blade, Anubis appeared once more, but looking more sage, a potential winner at Cruft's, sire of ten litters with a noble profile suggestive of one who thought that there were at least two sides to every question. John Spendrift sank the point lightly into his desk-blotter, and twirled it round and round. He then put the dangerous toy down, rose, sighed, and walked over to the faux-Japanese faux-blind, part of which was going to have to be replaced because he had accidentally poked it with the paper knife while deciding what to do about an irritating email. The email in question lay open on his laptop.

Sent by Professor Transom, Miles' Head of Department, it blamed the Librarian for the continued absence of the junior Lecturer in English from the campus. While this was not a hanging offence, for it was after all the summer break, the research term when papers were given at conferences, when books were read and even written, Miles Proctor had now been gone for some considerable time. *Why?* The Librarian sat down heavily and donned his glasses. Then he tapped at the keys.

> Dear George
> The fault is mine

Bugger that, there is no fault. And if there is, it isn't mine. The book world is a pretty strange world, at times, particularly at the Gothic and even more the occult end, where Miles has been foraging. Some of the buyers and collectors are difficult individuals. Unhinged, some of them. Spendrift remembered only too well the affair of the Lovecraft papers and all the rum goings-on that Visiting Professor from Miskatonic University had led them into. On nights with a full moon or following a late Feast in College, the Librarian still woke up screaming. Mind you, after a College Feast and an evening sat next to the Principal, there were plenty of reasons for that.

> Dear George
> Thank you for your email. I'm sure that Miles
> Proctor

Trouble is, I'm not. I'm not sure of anything. I've got a funny feeling about this one. And if I'm honest, which I never have been with you, so why break the habit of a lifetime, I think Miles has got himself into some kind of odd place where that rare book has led him. He's either got the book or he hasn't. We'll know about that, one way or the other, soon enough. But that letter he sent, marked 'Personal and Confidential', though even if it hadn't been I wouldn't tell *you*, you professional gargoyle, was so contorted in the wording it was clear that something was badly amiss. He could be sick. But they don't get sick at his age. They do other things, though. Fall in and out of love. And the mid-life career crisis happens at all ages and stages, now. These people are top of their tree, professionally speaking, but they aren't that well paid. It isn't like the States. So why am I pussyfooting around here? He typed at speed, as if to punish the keys.

> Look George, you know full well that Miles Proctor, like every other individual working on campus, from senior academics to junior gardeners is appointed by the *College* and not by the department, in this case the English Department.
>
> Miles has contractual responsibilities beyond his contribution to teaching, and his research projects (which are, *nota bene*, of some relevance here). The third area of responsibility, and again you can check this in his contract, is administration, and a readiness to conduct such business on behalf of the College as shall be demanded by senior officers of the institution.
>
> As College Librarian I am one of those officers – as I have had cause to remind you at virtually every single meeting of the Library & Information Committee – and I can assure you that the book search on which Dr Proctor is engaged falls definitively into the high-priority category. This would be a very significant acquisition for our Library. Nevertheless, as the book in question was not a product of the Middle Ages, I realize that a reasoned judgment, as in so many spheres of College activity, may lie beyond your area of scholarly and indeed human competence.
>
> As a coda, I might add that if staff at the College sent fewer, shorter, and less truculent and verbose emails, we would all get more work done, and the institution would be able to rise above both its reputation for eccentricity and parochialism, and the

respectable but stuck-in-the-mud position it currently occupies in the League Tables.

Cordially

JS

John Spendrift MA (Cantab.) PhD (London) FRSA FRHistS MCLIP
Chairman, Jane Austen Appreciation Society (West Surrey Branch)
Advisor, *www.KeepTheElginMarblesBritish.com*

Ping. A pair of silent minutes passed. Then John Spendrift sagged, his facial lines slowly caving in. I wish I hadn't done that. I should have a filter built into this thing so that I get a reminder to re-read my own emails before I send them. This morning I've upset the Head of English, the Finance Office and worst of all the Keeper of the Cellar, and it's only ten o'clock. I'm getting worse as I get older. Everything's getting worse as I get older. Perhaps I should make it up with the Finance Director. Schmooze the Head of Personnel. Another year of this and I'll be asking for their help. Is it time to solicit the brown envelope? Take the earlies. Has it really come to this? He sat gloomily and waited.

After a minute, it rang. The Librarian picked up the phone as might a practised fisherman an incensed lobster, and held it a good six inches away from his ear. It was George Transom all right, but a contrite Transom.

- It's all my fault, John. You're perfectly right to upbraid me. Sometimes I think I should just pack it in, go down to the green and work on my handicap, and never bother anyone again. I'm not even as good at that as I used to be. It all goes back to the Ellesmere, and the Hengwrt.

John Spendrift furrowed his brow and brought the phone nearer mouth and ear.

- The Ellesmere and the…

- Hengwrt. Sorry John. Chaucer-speak. I edited the complete works of Geoffrey Chaucer…

No, get away, you never did, well you kept that one quiet. Only mentioning it every bloody time we meet. Your first thought on waking, probably. Main topic of conversation during the day. And most likely your last thought on earth, when you finally peg it.

But then the Librarian felt sorry for thinking these things. George Transom had indeed edited the complete works of Chaucer. His was said to be the best edition since Robinson. And surely there are worse thoughts that could pass through the mind in its final moments of lucid awareness, than the thought of having achieved something. Of having changed people's, experts' perceptions of material they thought they knew well. That brought new approaches to old questions, bringing in new readers. How much had he, John Spendrift achieved, really, in his smooth, almost silent ascent through Library-world?

His left hand moved across the blotter, and found the handle of the paper knife. It was engraved with an image of Thoth, the Egyptian god of language, who is said in some accounts to have formed himself out of words.

- …and if you work on *The Canterbury Tales*, you either work from the Ellesmere or the Hengwrt. They're the earliest known copies. The Ellesmere's in the Huntington, in Pasadena. It's in very good nick. The Hengwrt's the best, forgive me, the better of the two, but the rats got at it some time in the later Middle Ages. It's in Aberystwyth…anyway, where am I going with this. It's my fault. I encouraged Miles to try out Pasadena. Take the exotic route. I sold him on the merits of the manuscript library and the rare books room in the Huntington, and I probably over-egged it, by going on at him about the Getty. I just wanted to help his career. Get him to make the right contacts. They'd love him over there. Though of course we want him to stay here. Miles is *terribly* bright. Fantastic potential. But modest to a fault. The confidence isn't quite there.

I don't think, chum, that he pays any attention to you. That isn't the issue. But you're being decent. I'm going to wind this up, we're quits. Spendrift said this, albeit more elegantly, and replaced the phone.

Not a bad old stick, George. World class scholar, too. That's one of the things about the College. We might go all around the houses, but we get there in the end. We'll fight tooth and nail over some piddling academic issue, about whether marking dissertations for the Institute should trigger incentive payments or be built into the workload, about the design on the label of the College port, or the Plant Scientists' glasshouses spoiling the view from the Principal's balcony. But when one of our own is in trouble, we stick together. That's because we're good - academics, students, even the gardeners. Especially the gardeners, come to think of it. Top-notch. But no soft touch, there's no easy ride here. And when push comes to shove, I'd like to think we're made of pretty stern stuff. He straightened his spine and stared fiercely ahead, moulded, for this moment at least, from stern stuff. Then his attention drifted away from Miles, Transom and the College, and back to the *Times* crossword.

2

Spendrift'll kill me. Transom will kick anything that's left after Spendrift's had a go. I need to buy some time. It's still only the middle of July, and the start of the Autumn Term is a good two months off. I made a hash of that letter, but it will have to do for now. I've got, what, ten weeks maximum to sort all this, before the students are back? The College diary he pulled from his pocket assured him without equivocation that term would start on October 4th. So, come October, I'm in trouble. The trouble with the prospect of more trouble is – I'm not sure I care, any more.

On an airless journey by Tube up to Charing Cross Road, he thought the man seated opposite in the carriage was looking at him oddly. Heavy-set, cropped hair, early twenties. You don't make eye contact on the Tube. But then these days Miles thought that everyone looked at him oddly, and that the gaze he cast back at the world was probably a little crazed. When he neared the top steps leading out of the Underground and into breathable air, the man was unexpectedly ahead, a bulky silhouette turning round to face him. This blocked Miles' path, at a point where he was positioned a couple of feet lower than the stranger. He couldn't sense the presence of a soul, let alone the usual human wave, coming up behind him.

In his right pocket sat a metal watchstrap that had been his father's and which Miles kept meaning to get mended, a clunky thing. The scholar son now curved it round his knuckles, in his pocket.

-   Are you Miles Proctor?

His fist curled inside the metal band.

-   Mmm.

Miles took the last three steps in one bound and moved sharply to the right.

-   So sorry, I didn't mean to get in your way. I'll clear off. Just that I heard you give a paper on Writers of the 1890s at our postgraduate conference. Last year. In Leeds. Hearing your paper was what decided me on an academic career. I just wanted to say, you know, thank you.

The younger man was starting to blush, as he hovered uncertainly.

-      I really admire your work.

Now Miles remembered the conference, and the postgrads. Good group, one of those years where a few sharp young people on their way up will, without realizing they're doing it, make each other sharper. He wasn't sure how much credit he could really take for that one. And oh how long, how very long ago that conference now seemed.

Abruptly conscious of his rudeness, he half-waved, trying to put an implied 'good luck' into it, but the other, younger man was already starting to cross Trafalgar Square, obscured immediately by a flock of teenage Italians being led towards the National Gallery or some other cave of marvels in which they had zero interest. Miles let his hand, palm clumsily bangled by the watch-strap, slowly fall.

He walked towards Fiddlers Court, wanting some answers from Redidivus. He was braced for a sign reading CLOSED FOR FUR-THER BUSINESS, but surely there'd be a number to which enqui-ries should be directed. It came as a surprise then, as he turned into the Court, to see, ten paces ahead, the broad back of a figure in a pinstriped suit he was pretty sure he recognized. A moon of bald-ness, from behind, a few remaining strands of hair patted repeatedly back across the skull as the bookseller walked and talked. Accom-panying him was one who, though the white hair and humped back made it clear he was decidedly older, managed a brisk enough pace. Their conversation was animated. If this second character is Mr Winthrope, the owner of the firm, thought Miles, the old man has staged a miraculous recovery. Or he was never sick in the first place.

As the two paused at the entrance to Redidivus Books, still locked deep in conversation, Miles pulled back and stepped into a door-way. The man in the blue pinstriped suit deferred to his elder, who produced a key. This had to be Winthrope. Miles sauntered across the Court, and stared blankly into the window of a curiosity shop selling coins, notes and medals. Pride of place, the last Tibetan 100

Srang note from the 1950s, serial number guaranteed hand-written by monks. A dollar bill issued by the Bank of Philadelphia, 1895. Roman currency, courtesy of a British metal detector. He then re-crossed the street and approached the closed door. Someone, or something, had destroyed the bottom left hand panel, which was barely secured by masking tape and a plastic Sainsbury's bag. Miles saw that the venerable bell-pull had gone too. He rapped on the door. No answer.

Staring at unresponsive wood and pondering next steps, Miles caught some faded lettering in the stone on the side of the door, where the bell-pull had hung. Mr Machen's – then a word seemingly beginning with M – Shop. Interesting as it would be to know the past history of this place, its present occupiers were Miles' concern, right now.

Feeling within his rights to pry a little, he scratched and poked the supermarket bag with foot then fingers, just above the level of the step. A sixth sense told him that he was under observation from further up the street. Turning, he beamed innocence at a watching shopkeeper, lifting his running shoe and the leg of his black jeans to show he had been tying his laces. The man disappeared indoors. Miles fingered the ripped plastic bag into enough of a mouth to reveal a fair-sized scattering of circulars and unopened envelopes on the fading hallway carpet. He tried the door, which was of course locked. He walked back down Fiddlers Court more pensively, then stepped into the red telephone kiosk at the corner.

Above the handset a calling card offered discreet personal services from an alleged French maid with an unconvincing portrait. Miles took Becky's business card from his wallet, where it lived, and dialled the bookshop's number, looking back along the street. Nothing. They were in there, all right. Evidently the phone had not been disconnected. What to do, fax them? Abseil from the rooftop? He felt sure they hadn't been aware of his following them. And they would be unlikely to have entered by the front door only to exit at once via the back entrance. In fact, come to think of it, there wouldn't be a back entrance, since this terraced row was half of a Janus-face arrangement with St Martin's Court, wasn't it?

St Martin's Place, yes, and the start of the theatre district. Which, like its New York counterpart, existed more and more to show the same atrocious musicals by the same double-barrelled Brit to the same corporate crowd. Put me in a time capsule, thought Miles, and take me forward. 2009 or thereabouts, that will do. Whatever is or isn't happening then, at least there won't be any more *Les Mis* or *Phantom of the Opera*. But Fiddlers Court was not that. Fiddlers Court was, is, a living bit of the old London. Very old. Tubby pinstripe man and ancient Winthrope. They're in there, all right. In deep.

Miles drifted emptily back towards the Tube. So near and yet so far. Statues offered silent advice. Fortitude. Devotion. Thank you, Edith Cavell. I hope someone shows me some, too. Then down the steps past a diminutive figure clad in a black duffle coat in the height of summer, face hidden by the hood. Get your *Evening Standard* here. News of all that Mr Blair (ever rising) and Mr Clinton (somewhat tarnished) hope for the new century. News of London's marvellous, and marvellously vague, Millennium Dome. To be built somewhere beyond the East End. Hackney and Whitechapel were exotic to Miles, brought up in a different Far East. The East End meant, what? Tailors. Gangsters. The Kray Twins. And the spectre of Jack the Ripper, stalking his research decade, the 1890s? No, late 1880s.

By now Miles was heading towards the Elephant and Castle, named improbably, and by a circuitous route, after a Spanish Princess. In every sense he was going round the houses, taking in the skein of London, its interconnections and underground links. *Mind the Gap*, advised the familiar voice down in the Tube, as an insect chirrup of metal announced the approach of the roaring train, though the accent seemed to carry a newly minted, even Scots, inflection. Maybe they'd changed the tape. Political correctness, and a need to reflect regional diversity? Unlikely. The tenuous connections of London. Where the oddest things are sometimes the most true. Then Miles himself did an odd thing. Instead of carrying on to the main line terminus he got off at Embankment and caught the Tube straight back to Charing Cross. A weary soldier, he nodded acknowledgment to the statue of Edith Cavell, raising his rolled newspaper, then took up his post at the corner of the Court, and imitated a man reading it. I can wait, he thought. I can wait.

His wait lasted twenty five minutes. This was the height of the English summer, and the sky soon clouded over. Then rain fell with a vengeance, and the young man standing there, getting drenched to the skin while reading a newspaper as its pages turned sodden and illegible, looked and felt silly. He went home.

3

In his dream, he and Becky were back in the Dodge Avenger, heading west out of LA towards Death Valley. It was snowing, hard. Great whirls and funnels of the stuff obscured the view, giving Miles a sense both of heightened danger and a snug, slightly dozy pleasure. That anaesthetizing quietness of snow, in the greyness of a dying afternoon.

- Look out for signs to Red Dusk. Red Dusk, then Bask. Then it's north, up to Calgary.

The slow-motion snow grew even heavier. For some reason this lifted the car off the road and into the air, every ten to twenty yards or so. Then it would land, smoothly, softly. Up. Down. Up again. Down again. Flying. And drowsing. A tingling.

The grey now had flashes of pink. The snow formed a tunnel. He couldn't make out the contours of anything much, but the windscreen had grown to a size more appropriate to a coach, and that helped. Becky looked cold, though, next to him in the driver's seat.

Although the windows were tightly shut, there were sparkles of snow all over her padded jacket, bobble hat and scarf, leaving only her eyes and nose uncovered. Her eyes were closed. Let her sleep. She's driving in a straight line, and there won't be any oncoming traffic. Miles unbuckled his seatbelt and rose to get a white cup of water from the stewardess on night-watch, but the car was only briefly a night flight before it was a coach they were back on, then up into air, then down and then tingle, all on our way to Caligari.

-    You're all fine, known quantities.

He wanted to reassure the full coach, and moving slowly down the aisle, patted the shoulder of one and then another. Some of them had saline drips attached. That's good. They would have dropped down from the panel above the seat, automatically. Adjust your own, before assisting anyone else. There would be lifejackets under the seats, but most seemed to be wearing their own, tatty black ones. Most of these people were dead, or thereabouts, or staring ahead as if sightless. That's OK, they're all old, even the young ones. The point, though, is that they're quiet. You shouldn't disturb the driver. Then a burst of fear in the dream: oh no, I forgot to count them! I have to count them or we'll crash.

-    Dad. Help me Dad. Please help me count them.

Miles gently patted his father's shoulder to wake him, but the old man's right arm came clean away in Miles' hand. The so-gently amputated arm was simultaneously the arm rest of his seat. That's a bit odd, and his elbow won't bend. It was wrapped in the shreds of a black bin-bag, when abruptly Miles saw a scarecrow in a field, black rags torn, but he was quite small again, now, and didn't want to see that face. It turned anyway, with a grin, to take him in. A half-moon scar, from lip to pumpkin ear. A feeling of utter loneliness and abandonment overtook him, as he moved in the flickering, mortuary light.

Approaching the back of the bus, he missed his father. Was careful to hold his dead father's arm above the level of the heart. Through the back window he could already see the towering walls of snow, the strewn trash, bits of shredded black tire from other crashes. All the stuff the Russians left. The setting sun showed him vast urine stains, down from the high walls of snow, running into potholes in the road, impacted snow floating in cakes in those massive pot-hole urinals. Dirty light slapped him, and he flinched. I can't see properly, to count. Miles could only make out the silhouettes and not yet the features of the two travellers on the back seat, one much smaller than the other. The man, he thought, must be wearing one of those fleecy hats with ear-flaps, though his ears were huge, and stuck out of the hat.

> \-   *Because there's a* slit *on each side, fool…and where there's*
>   *a* slit, *there's a way…*

The hands were vicious bands around his throat. He heard the bang of collision and the hiss of smashing glass from the front end of the bus, felt the vehicle soar into the air, before it flipped over. The hands slid away, regretfully and almost gently. And then he was waking, trapped in wet sheets, soaking in his own sweat, that didn't now feel like his own. Didn't feel right. Not right at all. Cold cold water, pure water. I need. Ugh. *Dad. Help me, Dad. Help me count them, or we'll crash.* Sweat ran down his spine, pooling at the base, and, standing naked in the middle of the bathroom, Miles started to tear up.

But stopped, immediately. Come on, it was only a nightmare. He took a shower, thinking up a plan, and drying himself, saw that it was after five. The sky grew reluctantly lighter, seemingly wary of premature exposure. Miles pulled on his long red dressing gown, and then turned the key to the door of his study, and retrieved the book from the special pocket that he had had sewn into his black wool jacket. A piece of thick card was also sewn into the lining of the dressing gown, so that he could risk sudden movements without fear of causing damage to his constant companion. Putting fire under the coffee pot, he sat, made notes, and read. He thought he would go back to the beginning of the book, which of course had changed again.

This treatise will set out to correct certain common errors that may delay the journey towards an understanding of the true relationship between Magic and Time. Even practitioners at the sixth and seventh levels, those whose aspirations to the status of Adept are far from baseless, those whose feet have often trod the magic line whereby the unseen world is no longer a dream, the seen world no longer a reality, even they, knocking so to say at the very threshold of power, do falter when clambering over this stile, this rude and obstreperous fact.

To practise the Art of Magic is not, we must indeed insist, may never be, to exert force against the world in order to change it on lines of mere Whim. Rather the alteration brought about by the agency of Magic takes place in the present, so as to bring about both a different Future, and a different Past. Let us first address, as we always must on this Time-bound globe, the Future. The practical effect of the act of Transmutational Magic will be so swift as to erase from memory the state of affairs which preceded it. Once having taken place, the act of Magic is one that can never, thereafter, lead the traveller on the journey to knowledge to a point where it has not already happened, nor to a point whereby it has yet to occur.

Resting the book on his raised knees, Miles played with the arm of the angle-poise reading lamp, turning the hinge with his finger so as to move the pool of light. He pondered several things. All these things involved pressing at what the book had termed the *threshold*.

4

Jack's Jazz was a combined café and CD shop. Situated on the floor above one of London's better-known bookstores, it offered low Moroccan-style banquettes and sofas grouped round even lower tables. These Miles never used. For him, the point of Jack's Jazz was the huge windows, the view diagonally down across Charing Cross Road to Fiddlers Court, and the long, wooden bar running the length of that wall, where he could perch on a high stool, nursing a coffee, working or watching undisturbed. He would stare out for minutes at a time, writing occasionally in a spiral-bound notebook, or consulting the other book that he would pull out of his jacket. The staff had him down as an aspiring novelist. He looked the part and he wasn't bothering anyone. This place is never full anyway. Nowhere near. Maya, who frequently brought him his coffee, had taken a shine to him.

- Refill, Mr Writer?

Miles turned. Shades in one hand, 501s weathered from black to charcoal, hair like a pelt turning pepper and salt. Always the black wool jacket, white shirt (unironed, and doesn't seem gay, so) and the remains of a tan he certainly didn't get here. I really would like to. I *really* would.

- I'd really like to read your novel. When it's finished. Or even…

- Novel. Absolutely.

- What's it about?

- It's sort of at the ideas stage. To be honest I'm still making notes.

He smiled and gestured helplessly around the notebook, gently bringing down his hand, fingers spread so as to block from view all he had written that morning.

- Another coffee would be good, yes. Thanks.

- You don't know how it's going to end then?

Miles turned so pale so quickly that she thought he might faint.

- No. I have absolutely no idea how all this is going to end. *Absolutely none.*

He had looked so bereft for a moment, she thought, I've said the wrong thing. I don't know how, and I didn't mean to, but I have. Then Miles looked straight back at her, colour returning, and smiled again.

- No. I'm toying with the idea that things don't have an ending. They keep beginning again, slightly differently each time. A bit like, oh I don't know…the day? The days. They're all the same. Yet not the same. Or a wave becoming a new wave. When it crests, hits the beach, it's gone. Lost to the next one. Maybe I'll call it *The Lost Wave.* So the book is a sequence of snapshots of things that are actually kind of like amnesia, starting again always, always from a slightly different angle. But that's only half the story. I'm not there yet.

Oh-kay, thought Maya, now it turns out I said the right thing, and I don't why. Que sera. Lost waves, no endings. Just beginnings. Cool.

- Well, Miles, I wish you waves of luck. *Oceans* of luck.

Damn, she does fancy him, thought Zeke at the other till, at the other end of the room, behind the racks, bagging a jazz CD then thrusting it vaguely at a customer. He slammed the till shut.

Miles liked Jack's Jazz, to the extent that he was aware of anything about it other than the big window. The coffee, though not up to

New York standards, was (for the most part) coffee. Soup, which he always had for lunch, was at least good enough for him to be vaguely aware of ingesting it on a daily basis. The vegetarian salads were works of art that looked fantastic, and contained wildly organic ingredients normally only seen when caught in the act of strangling hedgerows, or prior to compression into tablet form by teams of visionary scientists in Switzerland. There was just one problem, apart from the salads, and a seemingly insuperable one. Miles didn't like jazz. He was still obliged to listen to it all day long. Not much option, there.

-    You ought to bloody like it, with a name like yours.

So had ended his first attempt to engage Zeke in a spot of mild induction. He knew he irritated Zeke, but put this down to his inability to tolerate the later work of John Coltrane at Heathrow decibel-levels and a time of day when the brain was still shredding and filing the last bits of yesterday's dreams. The bookshop downstairs complained, and with increasing frequency. Zeke's usual response was to put on more, even later and longer Coltrane, or improvised pandemonium with titles like *Machine Gun* and *Balls*, productions of the 1970s European Free Jazz movement, which evidently stood somewhere high above the peaks of the Italian Renaissance, at least from Zeke's sectarian vantage point.

Two of the more intrepid members of the *Machine Gun* ensemble also put out a live album called *Schwarzwaldfahrt,* at the climax of which the musicians abandon their instruments altogether and attack each other with rocks and chunks of tree, while stumbling waist-deep in a stream in the German forest. Perversely, Miles had a soft spot for this one, and started to rattle on about the Northern European Romantic tradition, but Zeke said he'd lost him there, by which time Miles had concluded in any case that all of this jazz improvisation lark, taken in the round or viewed from the treetops, down in the water or from any more angled perspective, was indeed, *en fin de compte* and even when not involving machine guns, balls.

But jazz is basically American, he thought, and I'm, even more basically, British. Is that the problem? The trouble with American jazz was, if it wasn't fractured and atonal it was either nervy as hell – Charlie Parker might have had lightning coursing through his fingers, but he made Miles feel he was on his third coffee when he hadn't even finished his first – or it curdled and turned maudlin on you, trapped you in unwanted, breathy intimacy at the end of the bar in a 3 am bottle of bourbon, reeking of self-pity and slurring in slow motion. Maybe he needed to try harder. Let's give it one last chance.

- OK Zeke. Don't pull any punches. What is it people see, sorry, hear, in Coltrane?

He had learned enough to know that it was always surnames for Coltrane and Mingus and Monk, but first name for Ornette Coleman and for Miles' namesake. Charlie Parker was Parker, or 'Bird' if you were one of the near-extinction bearded seniors who called individuals of either sex 'man' and who even Zeke found eye-watering.

- Dunno Miles. I reckon it's probably the unsurpassed levels of innovation, taking on board, just from the technical perspective, the use of overblowing, fractional tones, and other sounds deemed mistakes by the squares at Juilliard, but which are now an integral part of saxophone tuition. Additionally there's his versatility in moving from the blues and ballads to lengthy works written by himself, carrying a philosophical and political inflection that helped make those times so incendiary, and all delivered with a complex, almost reluctant authority. Not to mention the high, the golden polish, of Coltrane's inimitable tone.

Miles pondered this in silence for a moment.

- You rate him, then.

- Zorright.

The two looked out silently over Charing Cross Road, while Maya, regarding them with affectionate pity from the serving hatch, reflectively wiped dry some giant mugs. This place is going to fold. We've got a geek who terrifies the customers, and who's managed to piss off the bookstore, who control the lease. The food should be hanging in an art gallery, the cook should be hung, period, and the one customer who comes in every day can't stand jazz, and has never bought a CD. We're gonna fold. They'll shut us down. She dried another mug.

Miles was into day five of the Jack's Jazz stakeout when the odd couple made a comeback. Vaulting down the stairs two at a time, he exited while Mr Balding Pinstripe and the more thinly elegant Winthrope walked to the turning into Fiddlers Court. He followed them, unseen. Again it was Winthrope who had the key. Miles shouted, but the two swiftly entered and closed their door against the world, without a sign of having heard. Again Miles rapped hard on the door, whose missing panel, still not replaced, had been secured a bit more firmly with nailed board. Again the fruitless waiting, and the walk back to the red phone box. A proliferation of cards above the handset offered a range of services, from French maids to dominatrices, taxis to hairstylists and tanning parlours. Appointments Not Always Necessary. Tell that to Redidivus. While listening to the ringtone, he pulled down an unusually expensive looking card, white with tiny flecks of colour somehow pressed into it. It read – no answer, here we go again – *Coming Soon…*but the reverse side of the card was blank. Miles idly replaced it, put down the phone, and returned to Jack's Jazz. He picked up some odd looks from the vicinity of the kitchen and the till, but no comment.

Of course, he thought, they knew they were being followed. They couldn't even get into their own damn building without him hammering on the door followed by a phone call two minutes later. Of course they know. What should he do? Stick a letter of complaint under the door? No. Next time he saw them he would not knock, he would not phone. He would wait outside the doorway of Redidivus Books, for however long it took. An hour or so later, he saw them walking up the road, perhaps from the Tube. They turned into the Court. Miles stayed in his seat. After a few minutes he settled the bill and put on his jacket.

Glancing out of the window for a final time, he thought he saw Becky. At last. Was it her? It was the tote bag he noticed first. That candy-stripe pattern was very familiar. Used for carrying first editions of Zane Grey. But not, in the end, a stranger, much stranger book, that had passed through the hands and libraries and rituals of Aleister Crowley and Felix Manto. He liked her walk. Extremely alert, as if engaged by everything she saw, very upright. A slight roll of the shoulders. And other features. He wanted her again, lust and comradeship pinioning anger.

Then he noticed the two young guys in tracksuits and bandanas, conferring right behind her. One dropped back but held her in his sights, while the other kept pace with Becky on the tote-bag side, hanging back slightly like a car waiting for the right moment to overtake. Miles thought he saw a hand move down towards the bag, then flash back. OK, I've reflected on my own latent tendencies to racial and social stereotyping. I haven't jumped to a conclusion, even though I think about this woman every day. But you are not going to do this. Go! Miles took the stairs three at a time, and hit the pavement. Sizing up the traffic in a split second, he shot across the road in time to see the first young man drop something into Becky's bag. Something white, an envelope maybe. As she turned into the Court a smile, a nanosecond of acknowledgment, seemed to flicker in the brilliant sunshine. But was she glancing at Miles, or the messenger?

He glided swiftly along the pavement, so near he could begin to catch the scent of her. He was going to close on her just after she knocked, or better still, just as her key was turning in the lock.

Today central London was as hot as Los Angeles. No air moved. Concern was fighting it out with the smarting feeling of not just being dropped, but not being let in on the bigger picture. Then she slowed and Miles hung back while she quickly read the note, crumpled and dropped it in the bag. First anger overtook him, then he overtook her, blocking her pathway to the door.

- Becky. You ditched me. In the fucking desert. Why, please?

No response. Becky stood stock still. Above the hint of cleavage, he saw a tiny drop of perspiration glide into a question mark. He had to repress the urge to put his tongue to it. To nuzzle. To do, what else. To do everything, everything else. Her perfume and the scent of her body, beneath. But it was Miles beneath that wave. He was standing, but he was down and in deep. In heat, and struggling in the maze-caprice of circumstance. Under the fickle and flowery moods of the English summer, desert perspiration and a woman who, even in her unexplained and protracted absence, could pull him like a magnet.

- What's going on? And who do you work for? That outfit in the West Village, or this place….

- I know, Miles. I know.

- You know *what?*

- They might want the book to be with you, but they don't want *me* to be with you. They said break it off, when you know it's mission accomplished. I didn't want to do that, of course I didn't. But if I hadn't, I guess…we might not be here. And there's something more important. It's about to happen.

For a second her eyes made a calculated sweep of the Court, then she dipped her hand into the bag. Miles smoothed the note, and read. *The guy you were worried about is OK. He always sits in the third floor café window on the south side of Charing Cross. He's seen Mr B and Mr W. He's in Jack's today and he should have seen you. The meeting's starting right now.* Before Miles could say another word, Becky Morrell grabbed both lapels of his jacket and pulled him down on to her, kissing him full on the mouth.

- Now get in there, Miles. And don't screw it up. Whatever you do, take the job. *Get that job!*

With her left arm she pushed open the unlocked door, and with her right almost threw him into the vestibule. Miles had time to think, wow, I'd forgotten how strong she is, before she slammed the door behind him and he was standing in semi-darkness, listening to a hum of voices, gathered in a further room.

The man who stepped out to greet him looked vaguely familiar. Significantly younger than the booksellers, but older than Miles by, what, a decade? Still good looking – craggy features, lived-in. The frame of someone who now worked out and looked after himself, but hadn't always. It dawned on Miles that he knew who this man was, though he had never met him. The intensely blue eyes he did expect, but they were smaller and more cagey. More lined than in the photographs. And the hair was much shorter, well-styled but grey at the temples. And a sharp, gunmetal grey suit, with skinny black leather necktie. A suit! That was a turn up for the books.

- Miles. At last. Welcome.

The man paused, to shake Miles' hand.

- Felix Manto.

5

Over the next couple of hours, Miles learned a great deal. Mostly what he learned about was guesswork. When you have to trust guesswork, tread gently on its fragile boards, but still have faith in them, so as to move yourself forward – and when to hold back for a moment, rethinking direction, because the next step forward will only drop you down, fast, through rotting splinters, nothing to clutch at but space. The way these people operated was an object lesson in how to step out with an amazing confidence, built from experience and daring, knowing full well that the board you just trod on *had* crumbled, was vanishing into the void. But always the one behind, never the one in front. That was the art. Or one of the arts, of what used to be called Magic.

As men who are dead go, the quondam rock star Manto seemed pretty much alive. The room was a tip, lit by candles. Whatever Redidivus may have been, it was no longer a functioning book dealership. Like Manto, Mr Winthrope seemed to possess more vim and vigour than Miles had been led to believe initially, though for most of the meeting he barely stirred, cocking his head at a listening angle, furrowing his brow, mind mostly elsewhere, one white hand occasionally adjusting a velvet bow-tie. Miles knew enough about bespoke three-piece suits to know that he couldn't afford one. Gauntlet cuffs and fabric-covered buttons don't come cheap. So this very old man was still something of a dandy. Miles took in the artfully swept-back white hair rising from the widow's peak, the equally white, pointed and manicured beard, and saw a mix of vanity and high intelligence. He looked like someone who gets irritated easily. Particularly when people don't do his bidding. Though that probably doesn't happen often.

The guessing game began right at the start. There was no mistaking the atmosphere of a job interview – and although Felix Manto had been or was a rock musician, he was obviously well used to chairing meetings. There the resemblance to normality ended. Only some of those present introduced themselves. The overweight, whey-faced man in the pinstriped suit, who, along with a certain unwitting Librarian had set Miles off on the wildest chase of his life so far, turned out to be Mr Boxer. No first name, just Mr Boxer. Miles felt instinctively that, despite the fact that their only conversation prior to this day had been packed with unspoken knowledge, wilful deception, and advice that would eventually put the younger man in physical danger, Mr Boxer was a man you could trust. In this new world many things were now, quite simply, turned upside down.

Readily intrigued by mysteries, Miles knew he was easily hooked. Which must be part of the reason why they had set this up. But when he thought about it, there was no magic, or even coincidence, in their knowing that he would end up here, in this candle-lit room, blinds closed against the day, with them, involved. Once they had been told he was at his usual post, all they had to do was get Becky to stroll up from the Tube. At a moment of their own choosing. With an eye-catching candy-stripe bag that Miles had seen her carry before, just to make doubly sure she would stand out from the crowd. They knew he'd come. Felix Manto released the top button of his white shirt and pulled the black tie slightly down, took off his gunmetal grey jacket, then rolled up his cuffs while looking Miles over. That blue gaze is as penetrating as an airport detector, thought Miles, but benignly inclined, I'd say – at least for now.

- Miles, it might be Magic, but it isn't rocket science. A lot of the time it isn't even Magic. It's just knowing. How people are likely to behave, going on their track record. You in this case, sure, but everyone's a creature of habit. Like that Scottish fellow who, shall we say, got under your skin a little. He's potentially lethal, but in many ways he's perfectly predictable…

- Felix, I think you should talk Miles through what we're going to do about his dark encounter outside this meeting…*if* we decide to go ahead, that is.

This from one of those who, without any rudeness, was clearly not about to disclose a name, but who from the timbre of his voice Miles felt sure was an East Coast bookseller to whom he had spoken by phone, and one instrumental in his moves.

- Yeah, that's helpful. We have a lot of business to get through, today. But just to revert to the last point briefly, a lot of what we do, a lot of what *you* would do, is based on simple laws of probability. Facts, timing, the right moves. It helps if you're physically fit. So that you can run like hell, if you have to. And you would have to. Symbolism and all that stuff, yadda-yadda, it's part and parcel of Magic. But at the end of the day, hey, it's like Freud said; sometimes a cigar is just a cigar.

This drew a token smile from those present, apart from Winthrope, who looked at Manto as if he'd lost his mind. Then it was Winthrope's turn. When he asked his question, the room went very quiet.

- Professor Proctor, notwithstanding all the points raised about the practical skills involved, and the symbolism of it all, the pentagrams, cyclopean eye, the pyramids, all that…apparatus, there is another side that we *all* acknowledge. Though it is terribly hard to talk about, in definite terms. The gift. *Your* gift, Miles. You seem to possess it, but not know that you possess it. At the moment, as the Viennese doctor might also have said, it's unconsciously at work. You say you don't remember…. being able to alter the course of events?

They all leaned forward. It was going to hang on this. Miles had time to file a question in his mind about where in the States this man hailed from. Something in the elongated *all* suggested the Boston area. Then a new voice intervened.

- Of course he doesn't remember, he's an *idiot savant.* Extremely useful to us, he's demonstrated that already, less useful to himself, he's shown that too. But he doesn't know he's done it, after the fact. He's like a drunk who wakes up and can't remember how he got home. He gets the right result, no doubt about it. But he couldn't take on Level B work, let alone top level projects. He has a gift, oh yes indeed. But he can't control his gift. He doesn't understand his own abilities. Hasn't learned himself, yet.

This from another who had not spoken so far. The woman, in her middle years, attractive in a regal way and with a mane of chestnut hair, reminded Miles of some of the more steely female Profs at Beltane College. Elbows on the table, she steepled her fingers, showing him long, intensely carmine nails. Then she slowly let her hands drop, and looked him straight in the eyes. In fact, he thought he might have seen her before, somewhere.

-   The group is well aware of your views, thank you. We need to hear from Miles himself. *Miles…*

There was almost a plea in Manto's voice. This really was an interview. Some of them were rooting for him, and some weren't. He could get the job, the real job, or he would be offered something further down the food chain. There was no way they would waste time on an encounter like this, only to send him away empty-handed. There'd be something that exploited his talent, this *gift*, whatever it was. Something that made him useful to them – for a time. With enough excitement to guarantee his silence and his loyalty. But then? Some potion or other, to make him forget. These upstanding citizens are past masters at that kind of thing. And then one fine day he'd wake up like the drunk, and think, what was that dream all about? How did I end up here? And it would all soak away into Normal Life, as if it had never been. Either that, or they'd tire of him and throw him to the dogs. Leave him to the Scotsman, the man with monster ears. An unpleasant picture came into his mind, but he was able to cancel it.

-   …you don't remember, say, being able to move the car

back into the right lane, on several occasions when Miss Morrell was almost asleep at the wheel? Just by force of will.

- That's a leading question. You're feeding him lines.

This from the dark brown voice of the female interrogator most in need of convincing.

- *Think,* Miles. Do you remember when the books were being loaded on to the truck, in Pasadena…?

Miles went back in his mind. I remember the light. There is nothing like the light in Southern California. And not just the light in those beautiful stone lanterns, which come on after the sun has set, so fast the change from red to blue to dark. But that's the sun being the sun, I can't control that. I can't make it rise and go down when I want to. And then with the peripheral vision that the mind has, as well as the eye, he saw smaller things that, yes, he could control. He saw a dog's lead whip in and out of sight, as a snake whips away across the desert.

- Yes. I do remember. There was a woman out jogging. She was trying to do two things at once. Her dog was running out of her control because of one of those extending leads, but she was also about to lose her jogging top, in fact she did drop her top, it was pink, and I…. No. She didn't lose. The pink top. I stopped that from happening.

They all sat back. He'd got the job.

He didn't feel the slightest exultancy. Miles felt sick to the pit of his stomach, because he knew that just now, when he searched inside his mind, like putting your hand down into the darkness to feel for something, his hand had found something with teeth. He'd need tuition, if he took this job on. And Becky wants me to take it, and I want it. And I want her. But can I have both? A sixth sense made him veil these thoughts, as he described instead other forms of thinking, ones more helpful to his audience in the room.

> - And, just now. A picture was forming in my mind. Not a pleasant one. So I pushed it aside. People say that, you know, "I put it to one side. I put it on the back burner". But it's more than that, with me. I can cause things to happen, or not happen. Sometimes. I just haven't wanted to believe it, because it makes me sound mad. I've thought of it as being like déjà-vu. Or like the way schizophrenics think they can hear voices. Something that happens, yet that isn't real. But…

As in all interviews, the interviewed became for a moment the interviewer.

> - How did *you* know about those alternative outcomes, those different scenarios? There's one where a pink top falls, and if my memory is correct, a gun goes off and injures someone. But other, different worlds, or *stories*. Where that doesn't happen. Because I was able to push it one way rather than the other. Move a driver back into the right lane – all those things happened so far away from here. You weren't there. How do *you* all come to have an overview of this?

This question didn't seem to faze them. The professor-type answered briskly, still matter-of-fact, but with more warmth in her voice than before. Again she looked him straight in the eyes. Her own didn't blink. Complex, thought Miles, trying to read her, as well as what she said. Something of the lecture hall, a little of Lauren Bacall. Both acquired, not instinctive, behaviours. So who is she really, and where is she from? That accent: Boston, again? The part of the States where America got started.

> - It showed up in the Dream Pool. Don't run before you can *walk*, Miles. Chairman, I think Dr Proctor needs to

step outside, and that we need to discuss…

-   Come on, Laura, who's chairing this meeting?

Laura had not wanted her name to be given away. Mistake, Felix. She rolled her eyes heavenward in exasperation. Felix sat in profile, mouth slightly ajar, clearly not knowing who had got the upper hand here. Evidently Magic dealt with but did not erase all human failings, and fallings-out. And yes again, I think, Boston, thought Miles, hearing the elongation as she spoke of Miles' *walk*, which seemed to incorporate woe, war and work, before its four letters were through. Perhaps that's what spending time with this strange band of people would feel like.

-   Come on, *Felix*, this isn't exactly a board meeting at Citicorps. I don't see anyone taking the *minutes*.

-   With Miles here, I dare say there wouldn't be any point. He'd push with that powerful mind of his and make the minutes rewrite themselves.

There was clearly much more to Mr Boxer than met the eye. He smiled, eyes hooded, professionally amicable, giving away less than nothing. Thanks in part to his intervention, the *idiot savant* was now the possessor of a powerful mind. One of us. This broke the tension, and shortly after, the meeting too broke up.

6

Miles walked slowly through the heat of the day back down the Court. They wanted him to work with them. Not work *for* them, work with them. I'd have liked that one on tape. There would be no problems at Beltane, and Winthrope would clear up the affair of the book. They had a few ideas about secondment to a certain American research institute where they had contacts, or a plan for applying for extended leave. But his career was a good cover.

In fact they already had one or two people in the College on their payroll. He'd find out.

The book, of course, was a vital factor. And much too big an issue for one meeting. When they had finished, Miles was to go back and talk to Felix about that and other matters, some routine, others weighty. All complex. Miles knew that his life had just turned a corner, and at speed. He also felt chastened. Those simple, practical things, not the symbolism, or his gift, but just the simple stuff. He wasn't always so great at that. Like when he was gently reminded that it is perfectly possible to get in and out of Fiddlers Court from the opposite end to the Tube. You wouldn't see it if you didn't already know it, but there is a gap between two buildings. Not technically a public thoroughfare, but not invisible either. You can walk through it, putting one foot in front of the other, in a non-magical but highly effective way. Sometimes a cigar is just a cigar. Winthrope and Boxer were in and out of the building all the time. But why then did I have to go through all this rigmarole, if they knew they might want me on board? I must have been followed. Vetted. And thoroughly. Leave that for later. You're working with us, they said. Not for us. They said.

They had suggested he go back to Jack's Jazz, and take five. He didn't really feel like going back there, right now. But if he was going to go for a stroll to get some air instead, he'd better let Felix know. Would the phone number work, this time? He stepped into the kiosk, and then thought: maybe I should just go back to Jack's. It's what we agreed. I don't want them to think I say one thing, and then run off and do something else. They need to know they can rely on me.

Cogitating, Miles glanced up at the ever-changing cards. *Coming Soon…* Idly he pulled the white card, with its scarlet flecks, down. That's a really unusual paper, for these days anyway. A dense weave, almost a late-Victorian paper. He flipped it over. It read, in red, *Red.* OK, great, Red's coming over. Crank up the old Victrola. Crack open the champagne. *Red.* Probably another restaurant. But then, before his eyes, the letters added to themselves. *Red Car.* With one part of his mind, Miles thought, I'm seeing things. *Red Car.* Letters don't just grow on business cards like flowers on a branch. Another part of his mind thought, yes they do. The group are testing me. Felix and Winthrope, and Laura who didn't want her name spoken out loud, they're doing this. The interview isn't quite over. Just a little written exercise. A little test to show us what you can do. It was Laura, I bet. She isn't convinced. I've got to show her I can be trusted to do Level B things. Or is this Level D, down in the pecking order of transcendental magic-in-action. Or, and the hairs were prickling now on the back of Miles' neck, is this Level A.

Red Car

Just within earshot, tyres screeched and horns blared. Usual Central London soundscape. But possibly not, on reflection. *Red Car.* Whatever the test is, I'm going to have to react fast. Then, as the roar of a car engine drew closer, (and though he couldn't see it yet, the colour of the car was hardly in doubt) the letters added to themselves again. *Red Carna* – please, let it be a misspelling of Carnival. Please. No. Please God, no! *Red Carnage.*

Red Carnage Coming

Miles turned, in time to see the young woman pushing a pram down the opposite side of Fiddlers Court. The Court was a pedestrianised zone, but the red Lamborghini was going to take its chances and try to get in anyway. A series of stills. Things took a turn for the worse. A man rushed forward in an attempt to pull the woman back to safety, but this only caused her to jerk in shock and let go the pram. The pram moved, as did the car travelling far too fast, the two about to meet, and in his mind's eye Miles saw something appalling, blood and bits spraying up the wall. He hadn't time to get out of the kiosk. On instinct he stared at the card. I can do this. Crack the champagne. *Red Carnation! Red Carnation!*

RED CARNATION.

Carnations, and champagne, and safety. A young woman reached out on the passenger side of the sports car, which stopped the pram from rolling any further forward. The Lamborghini had already braked and stopped abruptly, grazing slightly the stonework at the corner. But that was the only damage.

The driver stepped, or rather reeled out – a Hooray Henry, complete with striped blazer. He was holding a champagne bottle, from which he took a last swig, chucking it into the back of the open-top car. A theatrical bow, then he plucked the red carnation from his buttonhole, and made as if to offer it, with a flourish, to a mother whose attention was all elsewhere. Failing to gain a response, he spun round in time to pin it on one of the two policemen now running into the Court. Miles looked down at the card, which now read *Coming Soon* only. Then even these letters were gone, the card crumbling to cigarette paper thinness, then to dust, the dust on books in libraries and then nothing, the last motes and molecules falling from his hand.

One for the Dream Pool, Laura. *Idiot savant*, am I. Miles thought he was going to enjoy working with some of his new colleagues more than others. And would you have killed a child, just for the sake of a test? Killed a baby, to prove that the organization was in danger of not filling a junior post at the right level of expertise? The appointee looked at the scene outside the phone box. The police car had been joined by another. The small crowd, the flashing lights, the Lamborghini, all looked real enough. But so real that he could have been doing Laura, doing the group, an injustice. They were all on the same side, now. At least in principle.

So if there were trust issues here, there was also the power of reality to intervene, with its random accidents, drunk drivers, victims young and old. And there were other powers, powers of Magic, to make those truly ghastly things all right again. Let's look to the bright side, because these are my growing powers, and I will do my best.

7

- Oh, it was the best of times, it was the worst of times. Mostly being a rock god, as you are kind enough to phrase it, was great, sure. There was just one pretty insuperable problem. You may not get this one. Even with *your* powers of intuition.

The dead-alive rock star looked a little sheepish.

- I don't like rock music.

Miles laughed. He and Felix Manto were sitting in a corner of Jack's Jazz. Miles had told Maya and Zeke that someone very important was going to come in and sit with him. This was business. They needed peace and quiet, away from noise and anyone who might overhear. Maya immediately covered half a dozen tables in the vicinity of the corner with 'Reserved' signs, and Zeke put on muzak at decibel levels appropriate to an elevator heading for the penthouse. Maya had the older guy down as a publisher. Take his novel, Mr Publisher. Let this be Mr Bloomsbury. Let there be a movie. Let there be me and Miles, starring in it, together. Zeke thought the guy looked familiar, but couldn't quite place him. Got it. He's the cocktail lounge pianist from the Radisson Hotel. What the hell have he and Miles got to say to each other?

- I'm alive, by the way. If you were wondering…

- Well the evidence seemed to point in that direction.

- Yeah. The fishing line, dead-in-the-water caper was just a good way to bring that phase to an end. I couldn't stand it anymore. First the man takes cocaine. Just the occasional line, after dinner. Then maybe just when you're on tour. Then before you know it, bang, it's crack, and it's taken the man. I had to get right out of that one.

- And you hate rock music? That's incredible.

- I liked some of the musicians. Interesting people. Restless folks who want to know more.

- Out of the Brits….?

- Well, Jimmy Page…

- Is it true, about the connection with…

- Nah. Just fantasy. Gossip. Rock music's rumour mill grinding away, I guess. It helped sell a lot of papers as well as records, back in the day…

Felix sighed, momentarily wistful.

- …or the day before the day. We'll get on to the book in a moment. But, no. You get these really bright, inquisitive people, with a low boredom threshold, and a real appetite for life – but the music. Page was an exception. They don't have a background. They learned guitar copying *Smokestack Lightnin'* till their fingers bled. A lot of them can't read a note. All those songs in four-four time, cloppety, cloppety clop, with a backbeat. Mind you, I should have issued a public apology for that last album. No, I'm a jazz buff. Must take a look at the stock here, I haven't been in for a while.

- Do they know you here? They didn't seem…

- I grew a beard, after I drowned in that Scottish loch. Wore glasses, cut my hair. And by rock god standards, I was little league. People have short memories.

- I still think you want to be careful, you haven't been dead that long. Where are you from, you the living person?

- OK it's obviously my interview now. The US.

- Indeed, but more specifically?

Having seen New York, bits of LA and Death Valley, Miles felt he had the USA pretty firmly nailed down.

- The Yazoo Basin. I toned down my accent when y'all started typecastin' me as a good ol' boy...

- The Yazoo...

- Mississippi. Place called Clarksdale.

There was a rumble of distant thunder, and for a moment Miles could have sworn the air turned faintly blue. Felix seemed briefly lost in thought. Across from them, Maya was standing on one of the bar stools, reaching up to fix a plate to the picture rail, while holding another pile of crockery. The stool tipped over and the plate went flying, but Maya landed squarely on both feet, catwise, crockery intact, tucked into her left arm, and caught the plate casually, almost as if someone had thrown her a frisbee. Another strong woman. I like Maya. Then she put the whole lot down, bending over to locate a cardboard box.

Miles couldn't help but observe the movements of a marvellously curvaceous female bottom, gently agitated in exciting, albeit contrasting proportion to an otherwise lean and, as he had cause to know well, muscular frame. A number of fleeting thoughts passed through his consciousness, chief among them his own pride in the fact that he didn't stereotype women.

- Yeah, I had to get out of that one, too. It's still the poorest State in the Union. Anyways. The book. It likes you, it's taken a shine to you.

- You mean, I like...

- No, I mean it *likes* you. It spreads its pages for you, to let you in. It tries unusual positions, moves its own words around, leaves virgin spaces for you to fill in, with your own words. It's courting you. Patiently. For now. If you don't think my language appropriate, use the terms you would use, man of your age, your generation. Whatever. *The book wants you, Miles.*

They had spoken a little about the book in the meeting, about the way he would memorise the opening, yet find on returning that it had changed again – the capacity of *Transmutations* to constantly mutate. The words didn't politely stay still on the page, waiting inertly to be picked up, then put down. They danced, in fact they more than danced. They interacted. Miles probed gently.

-   The literature – well, it's scanty, but references to the book always describe it as cursed. I read that Aleister Crowley blamed it for his fall into poverty.

-   Oh the book must have hated Crowley. Everyone did, by the end. Of course he stained the book. I won't go into details, but that couldn't have gone down at all well. He was more of a rock star than I ever was. Before there was rock. The parties, the drugs, the women. And men. That overweening sense that you could control people. Great mountaineer. Serious chess player. Boundless energy, just took the wrong path. I think the book resented being dragged along for the ride, so it took action.

-   But then you owned the book, what did you –

Miles experienced a sudden moment of panic. Oh no, suppose he wants it back. The book's mine. His left arm closed protectively on the book's bespoke pocket. It just felt pleasantly warm. And not the slightest bit cursed. A soft hum, across his ribs.

-   The book and me got along fine. But not the way you two get on. It never changed its words around, for me. In any case I was in no fit state to read anything. My attention span was shot. Only thing I cared for was cocaine. I certainly remember that cover, who could forget it, but I guess the prose is awful Victorian. Never using one word where twenty will do? You're the expert. To tell you the honest truth, Miles, I never really got much beyond the cover. There's a lot I don't remember from that last phase. Before I drowned, and cleaned up. Plus I'm not a scholar, like you…

That's OK, Felix, thought Miles, I'm increasingly less sure I'm one of those any more, either.

- I just wasn't the one. I'm better at the practical side. Capers. I should have been a bank robber. So when I quote-unquote 'died', we thought we'd advertise. Trawl.

- But surely it could have attracted the attention of anybody, just anyone.

- Not when we only sent out three emails, it couldn't. That catalogue went to a *very* select group. The others were high-end sorcerers, with résumés that would stun an ox. But too old, it turned out. The game was up for them. In the end we decided we were mostly just looking for somebody with a bit of magical nous, sure, but somebody who had the normal human skills – mobility, both legs in working order, clean driver's license. Somebody…

Miles sat back, beaming, and waited for Felix Manto, who was searching the air for the right words, to compliment him on the skills he would bring to the group.

- …somebody young, who would do exactly what we wanted. But why me, you're going to ask. Well!

Felix seemed to find something extremely amusing, and laughed to himself. Miles failed entirely to see the joke. I don't like being played with.

- Let's say, you were mentioned in dispatches.

But suddenly, like a car turning a corner at speed, appearing out of nowhere, it was Felix who became deadly serious.

- Which leads me on to something important. I need you to hear this, loud and clear. You have a private life, and it's yours. When we pick things up on the radar, we can be very discrete. We know when to close the curtains, and tiptoe away. We've been learning you. It took some time. But we don't condone affairs between members of the group. We got burned once. A couple that thought one plus one equalled three, and that together they had the power to take us over. We can't support that kind of verticality. If it's gonna work, this has to be a loose group. Of individuals. *No office affairs.*

Miles felt sick. Knowing that it was important not to react badly, he watched with inner vision his heart sink, pulsing redly down into cold waves, while looking with bright candour at the boss. You don't show fear.

- I suppose I expected something along those lines. While we're on the subject of contractual, or I guess tacit, obligations, I wondered – what's my exit strategy? Because this is a form of project work…

Miles felt enough confidence in Felix to relay his worry about the second-class citizen, the one who would one day be slipped the potion of forgetfulness, and wake up the next morning thinking the whole thing had been a dream. That he might prove to be expendable. And then what? No, it seemed there was no potion – not as such.

- Actually, we're a very caring employer. Very postmodern. If we need to let someone go, we use a special psychosoftware. Just so they can't give anything away, even inadvertently. Our first duty is to protect our own people, before we rush out to help other folks. And we cushion any fall with a golden goodbye, so the person never knows they've been black bagged. We're not exactly under-resourced. Which leads me to ask …

Then the talk was of expenses, flights, of matters and feathers smoothed over. It was all going to be great fun. He's done it, he's got a contract, thought Maya, as the two shook hands. Miles was conscious of his heart pulsing, like sonar, down in cold depths. I'm not giving up Becky just because of their control-freakery about verticality and the good of the damned Firm. Forget it.

But the book left a warm feeling, humming on his ribs. As if to say, but I'm here. I was waiting for you in the desert. And *I* didn't abandon you; it wasn't *me* that let you go.

And I won't let you go now.

Hellhound On My Trail

1

The man went by the name of Kenneth McLeod. His name at birth may never be known. Born into a complex skein of fishing families in Oban, he weaved and glided his way through the alleyways of Glasgow, carving a name for himself in the razor gangs of the 50s and 60s. A profoundly violent man, even to his friends. Even to himself. When three rivals cornered him under the railway arch late one night in Sauchiehall Street, their spokesman offering to elongate his smile in time-honoured Glasgow fashion, McLeod was seen to take the switchblade away, and then to slowly slice, without flinching, a half-moon gash from his own mouth to his own ear. He then proceeded to shunt the blade under his adversary's jaw and up into his brain, twiddling it a bit. Railroading the two stooges into carrying the jerking body to the rear of his black Commer van, he then forced them at gunpoint to perform a number of actions they had not anticipated earlier that evening, including the posthumous decapitation of their mentor.

Jollying things along by way of a cheerful bout of pistol-whipping, he, bored by now as well as weary from blood-loss, shot them. By his own account, this involved forcing the two into close proximity, then despatching both with a single bullet and a brief if sombre homily directed at the consequences of same-sex dalliance. The head (the first head of the trio, that is) went on to enjoy a brief career starring in a goldfish bowl in The Office, a portakabin commandeered by McLeod as his headquarters and tucked away in the, by local standards, bucolic setting of a scrap merchant's yard. That massive crusher was a handy thing. The head became the butt of daily ventriloquist jokes, TV ventriloquists being strangely popular at the time. A spot of lunch hour football was also encouraged among McLeod's subordinates, both to keep them in trim, and to keep him in spiritual touch with the beautiful game. In the end the matted cranium was consigned to the crusher, along with the detritus from a complex mail-train robbery, and various other incriminating items including a couple of newish Skodas. In those days most car owners who'd bought a car made in Eastern Europe were happy to see them flattened, not long after purchase.

Head injuries were a speciality of his, as, soon, were bank jobs. Razors became *passé*, firearms *de rigueur*. Clydeside's version of the swinging sixties had kicked in. After blowing out the brains of a trussed security guard via the mouth, admittedly more by accident than design, McLeod was fascinated to observe that, due to the particular angle of ballistic entry, the victim experienced no pain at all, and was able to conduct rational conversation for a good half hour or so. When the guard finally expired, his killer wept copiously, nominating the deceased the best friend he'd never had, and voicing regret that he couldn't bring his new chum back to life, so that they could do it all over again. By the time McLeod came to shoot himself fatally some years later, he had perfected the technique, and most of what is known of his motivation and psychology derives from the cassette tape he made before his face slumped down into the ashtray, while whatever damaged remnants of his psyche could scrabble an escape, shot into the ether by way of the new chimney smoking in his skull.

Few suicides leave this world in a state of unbridled merriment, and McLeod was chronically depressed, by any standards. The depression and frustration were a function of his blindness.

What is now termed macular degeneration had begun to affect him in his thirties. A blot the size of a golf ball sat squarely in the centre of his visual field. He began to complain that he couldn't properly see what or who he was shooting at, and gang members accompanying him on bank jobs began to dread the moment when he let off his shotgun. Standing by the blackboard in The Office and asking for volunteers to drive the getaway car, he couldn't understand why every hand in the room flew up at once.

-   *But lads, lads, you'll miss all the excitement!*

He missed the *sotto voce* mutterings from the floor to the tune of Bingo, Ken, got it in one, bampot; no way Hamish, it's your turn; I'm still paying off the plastic surgeon, me, and other unheeded dwindlings of loyalty, as chair legs scraped the floor and Scotsmen fingered Russian hand guns.

So many members of the gang now carried scorched eyebrows and scars from embedded pellets, that their Edinburgh rivals automatically took these to be the fruits of an initiation ritual. While this did wonders for their reputation north of the border, morale was low around The Office. His vision went from bad to worse. When two unbribeable wags from CID cornered him in the outside privy to present him with a white stick and a pair of aviator shades, he broke the stick in two and exacted retribution, but, timing himself afterwards, realized that what should have been the work of a moment (particularly given that he'd not finished his business), had lasted a full half hour and entailed a fair few fumbles and lucky ones. He also had to bury a suspicion that one of the two had in fact died laughing. The golf ball in the centre of his vision now blotted out the human face, thereby removing much of the pleasure he derived from interacting with his peers. Then darkness supervened.

He had to go straight, or at least semi-legit. This was the direction the Kray Gang in London had been taking, prior to the *Götterdämmerung* triggered by Ronnie's lethal tantrums. To Kenneth, this world was going to the dogs. No honest, clean distinctions anymore. While some of his this-is-a-raid, chew-the-floor-folks cronies took to the construction business, the bright ones sharking their way into non-exec or even executive directorships, McLeod got deep into the really and truly coming thing. Computers.

His scams were entirely lawful. He started hiring out desktop computers to firms for periods of a fortnight or a month, inclusive of delivery and uplift, the latter triggered at the request of the user. A clause in the small print stipulated double-charging following any late return of machines. Firms would use the computers, get used to having them around, forget to return them by the deadline, and, this being the beginning of the Grand Age of Fecklessness, just shell out and sign up again. McLeod wrote the machines off after two years, but continued hiring them out beyond that age. The profits fell straight to the bottom line, like a concrete-footed corpse into the Clyde. Kenneth McLeod was hereby declared a millionaire, and in two years earned more from going legit than he had in decades of blood, sweat and tears (the first and the third other people's, the body odour his own). He railed at this blatant injustice.

The fact that sadomasochistic pornography flooded the Internet just at the point where his vision would not allow him to access it, could only have added insult to injury. Whoever it was that said life is not fair, had, in his view, spoken the unvarnished truth. McLeod did however enjoy a sort of saving grace. A hobby, and one even more absorbing than the football. He had always been fascinated by magic. Not so much the Aleister Crowley kind, blasting rival warlocks and rustling up succubi, but the simple pleasures of turning up as Uncle Kenny at a children's party, to find a shilling or florin or (special occasions!) half-crown behind a young boy or girl's ear, producing out of flourishes and sleeves a paper bouquet, or fanning exotic cards, the more convincingly to intone and pronounce on possible fortunes and futures.

McLeod loved this innocent magic, and despite the fact that he could not, technically speaking, read, even before the eye business, collected books by and about Thurston, Blackmore and the classic stage magicians, absorbing from diagrams anamorphically through a magnifying glass what he couldn't suck from words. He loved television magicians of the time, such as David Nixon. TV was better in the 1960s. (It was also better when he could still see it.) The team soon realized that if a magician or a ventriloquist were scheduled to appear on *Sunday Night at the London Palladium*, that was it. All bets off. That nice wee Post Office, nestling in Paisley. Sweet little tree-shaded branch of the Royal Bank of Scotland. All just asking to be pillaged, a virgin hope postponed until next week. *Stuff they Tiller Girls lads, did ye no see Nixon? And Ray Alan, with Little Tich? Magic!* Magic came first.

He loved to be asked to perform at parties for gang members' offspring, in the days when he could still see and not send the cups and balls flying, or liberate the rabbit prematurely. Such invitations were usually self-generated, and enforced. Associates used to get the heebie-jeebies in case the conjuror's bag, once opened, might reveal evidence of a bookie's getting behind with his payments, or just parts of a bookie's behind, all because the Boss had grabbed the wrong holdall. Many times Dad would gloomily agree to the birthday party conjuror, while Mam waited in the hall armed with a rolling pin in case it all went skew-whiff. One December, McLeod offered to appear as Santa Claus in full scarlet kit and fluffy beard, an offer that turned his lieutenants a little queasy, given that *Ho ho ho wee fellow-me-lad, look what I've got for you* had formed the theme in a different professional context only the previous day. Causing a drill set to have to be replaced.

McLeod had no children of his own. Never married, indeed, or showed signs of interest in any woman beyond his sister Meg, who handled the accounts. They lived together, no one knew exactly where. *Just drop me off at the lights, lads, the walk'll do me good.* In fact nobody ever clapped eyes on Meg, though her telephone manner was such that no one wanted to. At the inquest, however, her replies were barely audible, issuing in broken snuffles from behind a full black veil.

- Och, Kenny was a good man. What a shame, eh. He never did any of these terrible things ye're saying. So good with children. And sensitive…

- *Sensitive?*

- Aye, sensitive about his ears.

The ears were a strange phenomenon. Two strange phenomena. They carried on growing at speed when the man had in all other respects attained physical maturity, and the curling hairs as well as the bat-like northerly projection were a talking point, though only when the two phenomena were not in the immediate vicinity. As noted, Kenneth's interactions with others were apt to be abrasive.

With other grown-ups, at any rate. As far as even his worst detractors could see, Kenneth venerated childhood as a time apart, never abused or exploited either children or his own position of power while in their company, and loved, simply, to perform acts of magic, over decades. With decimalisation the coins may have changed, in the world outside Kenny's world, but the act stayed much the same. An even more cynical regime at the local CID planted a couple of hardened juniors, wise to the predilections of Uncle This and the fumblings of Uncle That, as bait around The Office. All he did was produce coins and sweets from behind their ears, with an injunction (received with genuine amazement) to be amazed.

The worst that could be said of his abilities as a conjurer was that it all seemed to be more for his own enjoyment, rather than that of his audience. Extravagant but essentially unthreatening in performance, he nevertheless seemed to be turning in a mirror, marvelling at himself. The magician McLeod didn't empathise with his captive audience, other than to assume, in some ways correctly, that the capacity for astonishment in the very young is higher than their elders'. However, their intuition is also reliable. No child ever asked to have that loud and strange magician back – though none could have articulated, precisely, the reasons why. Not precisely. McLeod turned, fabricating roses, in his own cold spotlight.

So that's what we're dealing with, thought Miles, consigning the read-and-destroy file to the flames of extinction with one flicker of his hand. His story isn't over. McLeod's in limbo, dead and yet not dead, looking for a way out – or a way back in. Searching for the book. Then, the book suddenly hot in his pocket, his heart lurched.

2

Miles had begun to worry a little about the book. For one thing, there was the similarity between the weave of the cover, with its curious flickers of stitching, and the card in the phone box that could prompt him to save lives and change outcomes in the world. He had even wondered whether the texture of the book's cover might not have thinned a little, following the incident of the red carnation, though the next day, it had, to his relief, filled out once again. Or it had never thinned in the first place. Miles felt his ability to trust his own judgment falter, in inverse proportion to the flowering of his special abilities. Blinking in the light and slightly tender to the touch, that was all – intent on expanding his visionary powers, just a little too prone to seeing things.

There were other worries, which – and this was now a matter of professional interest, as well as private anxiety – he couldn't suppress or erase. At odd moments he would sense that the book was opening him, reading him, when he didn't want to be the object of any other subject, let alone this one. At the onset of these phases of interloper thought, he would lift the book gingerly and gently from his pocket, and carry it carefully to a safe place in another room. He had begun to worry that his thoughts might be porous or leak out, feed the book in ways that might rebound on him as it grew stronger. He moved with meticulous care at such moments, veiling his thoughts, a parent carrying a sleeping infant back to its cot, following a fractious spell in the night. Miles craved neural privacy. Or was this needless anxiety, brought about by hectic changes in a life now far from normal, where the only potential mentors might also be competitors, or worse? To compound these anxieties, the book's own early life had started to trouble him.

In the beginning came that flash flood, which filled the printer's cellar in 1895, ruining the bulk of the first run. This he was sure he could verify, from different authors' memoirs and letters of the time – the accounts of divers hands, as well as the subsequent rarity of copies. Recent experience had however led him to question the normal assumptions about accident, and the normal ratios dictating probability. The book he now owned (assuming for a moment that he did own it, and not the other way round) could change events. This was also its theme, but his uncanny acquisition was not just a book about things. It was a book that did things, potentially violent things.

Suppose it had no interest in the other, the inert copies born dead in the same litter, weak and passive little books that could only be *about* and never *do*, heaped at the printer's in their deadweight, dreamless sleep. Did the book itself cast a localised spell of storm and flood, bring about the closing of the waters over the printer's cellar, over the numb and clueless spines of all but the siblings, who escaped? Spendrift had identified a further copy, one acquired by the British Library, but then permanently mislaid. Libraries do lose books, but was this particular copy doomed to be lost in any case, traced and subdued, knocked out of action by the magical reach of its counterpart? Books aren't supposed to be able to think for themselves – but let's face it, this one does. It rewrites itself every time I consult it.

And then there was the copy that allegedly went down with the *Titanic*, possibly mythical, possibly magical, possibly just paper. Was this an innocent, impotent book, cherished by a collector of late nineteenth century volumes, who in all likelihood never read them, valuing instead the fancy covers, illustrations – Turkish papers, as those swirls of marbled colour pasted to the inside of Victorian boards were known. Miles had dug around a little.

The owner of this second copy began to set off alarm bells. There were lacunae in the biography, and a developed interest in spiritualism – ectoplasm, table-tapping and Indian scout guides to the beyond – derided and exposed as fraudulent in due course, but at the time a sign of the avant-garde, the radical fringe of acceptable thought. He looked to Miles like one of them. Oh what am I thinking – he looked like one of *us*. Let us suppose for a moment that his copy could also, like mine, warm the heart, change its words, prompt different consequences. Let us further suppose that there was some kind of falling-out between the twin volumes. We know for a fact that the book's warmth could curdle, turning to jealousy or rage – Crowley had realized that, only too late. That warmth could mutate into destruction without conscience. Or an insane hubris, the mad relish for a challenge. Did the book destroy its only real rival, having planned the later annihilation of the British Library copy as a coda? Miles was aware of speculation running away with him, but he had to let it run. He hit not so much the buffers of thought as a real iceberg.

Mad as it seemed, the question had to be asked. Did this most potent book of spells bring about the sinking of the *Titanic*? The marvellous ship, the ship that could not sink. The cartoon image of a book enraged, book drowning book, seemed impossibly gothic but in this case, oddly possible. Could a book not only depict madness, but, in this unique case, go mad itself? Can books dream? Can one inflict nightmare on another? Was the paper voyager on the *Titanic* murdered, consigned to the waves, such powers as it may have possessed sinking helplessly to the ocean floor – or, shot skywards into empty air, through the funnels of the listing ship?

Let's look at this from another angle. Suppose this was a competition, a rerun of the Cain and Abel narrative of lethal struggle, played out in the technology of the 1890s, rather than by human, breathing brothers. Let's suppose, and his mood brightened, there were two copies of *Transmutations*, one good and sane, one darkly and deceptively intent on black magic – and the good book won. My copy won. But alternatively let's suppose – and at this thought Miles' hand fluttered to his throat – that the reverse is true.

No. Nonsense. Forget it. Felix had understood the book's liking for its new owner, the shared magical wavelength. Becky had good intuitions, and while she understood the closeness Miles felt for his acquisition, she had helped him secure it (admittedly in a geographically roundabout way) and was as absorbed as he in the growth of his powers. Any other way of thinking about it is mad, thought Miles. Barking. But no madder than so many things that have happened to me lately. No madder than the things I cause to happen. That potential has always been there. Inside me. Now it's barking, I'm out on the prowl. Prowling in the watches of the night.

He had, as recent changes had sunk into his consciousness, begun to grow in confidence, as much as watchfulness. Exultant, he would pad the streets in search of small adventures, stalling a car before it bumped another's fender, calming a teenage gang embroiled in turf wars, quelling some angry character's twitchy urge to rob, or hurt, or do stuff. But even the remote control he exercised so smoothly had started to trouble him a little. It was, exactly, control. Miles was policing London's minor-key moods, dulling anger or anxiety, fussing.

He began to feel after a few nights of this social juggling and smoothing of the eiderdown that his batteries were wearing out. And uncertainties hovering round the book did not make the book, his book, wrong on all points. He remembered its warnings that Magic was not to be the exertion of force against the world, in order to change it on lines of mere whim. Who was he to silence anger, to bring anaesthesia to the life of the streets? His scholar's conscience was long gone. Lost in some padded cell inside itself. Now his secret policeman had started to back off. Late at night the book would feel warm inside his pocket, or flex its words as a cat might stretch its claws then retract them again, prior to more dozing and dreaming. Miles concluded that he would calm his own anxieties too, and let them doze and dream, for as long as he could pull it off. The ride was just too interesting.

Felix Manto wanted him to drive, but one, he didn't want to be a gopher, or hang around gunning the motor while the big boys did the fun things, and secondly, he didn't care much for the automobile, unless it had Becky in it. In dreams he would drive, or Becky would, and that was just fine, and often mutated into sex or wild flying. He hadn't had a nightmare for a while now. But real cars depressed him. They were too like people, with their two headlight eyes, their fixed-grin grille, their Don't Bother Me air – I'm in my own world, here, so get out of my way– and that terrible imprisonment in forward, time-bound movement. This world would wear out because as a species we don't have eyes in the back of our heads. And as a species we need more true connection, less gridlock. A London traffic jam wasn't what even Henry Ford had anticipated, let alone aimed for. Smarting briefly with ethical indignation, (another side of himself that could easily be persuaded to doze and dream), the sorcerers' apprentice moved, yawning, to the bathroom. Today had been taken up with weapons training.

Something was staring him in the face that was not just the mirror of last thing at night. He brushed his teeth, and looked wearily into the glass. His arms and shoulders ached from the marksmanship exercises, and the work with loose weights that went with them. But he felt good. Fffm. Curious smell. Cigar smoke? It must be drifting up from the next flat down. But Helen's a retired schoolteacher, it's a bit late to take up smoking. And she lives alone. Could have a guest staying for the weekend, I suppose: a late night, cigar-smoking paramour. Stranger things happen at sea. Anyway, that whiff has gone now. Odd. He looked deep into the mirror. You've got bags under your bags, chum. What was it Dad used to say? It's a great life if you don't weaken. And then he'd say, but I think perhaps I weakened. Miles sighed, and put out the bedside light.

As he lay waiting for sleep, a warm arousing thought of Becky came into his mind. She had bought a new dress, shiny grey silk with a pattern of red diamonds. It accentuated her curves. It excited Miles. In his mind, he was pulling down the zipper, and planting kisses on the back of her neck. Then he moved his right hand, and did what people sometimes do in these situations.

He reached out and put the bedside light back on. Perhaps I'm too tired to fall asleep immediately. That does happen. He sat on the edge of the bed, and then with a slowed care that verged on reluctance, took out *Transmutations,* his guide to the light or darker worlds. It fell open in his hand, but at two facing blank pages, as if perhaps to say, do not pester the oracle. Respect me and read me when you're fresh, please, not in the last moments of wakefulness so that my words will be lost in the morning. But, thought Miles, risking a moment of light challenge, your words will have changed come the new dawn, in any case. The blank page took in Miles' equally blank gaze. Then he closed the book.

Then he opened it once more, he was sure at the same page, which now swarmed with words. Miles sensed obscurely that his book was not angry with him, that it sat once more comfortably within his possession, that any passing tension in the dynamic between them was trumped by the obligations of the text to discharge its duties. If the neophyte wanted to learn, the book must be ready to teach. Settling himself in receptive mode, Miles too felt a sense of renewed obligation, which in an indirect way proved to be the magic manual's theme, on that particular night.

> *The Adept in Magic passes daily through the city,*
> *seeing but unseen, mingling with the ordinary liv-*
> *ing, a man of the crowd. He catches their loves and*

woes sufficiently to draw knowledge and energy, yet knows himself at last to be apart, wrapped in the robe of a singular destiny. At times must he be mindful not of the living but of the walking dead, who likewise pass seeing but unseen, adding here to the numbers of the crowd, there flitting bat-like down some alley, on the tremulous fringes of vision.

Some resent their death, and did not wish it, or find that it leads not to the place they hoped. For them Death brings no peace, but only the urge to show others the mirror through which they have stepped back into this world – and haul in the innocent, lure them to their own demise. The Adept will learn to avoid these troubled souls, and if his glance should catch one, look immediately away. But other nightwalkers tread the city's thoroughfares. These are the grateful dead, contented ghosts, the Adept's helpmeets, servitors in dream whose earthly servitude has ended, wanting now only to assist, to magical ends, in time flowing later than their own. It is a small price they exact, merely the price of recognition, agreement that while it is gone, their own small time took place.

The Adept feels acutely as a warmth around the heart this obligation, flowing like the Styx between two worlds of life and death, where each man's his own Charon, hiding in a book, in a photograph, in music heard or painting seen, something that was lost but now recalled, bidden or unbidden, shining sweet counterweight to all that's lost in every tick of every moment, every passing sigh within the chambers of the heart.

Miles looked up from the page to the blankness of the ceiling, then down to the book in his lap, which appeared to have closed itself. Miles began to do the same, extinguished his reading light, and slept.

In Miles' dream, a bend in the river. A dream of a dull day. No one else around. Miles was standing on the shore, aware of water lapping, but only visually. No sound, at all. A heron flying over. The green of tall trees, darkening. Then a growing speck, making its way to where he stood, watching. A man, rowing. In no hurry, but heading this way. The man dressed in black. Large black Fedora, pulled down. I can't make out his face.

Whoaah there. One of those spasms that makes the whole body jerk, woke Miles up. He groaned, turned, and dived into sleep once again.

The river. A dark, slightly ominous day. A slight breeze, felt but again unheard, and dry enough, but something brooding like an air of silent thought, expressed in a fading of the light. Day's end, almost. Miles was standing on the shore, not going anywhere, or aware of having come from anywhere else. Just waiting, in the now. A heron flew over. Then the speck of a man appeared out of nowhere, growing by degrees. There was a coldness, too, in the air. The man rowing, without hurry, steadily towards him. He waited. The man was wearing black, a wide-brim Fedora shading his features. As the rowboat drew up a few feet from the shore, he raised his face, and looked at Miles.

African American. Getting on in years, the face quite lined, the mouth seemingly caught permanently in the act of pursing its lips. The man lifted the oars, and placed them slowly in the bottom of the black painted rowboat. Strong. Powerful hands. Would have to be, to lift those oars so carefully, lay them down so slowly, in the silence. The man looked at Miles, not at all unkindly, but quizzically. No negative vibes, but no words either. He then slowly raised one hand in graceful invitation, but Miles, though rooted to the spot, felt wary of accepting. Room for one more inside? Thanks all the same, but no, I don't think I will. Not this time. The hand slowly fell.

Now Miles felt less that the man was looking at him, as giving him an opportunity to look at the man. Who now removed his hat, as if in agreement. Raised his chin a little, almost posing. Turning the head to slowly let himself be seen in profile. And cocked an eyebrow, as if to say, over to you. The light was failing. The rower set his oars back in their rowlocks. A moment's pause. You're sure you won't? That's fine, everything in its own good time. Then he glided away at the same unbothered pace. Without a sound. The soundless small waves lapped the shore, as Miles looked down, then let his eye sweep the horizon. In the dream, night fell. How seldom this happens in dreams, which mostly take place, if a dream can be said to take place, in dull light.

Miles groaned in his sleep. High above the open curtains, the moon peered down. A white sickle moon, carving a grin in jet black sky. Miles dreamed no more dreams, that night. Or if he did, they were not the kind of dreams that demand an answer.

3

Something was staring him in the face, as he shaved, that signified more than the mirror of morning. He turned off the music of the taps, and began the rattle of cupboards and spoons and timers pinging that means breakfast. He hesitated, turned, and took a detour to his study, in search of a sound, trapped in a compact disc. No, it's too early, those recordings were made too early in the twentieth century. Then he found a chair, set it by a tall bookcase, and climbed up in order to retrieve, carefully and not without some teetering, a cardboard box. He emptied the vinyl, long-playing contents on to the carpet, and began to sift. To no avail. No, you need to go further back, much further. It was one of Dad's. This is Dad's generation – or even earlier. Wax cylinder era, maybe. Jack's Jazz might have it.

Zeke put thumb and index finger to his brow, momentarily shading his features.

Then he smiled.

-       Let me think. Yeah. They put it out again in a boxed set,
        with lots of other stuff. A couple of years back. It's in the
        store room. It's expensive and it didn't shift many copies,
        but. Yeah, anyway.

Zeke brought the large square red box out of the back room and,
handing it to Miles with one hand, opened and then slammed shut
immediately the drawer to the till.

-       On the house, mate.

We'll be closed by the end of the month if he goes on like this,
thought Maya, reluctantly moving from the serving hatch to deal
with a late-breakfasting boor who had just snapped his fingers in
the air. You can't stomach me and people like me, can you. You
hate us. You still think white's the sodding norm, and we should be
sat at the back of the bus. Sat on our hands in the back seat of life.

-       A refill? Of course, sir…. No, I was born here, actually.
        Londoner, born and bred…Well I suppose I *am,* now you
        mention it. Can't work in a kitchen and not eat, can you?
        Oh I am *so* sorry! What a butterfingers. And it's gone all
        over your trousers… Yeah, *you too.* And here it comes
        again. What *am* I thinking of?

Miles kept his head down in an effort to keep his face straight, and
hurried out of the shop, while a cherubic Zeke started to whistle
Greensleeves.

So this big red box is it. *The Anthology of American Folk Music.*
Damn, that's not the right song. But he's here, alright. And it was
one of Dad's. And somewhere on a river, quietly becalmed, in a
rowboat deep inside someone's dream, perhaps his own, the man
smiled, drawing a cigar out of its tube and rolling it reflectively.
Letting the leaf fibres crackle, in his ear. Sound was making its way

into the picture.

This old blues has got very strange lyrics. He sounds like a stage actor, croaking the lines, but it's a stage whisper. *Old times ain't now, nothing like they used to be. But I'll tell y'all the truth, oh you can take it from me.* This in an ironic cackle that suggested you'd do anything but. And that death-rattle voice. A real character. He sounds about a hundred and twelve. Miles turned the pages of the equally strange book that came with the red box to find out more about Rabbit Brown, who had recorded this blues in a New Orleans garage, back in the 1920s. Whoosh, no wonder he sounds old. Born in the American Civil War. Deep inside a thought, inside a boat, inside a dream, the man with the cigar had been joined by two friends. Three men in a boat. Rabbit Brown flapped his hand down and his eyebrows upward in a self-deprecating, aw-shucks movement that made the younger of his companions, a flighty looking individual with wide saucer eyes, laugh out loud. The third man laughed too, but a little more stiffly. He had a scarf tied tight around his neck, and his laughter soon turned to coughing.

The book in the box was entitled The Old Weird America. Miles was having trouble with some of Rabbit Brown's lyrics. Sometimes he seemed to be singing two different lines at once, superimposed. The meaning of first one, and then the other, would come through.

> *Well I bought the groceries, and I paid the rent.*

That fitted the song in some ways, a love turned sour and a home breaking up, but only if you wrote the words down. If you listened, you heard something else.

> *Well I burnt the ghost rail, and I played the rest.*

Something along those strange lines, anyway. Weird old America. What does that booklet, the one that comes with the box, think the lyric says? 'It isn't possible to make all the words out with certainty.' Thank you very much, Harry Smith.

It was Harry Smith who assembled the music, chose the tracks for this Anthology of curios, which got odder the more you listened to it. 'I bought gold ring. Paid rent.' was the best the liner notes could offer. No, no, no. Miles let his mind move now like a shark in deeper water, more dreaming than thinking, you *know* that isn't what he's singing. Miles played the track again for the umpteenth time. This time he heard it, loud and clear.

> *Well I board the ghost train, and I pay the man.*

Miles did some more digging around. Around old simple names, Richard 'Rabbit' Brown, Robert Johnson, Charley Patton. Harry Smith. Saucer-eyed Johnson learned the blues from Patton, who in the only known photograph sat wrapped up and stiff-necked from a razor wound inflicted by a lover. The father of the recorded Delta blues, but a man who knew he was dying of tuberculosis from the start of his career. And the old weird America, a ship in the mind that will not sink. And what the technical term is, when you mishear the words of a song. They were all connected. That, or a growing tolerance for tenuous connection was nudging Miles' tendency to see patterns in things even nearer its limit.

A lyric misheard, Miles learned, is a mondegreen. Lovely word, he thought, green-world: French and English, twined together in the bed of language. A word, it transpired, coined by some researcher in a music library, decades ago, working his or her way through crackling 78s of old Scottish and English ballads, who misheard a line, 'Oh they have slain the Earl of Moray, and laid him on the green', as 'Oh they have slain the Earl of Moray, and my Lady Mondegreen'. Miles was charmed by this, stored the word and the image in his mind, bringing out both to replay them, as now, shaving, peering into the morning glass and musing on reading, music, mystery and the day.

For a second he imagined himself at a masked ball, bowing to kiss the extended, bejewelled hand of Lady Mondegreen. Rising and falling slightly with her breath, a beautiful ball-gown, shiny grey silk with its pattern of diamonds and leaves, flowers and vines.

But then as the unheeded tap filled the basin, the gown in his mind rose and ballooned grotesquely, filling his vision and surrounding him, a giant air-bag that squeezed and held, his daydream stolen, noxious now and threatening to stifle him. Then the patterns in the silk drew back, allowing him just enough air to breathe, but forcing him to see a satyr's mask, half-hidden by the tracery of vine leaves. Miles was shaking now, standing in his own bathroom but invaded, holding a razor in mid-shave while Harry Smith's old weird music played on the machine in another room, but seeing only, as clear as the words on a page, a figure in the setting of a midnight ball starting to take off its mask. He saw the beginning of a sickle-shaped scar, running from ear to mouth.

Miles, don't look! Three men in a boat jumped to their feet, nearly capsizing it, shouting a warning. Joining hands, they brought their minds together, pushed forward to help Miles, shrinking the half-masked gargoyle face until it sagged, came apart, became just a blemish, then finally a micro-dot of pulsing dirt. As their boat shot forward it was as if they brought the whole river with them. Miles barely had time to glimpse the face behind the mask, what lay behind *that*, and immediately erase what he saw, when cleansing water from inside the dream in the mirror poured through it, adding to the overflowing water from the sink. A dream-wave of water knocked Miles over backwards, all for his own good. Then came a terrible howl like the Doppler effect of a speeding train, straight past his ear. Miles jerked his head, tried to faint, to not see or hear. Then all he could feel was his panting heart, all he could see was spinning ceiling, and all he could hear as he lay holding a razor on his own wet bathroom floor was once more the old-time music, rumbling and drifting along in magical waves, emanating from the other room, pouring in like water from the past.

When, later that day, he had found out more about Harry Smith in the British Library, Miles' mind was buzzing with connections. Some of the stories told by Smith about himself were blatant put-ons. That, for his twelfth birthday present, his father had given him a blacksmith's forge, together with the injunction to turn lead into gold: oh really? But Smith did practise alchemy. No doubt about that. His father taught him the signs of the Kabbalah, and other magical lore. He made films and many paintings, most of them destroyed. By him. He collected things. Painted Ukrainian eggs. He owned 20,000 gramophone records. Less conventionally, he owned the world's largest collection of paper planes, ditto string games: crazy. Miles sensed subterfuge. A biography building, a looping sequence of eccentricities that hid the man's real life. But many of these minor arcana, the strings and planes and what have you, were real enough, and followed the flight path of 1960s counterculture to land safely in the end in museums in DC.

What really gripped Miles' attention was that everything to do with the anthology was bound up with Magic. Every track, Smith wrote, had an occult connection to the next. The four groups of songs represented the four elements, of Earth, Water, Fire and Air. But as well as practising Magic, Smith was steeped in hermetic epistemology, and the centuries-old writings of English mystics such as another adept, Robert Fludd, a Smith of his own earlier period. Fludd was mentioned several times in *Transmutations* with near-reverence, and Miles had intended to find out more about him. The book did that. If you dithered, it pushed you, on to the next stage. In this instance, it pushed you towards the stage of the Memory Theatre.

Alive in the Elizabethan era, before the time when Isaac Newton put aside alchemy and took up instead the reins of science, Fludd had devised what he called a Memory Theatre. The aim of the Theatre was to store all knowledge of the universe, humanity, time – and make it accessible, to magicians. To this end he devised a system of alchemical and astrological symbols, arranged around the walls of an amphitheatre. Each symbol had a drawer or cabinet beneath, (some hidden) which, when opened by himself or another scholarly magician, would reveal a briefing on all existing knowledge of that subject, together with cross-references to other materials. Among its many intriguing functions, the Memory Theatre anticipated the computer, for if the symbols pointed back to a medieval, pre-scientific understanding of the universe, they also looked forward to the miniature memory theatre of today, the laptop with its icons.

What was meant to happen in the other half of the Memory Theatre was less clear to Miles at this point, though he had a feeling he was going to find out. Intuitively, he thought that in part of his being, he already knew. He was playing around in his mind with one or two other things that might shed light, if only will o'the wisp light that might lead down false trails. One was his hunch that old vinyl, as much as words written or pictures painted in the distant past, might have things to say about the maze he now occupied. The book had pointed him in that direction. He had discovered that one of the handful of recordings by Rabbit Brown to have survived was a song concerning the sinking of the *Titanic*. The other thing he had found out came as more of a surprise. The descriptions of the magical library fashioned in Elizabethan times were beginning to remind him of somewhere he once knew.

He was trying to recapture a memory from childhood, specifically the curious lay-out of his father's study, on the Scottish coast, where he had sometimes been allowed to play, trying and usually failing to pull down old leather bound books, their covers marked with stars, Celtic knots or other symbols. Trying to open drawers that were invariably locked. Miles would give up in the end, and climb with the aid of a footstool onto his father's high chair. Prompted by reading about the Memory Theatre, he remembered with increasing clarity the semi-circle of towering bookshelves, the cabinets with their inviting, curving drawers. His father sitting, deep in some volume, in his tall chair in the centre. His odd preference for reading by candlelight. And an empty space, like a pool, in front of the chair.

4

The two were sat, at midnight, in a bar opposite the Charing Cross Tube, Miles nursing a black coffee while Felix downed a Manhattan at record speed in order to get to the glacé cherry, then asked himself morosely if his scholarly companion would be likely to offer to buy him another.

-    Felix, help me out. You play the blues.

-    Played the blues. Start of my career, then again at the end. Blues is mostly about endings.

-    You started playing in Clarksdale?

-    There and thereabouts. Trouble with that place, you didn't take home more than a dime and a hangover. Only six people in the audience, three of them fighting drunk, and the other three played better than I ever could. I really got started in New Orleans. Though I'm forgetting. My first big break as a blues guitarist nearly happened right here, in London. I was supposed to play a UK tour backing Sonny Boy Williamson…

-    Wasn't he there the night Robert Johnson drank from the infamous bottle of whisky? That a jealous husband had topped up with strychnine? Johnson, who the myth says sold his soul to the devil for, have I got this right, the ability to play the blues like no one else. Are we down at the crossroads, at midnight?

-    No way Miles! How old you think I am! Well, OK, point taken. No, that was Sonny Boy Williamson the *First*. Robert Johnson's minder. Used to watch out for him. As you say, saw his friend about to take a sip from an opened bottle, and dashed it from his hand. But he couldn't watch him all night long. Didn't see Johnson take a hit from the second bottle, which had been opened and tampered with, until it was too late… Good looking guy, Robert Johnson. Big eyes. Nervy. A hit with the women…plenty of irate husbands with a reason to…

-   You do talk as if you knew him, as if you were there…

-   Wouldn't say I was *there*. But I saw it all in the Dream Pool.

They looked at each other in silence. Then Felix picked up the thread again, running a finger idly round the rim of his empty glass.

-   No, I was going to play behind Sonny Boy Williamson the *Second*. But he wasn't the easiest of people, something of a sharp tongue, so…

-   Didn't he try to burn down a hotel, or something?

-   Well there was an accident, that's true. Happened late at night, when he came back to his room, after a gig in Birmingham. The British one. He set his hotel room on fire. I believe he was trying to stew a rabbit in the coffee percolator.

Miles gave Felix an old-fashioned look, but the American gave every indication that he was not making this up. He set down his empty glass between the two of them, noisily.

-   Sonny Boy couldn't be bothered to rehearse. You know, he wasn't exactly complimentary about you English guys trying to play the blues. Let's face it, Miles, it is an American form. "Those English boys, they want to play the blues so bad…and they *do*, play the blues…so…*bad!*"

Felix laughed uproariously, slapping the table. Then he peered theatrically into his cocktail glass, as if astounded that the contents should have vanished, and looked quizzically at his companion.

Miles sat stone-faced, folding his arms. Oh they have slain the Earl of Moray, and laid him on the green. They have slain the Earl of Moray, and my Lady Mondegreen. But she that was slain, has now risen. As a spirit of unanticipated connection. There was a distant rumble of thunder, covering a myriad softer sounds, such as, had it still existed, a distant quill scratching on parchment in The Memory Theatre. Fludd's? Or my father's. Down in the flood. Ghost train crashed on the levee? Well, I board the ghost train, and I pay the man. Miles in his trance looked around. Someone's eyes were boring holes in the back of his head. There were presences in the night air pulling in on Miles' side. But there was at least one other presence.

- You OK, Miles?

His head suddenly ached. There was someone else inside it.

- *I like the English well enough. Don't mind Englishmen at all, no I don't. Very tasty – though always to be taken with a pinch of salt. And washed down with a wee dram of Bells, 'Afore ye go' - just like it says on the bottle. You're going, and ah'm taking you, Miles Proctor, down into the flood. You could do with a cold shower. I'm awful well-connected, I can get you an invite to the ghost train. A First-class, one-way ticket. Just say the word. I'm asking. You dancing?*

Blind himself, save to the rictus grin of a blind man's scarred face, a muddled Miles took a mistaken swing at his new employer, who ducked and up-ended the table, smashing glass and coffee cup, sending things flying. Bar staff helped Felix pull the unconscious young man to a sofa.

Felix had been intending to tell him about New Orleans, about Richard 'Rabbit' Brown - what little there was to know. That he couldn't survive on his wage as a musician, but made a living from taking tourists round Lake Pontchartrain, in his rowboat. About his growing up in Hell's Gate, a maze where the police didn't venture.

About smoke, and mirrors, and their role in Voodoo. The different strains of Magic. And the undertow in Rabbit Brown's song about the loss of the *Titanic*, a ship where any blacks would have worked without freedom of manoeuvre below decks. Cruelty, prophecy and the darkest, midnight comedy haunt many of those songs. But all of this was going to have to wait. The distant past was going to have to wait.

Miles had stirred up some old memories. Felix hadn't thought about Robert Johnson in an age. Maybe since before I drowned. There are mysteries in there, and not just the speed and the self-invented tunings. Johnson recorded his songs alone in a cheap hotel room in the first half of the twentieth century, facing the corner wall to get a better acoustic, nobody else around. He does say, though, at one point – on compact disc, download, on whatever is the latest sound-trap from the virtual, ghostly store – *No, I want to go on with our next one myself.* Forms of magic, hiding in plain sight. Miles needed to know about that.

Yes indeed, thought the ghost of Robert Johnson, who had seen and heard everything, standing at the window, Charing Cross Road behind him, the unconscious Miles Proctor in front. Mr Johnson had died young. Massive eyes, great spinning marbled catherine wheels. A dead man's hungry eyes, endlessly curious, and avid to make up for so much lost time. *He sure does. And what makes me doubt he's gonna get that from you, Felix. Plain sight's a complicated notion.* He stepped forward, a tall man in a long, almost floor-length coat, eyes whirling and closing, whirling and closing. First he raised his left hand abruptly, causing the surrounding scene to freeze, then placing one foot either side of Miles' supine form, middle finger topping his index finger, pointed down towards the centre of the forehead beneath him.

After some moments, he looked up again, exhaled at length, and smiled. *Now I get it. So that's what you're all about. Kindred spirit, after a fashion. Blues for me, book-work for you. Either way, a prac-*

tical aid to dreaming. *The same heightened receptivity to tenuous connection, we all got that in our extended family. Guess in my case it just hardened into fatedness. The still, sad music of humanity.*

Johnson let his gaze sweep round the packed bar-room. Another miniature everywhere.

- *We all have such a need to* escape. *An essential part of being human just seems to be the wish to be somethin' else. Escape from the Delta, that was me. I sung it to sling it into other people's futures, shooting me out of my own present. Well, at least that was the plan.*

Robert Johnson sighed, this next smile more rueful. *You need to escape from your co-workers, boy. Learn the same lesson I did. But this time do it* before *they open that bottle of whisky. Learn to read with your hands. We all crave escape. Alive, dead. Or just down in the hollow.* He turned to the window, made an ancient rapid sign, fingers fluttering, protecting his own, for a night, or for a moment. For the time being. Then he raised his left hand casually and let the ambient scene come back to life. Whispers floated once more on night air, groups crossed streets at the lights, neon turned to red and blue and silver balls in rain, papers rustled in the cabinets and drawers of eternity. *No, I want to go on with our next one myself – did I say that? I want to go on with* your *next one, and hang on in there. One or two friends are already on board. We'll need them. All aboard the ghost train.*

Then he slipped down the stairs and was barely there, a flicker in the peripheral vision of the unseeing eyes he overtook. *And what would you see, folks, if you could. Some dealer, some pimp in a stolen cashmere coat. I'm wicked science, voodoo mechanics - get used to it. Cognitive dissonance as cultural fast-forward –* lightning flashed, and he grinned – *that's what I'm talkin' about.* The thunder rolled, more angrily this time. Johnson's eyes grew wider accordingly, spun and shone, the zodiac whirling in each immense iris, long fingers testing the London air for future-facing signs. *I've been studying rain. There's one hell of a storm brewing.* He cast one final glance back up towards the bar, a tall, walking lighthouse, rotating its penetrant beam in dark fog. *Good luck, Miles, you'll need it.* Rain began to patter on the awning, a pianist trying scales. The dead man stepped out on to the pavement, blazed brightly for a second, and then vanished into night.

5

The book seemed less inclined to change its words. In fact of late it had started to resemble a training course or even a game, whereby you passed certain levels, with no need thereafter to return to them. Its current focus was the organization of the group engaged in Magic – in contemporary parlance, networks, support groups, resource issues. Miles looked for what the book had to say on how to broach this to his own group.

> *The ends of Magic are those of positive change; a restoration or a return to things past, the amelioration of which will issue in a brighter future, or a move into an altered future, which will, as the Adept looks back along the avenue of time now past, subtly rearrange its markers, its white stones and cypresses, to picture a story that can henceforth not be told in any other way. Both the ignorant and the supposedly wise talk of mysteries and of mysticism. There is no Mystery finally, only Nature, in a widened sense inclusive of the Spirit. What we are about is rearrangement, a better colligation, harmony. But this is to speak of the Adept, and to speak of wider worlds of Space and Time. In between the two stand the bridges of social organization.*
>
> *If these fail through age or are of poor construction, even the experienced and percipient practitioner of*

> *Magic may plunge, through no personal fault, into*
> *Error, or downward to Destruction. There is need of*
> *a group, with a base strong as that of the Aegyptian*
> *Pyramids, and a vigilant eye at its apex, to see, as*
> *it turns, all threats and opportunities that may be*
> *advancing below.*

He closed the book thoughtfully. It was time to tap and test, learn more about the capacity of the organization, starting with the Dream Pool. The book pushed you, prodded you on to the stage. Now it was time to push and prod the group, test the leadership. Find out whether that base was strong, that eye sufficiently vigilant. Because Miles had every intention of getting all that he needed and wanted from this.

The group agreed to meet at the erstwhile bookshop. Miles noticed as he approached that the lost panel had still not been replaced, and that vandals had spray-painted the door. If the organization is as well-funded as Felix claims, then come on, do it up. Bad decorative order risks drawing attention to the place – not a good idea, surely. I might bring this up. Things are getting a bit *too* erstwhile.

Today it seemed that the core group set to meet Miles around the table would consist of Messrs Manto, Boxer and Winthrope. Laura might or might not attend. Laura was, Mr Boxer's pursed lips inti-mated, somewhat mercurial. Felix, decidedly un-mercurial and never afraid of a style-statement appropriate to his nationality and previous career, roared up the pedestrianized Court on a Harley Davidson, and ostentatiously kept the studded jacket and leather mittens on, the whole way through the meeting.

Miles cleared his throat and began by asking to be inducted into the mysteries of the Dream Pool. Manto the Sunday-biker looked interrogatively at Boxer the failing bookseller, who looked cherubi-cally at Winthrope the éminence grise, and folded his white hands before him on the table. The silence that followed was freighted with unvoiced caution, but appeared to have tipped into assent.

However, the topic was evidently of little interest to Winthrope, whose eyes kept closing, carefully coiffeured head nodding forwards, until, when Miles had barely finished explaining what it was he wanted, the old man in a velvet suit appeared to have fallen sound asleep.

- OK. So we have one Member of the Board already there.

- *Oh*, I get it, Felix. I think.

- You need to fall asleep, Miles. This may not work the first time. It's going to be a hell of a lot easier for Winthrope here to drop off than it will be for you, simply on account of the age difference. Plus he's been skinny-dipping in the Dream Pool for decades. It's second nature to him. I also have to warn you that some people are extremely suggestible. You may experience the opposite problem, and then we'll have to put some effort in, collectively, to drag you back to wakefulness. You'll get the hang of it but there may be a few false starts.

- I don't feel sleepy.

- I think you'll drop off in a minute or two. You can faint in self-defence – I've seen you do it. And you can control your mind in order to get a handle on external events, and vary them. That's a *very* good indicator. You may simply be able to make yourself sleep, to order. It's just that you haven't ever tried before. Give it a whirl. Sleep well…and pleasant dreams.

Miles obediently closed his eyes. He was aware of the other people in the room. Too aware, in fact. Of chairs creaking. Of his colleagues' audible breathing. In fact, rather than feeling sleepy, he felt a heightened awareness of all the ambient noise that we produce, even when we think we're resting in silence. It occurred to Miles that there is no such thing as silence. And that we are never completely still.

All those scratchings, those little shuffles and half-sighs. He had wondered, when he read about sleep clinics, how they could possibly get people to sleep, to order. How could you drop off, with wires attached to your head, knowing that as soon as you were dead to the world a whole team of strangers was going to come in and watch you, and take notes? Surely you have to be alone, or with a partner, and comfortable, to really and truly sleep. When you sleep on a train, it isn't real sleep. It's just a form of absenting yourself. I just can't hack this. It's almost interesting, listening with my eyes shut, but it isn't what's supposed to be happening.

- Nothing doing, Felix. I'm not sure I can fall asleep to order.

- Just hang on in there, Miles. The longer Mr Winthrope stays in the Pool, the more he should be able to pull you in, too. You can't feel it yet, but he's searching for you. With his fingers.

Miles felt this was a bit creepy, but suppressed the reaction in case the sleeping senior could overhear his thought processes. They waited for several minutes.

- If I may make a suggestion, Felix, I shall join our colleague on the other end of the line, so to speak. I may be more attuned to the way the Proctor mind operates. If I may?

Felix nodded. Mr Boxer inclined his head, which moved in slow motion towards the table. Lank grey strands of hair were led by gravity to drift downwards too, landing alongside. Within seconds he was breathing stertorously. Miles closed his eyes again, and attempted to focus steadily on his own breathing, in order to slow it. While doing this, he also tried to observe his own consciousness, as one might a cinema or other screen across which images pass.

Good, bad or indifferent, just let those pictures go. Calm. Calm. Just non-judgmental watching, and waiting. Essentially, he thought, what I'm doing isn't any different from classic forms of meditation. But meditation is an end in itself, whereas here it's just the portal.

It was becoming increasingly evident that thinking about thinking was not something Miles could easily stop doing. Time was passing, but he was still as wakeful as ever.

- OK, Miles. I'm going to try to knock you out.

Miles watched with faint alarm as Felix launched himself half way across the table, then fell fast asleep, one leather-mittened hand hanging over the edge of it on Miles' side. Miles closed his eyes.

6

After a few minutes the woman called Laura quietly entered the room, and signalled to Miles with a finger to her lips. She took off her belted coat with 1980s-style padded shoulders, looked for somewhere to hang it, failed, shrugged and slipped it round her shoulders again, yawned once, then slowly sank from view and passed out on the floor. Miles examined his nails.

After half an hour or so, he felt he had had enough. It's been fun, guys, but. Winthrope was still in half-profile, chin on chest; Mr Boxer face down on the table; Felix Manto still fast asleep, and would feel stiff as the leather he was wearing when he woke up; Laura was an unseen version of Sleeping Beauty. Have I missed anyone? Miles checked under the table. Mr Boxer's hands rested, as usual, on his knees, white birds perching. All present and correct.

Now what do I do? Felix didn't give me any instructions. The only one out of his depth here is the one who stayed lounging by the pool-side. Do I wake them all up? One at a time? Then the others will know when one of them exits the system that this hasn't worked, and that they should prepare for landing. Fasten seat belts. But suppose the state they are in is more like sleepwalking. It could be dangerous to wake them – I have no idea. They must all be up to *something*, it's just stuff I can't see, because I'm awake and they're all cavorting in the vale of Morpheus.

The Dream Pool. The waters of sleep, presumably. Are they swimming? Maybe they need to towel off. However you think of it, I'm dependent on them. I'd better not wake them. It might hack the firm off, to find their collective dream cut short by the new boy. I'm beholden; entry level. Not even middle management. Yet. This one isn't really my call. Felix should have spilled all the dream-beans and told me. But then, he didn't think it would pan out like this.

He decided to cough. Out came a polite, slightly suppressed clearing of the throat, mildly embarrassed, and terribly British. Not a peep.

Miles walked to the door, brow furrowed, then quietly left the building, closing the door gently behind him. Immediately he was beyond Fiddlers Court his face lit up in a radiant smile. That had worked, so to speak, like a dream. He felt sure he had veiled his thoughts successfully, only letting out what they expected to pick up. He had made himself invisible to Winthrope, despite the ancient otter's years of dreaming in the Pool. Now back to real life.

7

They always met at Becky's, because they didn't want the book to overhear. Miles liked their brave new world. OK, there's a mad Scottish gangster out to kill me, and he's dead, sort of, and I can't go to bed with my girlfriend in my own flat in case a book gets jealous and drowns us. Meanwhile we're under surveillance from a dead rock star, but he's alive, one of a cadre of defunct antiquarian booksellers, who've paid for me to have weapons training. I get hypnagogic visions when I shave, and there's quite possibly at least one dead musician living in the bathroom mirror. It's the old, old story.

Then today I go to a staff meeting where everyone's asleep. Mind you, that happens in College. But, and it was a very big, beautiful but, we can also do *this*. As mystery deepened, Miles was learning to spread his wings. After plucking cars out of the air or stopping them from crashing, veiling his thoughts from the group while linking them to Becky's was a doddle. Or so he thought.

Back at the flat, now, he threw jacket onto chair with a cavalier flourish, then told Becky what had happened. Her shoulders dropping a little with relief, she locked one of his hands in hers, gently drew along one of Miles' eyebrows with her other index finger, and looked at him interrogatively.

- You choose, Becky. Where do you want to *go*, today?

- I was wondering about Barbados.

- You'd have to show me the book.

Becky let go of his hand, and walked to the bookcase where a large collection of travel guides and coffee table, large format books with colour photographs of exotic locations was growing magnificently.

- OK. Yep. Barbados it is.

They sat on the sofa, Becky's head on Miles' shoulder as they turned the pages. They had to both see the same pictures at the same time, and look at each for at least five seconds. She had a sense, though, that they were getting faster, and wondered if next week or month they would be able to flick through and jump straight into their shared, their telepathic dream. There were oceans of time to find out in. Each thought of the other, you are so clever. And you are so damned gorgeous. Miles put the book down, and raised an eyebrow: ready? Becky nodded and closed her eyes. He put her hand in his and they fell asleep together on the sofa. *Sigh.*

Instantly they were walking on white sand, at the very beginnings of sunset. Sunset moved fast, in these parts. Further along the beach, people were setting up barbecues, and the air became scented with smoke, lamb and herbs here, marlin or barracuda there. They walked to the end of the pier in Spightstown, then kissed in red-blue, changing light. Walking back to their apartment, Becky wondered should they swim before dinner. There's something we have to do first, said Miles, and led her, smiling, into the bedroom. He tossed his long shorts aside. He even took off his shades for once.

Becky unhooked the briefest of white tops, which caused Miles to instantly grow, noticeably. But then Magic has always been about defying gravity. Magic also means removing Becky's skirt: now you see it, now you don't. Vanished. Along with this beguiling if skimpy red garment, and then running his tongue down the length of her spine, and beyond. This is what Magic tastes like. The tip of the tongue on its warm travels meets a touch of salt, some from the sea air, some hers, meets pheromones. We take this one slowly, magic bringing the tongue alive in such different, but all her, velvet, red places. Into her upside down smile, where the tip of him just disappeared from view. As if by magic. Everything suddenly waits, suspended.

You're thinking something. Yes. Something nice. Then Miles withdrew, and, utterly delighted and besotted with each other, they reconfigured the ancient, most innocent and most experienced ceremony, so that Becky's ample and wonderfully curvaceous bottom was – in magical reality – on top of him, by way of a change. Whooping, she rode him and rode him, breasts bouncing, chestnut mane flowing and flying. Defying gravity. Thrilled to bits, thrilled to the bone, in a dream.

In another part of London, Felix awoke, and moved somewhat stiffly to another room, to perform that day's spot check in the customary way. Where is Miles, as of this minute? Let's gently adjust the firm's camera obscura, while holding in mind a picture of Miles, then wait for the picture to form, and bravo, he's…in the College library, writing a lecture. So this rather elaborate glass machine tells me. Fine. And Becky. There she goes, appointment at…the opticians. Fine also. OK.

The Dream Pool thing was irritating, though. Miles should have got there at the first pass, though I didn't say so at the time. We must build up his confidence. 'Tremendous talent, but lacks confidence.' That's what the secret reference from our contact in the College said. But Miles is now the first one on record who hasn't made it into the Dream Pool on the first attempt. And Winthrope was in there, looking for him. Winthrope could send anyone to sleep, in seconds. Maybe our young friend is not quite up to this.

Felix began to fret once again about the interview. That was a shambles – I didn't handle that one well, at all. Time hobbles your judgment, gives you too many nuances to factor in. So you forget other things that are actually more basic. It's gotten so very hard to weigh personalities, weigh circumstance.

He mooched his way back downstairs, tapping on the balustrade with a Hard Rock Café key-ring, and entered the room. Its door creaked, though not sufficiently to disturb either Mr Boxer, or Winthrope, both snoring, their heads now flung back. With a start he noticed Laura's protruding, sleeping feet. It's so hard to judge. And management is so damned difficult, compared to a career in music. But the hardest part of all is trying to identify really dynamic, motivated colleagues, like these people.

Miles and Becky awoke. Two experienced, innocent people who went all around the world each day. Tomorrow she thought, perhaps and why not, Lisbon? Never been. Wouldn't, in one sense, go, even if she went. Or Rhodes? Paris? Egypt? Whichever, back in time for lunch.

8

Vicksburg, Mississippi. Sometime in the 1940s. The rusting white Chevy parked in back of a thrift store, grey powder rising from gravel. The man who got out would have been recognizable ten years later as a beatnik, at home in parts of San Francisco, New York and Tangier, and attacked just about everywhere else. In Vicksburg in the 1940s he looked so completely other that he didn't attract any attention at all. He just wasn't on the radar. Alive and well, though barely visible as a phenomenon on the normal spectrum, Harry Smith glided silently into the thrift store.

Nodding to the owner, who didn't see anyone nod, he took in the usual, sad ephemera. The Negro minstrel moneybox. The wind-up gramophone with needles the size you'd expect to see sticking out of an addict. Grandma's Sunday clothes, now that Grandma's gone. A Kodak camera in a scratched leather box. Neckties adorned with fighter planes, candy-stripes, girls in Hawaiian grass skirts, short kipper neckties that only came half way down a man's chest. Pleated trousers that tried to climb half way up it. Smith paused briefly over a wide straw hat, then let it drop when his eye was caught by the box of 78 rpm phonograph records.

He flicked through them with the speed of a croupier, looking at the paper labels and only pausing on certain ones. *Paramount Records are recorded by the latest electric method. Greater volume, amazingly clear tone.* His eye lit on The Norfolk Jubilee Quartette's 'Way Down Yonder in Egypt-Land', The Hokum Boys' 'You Can't Get Enough of that Stuff'. Banana-in-your-fruit-bowl innuendo, think I'll pass. Aha, Blind Blake's 'Too Tight Blues'. An altogether better class of fruit bowl. One wrought with violets, and leaves of vine. Then the stardust instant, in this case (lucky strike!), Charley Patton's 'Jesus is a Dying-Bed Maker'. Harry Smith had two copies already, but there was always the possibility that more than half the lyric would be audible this time. Paramount Records claimed an amazingly clear tone. They lied. But then Charley Patton had enjoyed a real, if regional, celebrity. People played them to death, and the records just wore out.

Harry put the shellac disc reverently to one side. He lost himself once more in the heat of the chase, and his croupier flick. But when he looked down again, his record was gone.

Another white hipster was trying to buy it, from the jaded old gal in the turban. Not so fast. He looked like a kindred spirit. Shades. Taller, with a real beak on him. A Brit, by the sound.

- You already got a copy of this?

- No. Forgive me, I've never even heard it. I collect…sorry, I didn't realize…

- Then it's yours. If you can get all the words down, type them out and mail them to me. Harry Smith, Chelsea Hotel, New York City.

- Simon Proctor. Pleasure. I will.

9

The scene was now no longer a thrift store, but a place far from Vicksburg, and the thoughts and atmosphere that helped make the room special, make the space itself, stood at a distance from even the world's most elongated sense of what constitutes Far and Near. The man called Simon Proctor walked around the circle in this secret room, lighting the tall candles, and wearing a long red robe, inscribed with alchemical and other signs indicative of his interests. In a profound sense alone, in that he lacked all strictly human company, he paused to close a cabinet that he had absent-mindedly left open, as incense and the smoke of burning pine cones swirled in moving ovals, jets and circles. He divested himself of the robe with ritual slowness, and readied himself for the large pool that occupied the rest of the circular room. As he gazed at the space it began to fill with dream-water. Astral, it began to ripple, alive with many colours, many voices. Little bits of the stars, the skeletons of glowing leaves. Curlicues and dots of other lives, and minds, and music. He was already actively asleep as he let himself drop down.

Amazing, thought Harry Smith, now pacing his hotel room in New York City. Scratch the surface of this world, this spinning thing, and so much magic leaks out. You just can't always hear the words right. He rigged up his tape machine, and opened the window. This he did gently, and with a certain amount of finicky manoeuvring. Some of those painted Ukrainian eggs hadn't been blown in the first place. They were apt to explode. And his cave in the Chelsea, like most sub-millionaire level hotel rooms in Manhattan, was hardly grand in its dimensions. The fact that every spare inch was covered in piled-up 78rpm phonograph records or elaborate creations made from string simply added to the pleasures of the nest, the pleasures of the maze.

Harry Smith pressed the Record button on his BASF reel-to-reel tape machine, to catch the voices of the night, the tapestry of sounds in new-old West 23rd Street. The only way people will know how things were – how did that tune go, again? Where'd that life go? – would be if some other still-breathing body bothered to tape it or keep it, write it down or size it up, then pass it on. Though the bits that can't be fathomed, that were eyes and now are pearls, do tend in their opacity to be the most rewarding.

Harry Smith died at an advanced age. The taping project was still incomplete, but perhaps it could by its nature never be brought to a close. Some of the things that seemed strangest about him had passed like clouds of incense out into the culture, perfuming it, clinging, or turning out at day's end to be not smoke in mirrors, but prompts to social change. And so he didn't really have a day's end.

Therefore it is at least imaginable that, although deceased, he had no particular desire to leave New York City. Fortunately the Chelsea Hotel, a real building, albeit one familiar with cosmic flights of fancy, would surely still have welcomed him. Stanley Bard behind the lobby desk, Captain at the ship's motherboard. Raising no more than an eyebrow, while Harry floated up the stairs. The deep moans round with many voices. The sky does the same, and we glide by betwixt and between, ourselves a recording, at times hard to fathom, whistling an old tune whose notes are pricked in starlight, legible on skin, on sky, on water, whispered words, notes and hums urging our thinking on, optimistic flickers that transmute into encounter; friends – past, present, and future.

On the roof of the mind, it is equally imaginable that it would be about time for a quiet reunion. Everything is all about time. In such a case, Rabbit, Robert and Charley might be present and lounging in poses reminiscent, up to a certain point, of Manet's *Déjeuner Sur L'Herbe*. Harry had always been partial to *l'herbe*. Rabbit not saying much. Said it all when he was alive, why say it again now. Old times ain't now, nothing like they used to be. Robert blazing away as usual. A figure from the past, but all he was ever hungry for was the future. *If* such and such happened, then *this* would follow, and then if we did *that*, well who knows.

Of course, he saw things. Ghosts, flickers. Most of us do. Someone flitting, caught for a nano on the edge of visibility. Sometimes he used to see the same passer-by, floating up a wall or through a window, particularly when he was recording. Used to call him the phantom engineer. *I want to go on with our next one myself*, but thanks for dropping by.

Up on the roof, the ripple of a shiver, brief premonition of autumn in the air. Charley spluttering a little, as usual.

- How long you had that cough, Charley?

- Well, let's see, Robert L. Started in my thirties. Got worse. Then I kicked the bucket. How long I been dead, anyways? What year is it?

- You mean, how many years since….

- No, I mean what year is it. 1975? 2000?

All the years, all so alike, if only in their hospitality to sharp internal differences.

- Aw what's it matter. Read in a book someone wrote that I might or might not have been born in 1891.

- You should know, Charley, you were there…

- I was *there* but, cut me some slack, I was busy being born, I didn't *know.* Now I'm dead I *know* 'bout this and I know 'bout that, and I certainly know about the other, but what I'm sayin' is, one thing I know for sure is, I wasn't fully and properly *there.* Plus I'm not strictly *here*, either.

- What you sayin', you not here. You talking to us. At uncharacteristic length, in point of fact, though the divergence from custom and practice is not unwelcome.

- I'm *not here.* You're *not here*, Robert L, and you're *not here*, Rabbit. We're all of us in this together, and that means *we ain't here.* We're an illusion. Now pour me a drink. Thanks. By the way, how many of us illusions are up on the roof, tonight? And, it occurs to me to ask, anybody heard anything from Him? What year is it?

- Don't start that again. Him, you mean Harry, he's here, in a conjectural sense, that being his preferred *modus operandi*, just as it was when he was…

- No I don't mean Harry. I mean *Him.* Anybody heard anything.

Rabbit looked around carefully, poised his lit cigar on a saucer, then chipped in, in hushed tones.

-   He's asleep. Still sleepin'.

-   *Still?* Don't you think it's about time we woke Him?

You crazy, remember what happened the last time, don't shout you'll wake Him, well you can go first and I'll stand right behind you... Serious concern was vocalised, some of it tinged with reproof. Even Robert Johnson looked like he'd been hit by something unanticipated. He moved nearer his old friend, leaned forward and spoke earnestly.

-   Charley, you're troubled in mind.

-   Well, sure. Does a bear shit in the woods? Sounding troubled – I'm good at that, that was my professional posture. Interjections, arguing with myself, doin' the place in different voices – cookin' up a séance on a record. Troubled in my private life? Can't rightly remember. Isn't everyone? I'd have to read that book again. Though to my mind non-fiction don't always tell the truth.

-   Books and the truth and private life have all been moving around in my mind too, lately. Charley, you remember Miles?

-   He the young white guy we nearly drowned in his own bathroom? Water and mirrors, fine. Dreams and mirrors – or water – even better. But if we goin' do all three at once, I sure could do with more rehearsal time. All for his own good, but it's been a while since I had to perform *that* manoeuvre. It's a while since I performed, full stop.

-   We're each of us a voice and six steel strings. He's all books. One book. I guess we have words in common.

-   Unclear words are the best kind, to my mind – there's

more in them – though, speaking of books, recording is a *kind* of book, least the way I did it, that needle writing directly on to a wax master. While you'd just sit in a hotel room and press a button, Robert, I was jammed in a booth screamin' and hollerin' the blues into an eight foot long, sixty centimetre wide plywood horn that's attached to the needle. No wonder I sounded troubled in mind…. Felt strange, the first time. Like lots of things. Like the first conversation you have, once you've died. That sure feels strange. Where were we – what year is it again, Robert L?

-   'Bout a year later than when you started pronouncing. We got nothing but coughing fits for half a century, and now we get a disquisition on bears, blues and plywood. Just goes to show that things are…never over. Anyway, you ought to get someone to check it out. A cough can be hard to get rid of, once it's got a hold of you.

-   Hm-mm. I guess it's about time.

Eventually, like any of us thinking selves, they would call time, boat ready to drift off into the stars. Some stars are made of crystal and have beings inside, working late into the night, who wave. Had they got this far, they would have passed through clouds of stardust, making them sneeze, but clinging harmlessly afterwards to their clothes, tiny silver fireflies. In which case it follows that Rabbit must have done the rowing, because Rabbit always rowed.

10

Miles' sleep was troubled, that night. There's nothing so *unheimlich* as a quasi-dead Glaswegian gangster with unassuaged issues, most of them acutely bibliographic. How does he get into my head so easily? Is it through my dreams, or through my ears? Oh no, here we go again.

-   *Miles, you've read my mind. I want that book. I need you
    to read it to me. I'm no in your ears you wee bampot, I'm
    over here – left a bit, right a bit – aye, I'm over here in
    Hell, trying to get twenty winks. Counting sheep, but they
    keep catching fire. There's only so much roast lamb a man
    can take.*

Tah-dah. Leave me alone Kenny, I'm off duty. Actually no chum,
there is no off duty, is there, anymore? We're all on permanent
standby. I think we could both do with a weekend break. Where's
the nearest exit… I need ear-plugs for the mind.

-   *Listen up, Johnny English. Put your worries behind you
    and think about mine. The change'll do you good. I want
    the book. I loved the pain it gave me. It felt real. Let an
    old blind man have a feel. Tape the bloody thing, if you'd
    rather. I'll wipe the screams off a cassette, and send y'it,
    and I wilnae charge. How's that? If you dinnae hand it over,
    I'll willingly come and take it. I could do wi' a splore and a
    spot of skullduddery. Fresh air. This place is playing havoc
    with my asthma. And that makes me anxious.*

Cassettes for heaven's sake. What year is it?

-   *I don't like Hell, so I don't. It's no a patch on Glasgow. There
    are terrible gaps between the acts of violence where noth-
    ing much happens except tedious pleas for mercy, and the
    food's shite. They don't even want me here. They try to be
    unkind and vicious, but I can sense the pity behind the wee
    jabs. They say I'm betwixt and between, that I'm down in
    the hollow. I'm no even certain this is Hell. They're trying to
    dignify a bad experience by aggrandising it. I've had more
    fun in a railway station waiting room. Through the walls I
    can hear the tortures of the damned and it is so frustratin'
    not to be able to offer a helping hand to one side or the*

other. Tweak things. Know what I mean, eh? Customer focus. Results-driven agenda, all that management shite. I've been on a course. There's sod all else to do. But they wilnae employ me without a social security number, and ye cannae get one of them if there's the slightest sign of life in you. 'Ye cannae come in. Ye're not deid.' It's a stuck record. All I get is fobbed off wi' counselling sessions. Role- play. What you would *do, if you* were *dead. If you were real.*

Sadly Kenneth this is not an area in which I have either skill-sets, or one iota of interest. Get out of my head, you're squatting.

- *I'm not alone in my crepuscular half-life. There's third generation betwixters and betweeners, here. Some of them are going mental. But I'm in danger of straying off mes- sage. Let me have the book. You must know it off by heart by now, surely? Read a book once, and you've read it. You have* read *it, haven't you? I'm startin' to wonder what your game is. Meg sends her regards. She has coping strategies. She quite liked the look of you. There's no accountin' for taste. I can probably arrange something for you both, if the powers that be give me a level playing field, but there's things undreamt of in your philosophy you'll need to know. But I'm getting ahead of myself, as dear Mary Queen of Scots said to the executioner, sharpening his axe… Don't say I'm no willing to share. I want* to *share.*

Miles felt a reassuring purr across his ribs. This is not going to happen.

- *It's the only thing that just might tip me one way or the other, off to bye-byes for good. That's my preferred option. Or failing that, into some oneiric simulacrum of the good old, bad old razor days. 'Gillette - the best a man can get.' I'm no fussed. I don't fit in here, there's too many English. Bloody incomers.*

I'm not rising to this. I'm starting to drift. Drift, mind, drift. You can do it. Now I wish I'd learned how to fall asleep to order, after all. Now, what did Felix say.

- *I miss my kin. I dinnae know who they are, but. Family's terrible important. Everyone needs a family, a vortex to call their own. Family, a partial paralysis of, and a partial endorsement of the instincts, am I right? I need to relocate, though. It's puttin' me under duress. Under your dress, how's your father? Only met him once, in one of your nightmares. Not a classic of the genre, though I savoured the cultural references. Both of them. He's no exactly the life and soul of the party, is he? I know he's dead, but even so. I think there's maybe a bit missin'. Apart from the arm you pulled off. I'm no being sarcastic, I've had people fall apart on me too. We're awful alike, Miles, awful alike. It's no my fault I'm better lookin'.*

Words fail me. Worse, I'm getting accustomed to this. It's becoming like a recording of the waves on the shore, or the rain forest. Common British birds; just a tad more gothic. Night, all.

- *I cannae see, I cannae get a handle on the world. Cannae go back, and I canna go on. I can't even die. And that's something I thought I'd pulled off quite well. A jobbie well done. Mah self-esteem's awful low, awful low. Entre nous, Death, and the gatepost, I crave closure. GIVE ME THE BOOK. Yonder grimoire, yield it up. If not, then you and your wee paramour… I'm sure I dinnae have to complete the thought. She's an awfully big girl. Let's not go there. I wouldn't. Anyway, it's been a privilege. Quality time. I am so pleased to have been granted special Mind Reader's Rights, Miles. So gratified to have penetrated your inner circle. If you catch my drift. Forgive any infelicities of diction, I am so redoubtably Caledonian. But I dinnae like to put other people in boxes. On reflection, let me put that another way. I killed myself but didnae die, and both before my time. I've got bags of get up and go, I'm still wearing L-Plates. To tell the truth, I never learned to drive, never passed my Test. I ran over a father of ten in the Gorbals on my first outing. Not my fault I cannae see. I got a mite distracted, attempting my first driving lesson in a stolen Fiesta pursued by the Gartside Constabulary. Under the influence of macular degeneration. Och, I'm descending into anecdote, let's elevate our discourse. At least if I was a Satanist I'd be a Protestant Satanist. I don't need any intercessor between me and the deep shit. I'm worried now, but I won't be worried long… Anyway, precocious one, thanks for sharing. NOT. But have a wonderful night. AND MAKE SURE THE BUGS DON'T BITE! Miles? Miles? Gis a break. Gis the grimoire. MILES!*

11

The next day assumed the same general contours. Aside from the irritant of not being able to take Becky there, Miles liked his flat. Two minutes' walk from Camden High Street, and yet quiet. High up in a Victorian terrace. But today, in fact for the whole of the last week, he hadn't liked the overflowing bins in full view, down in the courtyard. He got the coffee pot going, looked down from his window at the bins, sighed and phoned Camden Borough Council. The voice that replied was linguistically that of contemporary Greater London in a young and female incarnation; all as expected. Miles cleared his throat but then realized that she was a recording.

- You have reached Camden Borough Council. We are arksing if you would be willing to take part in a survey. If you are willing to take part in our survey, please say 'Survey', now. (Pause. Miles remained silent.) Thank you for agreeing to take part in our survey. We will now arks you ten questions, of ascending complexity.

Miles put the phone down. Turned towards the kitchen. Came back, and looked down once more at the overflowing rubbish. He sighed again, irritated at himself as well as inadequate waste disposal, and pressed Last Number Redial.

- This is Camden Borough Council. We are arksing if you would be willing to take part in a survey. If you are willing to take part in our survey, please say 'Survey' now. (Pause. Miles remained silent.) Thank you for agreeing to take part in our survey. We will deal with your enquiry momentarily.

Miles now heard the first movement of the Third Brandenburg Concerto by Johann Sebastian Bach. In its entirety.

- If your telephone has a touch tone and you know the number of the person you are calling, you may key in the extension you require now. All of our calls are monitored for training and quality control purposes. If you wish to speak to the operator, press nine at any point during your call.

Oh, get on with it.

- If your enquiry concerns an abandoned vehicle, please say 'Abandoned Vehicle', now. If your enquiry concerns council tax, or drainage, please say 'Council Tax or Drainage', now. If your enquiry is regarding waste disposal, please say 'Waste Disposal' now.

- Waste disposal.

- I'm sorry, I didn't quite catch that.

- WASTE DISPOSAL!

- We are putting you through to one of our advisors. Calls may be monitored for quality control purposes. Calls

> to this number are charged at five pounds per minute,
> which is why I am arksing pointless questions, repeating
> myself like a complete ninny, playing music that you used
> to like and now can't stand because you associate it with
> faceless bureaucracy, and not using one word, or indeed
> two, three, or four, when ten will do.

Miles looked at the phone with a measure of concern, for it was no longer a boxy modern device with a little aerial, but a black thing that Alexander Graham Bell, or more likely the Spanish Inquisition, might have recognized. Am I awake. I believe so – I think this is happening. Interesting. Friend of Uncle Kenny's? No such thing. Unless it's Meg, which I utterly doubt. I think he's turning ventriloquist. Another kind of stage magic, I suppose. Why are there no stage ventriloquists anymore? Interesting thought. Then again, no, it isn't.

> - If you have recently moved to the area and have an
>   enquiry regarding schools, forget it. The schools round
>   here are all crap. If you would like to speak to an advisor,
>   you can't. Cheryl's sat next to me, but she can't come to
>   the phone right now. Not in the state she's in. If you want
>   to know the time, arks a policeman. If you want to hear
>   your own voice, calling piteously from the bottom of a
>   deep well, press six.

Miles weighed a few alternatives in his mind, but opted for silence. How is this going to play out, as if I didn't know. Last night he was in my head, now he's taken over my phone. Talking rubbish.

> - If your enquiry concerns self-harm, assisted suicide, or
>   you are simply feeling that your life lacks purpose and
>   you need a gentle push in the right direction, key in the
>   letters l-o-s-e-r, or visit our elegant Tube station, right
>   here in the heart of Camden, and jump onto the line. Do
>   this just before the train comes in, fool, not after it's left!

That way you will derive the maximum impact from the occasion, and be able, albeit briefly, to savour the driver's look of unqualified surprise. If your enquiry concerns the answer to the answer but you didn't hear the question, say 'Waste Disposal', now.

- Waste Disposal.

- I'm sorry, I couldn't quite catch that. Please wait, and you will be connected to an advisor. If you believe that papalistic followers of Rome have moved into your neighbourhood, why are you wasting time listening to me, go and do something about it. The price of petrol's coming down – so don't hang back. If you are a benighted retard or live south of the River Tweed, which comes to the same thing, please accept my condolences. (An explosive, ripping fart. Miles held the phone further off.) If your enquiry is social, and you want to arrange a surprise Orange March, or hire a *fantastic* magician for your child's birthday party, press…

- Waste Disposal. I want Waste Disposal. You're wasting my time. And I'm going to dispose of you.

Oh dear. Surely I can do better than that. I need to raise my game. There ensued a diplomatic silence, at the other end of the line.

- I'm sorry Miles, you're dropping your balls. I'll pretend I couldn't quite catch that. Please stay on the line, while I slip into something more comfortable…

Miles sighed, and patiently held the phone well away from his ear. An eighteen inch long tongue flicked out of it, tasted the air, deluging the general vicinity with rank, charnel-house spittle, then retreated. If Miles moved the phone a little nearer his ear, it began to peek out again. In. Out. In, out. Inoutinout. Shake it all about. He slammed the phone down into the cradle, to a muted squeak.

Yep, that was Kenny all right. Albeit with an enhanced range of stylistic hallmarks. Perhaps limbo suits him better than he thinks.

Miles poured boiling coffee in the kitchen, left it to cool in a Beltane College 100th Anniversary mug inscribed with the College motto, *Quid Agis?*, and looked out of the window. Let's keep our expectations low. Ah, here he comes. Magician, to ventriloquist, to drag act. Then again he loved those 1960s variety shows. I'm not looking forward to his Tiller Girl routine.

There was a noise from the courtyard, audible even at this height. An old lady on a Vespa Scooter, carrying a hamster's cage strapped to the backrest, shuddered to a halt by the overflowing bins. Dismounting, she bent down and opened the cage, allowing a family of plague-bearing rats easy access to their new abode, then grinned, curtsied and doffed her pink wig, exposing the dead white pate. Miles took in the thick brown stockings, the bluebell twinset. He opened the window and called down.

- You should be wearing a crash helmet. What you're doing is illegal.

- *Gis a break, Miles. If I wear the helmet, I cannae see with my ears. Believe you me, it disnae work. And there's no need to shout.*

- Sorry. And fair point. About the ears.

Miles closed the window, as the bald old lady waved and took off into the rush hour traffic. There was a metallic screech and a loud bang after she rounded the corner. Miles winced, shook his head, and padded into the kitchen to locate both the Air Freshener and the strong black coffee he needed.

At a safe distance from both *Transmutations* and the dead-undead Glaswegian gangster turned granny, he pondered the ways in which the benign and the menacing can blur or intertwine. One thing's for certain. This macabre truce cannot hold. Not with him.

And not with the others.

Bell, Book And Candle

1

\- Nothing in what you say surprises me, Miles.

Winthrope rose from the table at which the two were sitting, and moved slowly toward the window, pressing for support on an ornate lacquered walking stick. Miles would not be so impolite as to ask whether this new addition was a temporary or, from now on, a permanent aid. Something in the window area seemed to irritate the head of the firm. During none of Miles' visits to the building in Fiddlers Court had he seen the blinds to the street other than shut tight. Today the old man raised his black cane, its head a silver griffin, to try to reach and hook the loop of string with its plastic pearls that would have allowed the slats, had they been in good working order, to rise and fall and let in strips of light. All he succeeded in achieving was the propulsion of little clouds of dust into the air. Giving up with a gesture of irritation, he let his cane rattle onto the table, which he used to rotate himself back into his usual seat, and sat down stiffly. Though he might now have difficulty walking, there was no evidence that Winthrope had experienced difficulty in dressing, that morning. Unless someone else had assisted.

White hair swept back, three piece midnight blue suit buttoned and immaculate, the necktie today a loose black cravat held in place with a jewelled pin of the kind fashionable in Poe's time, he looked as impregnable, and as self-regarding, as ever. Winthrope turned his body stiffly in his seat to take Miles in, lips pursed, gaze opaque. Miles obligingly moved his chair, legs scraping the floor awkwardly, to make the old savant more comfortable. He had first seen Winthrope occupy that seat at his interview. This made him warm to the man, to the extent that it put them both on the same side. But for Miles his growing powers were a resource he both offered to and shielded from others.

- You shouldn't let your guard drop where McLeod is concerned. He's a vicious box of tricks. He may be the worst we've had to deal with in some considerable time. These apparent signs of weakness he's showing you are aimed at getting you to lower your guard, that's all. Remember, he's a magician. Of sorts. Well. He's trying to charm you. It's a music hall turn. Finding a quarter or a nickel in your ear. Pulling rabbits out of hats. Throwing out titbits that make him look vulnerable, and make you a little more trusting. Don't believe a word. If he thought it would get him the book, he'd slit your throat from ear to ear, without thinking twice. Without thinking about it *at all*.

Winthrope tapped out these last words with his long but immaculately filed and squared-off nails on the table. The accents of Beacon Hill made an *awl* of all, everything turned in three letters to a tool for piercing. Miles was barely listening. Though he was retaining the content, it was all entirely predictable. He let his mind wander undercover, the better to test the dynamics in the room, while reviewing his own loyalties. There were other ways of understanding his relationship with Winthrope. His sense of being beholden, for example – that probably needed to be sealed tight now and pushed overboard. But his sense of divided allegiances? That one needed to be opened up, so that some light could be shed on the different forks and veins that crossed the maps of alternative futures.

Miles had deceived this man quite deliberately, about the Dream Pool. He was running his own solo version, and it was strong enough to incorporate Becky. Their own private Paris, their night in Tunisia, Trieste or Tangier. Now he had to decide exactly how guilty or guiltless to feel about that sweet deception. He plumped for guiltless, without further thought. The house that Miles built he was now putting in order. Spring cleaning in August, with six weeks left before the start of the new academic year, about to tread again the worn-out boards, pin up posters for visiting speakers nobody needed to hear, or an Office Hours notification of when he could be tracked to his small lair, all ears to the new students bearing old problems.

- So what should I do, Mr Winthrope?

- Victor.

- Victor. If I turn off the tap, he's going to come in with all guns blazing. I could have put that better. There's a danger...

- No, I'm with you. You're right, Miles, you have to keep the channels of communication open. He will not attack you, not *seriously* attack, while he still sees you as his sole means of getting to the book. If he ever found a way to get his hands on it without going through you first, then...

- That isn't going to happen, Victor.

- No. I believe you're right on that one.

His necromantic senior looked at Miles with a flicker of jealousy, almost of anger, that the younger man was quick enough to catch and retain for filing before it vanished in a web of wrinkled laughter-lines.

- No, we're pretty certain that no-one can really get a handle on what's in that book while *you're* around. And that no-one could ever stand a real chance of getting to *you*, not in any truly malevolent way, while that book is still there to protect you. How *is* the book, by the way?

Winthrope asked this in the tone one might use in order to ask how a rich, querulous and elderly relative was getting along, someone the whole family knew of old, but access to whose bounty was denied, to all but one member, her favourite.

- 	Oh, the book's fine. Thanks.

I have to be extremely careful what I say next. The book had been owned by Felix Manto. Winthrope the warlock and book-dealer managed to let the single remaining copy of a unique magical treatise slip through his fingers, because he failed to realize that it mattered not only what was in the book, but who read it. This book was fickle.

In his mind Miles veiled deliberately, sketching a blank grey wall that stretched to the sky, and in front of it, rope tied to waist, a mini-Winthrope: hapless little pendulum, swinging sans purchase or progress.

- 	It lives up to its title. It comes from a distant era, but for me at least, it keeps changing, in the now. The changes aren't random, and it isn't going round and round in circles. Reading it – working with it – is a little like…

Miles peered into his own thought-processes, as might a newly-fledged fisher of souls, peering over the mossed lip of an ancient well, whence called ambiguous voices. This time the blackness returned no firm answer. So much had happened, he was unsure of what images to conjure. So what *did* it feel like, interacting with and learning from his workbook? He could sense Winthrope's mind probing, colonising his hesitation and diminished ability to veil, growing claws and crampons, a reversed Dracula inching his way up the blank grey wall that Miles had built to keep him out.

Instantly Miles brought the temperature of his self-defensive day-dream crashing down, sending the tiny climber skittering down mirrors of sheet ice, while here in the dusty London room he heard himself babble conciliatory nonsense.

- It's like being in a round, tall tower. I'm walking up and up the spiral staircase, and on every new level there's a window. When I reach the level of the window and look out, it's a view of, well whatever the view is at that point, on that day, and it's…

- What *is* the view, Miles? What do you see, when you look out of your high tower?

The warlock had a wistful look, and his question was as real as, simultaneously, were his mental efforts to turn the ice wall horizontal, make of it a navigable pond. Briefly, in their shared mind, Winthrope had the upper hand. Briefly Winthrope skated, visually gallant, emblem and guardian of Enlightenment, hands folded serenely behind a dapper frock coat, needing no cane. His pointy beard a dagger of self-certainty in the self-conjured breeze.

In hot pursuit, Miles fumbled and blurred his desired mode of transport, finding himself mentally in a fire engine, already losing control of the vehicle slightly, its clanging horn changing to a wily old serpent, wheels hissing too on the ice as it cracked and Winthrope's lugubrious laughter boomed, distortion piled on distortion, threatening a shifting of tectonic plates, down in the depths of the Dream Pool. In the nick of time Miles sprang free from the fire engine as it sank beneath the ice, and wiped his mind scrupulously clean by compressing what had happened into a mental postcard. This he marked Lucky Escape, throwing it nonchalantly into a newly blazing mind-made fire, continuing in London time to opine at the ceiling, mouthing a plausible rejoinder.

- I can see all the way to the horizon. A long level plain. Populated with cities, rivers, occasional wild areas.

Mountains. Then the horizon. I see more, because I'm getting higher in the air, leaving the ground behind. And I know more. So the horizon gets further away. I'm learning. It's exciting.

Too bloody exciting, was the next thought Miles veiled. My little closed world of intrigue, the size of a snowstorm paperweight, packed with too many actors and motives and magic. Shake it and the whole thing might explode, paperweight turning to grenade. Actually, I could really do with some quality me-time on the top of a high tower. They were both silent, minds retreating from inside each other's.

Winthrope rose slowly to his feet. From his vest pocket he drew a box of matches, leaned forward gravely, and lit a candle. Blowing the match out, smoke rising briefly in a halo, he took on the air of a high priest, engaged in ritual ceremony. Perhaps at this moment he was. Then he plonked the wax-encrusted Chianti bottle squarely on the table between them. You're populating your world, thought Victor, more or less to himself alone, but not worried this time about clairvoyance. That's what youth is there to do. Climb. Your little tower image was meant to distract me, but as people instinctively do, you told a form of truth. Look out of the slits, and get to the top. There are only so many stories in this world, and they're all of them about pilgrimage. Spiral ascent, my son. Do I see something of myself in you? Given the – *singularity* of the work in which we are engaged – I guess I'd be bound to.

Winthrope, born in Boston, now embedded in London, but resident at one time or another in most parts of the globe, had pretty nearly reached the summit of his tower. Not that he was a tower man, when psychic push came to real shove; that symbol was for Miles. Yes, Miles is more of a Jungian type. My mind's still full of books, maps, signs, spread out across the floor. Lateral connections, years of travel; moving on, moving forward – not up, as such. What could up mean, now. Now I am old, neither young nor Jungian, and it takes a hell of a lot to frighten me. Something about this Scotsman beyond his sell-by date does bother me, though. He's working on a lot of different levels, and he isn't climbing any damned tower. He's on all of those levels all at the same time. He's hungry, and he's angry.

Best not to frighten Miles too much, he veiled. He's skittish, for all the hauteur, his new seen-it-all bravura. And the balance of probabilities is not on his side – which means, potentially, not on ours. Not on *my* side. The slippery luck of the young, Nature's favourites; that's his best weapon. His inner eye caught sight of the phrase Lucky Escape, but the words themselves were already escaping, up a chimney. But if Miles truly knew himself, then he'd have to know his limitations; and pouf, in that moment his magic might wane. He wouldn't be so young, any more. And then he might not be so damned lucky.

Miles' optimism returning, he too veiled again, then reviewed his clichéd answer and, as is the case with clichés, saw there was some truth in it. Yes, actually, reading the book, working with it, does feel like climbing the steps of a tower, but a twisted and tightly wound tower. An element of claustrophobia seems to come with the magical territory. There's no going back – I can't say to myself, that's fine, I've reached level six now, I like the view from here. I'm going to sit and enjoy it for a while, eat my packed lunch, then go back down the stairs to old reality, back to dear old Beltane, back the way I came. Then he felt a chill because he knew, deep down in his innermost being, that there would be no going back. Not because of an exceptional destiny but rather, he thought, because there is no such thing as return, not for anyone. If Miles was going to go back to the past, his intuition told him, the route would have to be magical, and the destination would be…not as it had been. This thought he saved for later.

Equally he felt with autumnal certainty that if he were ever to glance behind him, the steps he had taken would now have vanished. So where does that leave me. Pausing to take in the view, while hanging in mid-air? What would he do when he got to the top of the tower, if there was no going back? He hadn't thought that far. *Suppose the tower has no top, and my climbing no end.* He suddenly felt infinitely weary.

- So, Miles. You'll keep on working with the book.

Victor's face wore a look of professional respect, the resigned OK-you-win of a tutor whose student has just outstripped him, left his knowledge far behind, and exposed its old-fashioned limitations, strewing the cummerbunds, dentures and stays across the knowledge highway. Miles meanwhile crossed his ankles, troubled in mind by a fleeting image of Wily Coyote, stepping off the cliff with legs racing to keep himself aloft before the inevitable fall. Knowledge always brings a fall. Or at the very least, an enhanced gravity.

- And we'll keep the channels of communication open vis-à-vis our unpleasant friend, at least for the time being. There's a further reason to do this. Apart from the fact that it staves off the moment when he seriously attacks you. And he *will* go for you, make no mistake…

Yes, yes. Do you think I'm dim. One fine midnight there really will be a slavering hellhound with eyes like gig-lamps heading for my throat while I lie immobilised on Bodmin Moor by an arrowhead tipped in curare. That's blindingly obvious. Or a nightmare version of Becky will catch me with my defences and my trousers down, then slip into something more Transylvanian, and go for the boneless bits first.

Or, and this is most likely, Kenny will have wormed out in his blue-cheese brain the way he can really get to me, because the real way to get to someone is precisely not by way of their worst nightmare. You run through your worst nightmare at some point every week, maybe every day. You own it so completely that you know it inside out. He suddenly thought of the mother, who had nearly lost her baby to the drunk in the careening red sports car. Her worst nightmare nearly happened. But she was in, then quickly out of crisis, on that day at least. That one was in essence about me. Or it was a lesson from the beyond, that the allegedly Beyond is always just around the corner of the Here. What was nowhere is now here. Easy as moving a letter or two, in the mind. A world of life to death and back again, Miles and a lone mother, cars and carnations, merely illustrations.

So the way to catch me will always be to enter by the portal that I least expect, not the window that I have fastened securely, where the garlic and wolf's bane are in place. It's while you're fiddling with window-catch and winter aconite, peering fearfully out towards the setting sun, that the Thing is most likely to be standing right behind you. Not for the first time he thought, we could do with eyes in the backs of our heads. Anyway, Victor. You are about to tell me that if we keep in dialogue with bat-ears he will reveal more about himself, which will give us power over him, rather than the other way about. Because all of this, at the end of the day, is about power.

- I know that your relationship with the book is very special. None of us is going to interfere with that. But does the book know that you're in danger, from this shape-changer, this lost soul who wants to kill and kill again, but also die himself? His death-drive is incredibly strong. He can't ultimately tell the difference between murder and self-harm. Does the book really understand this?

Victor, I apologise. You have retained a capacity to surprise. I must remember to watch out for that, along the dark and winding stairs ahead. For now at least, the sorcerer still has the power to startle his apprentice. The veiling, the false front of his mind, turned this into a fractal, a myriad bowing sorcerers in robes and starry hats, good-humoured, respectful, young, tiny and infinite in number.

- We know that the book protected you in Death Valley. Or do we? Was McLeod simply unable to survive comfortably in the vicinity of the book – which isn't the same thing?

Miles wasn't hearing anything he hadn't asked himself already, but before he could conjure a suave evasion, summon from the reaches of his non-verbal mind a new fractal, or sketch a new blank wall, Winthrope himself was changing the subject, and with immense force. He did this by altering the scene in his mind in such intricate detail that Miles' mind was captured, pinned deep inside that scene as it unfolded.

Internally Miles' world was turned against his will into that of a black-and-white movie, more specifically, the final scene of an old *noir* thriller, where the psychiatrist steps towards the camera, to explain all to a cinema audience in dire need of answers as to why an axe-wielding murderer should have come to plague this small town in Maine, one indifferent summer. In tuxedo, hair slicked back, beard trimmed to hyper-professional suavity and sporting the heavy black glasses of the 1950s, Winthrope, in this hallucination the medically qualified authority on all things twisted and macabre, stepped forward, imposing head filling the screen.

To a non-existent drive-in audience on a warm summer's midnight in the early 1950s, some rapt, some wrapped round each other, some slugging Coca Cola or asleep, he began intoning *sententiae* that shed light on dark corners in psyche and old dark house, cellar and psychology alike. Only the psychiatric authority, not the dim-witted police, not the handsome but intellectually challenged male lead, could shine a real spotlight on the family romance. The millionaire Father, upright but wheelchair-bound, impotent – derided by the scheming son. His Mother, meanwhile, only too present, and ready to sharpen the axe: an Oedipal carry-on.

Marvelled at by chain-smoking reporters and open-mouthed townsfolk, Victor Winthrope MD carried on his own stroll towards and beyond the camera, as if it were not enough simply to stun the cast of characters, but as if he had to win over the drive-in audience too. Carefully, he climbed out of the screen altogether and, still explaining and rationalising, began to wander at random through the darkness of his dreamed and moonlit drive-in, here rapping on a car window to startle a young couple exceeding first-base, there plucking hand-rolled pungency from the mouth of a red-eyed roadster, grinding his heel on its final sparks, drenching his audience on-screen and off with a bracing shower of textbook pseudo-eloquence. What or who is he looking for, thought Miles, unable to either intervene or escape, but only to watch. I think he's looking for Kenneth McLeod. I do believe he's trying – even though he's trapped me in his own thought-processes - to help me.

Back in the drive-in, and from an abandoned, flat-tired Oldsmobile invisible to both Miles and Victor, where he dallied idly with a carton of popcorn, a bat-eared silhouette was busy putting Winthrope's Manhattanese schtick onto reel-to-reel tape, scanning him meanwhile through binoculars, 'Death' scratched on both of its black lenses with the diamond from a ring, one stolen long ago. He absent-mindedly placed the ill-gotten jewel beneath his tongue as if it were another form of popcorn, aspirin or host, and then, breaking it up with loud cracks from his molars, swallowed, coughed, and then muttering imprecations, fiddled with the dials on the tape machine.

Miles himself had by this point appeared on screen, albeit with visible reluctance, ingénue college boy in loafers, hands jammed awkwardly in the pockets of his tennis shorts while Winthrope dulled his senses with lines about crime and time, a long lost will, a squalid family squabble. Meanwhile liver-spotted, long-nailed hands in the Oldsmobile succeeded in cranking up the volume on the recording equipment, as a foul mouth emitted notes of rising incredulity. Having scoured the scene but missed McLeod, Winthrope climbed back, frowning, into the safety of the screen he had imagined and populated, gently pushing Miles, a widow exuding crocodile tears, and a flummoxed family retainer from its centre.

I've got to be careful with him, here, he veiled, facing Miles in London. I can't let him know what my real fear is. I can barely admit it to myself. He let Miles' psyche wriggle back by degrees to Fiddlers Court, without granting him, as yet, any right to reply.

- Psychopathic killers can be urbane, charming, brilliant – learn all the tricks that will help them wangle their way through the door – but they have no empathy, no capacity for identification. Or at least it's a tap they can turn off at will. What spooks me about our friend is that he has no empathy with *himself*. He positively wants to die. And yet he identifies, somehow, with you. I just don't get that bit. So there is a danger…let me put it another way. It will help to keep him talking. Just like, well, just like in the movies!

He smiled with supercilious benignity at the young magician, now caught passively between Fiddlers Court and an imagined outdoor cinema of the 1950s, unable to speak in either zone. Yah, that's the way to spin it. There are only so many stories in the movies, and this is the one with the neat, upbeat ending. And Miles is a simple soul. Winthrope beamed again. In his dream-spun drive-in, all was stilled now apart from the hypnotic intoning of the psychiatrist, and the bat-eared occupant of the Oldsmobile, now loading a shotgun and shouting blue murder.

- You know, like a movie, where someone keeps the killer talking on the phone, which gives the police their chance to race round and catch him. His location has been traced. They know where he's calling from. What we need to know, though, Miles, is…who *are* the police here? Who's the operator? What are the limits on the powers of the book, in terms of its self-understanding? Who's the agent? Is it you, or us, or the book-and-you? Who's in the driving seat?

In trying not to say too much, Winthrope had painted himself into truth's awkward corner. But then why, he thought, am I surprised. There will be lies in there, naturally. We can keep things from each other, even to some extent from ourselves. But really, if you had a tape recording of all the conversations that have ever taken place in the history of the world, what you would hear, for the most part, is a vast horde of people telling each other the truth. Most of the time we convey the truth of our own natures more to each other than we do to our own self. And so the more we can keep old bat-ears chatting, the more we find out about him. So we gain power over him. Because, at the end of the day, all of this is about power. And we are the group. He is a one-off from the dark zone – but a loner, nonetheless.

Miles, who had re-charged his batteries, recovered his senses in their overlapping minds, by sheer willpower forcing the credits to roll; unstoppable Winthrope continued to mouth off in silence, spewing Cold War, cod Freud in the lap of a smiling DA.

Abruptly they were facing each other, eyes closed and foreheads almost touching, at the table in Fiddlers Court. Each jerked to attention, expert chess players heeding a bell. OK it's stalemate. Good game, Miles. Good game, Victor.

- So just be careful, Miles. I wish you the best of luck. And be reassured…

Here Victor smiled, and extended a banker's handshake.

- …be reassured, that nothing you've said this morning surprises me.

Infuriated by this last remark, Miles smiled brightly. He got up to shake the old boy's hand. When you interviewed me, chum, we were sitting on opposite sides of the table. Then you gave me the job, which rotated me, Miles as chess player, no longer piece, round to your side. I was quids in with the high rollers. Working with, and not for, you said. White knight was now dark player. But, either way, you just admitted you still want to use me, and as a pawn, not a knight. This is really about you, and power. Power you let slip from under your nose, when Manto let go of the book, that's now made its way into my world.

If the book has to come to my rescue, then that will add to your knowledge. You'll probably want it so badly by then that if I can wriggle out of McLeod's reach unharmed, then you'll go for me, at that exact moment. But if the book can't help me, and I'm ripped to scarlet shreds by Dr Death, you'll learn something from that too. And you'll come to my funeral and get the book anyway. You'll try to prise its truths open. It won't put up with that, it won't let you. Perversely I can't help but like you, Victor, even though a little goes a terribly long way. But I don't trust you. I'm glad I held things back from you. My instincts were right.

And so the two parted on excellent terms, reassured by their discussion and cerebral jousting that what each had thought in the first place had just been confirmed as true. Meanwhile in a rapidly fading, nocturnal cinema of hallucination, the driver of the Oldsmobile was engaged in heated argument with a terrified youth in a peaked cap and bow-tie, holding him upside down as dimes and quarters squirted from his shoulder bag, endeavouring to recoup the cost of admission to what had proved a disappointing midnight movie. Then the screen became stygian, was gone with the wind, its plug pulled.

Once Winthrope had heard the door to the street close, he tapped on the wall furthest from the Court. Mr Boxer immediately joined him at the table.

- Dunno how much of that you heard, Boxer.

- In all candour, not a great deal, sir. My preference is not to eavesdrop. And I was, in any case, anxious – *am* anxious, to hear you voice your thoughts. You have been

around the block, to use contemporary parlance. I doubt
that young Proctor brought much that was surprising
to the table.

You always were an unctuous little so-and-so, and long winded
with it. But you know which side your bread's buttered. And to be
fair, your own instincts are pretty shrewd. Let's shoot from the hip.

- No he didn't. I stick with what I said earlier. However
  perverse it is of me, I like Miles, though a little does
  go a terribly long way - but I don't trust him. He only
  cares about the book. He's an ambitious freshman, who
  knows he'll make professor if he works at it. Cocky. He's
  pretty sure that if he studies hard enough, he'll crack all
  the codes, gain his doctorate in Magic. And then? Pouf,
  gone. We won't see him for dust.

- And you are absolutely sure you saw him in the Dream
  Pool? Hiding his thinking from us?

- It was him alright, down there in the Pool. I wouldn't
  exactly say I *saw* him. I had him by the nose at one
  point. He couldn't tell. He's pretty good at veiling, and
  also at blocking with cartoon scenarios. He tried it on
  just now. But aren't they all good at veiling, the smart
  young guns – just not as sharp as I, my dear Mr Boxer,
  just not as sharp as I am.

You are wise and shrewd, thought Mr Boxer. In one zone or another,
in and out of worlds and dreams, spaces which appear on no map, in
no book, not at any rate the ones with barcodes, you have witnessed
just about every kind of human, inhuman and beyond-human
behaviour. And that has brought a wealth of knowledge into this
organization. You have lived so long. But perhaps, and here Mr
Boxer also veiled – if one were to offer a direct and honest appraisal,
you have lived just a little *too* long.

2

If Miles' inner life was a progression up the stone steps of a tower, then it was not this tower. Climbing the stairs to his office, on the fifth floor of Bertrand Russell, he didn't want to be in College at all. He wanted to be at home on her sofa with Becky, asleep and unmoving while travelling the world with her, voyaging ever further. Diving in the chambers of the heart, which only exist in the mind but which are cave-painted with real signs, complicated signs that mean in the end one simple thing; that this is it. This is the one. And he certainly didn't want to be teaching.

For the most part the College campus stood empty of undergraduates in the summer months, their rooms let at this point to Italian summer-school teenagers, interested only in each other and, for want of better entertainment, in setting off the fire alarms by night. These teens were forcibly taught estuary English by the STDs – Supernumerary Tutors and Demonstrators – until their linguistic competence deteriorated to a level so embarrassing to the institution as to mandate swift repatriation. Then it would be time for Estates Management to check the carpets and curtains for cigarette burns, then bus in the contract cleaners, readying the College for a brief September flurry of academic conferences, before the new wave of undergraduate students hit. These freshers, all thought of serious study postponed until at least the following year, focussed mainly on each other and on getting hammered each night in the Students' Union, and would also be taught largely by the STDs.

Malcolm Coates was one of Miles' PhD students, and he had phoned to say he was stuck, part-way into a chapter of his doctoral thesis. As an STD he was also weary from getting up at one a.m. to see if he could nab Fabrizio and Lucrezia in the vicinity of the fire alarm that had just woken him, and do so without risking serious injury, because they had also covered the stairs with diluted Fairy Liquid in the Hall of Residence where he was Junior Warden. The PhD situation plus the STD tuition, topped off with night-watch duties, had generated fairly hefty bags under the eyes. His student looked older than Miles, whom he was disgusted to see was thin as a rapier, tanned, and possessed only those lighter shadows round the eyes that come from doing other things.

At twenty three, and a martyr to comfort food, Malcolm had stopped weighing, choosing instead to believe that the tyre-like overhang featuring a ring in its substantial navel could be taken as indicator of a free spirit, rather than the fashion crime silently diagnosed by his peers. Malcolm was beholden to Miles' patronage and intellectual esteem, while knowing that he and his mates had the College over a barrel. The STDs were doing most of the teaching, and taking a fair bit off the shoulders of Security, the Hall Wardens, and even the Counselling Service. The academics could be snotty, but the Principal always sent the STDs a personally signed Christmas Card. All four hundred of them.

Miles' student sat patiently, crossing his sizeable white legs. These were dotted with ginger hair and rendered bare from the knee by the camouflage long shorts, which failed to match either the once white tee-shirt or the sockless running shoes, not that this student-tutor was much given to rapid movement. Malcolm's naturally ginger hair had been shaved, sculpted and cajoled into a dyed-green Mohawk, giving him the air of a majestic giant rooster. He fiddled idly with one ear-ring, waiting for Miles to find his notes before Malcolm sketched the contours of the latest intellectual buffers he sensed he might have hit.

Malcolm had begun with a promising, if narrow, topic for his thesis: 'The Role of Nocturnal Footsteps as Leitmotif in Novels of the Mid-1860s'. With Miles' encouragement he had broadened this somewhat, first with a disastrous sideways move, putatively titled 'Madwomen Leaving the Attic: Defenestration, Literature and Empowerment' – a topic deriving ultimately from Malcolm's unreciprocated devotion to Mandy Smitten, a fellow postgrad, who, after years of cultivated vagueness leading up to her own

PhD dissertation, entitled 'Navigating Otherness: Notes towards the Post-Postcolonial', had abruptly locked onto a tenure-track professorship at Stanford with the unnerving precision of a Cruise Missile. Latterly, Malcolm had reverted to his first topic, but had broadened it on pragmatic grounds to include more detective fiction and supernatural mysteries of various sorts. While Miles saw little that was original in this approach, he thought he could see a publishable article or two in the making. Meanwhile, Malcolm thought he could see Paolo and Francesca messing about, first with each other and then with the fire alarm, and hadn't really got any further than that, not this week.

- What sounds you listening to these days, Malcolm?

Miles, playing for time while trying to make sense of his scribbled notes and attempting to manage his bad mood down into a state of affability, had noticed a set of earphones that trailed into the breast pocket of his postgrad's camouflage jacket. As he recalled from a drunken party at Malc's where Miles had cast an eye over the CDs, Coates' taste in music ran from Heavy Metal through Even Heavier to Nouveau Thrash. (Fingering his way around the shelves and cardboard boxes, Miles had also discovered a hefty quantity of herbal cannabis and an equally sizeable, chewed chunk of six months old pizza, the combination of which lent Malcolm's music collection a curiously synaesthetic whiff.) There are certainly a few things I could tell you about Felix Manto, thought Miles, collating his professional thoughts on Malcolm's critical methodology, prose style, and command of the Victorian literary canon.

- Sounds? Oh it's not music I'm listening to. It's Dickens.

- *Dickens?*

- Yeah. Here, look.

With a flourish, Malcolm proceeded to extricate from within his camouflage jacket an Audiobook of Charles Dickens' last novel, 'The

Mystery of Edwin Drood'. Miles accepted it with all the pleasure he might have derived from sampling a handful of fish innards.

- Malcolm, I'm amazed. You weren't going to listen to the tape as a way of getting round having to read the book, were you?

No of course not, Malcolm lied, running one hand nervously through his burgeoning Mohawk. Left for dead in a broom cupboard of the mind, Miles' scholarly conscience abruptly burst its bonds, hammering and yelling *Let Me At Him, I'll Take Him!*

- I'm shocked. Seriously. Surely the act of reading is…how to say? A silent, cerebral communion…or it's nothing. Surely. This is like seeing the film of a book. It might be fun, but it isn't the same, it isn't The Book. I thought you'd be listening to – I don't know – Black Sabbath.

Black Sabbath? Get a grip, how old do you think I am? Malcolm's idol was an only recently deceased musician, much mourned, at least by Coates, but he wasn't going to sully the name of Felix Manto by dropping it into this conversation, particularly since Miles would never have heard of him anyway. His postgrad had Miles down as a jazz buff. Holding forth authoritatively about BeBop, Hard Bop and Post-Bop to impress his latest blonde waif. Bloody academics. You might not get this, *Doctor* Proctor, he fumed, pulling some fractured thoughts on Jane Eyre from out of his rucksack, but I don't want to be an academic. Not really. Clearing his throat, Malcolm briefly acknowledged his inmost dream, the roar of the crowd, and windmilled a power chord on his Stratocaster.

Just then the phone rang. John Spendrift had glimpsed young Proctor from across the quad. He had spent the morning measuring up in the entry level of the main Library, costing some new glass-topped display cases, and pulling out items from the Victorian Studies section in the Rare Books and Manuscripts Room. The bust of Queen Victoria in the atrium, before you reached the Issue Desk

– that had set him thinking. But if this exhibition to mark the start of the new academic session was really going to work, it needed a centrepiece, or pieces.

Spendrift had padded around every College gallery, corridor and alcove, returning the painted and for the most part imprisoned gaze of early Principals, and pondering the faux-Middle Ages of later nineteenth century escapism. Miss Evershed? She was different, the first Principal of the new College, toughest of cookies, vocal in the cause of female emancipation, and one who had thrice climbed the Matterhorn, the last time with fatal consequences. No. It's a great portrait, but nobody's heard of her who isn't interested in College lore. OK then: the College bronzes. Pride of place, a life-size naked woman, writhing with a snake in sculptured synergy. Sculptor, Maxim Du Vertige, 1888. I like her, I like them, but a female student has tried to deface her on more than one occasion, a male student knocked her off her pedestal while attempting something else, and the last time I had her moved into the foyer someone wrapped a College scarf round her neck and gave the snake a Spurs supporter's bobble hat. She's just too precious. It's too precious. So what else is there?

Spendrift walked around the Music Library, footsteps echoing, fingering the yellowed pages published by Boosey & Hawkes, and Busoni. Tennyson's 'Come into the Garden, Maud', in an arrangement for voice and piano. Hmm. A Victorian evening at home? The Music and Drama Societies between them could pull it off, but that might risk going down the food-and-drink route, which he wanted to keep clear of the Library for as long as he had strength to fight that quiet rearguard action.

Letters, then. There was a witty one from Oscar Wilde, informing a board of theatre managers that, while their staging and seating facilities were perfect, the building itself would have to be moved prior to first night, due to the poor angle at which the light would strike his profile as he was carried in by cheering crowds. The only other letter from Oscar was a routine query about expenses. The Bram Stoker letters were of some historical interest, but written in his capacity as gopher for the actor Irving, rather than as creator of the undead. There was of course the voice of Henry Irving himself, a memorable if booming Prince of Elsinore, but the recording had been done on a primitive wax cylinder so distorting that everyone had been sure until recent days, and the purchase of some clever new software by the Linguistics Department, that these eruptions in fact constituted the sole remains of Irving's Prospero.

What treasures were left? To show off Beltane College's single canvas by Dante Gabriel Rossetti, yet again? Only if it was balanced by something or things decidedly un-decadent. Alternatively, what about a stodgy centrepiece with decadent wings. Getting there. In different media. Three boxes ticked. The George Eliot letters? Beyond tedious, but nothing if not voluminously beyond tedious, and therefore by definition a scholarly resource. Otherwise, Rossetti's painting of Ophelia drifting downstream it would have to be; more ball-gowned sorceress on laudanum than love-crazed suicide, but that was the Victorians for you. Oh what am I thinking, go back to square one. Admit the obvious. Box three, in the alcove, under the bust of Queenie, new glass-topped case, couple of new spotlights, what could there be, what could there *ever* have been, but the book. Miles Proctor's book.

- I'm teaching right now, John. Yes, a postgrad, that's right. Yes indeed. Summer's lease hath all too short a date. It certainly hath. I'll get back to you on the hour.

Miles looked so thoughtful, so utterly absorbed as Malcolm read out his notes that he began to feel much better about both himself and his research supervisor. That was the thing about Dr Proctor, he always put the needs of the student first. He'd probably rather be in the Library having an elevated conversation with John Spendrift, or more likely working on his own world-leading research, but he's come in specially. Just to help me.

A few minutes before the College bells pealed out the hour, Malcolm was zipping up his rucksack as the phone rang again. No, I'll leave him to it, thought Malcolm: thanks, Miles. Malcolm tiptoed out. Miles, facing the window to the quad thought, John, this will be you. Now what am I going to say, and how am I going to say it. He picked up the phone.

-    Miles, it's Laura…Laura Winthrope.

3

He made his way out of Bertrand Russell, and walked downhill past Maynard Keynes, having arranged to meet Laura Winthrope in The SteakOut. During term time, this shrine to mild gastritis would be heaving, but at this point in the boom and bust cycle of the academic year they should at least be able to get some privacy. Plus, nowhere else was open.

So: she has to be the old man's daughter. Interesting. What will she want from me? She won't want to *tell* me anything, because this lot never let anything slip out. That's the firm's motto. Hug it to your chest, even if it's something the group needs to know. Especially then. You have to find everything out for yourself. And watch your back, while hugging your chest – awkward, but you'll get the hang of it. Most likely scenario, he will be using her as a way to get the book from me. It's the one volume left in the world that this learned antiquarian can't read. He knows that it's sitting in a flat in Camden, just a few miles away from him, but that it might as well be in an alternative universe. It *is* in an alternative universe. And he just can't bear it.

So Laura will be a ruse, a different angle of entry. She will want to borrow it for such a short time. Just for a little while; *please*, Miles. Old Father Winthrope will of course have forbidden her to do any such thing, do not do that, Laura, which is why she uses my number on campus and doesn't want to meet the *idiot savant* (and that one still smarts) where Daddy might be at work, sleeping, eavesdropping, or a combination of all three. But intuitively, and Miles was more and more a creature of intuition, that doesn't feel right. I'm not sure you could forbid or pressure Laura to do anything. But what do I know. Maybe I'm about to find out.

More troubling is the question as to how she knew that I would in fact be on campus today. And if I can be traced here so easily, am I being followed when I visit – be still my beating heart – more sensitive destinations. I need – we need – to take more precautions. Worst case scenario, see a little less of each other, just for a while. But I couldn't bear that.

Spot of rain in the air. The air itself beginning to darken, thickening into smoky viscosity. He walked up the steps to The SteakOut. This was always, to Beltane regulars but even more to first-time visitors, a slightly unnerving moment. The sign on the glass read Automatic Doors, but the invisible trigger which controlled their opening was for some reason set a little too near the glass for comfort. People would shuffle uncertainly around the general vicinity of the entrance waiting for something to happen, before sidling in on the coattails of a regular who breezed straight at the sign, without fear. Miles walked confidently straight towards the glass, which duly parted its vertical lips to admit him. Not a soul to be seen. No customers, no one even serving. Hello? And again, louder.

Footsteps echoing, he crossed the blue line in the flooring, and peered through a porthole into the kitchen. A couple of STDs in white coats and hairnets were further supplementing their income by washing and chopping, in a desultory way, the ingredients of today's Salad Special. Well, at least that means The SteakOut is open. I didn't think it would be this quiet. Although you need a degree of privacy when you really need to talk to someone, it actually feels a bit spooky to be the only customers. What with that and the dodgy doors, she might well jump to the conclusion that this place is closed. And anyway, the courteous thing for me to do would be to wait outside. He turned around to do exactly that, but found himself gazing straight into her eyes.

Later he would ask himself how long she might have been standing there. For now, it was Laura Winthrope's eyes that claimed his whole attention. Green, he thought in retrospect. Grey green. Not a blend of the two, but first green and then grey, grey and then green. He was reminded of stormy light, falling through trees on to a pond where he had paddled his small boat, as a child: where he had been warned of the dangers of drowning, even in shallow water. The whisper of rain on leaves. Time to get under cover. Before bullets of rain break the soil and cause new things to grow. He thought of the eyes of an animal, also. Predators projected the colour of their eyes for purposes that only members of their own species, or their victims, could interpret.

-   Hello, Miles. Thank you for this.

He put out his hand, which she took only to let drop in favour of a perfunctory and perfumed air-kiss, both moves accomplished adroitly and both making him feel clumsy. Side by side, they walked by more glass, to the interior. The moment had a ritual feel to it. So excited and uncertain did Miles feel about the reasons for his summons, which was what it was, that for a few moments he let their wordless progress take on a solemn, almost bride and bridegroom feel. And then moving from kaleidoscope eyes to the somewhat randomly stained glass of The SteakOut's interior, fitfully catching the light before a storm, he was reminded by the bounce and swerve of memory of some stained glass windows he had once seen in a church, windows stoned out by Roundheads in the Civil War.

The congregation had lovingly kept the smashed fragments and put the windows back, with the restoration of the monarchy. But the Restoration couldn't put Humpty together again. The unnumbered fragments had been hoarded, with reverence, but higgledy-piggledy.

They couldn't get the angels and apostles, the visor or the patient hound beneath the knightly feet, back into their proper order. Here, half a saintly profile looked hopefully up to a fractured heaven, while over there, in the wrong place, fell the rays of transcendent illumination. The stone fronting the Saviour's tomb had not only rolled away; half of it had disappeared. There in a corner lay parts of a robe, though the face that might have identified the wearer was broken into the shards and glancing lights of an abstract expressionism. In fact at first glance the windows did look modern, and deliberately abstract. They were still very beautiful. Perhaps more so.

Miles was never sure whether he preferred order to fragmentation; it depended what sort, in either case. He knew he had always had an attachment to figures. If one childhood morning he had woken to find that the model soldiers who had been poised for battle as he drifted off to sleep were by some catastrophic agency, such as his brother, broken when he woke, he would have patiently glued them together again, rather than ask for a new model army. As an academic, although scholar of a relatively recent period, he liked the old ways, at least some of them, or fondly and mistakenly thought he did.

His mother had brought her sons up at the high, somewhat vague end of Anglican worship; smells and bells, as those suspicious of both say. He still liked both, or at least their aesthetic echo, finding in his memory of the bell during prayers and the heavy, almost claustrophobic scent of incense, something true to the mysteries of the world, and yet comforting in its insistence that those mysteries were benign, in the end, and could be navigated. He had needed that sense of the ultimate benignity of things as a crutch during some of his recent near-tumbles, though the larger question of how, if at all, his recent experiences could be or should be squared with any form of traditional belief was one he was locked in too tightly, right now, to be able to stand back and see with any clarity. Perhaps if I persevere and stick with what I think is right, he thought, the answer to these things will come to me. What his father had precisely thought about such matters he had gathered only in hints and signals. His father was inclined to mysticism and, Miles was beginning to intuit, his own understanding of magic. But then the bells and heavy scents, or the high bookshelves and locked cabinets of his father's study, were themselves only hints and signals.

And anyway, he had a positive relish for fragmentation, for the things the day throws in from left-field, for unfinished magical jigsaws that kept his mind honed. In the joyous and grown-up parts of his being, Miles loved the overthrow of order, the getting out from under all the dross that had messed up his father, and his father's generation, and that seemed to find its latest incarnation in the world, occult to him, of management. Laura Winthrope by his side, he proceeded into The SteakOut. This unpaid, unsafe, unseen and nightmare-inducing new job – how *exciting* it all is. It points me towards hidden order, then throws strange new fragments my way.

Aware of Laura's breathing and her locking step with his, Miles thought, characteristically, that perhaps there was a way to reconcile all this. Maybe the world is fragments, unconnected things and events, moving through time. A lot of it random happenstance, chance encounter: stuff. And maybe the opposite is also true. There are hidden patterns, and meanings, and echoes – the skein of connection. And perhaps it's all the same world, whichever way you read it. So if patterns make you happier, or seem to make the world clearer or better – do it. Think in that way, and the world will happily play itself back to you, on that wavelength. Was this meeting with Laura a one-off, or part of a pattern, a jigsaw piece? I think I'll go for pattern. These days I generally do. It's more mind-bending, in the beginning. But more healing in the end. But why think of healing in this current moment, this current meeting?

The world is so strange. Not just poetry and dreams, but real mirrors, real clouded towers and solemn courtyards; the twists in water as it falls and flows away. The curious watching stillness of the trees, as if bending in a tree-world lens to view you. Clouds drifting, like pursuer and pursued across the moon. Or old black and white photographs, that in fading, start to register something beyond the intended. London streets from a very high building, pathos in the silence and slowness of traffic, seen from that height. A silence as heavy as presence, inside the apartment, as you unlock the door and enter on some sunlit morning. Almost as if the now stilled chairs and curtains had been up to something, conversing, hadn't been expecting you to come back until later. Animals, who seem at times only to be playing at being animals, as if they found us amusing and would say so, the moment our backs were turned. And eyes.

Her eyes were very beautiful. He hadn't quite realized, before today. If they were windows, this soul was illegible, not in any way to be fathomed, with here a green undersea play of light and shadow, there a steely mirror that repudiated bravely all attempts to seize or capture. There were colours and lights there that held your own gaze. Stole it perhaps, to see through you later, in private. But to what purpose, she had not as yet hinted. Again he questioned allegiances, again he reverted to predators – the fierceness of colour, the brutal precision of desert and jungle.

> - I wasn't sure that you would come. That you would have the time to spare. For me.

Her tongue flicked out for a second, under the very white and perfect teeth, made more so by her deep red lip gloss. Though gloss was not quite right. It was her teeth themselves which shone with the natural gloss of health, while her lipstick was a deeper shade of carmine. Peripheral vision told Miles that a server in white had now configured them as a triangle. The man was waiting patiently. Coming out of his paralysis, Miles felt that he must have been standing there as if turned to stone. Indeed, he half expected, as he turned, to see a mocking smile, but the man, youngish, and he would recall later, so intense now his awareness of detail, unshaven, dark skin tone, perhaps Mediterranean, was simply and blankly looking, between and not at them. No sound. No one else in The SteakOut. *Coffee*, she said. Black. Miles nodded, as the waiter inclined his head, turning on his heel.

And, no, he couldn't read today's Laura. The pages were all flying open, at speed, but the words broke apart into whirling black letters that he couldn't piece together in the correct order. They flew around in tiny sighing clouds. Although the conversation they were about to have would stray into symbols and thickets of literature, Miles did not believe, retracing this strange encounter subsequently, and obsessively, that she ever made a single reference to *the* book, to his book.

The conversation began by moving along customary lines, as they sat at one of the small, glass-topped tables. Clichés can be very important. They contain truth, for one thing, but for another, suture over pain. Twin wicker chairs contained the couple, curved a little, high-backed, the arm rests also high. She sat upright in a classically professorial pose, and indeed, it emerged that she was a Professor of Near Eastern Studies at one of the other London colleges. She had simply located his office extension in the British Library Directory; no deception there. And the odd sense of déjà-vu he had experienced on meeting her first at his interview? Well yes, they probably had seen each other at some point, across a crowded seminar. At the School of Advanced Research, or some other haunt of fine distinctions. So far, so perfectly explicable.

It was at this point that he felt heat across his ribs so powerful that he almost expected to see smoke pour from his clothing. Ectopic heartbeats made him feel as if the book in his pocket were shocking him electrically, or vibrating like the mobile phones that it was rumoured had been invented, but which governments world-wide had held back from general issue, for reasons so far unexplained. Excusing himself, he walked stiffly but at speed along the dotted line that marked the floor between tables until he came to the sign of a matchstick man without features, legs akimbo, high on a purple door. Entering, he read above the sink the instruction Now Wash Your Hands, and did so scrupulously and immediately, drying them with even more care, and pulling spare tissues from the box fixed to the wall. Only then did he slip into a cubicle, opening the door and then locking it behind him with tissue-swathed fingers, before removing from his inner jacket pocket, and inspecting, the book that must retain its pristine state.

Leaning with his back to the door of his enclosure he read the opening words of a chapter he had no prior recollection of reading. It sounded a warning.

> *Now, at the moment when the Adept feels as secure in his knowledge as One who surveys his lands from the highest Tower of the Castle, now when all threat seems it might be ground under foot, a snake never to bite again; now is the moment of greatest danger, when the tall mirror of Pride in Magical Prowess, rather than shewing the Adept a true reflection, risks blinding him to what lurks behind the glass. Nor must it be of necessity the case that the threat is a secret hoarded by an enemy. Now is the moment when Friend may, all unknowing, no longer be so, and worse, when Strangers may be drawn, even against their better judgment, even against their Knowledge…*

Miles' heart lurched. It was as if the book's words were now more than words, were the script for an inner voice to play back to him, filling his eyes, his ears, with an amplified warning of danger. But could Laura Winthrope really be that dangerous? Strange, yes, and in her strangeness beautiful, yes again, but *dangerous*? He calmed himself and prepared to reread those last lines, but of course they had changed again:

> *Nor is the obvious Enemy, be he thief in the night*

or accuser by day, the worst Opponent of the Adept. His magical powers may be led from their true and purposeful path by a purported friend, a second person now possessed for a season or a moment by the dark mind of a third. Fear the Opponent who works through the Friend. Yet above all fear the Stranger, who may be drawn against their better judgment, yea, even without their own Knowledge, to throw harm in the way of Magic, bring down the high tower, murder the Adept even as he sleeps. Worse, they may murder the Magical King as they themselves sleep, *active in malice at midnight but breathing as innocent as new-borns in their unstained cloud of not-knowing.*

The rest of the page remained blank; Miles stayed rooted, spooked, mind whirling in a Gents' in Greater London. Slowly and with infinite care, he replaced the book in his inner jacket pocket, collected himself, and, after gazing for a moment into the unused toilet bowl as if terrible danger might lurk there or come bubbling up the u-bend, walked once again to the sink, washing, this time, not just his hands but his face, and in cold water. As he bent towards the sink to turn on the tap, the words Now Wash Your Hands changed, unseen by him, to stark Gothic script that read **Now Watch Your Back**, but the letters vanished as he raised his head to force some composure into the eyes that looked back at him from the mirror. Now wash my hands of Laura? Or the whole firm? He was in too deep to pull out now without starting a chase in the Dream Pool that might end in drowning.

As he turned to dry his hands with more tissues pulled from the box on the wall, he thought he saw out of the corner of his eye and barely for a moment the letters *HEL* appear in lipstick on the mirror. HELP ME? Or HELL? Remembering red cars and red carnations, he closed his eyes and tried to pin down, and if possible nudge and ameliorate, circumstance. But it was no good, he was too rattled, and too aware of keeping his companion waiting. Miles put his hand to his chest, but felt, now, only a slight warmth across his ribs. He opened the black door with its little sign-man, legs pressed studiously together, and strolled with as much nonchalance as he could muster back to the tables, following the little arrows in the flooring. Had he glanced through the port hole of glass into the kitchens, he might have seen the two STDs, gender obscured by hairnets and clothing suggestive of operating theatre greens, locked in a passionate tongue-twined embrace, oblivious to an overflowing sink and to the fate of a large bowl of tuna niçoise their movements had knocked to the floor. Instead it hit him how powerful her personality, her *mind* was – it seemed to be dictating the whole context in which they sat talking, down to the weather, down to an odd sense of claustrophobia, leavened with rapt fascination.

She took it, Laura observed dryly, that Miles was becoming adept at dealing with this necessary segregation of affiliations, these separate lines of life? And how did it feel to be following his new career-path? The crisp tone she had adopted at his interview, with its hints of suspicion and the academy's version of the *grande dame* were still in play, but at variance with the other, opaque signals that criss-crossed the, by now, utterly charged air. She threw back her head, smashed eyes unreadable. Rain started typing short lines on the window.

Again she tossed her hair, her mane, chestnut with silver sparks, and ran a bejewelled hand through it. An amethyst the size of? Of itself. One moment she seemed restless, as if, Miles thought, annoyed with him, at other moments focussed on him utterly, but solely through the prism of a gaze he could not penetrate. Was she coming on to him? Unlikely. Anyway, although completely hypnotised, he didn't desire her. Did he? There was not one inch of unoccupied space in his life, no room for more desire. In any case, hadn't she been the one who had begun by reminding him of the strict necessity to keep things clean, and separate. Though that of course entailed secrecy.

Laura was wearing a hound's tooth jacket, over a tight silk waistcoat. This and a degree of agitation couldn't help but draw Miles' attention to what would surely be heavily beautiful, eminently cuppable, breasts. Decently into her forties, she looked great. There was nothing girlish about her, and she didn't flirt – at least, not in the usual ways. Today in a white shirt, seemingly a man's cotton shirt in a dense weave, French cuffs and jewel cufflinks. The chair creaked, as she leaned forward. Laura also creaked, a little. Or rather, her trousers, made out of black leather hide, creaked. She looked at him dreamily.

-    Miles, do you mind if I ask you a question?

-    Of course not. Fire away.

For a second, her eyes looked like they might roll up into her head, and he have to catch her from falling. Then she laughed, darkly. Scant resemblance to the Father. It was partly the face of his interviewer he now saw once again, the academic fencing mistress who could cut new red lines in your unmasked face, if she chose. But added to that, today, this dream-intimacy. Forever afterwards, Miles would be able to summon up a vivid recollection of her skin, the essential pallor made even more attractive by the clusters and dots of dark, of varied, pigmentation. The veins in her strong hands, and the deep red nail polish. Perhaps this louche dreaminess was really a way to rebalance the dynamic between them. Making herself unreadable would perhaps give her the power to focus him on exactly the points she wanted to come to.

Again she drew one long-nailed finger slowly through her chestnut hair. He knew with an unjustifiable but absolute certainty that she would have at least one or two larger moles on her shoulders and back. He felt sure he could see certain other things. The aureoles around her nipples would be large. And grape-shaded. There. Damn. He did desire her. Damn.

Miles half-felt she knew that she had him, half thought she might be asking the question of herself:

-	Do you ever have the urge…the urge to confess some-
	thing, to a complete stranger?

Miles reminded himself, not for the first time of late, be careful
how you answer. He probed his own mind to find a secure magic
circle in which to retreat from giving too much away, but his earlier
efforts of that kind had left him tired, today. His mind, into which
he now peered, seemed clear and bare, but dangerously unfenced,
without conning tower or watchman.

-	Confession as in the box and the priest, no. If I'd been
	brought up in that particular faith, then, who knows.
	And of course there's psychoanalysis. The literature's
	always interested me, and in Eng Lit we all dip in and
	out of Freud, one way or another.

And what, he couldn't help but think, would the interpreter of
dream make of this, and of you. Of my reaction to you. Sometimes a cigar is just a cigar. Sometimes a mind is an ocean with
no solid floor, none whatsoever. What in my mind is at work? He
had a sudden vision of a classical statue in the deep green sea that
reared up, whitely from green seaweed, blind eyes flashing, mouth
gaping. He shivered. I'm picking up fragments from her thoughts.
Pull yourself together. Get a grip. Remember the interview. Get it
into your psyche that any conversation you have with this woman,
however wayward, is a continuation of interview.

-	But no, no, Laura, I wouldn't. Not confess something
	important to a stranger. I do believe that…that we're
	all, always, in some kind of give and take, push and pull
	with each other, you know, I'll risk giving you this if you
	offer me that…

Oh bloody hell, this is true, but it's the last thing I wanted to say.
And I'm waving my hands around, which I do when I'm nervous,

and that's probably not a good idea, either. Miles stuck both his hands between his legs.

> - …and, so. Where am I headed with this. You wouldn't want to waste that *transaction* which is such an important part of life, on a stranger. You'd be throwing something valuable away. Because a stranger doesn't know you, so what could they possibly give you in return?

Miles thought he had now got away with that one, and got things back on an even track. A card advertising the services of a dominatrix came disconcertingly into his mind, but he successfully pushed that card back into the deck. Laura creaked, and leaned forward. Miles was aware of their knees just about touching, under the table, at that precisely calibrated, or indeed completely accidental level of intimacy, where it is perfectly possible for one person not to be aware of the touch the other feels. Or, alternatively, where both can be completely certain that the other knows they can feel this, but where neither is about to withdraw, let alone say anything, because this is, when all is said and done, pleasant. Pleasant in conjuring thoughts, as it does, harmless thoughts because unvoiced, just resting there like limbs briefly touching or the glimpse of a tongue on white teeth; thoughts of what might also be pleasant, some other time, and in some much more private place.

> - So why do I feel this – when I'm in the company of a total stranger, this *drive* to confess?

At least she isn't telling me *what* it is she wants to confess. If she does that then we're really in deep water. Because the process of transaction will have been started, whether I want it to or not, and I'll have to give her something back, in return. Yield something up. Quick, fake something.

Miles, who was not very good at this, who had not even flirted, who had moved as carefully in a tight situation and with as much dexterity as gaucherie could muster, felt guilty about Becky, guilty about desiring another woman even for a moment, and wondered miserably how he was going to extricate himself from this. It was harder to deal with the daughter than the father. The rain too came down harder. Neither of them had an umbrella, or even a coat. They were islanded here, for some time. He was almost certainly going to have to offer to buy her lunch. He looked morosely at the napkins and steak knives and spoons set before them. On current form, she would control the situation by insisting he ate, while she sat nursing a second black coffee in those beautiful talons. He poured them both a glass of water, aware that the hand that did the pouring trembled slightly. Ice tut-tutted as its small blocks hit the glass, drops of water darkening the tablecloth.

- It could be different versions of you, catching up with each other. If you feel driven to confess something to a stranger, could it be a way of admitting that there's more than one you, there's you as you are now, but there's you as you were then. However long ago 'then' was.

Laura appeared to weigh his words serenely, as if to say that, while I'm not at all sure that you are either old enough or sufficiently damaged to touch me emotionally, I do accept that you are doing me the courtesy of taking me and my tactical and other forms of divine madness seriously.

- And so actually…

Miles now felt for a brief and illusory moment that he was Doctor Miles, on a roll, on the breakfast news, sure that cures for all bad things waited just around the corner, that life was so much more than death's waiting-room, that everything in the garden was if not lovely then do-able with serious husbandry, all fundamentally OK.

- Actually, your urge to confess something to a stranger – which seems dangerous at first glance, is a way of normalizing the plight we're all in. We're not the same people now that we were then – you yourself reminded

me of this when we started this conversation, which by
the way it's a pleasure to be…having…

Stupid boy, they both thought.

-    …when you reminded me that in this new, magical life
     I have to be careful to keep everything pretty strictly
     compartmentalised. Confessing serious matters to a
     stranger could be a good way to reconcile things in your
     own mind. About yourself. You're strangers on a train
     or plane, whatever – and then you get off, and you go
     your separate ways. Confession over. Pressure released.
     How much harder it would be to confess the then-now
     differences to someone you are close to, like say family…

Warmer, they both thought. Bright bunny, Miles. Though if you go
talking to strangers about even the bare bones of what we all get
up to, back in Fiddlers Court, you're fired – or worse. But family?
Fuck family, she thought. I'm fucking familied out.

-    Because after all, confessing doesn't cost anything…

A blurred image came into Miles' mind, wherein the dominatrix
and the psychoanalyst and in his different way the priest were
all presenting their own versions of an invoice. He knocked the
thought aside, and tried to focus on making his eyes smile, the conversation flow – and would the waiter please wake up, and serve us.

Laura jerked her head, suddenly, up, and Miles could see the vein
pulsing by the side and down from the tight central column of her
throat. She swallowed hard, put her hand to her temple, and held
his gaze, eyes widening, and seeming to look right through him. To
what place? A site of terror, or elation? There's no way round this.
I have to. Gently does it.

-    I wonder, just in broad terms, what kind of thing it is
     that you would want to confess, Laura?

A crash of thunder and the air turned heavy, pressure changing yet again. Laura smirked, and casually pulling a sachet filled with white sugar from the bowl between them, tore it open slowly, and just as thoughtfully-cum-mindlessly spilled the white contents on the table, turning her finger around and around in the small heap of moon-dust. A second crash, nearer this time. The thunder warned, but the thunder knew nothing, was just trying out its latest words for rain, while flashing light hit shifting air. It is just the same with everything else, and we build our frail houses and hopes on the cusp.

- That's the thing. I don't know. I get the urge to do this, but (*very small voice*) don't know what it is that I want to (*looking straight at him, now*) be rid of. My partner said I had a gaze that could cure meat. (*What? Let that one go.*) He'd hunch at his easel, painting, abandoning, painting again, painting over – it drove me insane…or stay locked in his room. Playing Mr Unappeasable. A part he was born to play. We had a weekend retreat. In…

Her inward gaze seemed to roam for a moment round the spilled sugar pyramids and ranges of the whole United States, here flattening Wyoming, there tarrying with Pensacola, flicking the Cape, but coming home always to the old East Coast.

- …in, oah, Massachusetts. Last time I was there, they pulled me over for speeding. But you have to shrink the past right down to manageable, bite-sized portions. He probably wasn't in his most magnanimous phase, at that point. Or I on my best behaviour. But when they pulled me over, I thought, it's just, ah, Massachusetts, it's just Concord, it isn't all of…life. I had to put him in my pocket, and move on. But confess? *Confess?* Heavens, no!

It was as if she had turned the table; as if Miles, and not she, had said shocking things. Then Laura began picking again at her pyramid of sugar. She seemed to relax, move away from dangerous territory, and Miles relaxed, too. A little.

- Of course I used to start fires.

For a second she resembled a still-beautiful grandmother, who concedes that well, yes, I may have had a *teensy* drop to drink, and then crashes out of consciousness to the horror of three generations arriving for her surprise party, the by now empty sherry bottle rolling noisily across the kitchen flags. But there was no whiff on her breath. Of course there are pocket sprays that hide the altered liver count. Equally he was dead sure that, yes, she had been a youthful fire-starter. *No*, Laura sat bolt upright, correcting herself as she might a student in a lecture hall audience who had unwisely interrupted.

- *Set*. That's the word, isn't it? I set fires. I started them and set them. Game, *set*, and *match*. All played according to my rules. And then I stayed to see the fun. The gates of heaven are open, sometimes. But Miles, Miles… I never saw you there. Not even once. I looked for you, once, before we met, knowing I would meet you.

Her tone had rapidly become maudlin and he thought, no, she might be intoxicated, might be about to cry, and so he inwardly prepared himself for this by starting to bring his hands, all butterfly fingers and thumbs, to the table.

- But Miles…

Here it comes. She moved the condiments. Pepper to salt; checkmate. The hand that was shaking he moved back beneath the table to his equally vibrating knee, commanding calm. Laura shook herself.

- That wouldn't be the *thrust* of my confession. What do you make of your new colleagues? Start with Felix.

Thank God, she's changing the subject.

- Oh Felix is great. A fund of stories. And he's always upbeat. I'm not, so I like it when other people are. I haven't quite been able to work out his exact role in the organization, other than that he seems to be the glue, or the one that runs around and organizes everybody else.

But, Miles was about to stress, yes, I like him. He's fun. Good company. Your father isn't good company, he's a sly old fox and I trust him not a jot. So you could either be Manto's squeeze – or a chip off the old block.

- You shouldn't get too close to them, Miles. You need to be careful. Don't let them charm you. I'd step back a little if I were you. If I were you. Odd thought, that. To think that you and I might be each other.

She snorted. Rain hit the floor-to-ceiling glass windows, streaking the room with moving shadows. Grey soldiers in breaking ranks advancing. The air grew heavier. She looked around as if the next thing she uttered might be dangerous, if overheard.

- You're an English scholar, aren't you?

He could have responded, no, I'm a Condensed Matter Physicist, and it would have bounced right off whatever it was Laura had to say to him, in whatever oblique way she would choose to say it. He was just going to have to take all this in for now, and sift it later. Ask Becky to interpret. No. On second thoughts he would not be telling Becky about Laura, absolutely not. She stared at him, eyes firing something on the edge of savage.

- 'They flee from me, that sometime did me seek.'

Well, cryptic lady, first you make me think you're cracking up, and then you hit me with a line from Tudor poetry. He realized that the Mediterranean waiter was now standing almost pressed against their table, although any question of appetite, at least appetite for food, had clearly vanished. The waiter moved slightly away, talking silently to himself and swatting with a napkin at some non-existent fly.

-      'They flee from me, that sometime did me seek,
        With naked foot, *stalking in my chamber…*'

Something in the centuries-old poem seemed to suddenly come alive, and in a way Miles couldn't yet fathom. He thought his way back to Thomas Wyatt, author of this dream-like and mysterious poem, but only saw more mystery, more dreams and closed doors to hidden chambers. But something was happening to Laura Winthrope. Distraught, she had a hand to each temple, red mouth open like a letterbox. Help a lady in distress, Miles. Before she loses the last shred of sanity. And takes yours with it.

-      Thomas Wyatt, well remembered.

Miles leaned forward protectively, to hold her hands if necessary, if it seemed that a gesture of comfort would bring her back to earth. And then they both chanted, in low voices, like Japanese office workers pledging a daily oath of loyalty to the company, the same lines from the same Tudor poet. The server danced around their table, oblivious, smiling and swatting.

-      'I have seen them gentle, tame and meek,
        That now are wild, and do not once remember…'

She stopped and blanked, unspoken anguish in her eyes and on her velvet lips, and then, to his horror, brought one of her hands up to her mouth at lightning speed, then bit down, hard. Her hand in her mouth, eyes staring, blank as an animal's while feeding, stifled the scream.

Something shifted, and her mind came forward, open to him, only for her to recede and shoot back into the past. Though their faces were separated only by inches, he could only catch sight of her now at the far end of a long dark tunnel, the tunnel running way back, into an old house and a childhood of boredom and terror, that much he could intuit, that much anyone could see, such vast sadness. *Do not once remember, do not once remember...* Miles could suddenly see into the past she had no wish to recall, but seeing what he saw, wished he had not. Victor Winthrope was the father all right, in a manner of speaking, but something else as well.

Miles saw a dark house, very old by American standards, with gambrel roof and other signs of the colonial era. The door swung open, creaking, to admit him. The first thing he saw was a portrait of Winthrope in the plain blacks and whites of the Puritan era. Next to him sat an unsmiling young woman with a strong resemblance to Laura. Miles moved on, though seemingly it was the house that moved him on, showing him first this picture, then that portrait of the family, but there were only ever two members of the family, and by the time Miles had been shown the Victorian parlour portrait of Winthrope resting his heavily-ringed hand on the young woman's shoulder, as if to both keep the world away from her and restrain her in his own, and then seen the 1920s flapper not dancing or socialising but waiting in the dark for the white-faced old man to come closer, and finally when he had seen another picture which hung above the double bed in the topmost room, he knew he had seen more than enough.

He closed the door of the old dark house, relieved to be moving back into his own mind. What could he *change* – what could he do, to undo this? There was nothing in the world that he could do to alter any of it. No magic, only sadness. But then suddenly the moment shifted. Laura gazed at Miles with eyes as innocent as the eyes of a little girl, laughing lightly, in a restored and open way. He sat back. She smiled the most beautiful smile. Then the eyes rolled up as she brought the steak knife down with lethal force into the space vacated only a split second earlier by Miles' hand.

The paramedics declined to pronounce, though they arrived swiftly enough. As they strapped her to the gurney, she trustingly put one hand, the hand that had brought down the steak knife before it shattered, into his hand, the one that had nearly been speared on the now cracked, glass topped table.

-    This kind of suction. It keeps happening. My mind goes back and back. I dream that I have murdered someone. Then I wake up. I haven't, Miles. I haven't murdered anyone. I wouldn't ever want to hurt you. My mind his mind just keeps on, makes me not remember. But keep away from…Miles, steer well clear…

And then she was mentally gone. Tall doors in the dirty green-and-yellow back of the ambulance were closed, to take Laura away. Miles felt a hand on his shoulder.

-    She'll be all right mate. Your friend.

The unshaven, previously silent waiter was now affability itself. He wandered back up the steps into the eatery, whistling. And swatting still at non-existent flies. The STDs, divested of hairnets and white aprons, skipped out of The SteakOut, their rucksacks bulging with a week's worth of purloined foodstuff. A figure he recognized as the College Matron beamed at Miles roguishly, as she waddled past him. Miles thought to himself: I have one friend, and one friend only.

I only have one friend. No, make that two. One human and living. The other not human. But living.

You Go To My Head

1

- So, where would you like to go today?

- We're out of coffee. Paris?

- What would happen if we went somewhere we've already been, Miles. Miles?

- Yeah?

- There you are. I thought you'd dropped off the planet. Mm, that's nice. Don't stop. Anyway, what would happen if, instead of…That's even nicer, but I'm trying to think straight here. What would happen if we just went on memories, rather than using the photos, to get to where want to go? Use our own memories, then see if we could meet up, at a place we both know?

- I'd be in two minds about it. Ho-ho. Look, we're even out of peppermint.

- I suppose there might be a danger of our missing each other. We were going to do a supermarket shop, what happened there. Maybe it's not such a great idea. I'm not sure that people's memories of quote-unquote the same event, or the same place, ever coincide – not really.

- We've never quite cracked that one, have we? We agree to meet at some café one of us vaguely remembers. It's hazy mental snapshots of continental holidays, gap year stuff. It's on the corner of Rue Vaugirard and Rue Madame. Of course it is. I remember it so clearly. But it's not there at all, it's near the Gare du Nord, and then we lose each other.

Knives chattered to forks in a closing drawer. A timer pinged, then slept.

- And it might be a bit too spooky, for each of us to be locked in our own dream, looking for the shared one. It's important somehow that we dive down, and that we come up for air, at the same moment? At the same pace, anyway. I think so. I don't think I'm saying that just because I enjoy it. We have to be in synch for this to work.

They moved to the sofa. Becky looked over to the books, back to Miles, and pondered. She was wearing one of his shirts. Consciously or otherwise, and increasingly the life they lived was otherwise, they wore the same styles and colours, based around black, and a single shared pair of ear-rings. Just as, in the old days, lovers who were parted from each other for a spell would agree to gaze at the moon at the same time, settling for a second best form of togetherness, so Becky, for safety's sake as well as sentiment, had wondered if something or some things shared, like jewellery, if one of them got lost in some dark forest, might bring the other hurrying, if touched. Ear-ring walkie-talkies for the dream world.

- I don't know. I'm not sure we can risk it. Either one of us would be weaker on our own. And vulnerable to eavesdropping.

- Or worse. Yes. But suppose we look at some pictures of

a place we both know well in any case.

-    Possible. Yes. Consolidated memories. We share the same dream-pool, with a small d small p, but if something goes wrong, there's the insurance of personal memory to fall back on. So there's more chance we could find our way back to each other.

-    Find our way back to each other, yes. I think so.

Particularly given that they were out of coffee, a quick trip to New York and back didn't seem a bad idea.

Since there was already going to be a measure of experiment in this expedition, Becky memorised as much as she could of its distinctive lettering while placing the foil-wrapped bag of Kenyan beans in her own bag, then stepped in a silver mind-flash out of Zabar's Deli and onto Broadway, heading south towards the 79th Street subway to meet Miles. She urged herself to remember the bagging of the beans, and, because this was her experiment, decided not to tell him. In any case there seemed already to be something additional in the air, on this particular jaunt. Sounds, colours, lights, action – all of these, in abundance, but something more besides. Perhaps it was just that the trip-hammer life of New York, be it in movies, memories or real life, had a compacted intensity, was just more than other places. More hurrying dots of life, more vertically layered life. Life upon life.

Or was it less to do with Manhattan, and more to do with Miles' and her enhanced capacity to dream? She realized now just how bare some of their early dreams had been. It might have been unconscious, she now thought, but perhaps that was why they tended to choose beaches or other waterside destinations. Sand and big waves were a hell of a lot easier to dream than neon signs in Mandarin Chinese.

This new New York of theirs seemed indistinguishable from the real thing. They could leave each other now for minutes at a time, without any diminution of apparent reality. Not that either particularly wanted to. Plus, they were making discoveries on the pulses. Evidently there was such a thing as passive memory. This meant that Miles, who had heard Japanese spoken when he was a child, but never learned to speak it himself, could now hear it spoken in dream with perfect clarity by camera-wielding tourists, while still not understanding a word. And, evidently, there was such a thing as peripheral memory, akin to peripheral vision. They would recollect and re-experience things seen only briefly, on the fly, in previous dream-excursions, prolonging the encounter, this time teasing out details.

Their shared commitment to dreaming New York accurately meant that Becky would pull him, or Miles would pull her, back onto the sidewalk just in time to avoid being run over by some impatient New York City cabbie or police car. Each did this instinctively. What would happen, she wondered, if I just walked out into the screaming traffic, and let myself be crushed? Would I pop up, unhurt? Would I glide through it all like a ghost, terrifying the tourists and seniors on the bus curving into West Third Street, as I appear through the moving floor, smiling and waving, only to vanish again through the far side of the vehicle? Onwards, into yet more dream collisions. Police shootouts, where I prance around in the crossfire having robbed the Bank of America, then blow them all a farewell kiss then float away – vanish through a wall, or through the clouds. We could be the new Bonnie and Clyde, though the pristine greenbacks might wither in the real-time air of Camden.

And in any case, if we start to behave in a profligate or mocking fashion, it's cheating. It's like when you dream one of those dreams in which you know it's a dream – all too soon, you wake. If we go about our dreaming churlishly, as if to say we know it all, we know in our jaded way that our dream is just that, then that might corrupt our sleep; and the lightened, less detailed dreaming sleep will make us more likely to wake, will pick away at all our warmth and safety.

It isn't just about being able to have sex, be on our own, dive deep and escape from surveillance. Wonderful as all that is. It's about loving the setting where we walk, or say yes to some little adventure. In fact, setting underestimates it. The set has got to be more than a backdrop. This isn't a landscape painting, nymph with shepherd approaching, while the light of a fading sun falls on a hilltop temple. Better to pull Miles back, just as the lights change. Pretend to believe in New York, in the dream, and the more real will it be.

They walked across Central Park. It looked just as it does in the movies, some of which are indeed shot on location, although, particularly in Universal Studios productions, scenes just as plausible and set in the Park are in fact shot in Los Angeles. Becky knew she knew this, because she had read it in the *New York Times*, during a recent dream. It all looked so real by the boating lake it hardly mattered. They headed for the Park's perimeter.

The more we do this, the more we hallucinate New York, the more like real life it becomes. This is giving me goose-bumps. Right now, thought Becky, I could spring from the top of the Empire State Building and not come to any harm, float my way down, execute a perfect double somersault and, just in the nick of time, command an open truck carrying feather bedded mattresses to catch my swansdown landing. But suppose we keep coming back here, every trip intensifying? What's the logical conclusion of this, both thought, Becky glancing at Miles, who was squinting up at the vast Metropolitan Museum of Art, pausing for a moment as they shouldered a slow and companionable way through the crowd. If our dreams become more real as time goes by…

-    Miles, isn't the logic of this that if our dreaming gets more real, as time goes by…

Yes, I've been having the same thought, he thought without replying. Right now I could throw myself off some high building like the Met here, one of these soaring New York towers, and not die. I'm pretty sure of that. Once or twice I've grazed my hand on these trips and watched the cut turn patchily invisible, then heal in seconds. If I jumped, what would most likely happen? I'd dissolve back into being awake. But…

-    Yes, I've been having the same thought. The more intense the dream, the less *like* a dream it is…so yes, I guess there'll come a point when if one of us accidentally steps out under a truck…We might bleed, or have to go to hospital, before we got each other back.

Twin nuns approaching the couple gave them an odd look. One muttered to the other.

The dreams will be progressively more real. More cause and effect. More nuanced consequences. Operations, credit cards. Life support machines, and when or if to turn them off. And we don't have private healthcare, in the dream world. Or in any other world, he added to himself. The nuns glided past them and onwards.

We could die, each thought separately. I could die, or you could. If you were killed in the dream, I might have to die myself, before I got you back. *If* there's an afterlife. *If* I got you back. They walked on, silent for a while. Both, thinking their thoughts, some coinciding, some divergent, moved forward through the bright and noisy day – the hot dog seller with his bottles of Poland Spring, the students, the tourists, a team of morose looking clowns handing out flyers, choppers cawing overhead, intestinal subway grumbling and shuddering – the Moloch-maze, retinal noise of New York City.

Behind them, and they did not see this, partly because there was so much less to see, the street-pageant faded into insubstantiality, first sound and then faces and then colour draining out of it. As they moved forwards, the street died, backwards. Behind them and unseen, everything fell away to nothing. Here a lonesome hotdog, without benefit of roll or mustard, moved north towards a fading open mouth. There a hand, about to pick a pocket, evaporated into dotted lines then air, while the evanescent pocket jogged away, itself dissolving in the measureless void. Behind them, buildings wobbled, sighed back into architect's pencil lines, drawn by the draughtsman of not-today. The dream's over, people. Go home, there's nothing left to see. There's nothing left to dream. Out of the corner of one troubled eye, Becky slightly saw backward, into the great wave of zero that streamed out behind them. Unable to bear the thought of nothing, she erased it from her mind. Her memory filled it with something.

Our lives now are a walk along a tightrope. Perhaps, still, there is some wiser, broader Nature that can encompass it all, can make it mean right and true things, from the outermost sidereal to the steep reeling inside, then all the way down to the deep inside real. Perhaps. Which myth was it that pictured the world on a giant turtle's back, on the back of another, then another, then another turtle? So comforting, the sense of spinning cosmic plates, never dropped and magically balancing. How loose those plates seem to me now.

At this point a childhood memory of something she'd once seen on the West Side transposed itself to the East Side of Manhattan, and they came across a shop. The shop sold bones and flotsam of the ancient world, little bottles and sacerdotal vessels from Egypt, African masks, fossils and grotesque things. Becky wanted to buy presents, for someone or other, but realized, slightly forlorn, that the trilobite might vanish in an instant when she woke, and that anyway, who was there now to hunt down presents for? Just Miles. She had burned her boats. Driftwood thoughts. Her hand trembled, clutching the bag of coffee beans tightly, as if it were the last remnant of some splendid civilization. Last trace of the Zabar tribe. Last fleeting glimpses of the independent me.

Then something jerked in her vision – these glitches happened, nothing to worry about – and they were airlifted out of the cavern of curios and poised in bright sunlight, leaning on railings in the roof garden. Here, high up at the Met, some fanciful structures by Sol LeWitt did their decidedly un-level best to compete with the view. Then something jerked in Miles' vision – these glitches happened, nothing to worry about – and they were waiting in line, chatting to a couple from Des Moines, waiting their turn, to get to the topmost tip of the World Trade Center.

2

She awoke, slightly stiff, back in her apartment. My flat. I am learning the Queen's English. Welcome to my flat, Your Queenship. Our flat, where we come to sleep, and so to travel. Becky looked over at Miles, and could see his eyelids – so long – beginning to quiver, like, she thought, an exotic butterfly, out of its cocoon, settling on a leaf, questing again in the upper world. His diver's mind about to break the surface. The desire of the moth for the star? Who said that? Wrote that? Who was that masked man? Thinking cleared like mist from English fields, as she stepped lightly to her London window.

Becky placed one hand on the coffee pot, then paused. We're out of coffee. Then a thought stirred. What prompt, what bandanna did I tie, around which wrist, and why? I reminded myself to remember something, to retrieve and hold on to that memory. It was an experiment; to see if something dreamed could become real, here in London town. She let her mind roam over the details of the latest trip. They had covered a fair amount of ground, this time, treading the mountainous island. She remembered the nuns – identical twins, how rare can that be – up on the roof garden of the Met, smiling and unexpectedly insistent that the young couple pose for a photo.

She remembered walking round Battery Park City with Miles. Skateboarders skateboarding. Lunch hour office workers eating their sandwiches in imitation Japanese pagodas. A welcome breeze from the river. Leaning on the rail and looking out, to the Statue of Liberty verdigris-green on blue water; the baritone greeting of a ferry from Staten Island; the big clock, like a child's bedroom clock from long ago, way over on the Jersey shore. How they had stepped back, walking backwards laughing, to make out the words of the letters sculpted into the railings in front of them, words from poems by Frank O'Hara, by Walt Whitman, in praise of the city, in praise of freedom: in praise of each, found in the other. Until, moving on, they had trespassed on the urban freedoms of a speeding cyclist. She remembered his stern profile under the white helmet, the taut muscles in his thighs and the black Lycra shorts, his cursing them mildly as he braked, but no harm done, and so she turned, briefly, but there, to the north, right behind them, was nothing. A big wave of nothing. Her hand quivered. Back in the now, she thought, I hope I can make something out of that nothing.

The little bag of beans faded then vanished in her hand, but not before she caught the bright orange lettering. Kenyan AA. $6.95. Miles put his index finger gently to her pulse, wondering why his wife-to-be was staring, brow furrowed, at her perfectly empty right hand.

She didn't feel like travelling, today.

3

It was while they were browsing in the coffees and teas aisle that she broke down and started to cry. It was nothing. Then as they left the supermarket her brown eyes filled again, and she had to call up something, something to cap her own well of sadness as much as to satisfy Miles.

-   I so miss Mom, and Dad.

This wasn't strictly true. Mom, a bewigged, energetic, round bunny of a woman was great in small doses, when the energy rubbed off on you, less great after a few days' constant exposure, when she started to sap yours. Dad was lean and flinty, a Virginian by birth, with a lean Virginian look, that spoke volumes – thin, lean volumes admittedly – about the condition of his flintiness, inside and out, about how little you could expect to take away, but how utterly honest and true what he was, was. He was the one tree that even the great storm of whenever just could not blow down. No one could ever forget his piercing blue eyes, which were in reality as brown as his daughter's.

He had wanted a boy, and had wanted to be a professional sportsman himself, which accounted in her early years for Becky's muscular frame. When Miles ran a finger down or marvelled at taut curves, all she could remember was panting on the baseball diamond. Cape Cod is washed by two oceans, one of them safe. All she could summon was a memory of the other one; the breath-sucking crash of the Atlantic on her ribcage. She did miss them, though, it was true. At the end of the day, without saying one explicit thing, Frank the sports coach *manqué* had got over whatever unreal expectation it was that he'd had. And Suse knew that she was a bit much, sometimes. But, Miles, you'll just love them. And they will *adore* you. All I have ever got from them has been pure, unconditional love. That's all there is, at day's end. Love's the biggest ocean of them all. Miles smiled at her fondly. Genuinely rapt. Terrified.

Becky had to broach the subject. It was all so odd.

- Don't you ever miss your father? Your mother? You don't talk about them much.

- Not sure there's much to talk about.

Oh no you don't, not this time. I'm going to persevere, and you're going to talk.

- Your Dad got sick. Invalided out of the Forces – but not because he'd been injured in action, he just got sick? That's as far as I've got.

- He was in the Navy, yes. When he was called up. He did see some action, though he didn't talk about it much. He didn't talk about anything much.

- My Father's the same.

Becky had been asking herself lately if she might be old enough to have earned the right to sound wise. She ventured.

- It's that generation. Depression in the thirties, war in the forties. By the time they were barely grown up, some of them had seen enough to last a lifetime. Seen enough really major insecurity…

- On top of the blood and guts stuff, exactly.

- So after the war, I mean, we still see things kind-of from a nineteen sixties perspective, because that time was so great.

- I'm coming more and more to think it was the great age of paranoia too, but it was a paradigm shift. Huge. We're still building on it. I'm not sure we're equal to it, let alone clear of it.

Damn it, Becky thought, I didn't want this to turn into a tutorial. I'm not one of your students. She persevered.

- So everyone forgets the fifties. Or they mock it – you know, the car, the huge refrigerator, the dreaming burbs. But you'd have wanted a nice house too, and a good car and all those modern things, if you'd…but we're getting off the subject of your father. Anyway, that's probably what you wanted. I'm sorry. I didn't mean to pry.

She took her coffee mug to the dishwasher, couldn't for some reason get the door open, and almost threw the mug into the sink. No you're right, he thought. We're going to get married, or at least we've said we are, and you don't properly know me yet. We've only been together for a matter of weeks. Intense weeks, admittedly. You know things about me that other people don't even know about themselves, but the usual things: no. You know too much about the steeply, deeply unusual, and nowhere near enough about the normal. I don't give you enough. Maybe we're moving too quickly. But then maybe I'm not as sure what really happened, now, as I thought I was. He drew her gently back to the sofa, placing one hand on hers.

- He worked on submarines. Electrical engineer. Then he moved into surveillance, starting as far as I can tell with the Axis Powers' subs. Sonar and all that. I know he must have been to the States quite often in the nineteen forties because of all the stuff he brought back that was still lying around the house, years later. A lot of Navy people did bring things back. Records – boxes and boxes of those – ties, modern kitchen utensils. Things they couldn't get at home in, what did he call Britain? Blighty. Then they lived in Japan, during the occupation. Back and forth, over the years later on, with me. By now, obviously, he must have been working in some measure *for* the US, not just with Americans…

- And I guess he couldn't talk about his work.

- The trouble was, Becky…

Miles looked so deeply sad that she regretted asking, while needing as never before to know more. He briefly put his fingers to his temples.

- It wasn't just that he couldn't talk about his work. He couldn't *remember doing it.* Not after a while. He didn't know what it was that he had been working on. Only in the barest detail. Actually he probably said or at least showed me more than he should have done, when I was young. You probably think he was distant, a hands-off father. But he wasn't: at least not then. He might have been old to be a father, and my mother was much younger than him, but he wasn't the armchair and slippers type. He was a brilliant draughtsman. What he really enjoyed was drawing. He could lose himself in it for hours. I remember, I must have been about six or seven years old – he'd been invalided out, by this stage. We were back in the UK, for good. Living in this big, rambling pile with what the Scots call a steadings, on the coast, the East Neuk of Fife. It had been in the family for aeons. My grandparents' parents had lived there – that side of the family, the Proctors, were originally a fishing family, believe it or not…

Becky thought, well, OK, he's come out with more about his childhood in the last few minutes than in the last few weeks. There's some tragedy around his father, but I don't sense that there's anything contagious, that might skip a generation. That's what was bothering me, and I've only just realized.

- And he was in this odd, transitional state. He was losing his memory. It could have been dementia. It got progressively worse, and some of the symptoms certainly correspond to what we now call Alzheimer's. Then again, it doesn't run in the family, you'll be pleased to know, not on either side. But anyway, he was in this twilight zone where he couldn't remember, but he *knew* that he couldn't remember. He was aware of having lost his memory. Or chunks of it. And one day, we'd gone up into the loft because rainwater had got in. That east coast bump, the Neuk, gets absolutely hammered by storms. He found some drawings. Work drawings. Rocketry. Parts of the innards of submarines. And rockets to be fired from submarines. Beautiful drawings, tied loosely with ribbon. And I was outraged for him, absolutely outraged, because some fool had scribbled all over his drawings, in crayon. I could have killed whoever it was. His drawings, so fantastically painstaking, and elegantly done. And some complete imbecile had gone and scrawled all over them, just vandalised them.

Miles' eyes had been filling up a little, but now he smiled at her.

- And he just laughed, and told me it had been me, me-as-toddler, that had done it. So I said, weren't you angry with me, and he said – and I can remember this as clearly as anything in my life, as clearly as things we did in New York yesterday. He said, Miles, you were never, ever any trouble. You have never made me angry, not once, and nothing you will ever do will ever make me angry. He promised that, and he said, anyway, what are these worth, now? To anyone? Just a lot of old drawings. And we burnt them, together. He asked me to stay with him, while he burnt them. We used an old dustbin where the bottom had rusted out. I remember dancing round it.

- It sounds as if he remembered enough to think they might be dangerous in the wrong hands.

- This was the sad bit. He said that he didn't regret his role in the World War, because it was a just war, the one war that absolutely had to be fought. But he felt he was being punished...

- *Punished?*

- By forces greater than himself. He had some quasi-mystical beliefs I never got to the bottom of. Punished because when the war ended for other people, he had chosen to go on fighting his. That was the way he put it. And the things that he worked on were only created in order to destroy. To hurt people or kill them – or contain them.

When he'd had his choice, he had taken the wrong path.

- Weapons.

- Weapons. And surveillance.

4

They were sitting in Jack's Jazz. This put them in exceedingly select company, as the inevitable closing down sale had depleted the bins and trays of almost everything, bar anthologies of Weather Report and the midnight analgesic that is Smooth Jazz. The lunch tables were likewise denuded. Maya adjusted a framed poster of Thelonious Monk, hitting the keys at the Village Vanguard or some other hipster's haunt, a cigarette hung louchely from his corner lip. I could never do that, Maya thought, back in the days when I smoked. The smoke just got in my eye.

What a name; you couldn't make it up. And he hadn't. On first being presented with her sizeable, Buddha-round baby, his delighted mother had immediately named him Thelonious Sphere Monk. A blue sphere hung in Jack's Jazz, amid other round lights. Maya placed coffee carefully by Miles' hand, and then with a studied and equal care, by Becky's. And no, she had told them, she did not know what she would do. Something would come up. Zeke seemed to have something on his mind that he wanted to get off it, and so kept taking hesitant steps forward and back, or fiddling pointlessly in what remained of Mainstream or Easy Listening. It was also Monk spilling out of the big Wharfedale speakers. A whole monastery. *Round Midnight. Misterioso. Everything Happens to Me.* Great stuff, thought Miles, strange chords and crazy paving and shoots off in all directions, but always finds the right way home. He reflected briefly on the irony of his belated conversion to Monk's music just as Jack's Jazz was about to vanish, then tapped his foot and fell back into listening.

- I don't know whether you're aware that you do this,
  Miles…

I wish you wouldn't say that so often, he thought, a trifle glum. It's OK if I'm quietly being told I've got spinach on my teeth, but sometimes I get the impression I'm being groomed. However, what Becky went on to say was as much about his father as it was about him.

- …but you always qualify what you say about your father
  having lost his memory. You say instead that he'd half
  lost it – or lost half of it – I don't get it.

- Sometimes I think he had dementia. But that the phases
  of doing terrible things in public, or becoming completely terrified, that people report in elderly parents, just
  mercifully didn't come his way. Partly because he was so
  gentle… I think whatever happened *gentled* him…but
  then he'd always been…

For a while he was as lost in thought as one lost in sleep, and then he was back in the room and fully with her, having roamed some-where in time long past, bringing some jigsaw piece up from the underworld.

- You need to talk to my brother. We both do.

- I look forward to meeting Philip…

Becky thought the future-seller, hedger, banker or whatever he was, sounded like the worst kind of pinstripe and red-suspenders trickster, but you have to take on the family too, and that's that.

- Philip is convinced that Dad didn't lose his memory. It
  was taken from him.

- *What?*

- I know, I know. They took it.

- Who are They?

- You know. They.

They. The people you thought you were working with. But you weren't working with them, not really. You worked for them. Them, or an unseen they, behind them. Of course you get on with individuals, and they share things with you. Sometimes unexpected things, Miles thought ruefully. But if they have really got this far with you, it's probably too late. If they've started to share, so have you. That means you're one of them now. As long as they want something from you. But come the day they don't….

- He knew too much. The circuitry of rockets, the future of weapons. The fine, fine detail of destruction. So they stole his memory. His own circuitry was property of the company.

Becky thought her way back through thickets of patchy knowledge, here U Boats and V2s, there the A and H Bombs. And brainwashing. She put her hand back in his, and asked her question quietly.

- Do you think he was tortured? Did they damage him, physically?

- Far too crude. Or at least, they didn't pull his nails out with pliers. It occurred to me that they might have given him a dose of LSD strong enough to wipe his mental hard drive.

Becky winced. Then she tried to remember what she could about lysergic acid diethylamide 25. Not really her generation.

- The drug itself wasn't illegal till, I'm not sure, the mid to late sixties? The US military had used it on volunteers. But it would have been a pretty blunt instrument, Miles, if what they wanted was to ensure that he only forgot certain detailed information.

- Yeah. It would have been more likely to fry the cells that hold short-term memory, not the medium to long term: all that accumulated know-how he had built up. No. I wonder about computers.

- But in those days a computer could fill an entire room.

- *Exactly* my thought. I've been finding out more about Harry Smith…

- Don't I know it.

- Smith was described as being ahead of his time because he would use language that was esoteric for those days, drawn from computer programming – like the word itself. Harry Smith was probably the first person to talk about people being 'programmed' to do things. But Philip says Dad used to talk like that, too. Philip thinks Dad was programmed to forget. Philip can also remember my mother talking about how excited Dad was…this would be when they knew we would stay in Fife…about getting the chance to see a big room underground, with lots of kit in it…

- Your mother died a long time ago.

- I barely remember her. I was too young. Afterwards when I was trying to piece Dad's life together I jumped to the conclusion, prematurely I now think, that the big underground room was a nuclear bunker. As a family we had the right to a place in a bunker, in the event of nuclear attack, because of his work for the Ministry of Defence. What fun for all the family that would have been. When he died, we found the details on a card sewn into the lining of his jacket. It had directions on it. The bunker was just a few miles away from us. Somewhere off the Anstruther road, or next to the old airfield at

Crail, I forget.

-   But now you think the big room...

-   Might have housed a computer. That held exactly the
    kind of classified information he carried around in his
    head.

There was briefly a commotion nearer the kitchen area. A bird
had flown in through the open window, and was helplessly trying
to negotiate walls, a ceiling, and the alien kerfuffle set going by
Thelonious Sphere Monk and friends, approaching the end of the
quicksilver tightrope that is *Four in One*. Miles pointed, and whispered a phrase while placing the middle fingertip of his outstretched
right hand over his index finger, which gently flew the bird out
backwards through the window. The window promptly closed itself.
Becky noticed Maya noticing. Zeke, unnoticed, also saw. The bird,
not being human, flew straight from panic into amnesia without
passing through grateful thanks. None of these animate creatures
exhibited surprise. Thelonious Monk sounded surprised by absolutely everything, even while something else told you he'd seen all
there is to see, heard all there is to hear. Perhaps he was working
covertly for the restoration of surprise.

5

Becky was completing routine paperwork, to do with the search
for, and the sale of, recondite old books, esteemed in the main
by old and recondite people. Redidivus was winding down, was
almost out, but Winthrope still had schemes and scams. The
next Redidivus catalogue would be a fake, aimed at flushing out
evidence that certain individuals were or were no longer biologi-
cally or magically viable. Some of the books that were listed didn't
exist, or were worthless, but the response to the catalogue would
trigger a nuanced exchange of information that had relevance to

some project, and that project would be real. Everything led back to Winthrope, then out into a dotty and decidedly senior world where, as far as she could see, the boss was more intent on settling old scores than finding new ones; that, and maintaining a fearsome reputation for labyrinthine method.

Some of the books she was cataloguing did exist, and did concern the practice of magic, but were deemed by Messrs Winthrope and Boxer (Felix Manto having little time for reading) to have been written in code during their own period of composition, lacking therefore in any usefulness for the present. Some of the books did exist, did concern magic, and were either not written in code, or were evidently written in a code that could be cracked. For these clients, Winthrope seemed to be running a circulating library masquerading as a bookshop, in that the individual who purchased an item often sold it back to the firm again, once some occult use had been made of it. Some books were clearly hot potatoes. She could see why no one would want to hang on to some of them for long periods.

Some were rat-gnawed, or covered in furry mould. Some stank. A few, reputedly, could burn skin, and so could only be handled wearing a unique pair of gloves designed for this purpose, and made out of netting with little brass plates across the palms and finger joints and fingertips. Becky couldn't stand these, as they made wrapping the parcel almost impossible, though she had noticed that Miles was fascinated, maybe turned on by them. One especially noxious volume exploded. She was still finding traces of soot on the furnishings and walls, weeks later.

As the prices seemed to be decided on whim, it would have been exhausting and probably fruitless to mount a conventional audit or even keep a balance sheet. Becky worked on the principle that Winthrope set a value on the transactions which could not be summarised in terms of short term profit, but which played out as a long, indeed very long term strategy in his head. Everything, in essence, was a loss leader. Although she had come to respect his perspicacity in dealing with others, she couldn't help but notice that while the New York premises had been kept spick and span, and this in a neighbourhood with high and rising rents, the London base was, literally, falling apart.

And the demographic was alarming. More than one book search request had come from wizards on Saga cruises in the Med or the West Indies who pegged it from natural causes before the transaction could go through. An urgent fax had just come in from one such sunset voyager, in desperate need of spells with which to rebuff the pirates heading for his cruise ship, drifting and exposed, somewhere off the coast of East Africa.

Moreover, there were questionable aspects to the purposes for which these textual arcana were used. A voluminous correspondence between Victor, a purchaser and a third party, numbers two and three being in a race to get the book (a race which, for once, had galvanized Winthrope into price-hike mode), had seemingly ended in the violent death of number three after number two had bagged the item, save for the fact that three then got back in touch (handwriting a little shaky) congratulating the others on their ingenuity and promising a return bout, once, and this is what spooked Becky, he had progressed to its conclusion a century's worth of other business.

Of course this was most likely a figure of speech, but then again, this was the client whose correspondence with Becky was deliverable only by moonlight, utilising the services of a doddery owl with terrible digestion issues, or on one appalling occasion, demon emissary wood squirrels, who tipped rubbish all over the kitchen, tried on, chewed and wouldn't hand back underwear and items of sentimental value, adding insult to injury by hanging upside down from the light fittings gibbering and singing, until Miles took one of them out with an invisible scimitar used to powerful effect during the sacking of Constantinople. At this point, in deference to their fallen comrade, the squirrels climbed down and walked out of the flat silently, and in single file. The last one through looked daggers at Miles, jerked a claw upwards as it left, and then jumped on the shoulders of its predecessor in order to turn and close the door.

Miles and Becky sat for a while on the sofa, equally silent, staring at the wreckage of the lounge. After some minutes had passed, Miles observed that, while teaching literature in Beltane College had preserved him in an airless ivory tower, now he could see how the other half lived. He went to put the invisible scimitar back in its invisible case, which took some time as he had failed to make a mental note of where the weapon had been put down, while Becky made her way with painstaking caution to the bathroom, where she washed the yellow spray and gunk from her lenses.

Becky rehearsed some of these incidents, frequently troubling in their implications, as she wrapped with great care a fragile volume, prior to despatching it by courier to an imposing address in the Carpathian Mountains. The courier was a young conveyancing specialist called Jonathon, with other business to conduct. That was another problem. You never quite knew who was ultimately on which payroll, or finally accountable to which agency. Her only point of constancy in this otherworldly merry-go-round was of course Miles, though the deeper their involvement, the less she felt able to step outside herself and look to him for guidelines. Slowly writing out in block capitals an address in the Borgo Pass, she let her mind roam. Perhaps she would need to be even more involved with, involved in, Miles. In his identity. The crux of it all was that their future could not be seen clearly until his past was fathomed.

The father-embroiling Cold War seemed to be over, at least for now. The fall of the Berlin Wall and the subsequent break-up of the Eastern Bloc into hopeful fiefdoms, bobbing in the murky global swirl, meant that the generation that might have stolen her late, about to be father-in-law's mind, were themselves dead, drowsing on a Texas porch, or in their dachas. The new mushrooms would be burrowing, unseen, in their new mycelium, way down yonder in Rio, or up in the Afghan hills. She moved to the window, and looked down on London. But there's something back there that needs to be plumbed. Where and in whom do you place trust. Had it ever been different. She saw one of the organization's eyes and ears, a young gopher in an outsize hoodie, Los Angeles Raiders, studiously not observing her window. One day they were going to get caught out. Deep down she suspected that those guys knew all about their trysts, but were not minded to act. A motorcycle courier paused, enquiring x or y of the young man, who nodded. Who do you really work for? Yourself. Who do you trust? Yourself. Who gets to share your finite reserves? Of trust, of love, of the accumulated stuff: the government bonds, grandpa's watch chain and the smart new sofa. Miles. But only if, bound in so tight now, he also is in some conclusive measure, yourself also.

She watched from the window as the courier sped away to who knows where, while the LA Raider turned and sauntered away in the opposite direction, match in one corner of his mouth, putting in earbuds. Then Becky sat on the sofa and stared. Miles, she asked him, in her mind, you must have memorabilia. Your father's special things. And surely Miles, surely, you must have photographs, of that rambling house on the coast of Fife, with its, what odd word did he use – not stables – steadings. Where there's a photograph, there's the possibility of travel. But can we go back into the past? Can we dream our way back, and return to the present, safe and sound? I'm sorry that I never met your father. But do I really want to meet him, knowing that he's dead? I had a dream about him, once. I didn't tell you because it seemed so depressing.

I was driving a car across California towards Nevada, towards Death Valley. Except that it was freezing cold, more like Canada or Minnesota, and the car was also a coach, somehow. Worse, I was asleep, but knew I was sleeping. I just prayed that driving on a lonely road in a straight line, we'd somehow make it, and not crash. You said you had to go to the other end of the coach, because you'd just now seen two old friends chatting on the back seat. So you were gone, and I remember thinking, well, if I do hit something, then maybe Miles will be saved by virtue of being so far back in the coach. And then I somehow picked up that the couple on the back seat were not your friends, but would kill you if they could, and that your father was on the bus, but he couldn't get through to warn you, because he was dead.

I could hear him trying to whisper in my ear, but the cold was so intense it blocked my hearing, and I remember thinking too that I couldn't hear voices in my head properly because I'd pulled my woollen hat down too tight. It was blocking out signals. But your father was on the coach, and needed you to know that he was watching out for you, and that he had something to give you, a book, or perhaps it was a box, to protect you. But when I finally got my hand free of the wheel, which took forever, to get my hat off my ears, I lost control, and we crashed, and I woke up.

Remembering the nightmare Becky sat forward, moving one hand to cover one side of her face, as if suffering from a migraine, or visual disturbance in one eye.

6

They met later at his place. Miles stared into the bathroom mirror for a while, leaving plausible visual simulacra of their current and obviously separate whereabouts to seep through the mercury and over to the four-dimensional camera obscura that Redidivus used for surveillance. Miles always began by focussing on the reverse imaging provided by all mirrored surfaces, then planted the seeds of different images, inside that directional reversal. Winthrope's glass would in consequence show them to be precisely where they were not. As with many other things, he was improving with practice. The couple sat cross-legged, knees touching, to talk it all through.

-   I think it's a really, really bad idea. You're asking me to break the barrier between life and death. My only real experience of that is our friend Kenneth, and that hasn't exactly been pleasant. I've got used to my dear old Dad being dead. There are mysteries there that I would really like to get to the bottom of, but frankly I really do not want to meet him. Not on this side of my own death. When I'm dead too, fine. We'll have all the time in the world to talk then. Hopefully-maybe. Although to be honest…

-   When you put it like that, it doesn't sound such a great notion, I have to agree. What about, you go back in time, but you don't try to meet him. You must have photos of the house. You go back, you walk around. Maybe you find clues.

-   But clues to what? The whole point is that the information was in his head. I might find a few more drawings, I suppose, but so what. For one, I couldn't interpret them, I'm not trained as an electrical engineer. For another, that technology is most likely obsolete. They have these Cruise Missiles now, you remember the Gulf War…

-   That can fly down a particular chimney, and target a certain enemy group, and leave the houses on either side standing, sure, though they seem in practice just to have indiscriminately blown up three generations of the same family, as usual…

-   Exactly. So if I discover that my Dad helped design a prototype Cruise Missile, I'm going to wish I hadn't bothered. I just think this trip could just make me sad. And not really teach us anything.

I know, she thought, I know. I don't know why I want you to go. I don't know why I want you to go and not take me. It's just a fingertip pressure from some otherwhere, some subtle prompting like a whisper in a dream that says, do this, children, go.

- Plus, Becky, there's chaos theory. You know, a butterfly lands on one flower rather than another, a something else happens rather than a different something else, and before you know it, bang, you've got a whole different history. For want of a nail, how does it go, the shoe was lost, for want of a whatever comes next…until finally…

- I know. You could crush an ox-eye daisy underfoot in bygone Fife, and trigger World War Three, starting tomorrow. I know. At least I think that's what they think, now. That's what they say.

- But then again, what do they know, Becky?. And they don't always tell all they know. Misinformation. Disinformation. I think we need to get a sense of where I could go that I would recognize, with sufficient clarity to be sure I *could* learn something. Maybe I'm being too cautious and I should just try. But I can't just go in there rolling the dice of adventure. Set the destruction of the world in motion, and then when I'm called to posthumous account, say my fiancée thought that if I travelled backwards in time and looked round my dead father's house it might sort out some problems in the present that I'm not even sure I'm fully aware of, yet.

Fiancée? Bring on the antimacassars and the lace doilies. She got up briskly, and pulled down a photograph album. Here, sleuth. Go forage. They moved to the sofa, and for a while Miles turned pages, grunting occasionally.

Maybe this isn't such a great idea, thought Becky after a while. Are we on a hiding to nothing here. Come on, Miles.

- What is a steadings, anyway?

-   Oh, the steadings. They were originally farm buildings, and then when the farms lost their original function they got converted, for other uses. They're all over Fife. All over Scotland and the islands. Bed and breakfasts, granny flats, craft shops on the Isle of Mull…

-   And yours was what exactly?

-   My Dad's study and library. I wasn't really allowed in, it was his special space. Amazing room – a semi-circular arrangement of cabinets and drawers with the signs of the Zodiac and all sorts on them – a huge chair, or it seemed huge to me – more old books than Redidivus….

-   Photo?

Miles put a finger to his tongue. Then he turned pages.

-   Yep. Here we are. It's probably smaller than I remember it. But it's not! Oh no. Oh Dad.

-   Miles? Miles!

Miles was staring straight ahead, verbalising, plumbing his scholarly knowledge, partly in an attempt to think his way across centuries, partly as a way to postpone looking directly at an image of his father.

-   Think Elizabethan. Knowledge at that time was a really creative mess. A blur of magic and rationality, supernatural law and the laws obtaining in the courts. You could legitimately talk about, oh I don't know, the poetic organization of a given argument, or the philosophical and mystical assumptions underpinning the recipes in a herbal. So, this was a time of, call it holistic magic…

Get on with it, Miles.

-   …and one particular magician-philosopher, Robert

Fludd, aimed to devise what he called a Memory Theatre. A room which could hold printed knowledge of all
realms, seen and unseen, that could be summarised and
filed in cabinets and drawers, some hidden, arranged in
a semi-circle. Astrological symbols, alchemical formulae
to make access easier, and…

Miles suddenly paled.

- …help to link tenuous connections. I'd been thinking
  as I read more about Fludd's amphitheatre that what
  it was trying to achieve was something like the Dream
  Pool, some great collective library of imagery. But then
  I started to think about a different library. One I knew.
  My Dad's. It's a long time ago and my memories are
  patchy, but it looks like something that starts with the
  Elizabethans, maybe goes quiet or goes underground
  for a century, two centuries, starts to flower again in the
  1890s, and then…finds its way into a steadings in Fife?
  It's bizarre, but… Is all this…?

Miles made several rapid passes with one hand, causing tottering
piles of books to rearrange themselves, lights come off and on, windows open briefly and then close. Becky was now well used to this
magical variation on domestic routine, which so rarely extended
to washing and ironing, but felt worried for him.

- Becky, is all this genetic? When I do these things – am
  I my father's son? 'It is all one to me where I begin; for I
  shall come back there again'.

- Fludd? Sounds more like Alice in Wonderland.

- No. The Fragments of Parmenides – in a Victorian trans-
  lation, admittedly.

You're a show-off, but OK, you win. I'm getting dizzy. Lighten up, buddy.

- You're telling me your father was an Elizabethan? How old do you think you are?

- Steady the buffs, as my Dad would have said. What I mean is this, right here. *That's* what I'm talking about.

And then Miles handed her the photo he had found of a man in a dressing gown, sitting in an ornate chair, head down, perusing an enormous chain-bound book. Behind him in a semi-circle towered an array of drawers and cabinets about twelve feet in height and over twice that in circumference, inscribed with quasi-cabbalistic signs, some zodiacal, some Celtic knots, some chalked in private code. Also in the room, in front of the man's, in front of Miles' father's feet, was, or was what looked like: water.

- That's my own father. This is where I'm from. He's part of where I'm from. It can't be wrong to go back, can it, if I'm only going back to where I began. Going back to what's a part of me anyway. I mean, we might want to go back and live there one day.

He's mad. I love him to bits, and he's mad.

- Sorry, I'm getting carried away. Too attached to my roots.

Some of your roots are in the Victorian, sooty world of letters, some are in Magic for Beginners. I've got you by your manly roots, and by the way, we're staying in London.

- Sure thing, Miles. You were saying?

- I mean, what's the difference between travelling, in our sense, to last week's Manhattan, or to the Fife of twenty years ago? I'll be off then. Quick scout around.

He flicked through the leather-bound, brown album. Staring briefly at a photo of his erstwhile home, Miles sat with it clutched it to his chest, and fell asleep.

7

Altogether elsewhere and unbeknownst to Miles and Becky, a young man in traditional robes and an armed police officer stood outside Fishawi's coffee house, in the Khan al-Khalili district of Islamic Cairo. The café was open, and indeed it would be surprising if it had not been, as Fishawi's has been continuously open for the last two hundred years, except of course on Ramadan, when all true believers are fasting. A blind man selling carved walking canes barged into the policeman, who shoved him in the chest and shouted something. Then the two carried on with their site-visit, eyeing up Fishawi's, working out distances.

The young man pointed to the huge ancient mirrors hanging in Fishawi's, made an everything-up-in-the-air gesture with his hands, and shook his head in a vigorous no. The police officer nodded, and together they trudged a little further north, conversing, past scaffolding, bazaars and caravanserais from the Mamluk era. Past the sober young men in the madrassars. No, we've gone a bit too far. They walked back in the direction of Fishawi's, and looked around.

The two men turned into an alley. A very small café called Hassan's allowed them a view that they seemed to find satisfactory. The police officer moved on, while the young man sidled in and ordered a mint tea. It came in a high-sided glass, couched in a tin clasp. Thoughtfully he stirred the emerald leaves of spearmint down into the black Egyptian tealeaves. After drinking his tea, the young man left Hassan's café, and, counting his steps carefully and looking at his watch, walked to the jeweller's, straight opposite. This building was pencil-thin, its single window small. Nestled amid the bustle of everyday Cairo, the jeweller's had few customers. Everyone pressing the bell was scrutinised remotely, but very few would ever gain admittance. And anyone who did would be fully aware not only of the discreet but massive security within, but also of the inadvisability of tarrying, let alone trying the patience of these particular jewellers, themselves in thrall to the ultimate owners.

The objects on display were also few in number, as were those individuals or groups who could afford these prices, not that the latter were discernible from anything so vulgar as a visible bit of paper. Two items only could be glimpsed at the rear of the window, perched on black baize, effectively invisible, save to one who had come searching. But to one who had come expressly to look, the green of the beautiful emerald brooch, whose setting took the form of a scarab beetle, sat next to a matching ring, seemed to grow in vibrancy, the longer it held the eye.

The young man re-entered Hassan's café on the following morning, perspiring heavily, though the battered old suitcase he carried was quite small. He sat hunched in the window seat, resting the case on the ledge. He ordered a mint tea, but did not touch it, walking immediately to the lavatories at the back of the café, where he waited his turn, shifting from foot to foot, hurriedly paid the attendant beggar some baksheesh, and had just time to get into the closet with its squatting toilet and water spray when the explosion occurred.

While no one was killed by the small explosive device, the consternation was enough to clear the café and part of the street, where the windows of Hassan's, like others in the vicinity, were blown out. These included the jeweller's window, from which the young man now snatched the glowing scarab emerald and its companion ring, while those around sought safety at full speed. As policemen ran into the street, he recognized, as planned, his co-inspector of the scene the previous day, and made a quick sign, but was profoundly shocked when the officer shot him on sight, in the chest, causing a poppy outpouring to crimson his djellabah. Before dying, he just had time to register an equally profound dismay at being shot a second time, full in the face, an insult which had the supplementary effect of stopping his heart.

The police officer shouted that there was a second bomb, and threw himself down so as to cover the jerking corpse. While any remaining stragglers fled, he swiftly rifled the young man's pocket, snatched the jewellery, and lost himself in the ambient disarray, firing over his head and yelling, in order to clear a path. Eventually he steadied his pace, and by the time he had emerged from the market area onto the main street, opposite the ancient mosque, the murderer's pace had slowed to a watchful saunter. When the black Mercedes pulled up, he climbed into the back seat without a word, immediately handed over the jewels to the man on his left, and waited for his reward. Quite unexpected, it began to take effect as soon as a small needle had been pushed into the side of his left thigh. Narcotized to the point of expiry, the middle-man maintained an upright posture all the way back to the five star hotel beneath the Pyramids, where, as key players met to discuss timelines, next steps and areas of responsibility, the chauffeur got out to stretch his legs and smoke a cigarette, before driving the corpse away to be divided, bagged and dropped into the already protein-rich Nile from the side of a felucca.

8

Oh no. Please God, let this not be happening. I've died. I've died. I have totally blown it. I'm dead.

Nothing.

It isn't fog. It's not night. There's nothing. Absolute zero to see. But I can hear: the lapping of the water. Seagulls. Oh and a stiff sea-breeze. And I can smell it, taste it. Ozone. How much of what you taste is smell, and vice versa. They say that hearing is the last sense to go, when you're dying. I may be about to find out. I can hear. But I'm blind. Back in the past, I can't see.

Miles intuited blue on the edge of his vision, and half-turned. Craning his head and glancing backwards, he was intensely relieved to make out the contours of his childhood home. So I can see backwards, but not forwards. He was granted a nano-second in which to feel relief, when the ground crumbled beneath his feet, and, feeling his heart pound and himself to be once more at the edge of death, he faced once more forwards, and because he faced forwards, was once again blind.

Miles took a deep breath to steady himself. He could hear, but not see, the crash of waves. Somewhat closer were the seagulls on the cliff-side, whose nest he had part-broken with one flailing hand, to save himself and get a grip on something. He could sense them. He heard their skriking, and was not one whit reassured when he heard the most vocal fly up and away, rather than nipping at him viciously, as their young were doing. Seagulls on a populated beach do little harm to humans. They might snatch the fish in your chips, if they think they can get away with it. But high above the humans' street, for example when workmen climb up the tall tower of St Salvator's in St Andrews to mend the clock, they will attack, and go for eyes or ungloved hands. And if, as Miles had just ensured, albeit inadvertently, they feel that their own territory has been invaded by a human, they fly straight down and very fast at forty five degrees, aiming straight at the skull. Welcome to the East Neuk of Fife.

It came to Miles that he was probably about to die, in a manner of speaking, in his sleep. In front of his gaze was nothing visible, but had the power of sight been restored, there would have been little to see beyond ocean and clouds between his dreaming face and Norway. The stones that dug into his back as he just about held to the cliff face, though painfully sharp, were crumbling. At least one seabird was about to attack, to either take out an eye or trigger his fall onto the rocks a hundred feet below.

Miles focussed all his attention on altering the circumstances by magic, but where in Southern California his ability to move persons and objects had been assisted by a mood of calm and uninterrupted watchfulness, and where his focus on the changing words across a card that would eventually save an infant's life had been heightened by a form of moral panic, and where in subsequent scene changes, his own increased sense of developing skill had granted him a confidence whose foundation was almost stylistic, here he merely felt small and under threat. He started to cry, reduced once again to a child. This journey, which was about his father, looked as if it was going to close with his own death. Inevitably, it was his mother he wanted.

What to do, when travel through dream in the present makes what's behind you a blank nothing, but lets you look forward – whereas travel to the past reverses this balance of blindness and sight. But there was no do, now, not now he was done with doing, and could now only be done-to. Miles thought with an intensity he rarely brought to the world in which he daily lived, of the mother he barely remembered. His mother, and safety. *Oh*: I'm moving. Spinning – and facing the other way. I can see again! Miles could also feel that he was shrinking.

- 	*Miles!* How on earth did you get so far? Come here lovey. It's not safe to go so near the cliffs. Come to mum. Oh you're heavy. You are *so* heavy these days!

Miles laughed, delighted, his mother rubbing his nose back and forth against the tip of hers. He thought, I'm saved, I've been moved; I fell, but I was picked up and saved. What came out of his mouth was *little piggy*! He tried to say *And this little piggy went*, as they moved towards the cliff-side house, but the thought was blown away on the East Neuk wind he saw lifting his father's white shirts and his own small socks and vests along the line.

- 	Daddy?

More doubtful, this Daddy, a man not always to be seen, even when somewhere in the house.

-　You want to see Daddy? Well we could go and look, he might be there. Here, let me put you down: oof. Take mum's hand. Come on!

-　Clawfpoff. Home.

So he walked, sometimes stumbling a little, his hand in his mother's hand, back to his home, on a bright windy day, able now to see straight in front, sometimes gazing up at the high sky, most likely to stumble a little at such moments, but perfectly happy, now, and expectant, not looking back.

He took a few steps on his own along the cool dark hallway, hearing his mother close the door behind him. Sam heard too, and lifted his black head briefly from his basket, then grunted, flicked his tail, got up and shook himself. The dog ambled behind them, nails clattering lightly on the hardwood floor. They walked from the house to the steadings.

The grown man preferred cats, finding something opaquely magical in their poise and otherness, but Miles at this beginning stage knew cats only from books. His father had books too, but they were grown-up books you weren't allowed to touch, and most of them were too heavy to lift anyway. Now he was ahead again, and trying to stretch up on tiptoe, to see through the keyhole of the circular room, built in that shape so that camellias could be grown up the walls, or so he now remembered he was told, later. This room with the empty and ancient indoor pool, this library, was constructed so that his father could re-draw the lost connections of hermetic epistemology for purposes of magic, before his memory was stolen from him by night's dark agents: so the grown up Miles would be minded to tell himself. Unable to think these things through in his present form, the young Miles burst into the room, the door to which his mother had now opened.

With infinite regret, Miles put it to himself that he needed now to see whatever was in this room of secrets through the eyes of his grown-up self, not the eyes of a child. If his mother, at this moment herself both real and unreal, had looked directly at her son and not forward into the room, seeking to catch sight of her husband, she would have seen a curious thing. She would have seen her son's shadow detach itself from his material body, and pulsing, grow taller. The tall shadow-man, amazed by what he was seeing, glided at speed towards the books and cabinets and instruments, the astrolabe and crucible, the glass ball, the major and minor arcana. Rapt, thus, he failed to look down, and in an unheard, unseen second, slipped and fell into the pool, with an almighty dream-drenched splash of which only he was aware. His mother had no sense at all of the shadow or the splash, intent as she was on reaching for her little one as he ran laughing, as he loved to do, round the rim of the pool, empty of real water, but still quite deep enough to bring about dangerous falls.

Outside, by the cliff edge, a baffled seagull hesitated before once again preparing to gouge the hated outline of the tall creature that kept on fading, appearing then fading again from view, where it had tried to steal her eggs. It was gone again. Not being human, she forgot the slight, moving straight into foraging and instinct, calling on the wind, swirling in an arc as might imperiously a wizard swirl his or her cape, flying and diving – into the sky, and out of harm's reach, out of mystery.

Everything's Under Control

1

The Chief of Police had a problem. Lighting an untipped Rameses, he took a deep lungful and curved the grainy photographs and papers into a fan around his desk. A bomb had gone off in a small café, slightly away from the main tourist sites and mosques of the Khan al-Khalili. There were no reported deaths – at least, not from the explosion. A young man called Tariq had been shot dead by what were almost certainly police bullets. One of his own men, Officer Abdul, a peppery individual with a tendency to blur the boundaries but essentially a loyal employee, had disappeared. One or two shops had reported minor looting, but the main and thankfully low-level damage was to windows, not persons. Apart from Hassan's café itself, a barber's next to a jeweller's had taken the brunt.

The young man Tariq was reasonably well known around the bazaar and the mosque. He appeared to have been a different person on different days, or depending to whom you spoke. He was a firebrand. He lived locally, rarely expressed an opinion or left the neighbourhood, and was devoted to his mother. He had been abroad or otherwise absent for lengthy periods of time. The mother seemed curiously unemotional, perhaps honouring secrets, perhaps not, in her reaction to the loss.

On one point she was credibly vehement. Tariq had not only wavered in his faith, but had developed an unhealthy interest in ancient Egyptian religion. He had started to talk of studying archaeology, arguing that the study of mummification and burial places was in its infancy, nowhere near its end. And that the end, when it came, would usher in a new beginning. Where to go with all of this. The Chief of Police stepped to the window, and looked downward to the bridge that crossed the Nile. Lorries and private cars sped through red lights, most drivers honking their horns every few seconds simply because, in the *joie de vivre* of the swarm, that was what you did. A continuously depressed horn signalled that, no, I really mean this – people, get out of the way, or risk death. An old man led a herd of goats through this mêlée, patiently, miraculously, to safety.

2

Laura Winthrope awoke in a quiet room in a hospital. She had sufficient levels of awareness to know only that she had been heavily sedated. Attempting to move, and turning her head with painful slowness to look down, she saw that her arms were lightly pinioned to the rails that framed the bed. Hearing a low cough, she looked straight in front, where a middle-aged man in a white coat with a stethoscope around his neck stood gazing at her, one eyebrow raised, seemingly in compassionate interest. His trousers, neatly folded, hung over the side of a visitor's chair, while he stood in silence, masturbating thoughtfully. Laura slid back into unconsciousness.

3

-    If it is what I *believe* it is…

Victor Winthrope moved in agitated circles around a seldom-used and dusty upper room, one hand anchored by his cane, the other touching, almost ritualistically, objects and furnishings, an escritoire here or velvet curtains there, as if they might be about to vanish, lost to the weight of what troubled him. Between two of the worm-eaten bookcases hung a morosely slender mirror, presenting its reflective credentials from inside a tarnished frame of gilt. Marks of age pocking the glass became liver spots, ageing further those who looked into it. Winthrope came to a trembling halt, leaning his cane against the wall, and placed one hand on Mr Boxer's shoulder, the other on Felix Manto's, addressing his remarks to both through the space in between, facing the mirror.

- If it is what I now think it is, the scarab is the key item. If, *if* I am right, it is nothing less than the sacred amulet, caused to have been fashioned by Horus for his grieving mother, the goddess Isis, following the murder of his father, and her husband, Osiris.

- Might I ask whether the value of this remarkable object resides more within the magical than the monetary realm?

- Indeed, Mr Boxer. The answer is, yes to both. An emerald the size of a plover's egg is clearly of immense cash value. As a highly significant item in the annals of Near Eastern antiquity it is of course a world treasure, a museum piece. Priceless. The salve to my conscience in seeking to…hold onto it for my, for our, purposes, rather than donating it to the British Museum or perhaps better, the Museum of Cairo, lies in the fact that it…has certain special properties. Though at present it actually has none at all.

- Make sense, Winthrope.

Felix Manto shook off the old man's grip, and walked towards the mirror, running his hand through his hair. When he looked in the flecked glass at Winthrope he caught a look of irritation that Felix also shared from his side.

- How curious it is that one so *supposedly* up to his neck in magic should insist so very loudly, and frequently, on the necessity for prosaic explanation…

- Yeah, this is benighted of the swamps calling. Lead me to the light, Yankee.

- Very well.

Winthrope put one hand carefully into the outside pocket of his midnight-blue jacket, and pulled out precisely nothing. Looking at the old man's reflection in the mirror, Felix saw him holding, simply, the finger and thumb of his right hand at eye level height, and a centimetre or two apart, face shining in triumph. And that was all. Frowning and turning towards Winthrope in order to volley something that might puncture the Boston Brahmin's *hauteur*, he now saw him to be holding aloft a beautiful necklace of green stones. Turning once again to take in the mirror view, he once again saw nothing. Ah.

- Precisely.

- OK, I take it back. You've got me. Now explain.

The old man wrapped the necklace of emeralds slowly and with reverence around his fingers.

- The amulet, the scarab, was stolen from the house of a collector and fellow-practitioner, Dr Aziz…

- What? *The* Dr Aziz? The first magician to design a credible, all-weather invisibility suit? The most renowned magician in Egypt, if not the world?

- The same.

- The man who lived for years undetected in the Great

Pyramid, turned himself into a wraith in order to steal the infamous topaz from The Place Whose Name Cannot Be Uttered, the guy who…

- Felix, please.

- Dr Aziz. Wow. He wouldn't take kindly to being burglarized.

- Retribution, as you are intimating, reached a high order of severity.

Winthrope shuddered slightly, and looked pensively for a moment at the necklace. What a high price we place on inert things, he thought to himself, and how little we value life itself. We are a supremely clever, and a disgusting species. He slid the necklace back into his pocket, and patted it lightly. Not that this pretty thing is wholly inert. He sat down, with painstaking slowness, but his eyes were shining.

- The point, gentlemen, is that the amulet doesn't *work*, except when worn in conjunction with the necklace, which you have seen, and which has in itself some remarkable, if limited, properties, the third piece in the jigsaw being a matching emerald ring. We have the necklace. I have the necklace. The amulet is now on its way to us. At least I hope so. The ring is: somewhere. Best case scenario, it's with the amulet. Worst, in a place as yet unknown. In which case, patience is, or so they endeavour to persuade us, a virtue.

- Could it be lost, sir?

- In a casual sense, yes, Mr Boxer. The ring may be lost. However, I don't believe that an artefact of such power *can* be lost, in the ultimate scheme of things. The ring has been in hiding, and for some considerable time.

Dormant, if you like.

Bostonian pronunciation stretched *dormant* out almost so as to add a door to it, one that was closed for now, but one which Winthrope hoped he would live to prise open. In extreme old age some put their house in order, some try to boss others into doing it, and some just want the newest, highest, grandest house, by fair means or foul, now. All these were in play.

- If I were a betting man, which indeed I am when I can rig the way the wheel spins, I would wager that…well, deep calls to deep. The combined force of the two pieces will if necessary cause the third to surface. In my view.

- You said that the amulet would not 'work', sir. Not without its sibling artefacts. The precise nature of the work involved being, what exactly?

- Oh, just the same work we are all engaged in, when we speak of losing ourselves *in* our work, when we have children, or write stories, drink wine to forget, pay for – what's the phrase they use these days? – cosmetic surgery. We're all human. We know we're going to die. So we want to arrest time. Sure, we'll buy more. We're ready to pay. Believe me, I've paid. Stockpile.

- And so the amulet can bring a stay of execution?

- Yes, in the sense that all magic aims in that direction. More precisely, the amulet was made by Horus, the bereaved son, to comfort his mother, Isis. You need to ask yourself, what is the comfort that would bring most consolation to someone who has lost another someone?

- To bring the dead back to life.

- In the case of Osiris, that would be a trifle problematic. If you remember the myth correctly, you will recall that he…rather went to pieces. But, yes, that is what the amulet can do, after a fashion. When it is once more linked to the necklace and the ring. It can turn back time. And isn't that, really and truly, what we would all like to do?

Cello notes of tentative hope decayed in the squeezed air of thought. Three sad men, who would die, one day, in one way or another, and who perhaps had, in one way or another, already died, stood in shared silence in the room. Velvet curtains warmed and faded imperceptibly in one more day's uneven English light. Dust motes drifted down. All of our stories are tales from the crypt.

4

Laura awoke, to hear deep breathing, and feel fingers probing her lips and teeth. Carefully, she opened her eyes, an action she performed as slowly as if she had been lifting the heavy lid of a heavier chest. She found herself looking into the entranced stare of the doctor, a man with terribly pale skin, and a profusion of black curly hair, breathing heavily. She could see, though she had absolutely no wish to, the curved hairs of jet black protruding from his nostrils, and those zones on upper lip and lower jowls where that morning's shave had missed small fields of rising dots and spikes. He pushed a tablet under her tongue with his fingers, while raising the index finger of the other hand to his mouth, shushing her into silence. Lacking the energy, in any case, to scream, Laura once again fell down into the dark.

5

The Chief of Police stubbed out his cigarette brusquely, drummed his fingers on the desk, and lit another. Then he lifted the black receiver of the telephone, but immediately set it back down in its cradle. He called out irritably to an overweight lieutenant whom he could hear in an adjoining office, who entered, hands full of papers, sweat stains under the arms of a shirt that came out of his trousers on one side. This individual had his limitations, but his virtues included a compendious memory for the mysteries and byways of Cairo. They revolved intuitions for a while. Dropping their voices, they came back in tones of increasing conviction to a certain Dr Aziz.

Dr Aziz was known to have been the victim of theft recently. That extraordinary, and extraordinarily proud man, would have been at least as wounded by the insult to his reputation as by the loss of whatever was taken. Aziz. I thought as much. The Chief of Police weighed the balancing claims of action and inaction in his mind, then curved the fan of papers on his desk back into a neat vertical pile, which he handed to his companion, deciding to forget about them. If the good doctor is at the bottom of all this, it is better not to know. He has his own methods, and it will all be sorted out, in the end. But it would be better not to know precisely how. Aziz has helped us, from time to time. Several assassinations at least had been averted by the use of charts and prisms, where conventional policing had come to a perspiring halt. We leave him to his own devices, this time. I will mourn Abdul. Briefly. But just at this moment we are all moving at different levels on eternity's stairway.

6

- Most likely, Felix, the thief didn't know who he was dealing with. He got lucky. Then very unlucky. To him it was just a fat emerald. Dr Aziz had perhaps grown a trifle lax in his habits. Maybe he assumed that because he is who he is, no one would dare steal from him. Alternatively, it may be that the thief had not only some occult knowledge, but an occult ring, the one that goes with the necklace. Perhaps he was able to use the powers of the second to lead him to the first. But he didn't have the necklace, and he did need cash, so he sold them on. That's the kind of missing information we should be able to piece together, eventually. Soon, I hope.

- But I don't quite get it, Victor. Why would Aziz not just use his own powers to take the amulet back? How come it had to go through a whole chain of people and rigmarole, before the gang you seem to be in contact with got hold of it?

Winthrope's failure to reply did nothing to allay their sense of an impending storm. He was up and moving twitchily around the room again, touching objects, rearranging them to no obvious purpose. He seemed to all the members of the firm to have become uncharacteristically agitated of late. The cane was new. Its owner was old. Dark lightning was about to strike; strike them, or him. At such moments loyalty shrugs, and allegiance to anything other than self must tiptoe regretfully away.

- Remember the themes of the myth. Theft, dismemberment, murder. And separated by theft for many years, the three jewels have lain dormant. But now the process of reuniting them has been rekindled. The sleepers awake. Aziz won't only want his scarab back. He's proud, he'll want to turn his loss into spectacular success. He'll want the complete set. With each stage of the journey to reuniting the jewels there has to be at least one death, essentially a ritual propitiation. Then the grand prize, the ability to turn back time, passes into the hands of the final owner. But there is one last twist in the tale. As the jewels are reunited, so will be the spirit of whoever was sacrificed at the time they were first imbued with magic. That soul has been trapped and powerless, locked inside the jewels, craving escape, and for the longest time. It is that first murdered soul, grateful for release, which bestows the gift of turning back the clock's uncaring hands – as it flies away to freedom.

Felix Manto was troubled. For one thing, he could begin to see, though he had absolutely no wish to, the emerging contours of his own role in this maze.

- Yes Felix, as usual, I can read your mind. Not to put too fine a point on it, your job is to shoot the messenger. They want the necklace as badly as I want the scarab. We all want the ring. Their 'negotiator' will most likely be a company assassin. When it comes to turning back the hands of the clock, I don't know what their game is. Might depend on the cut of their politics, or their masters'. To turn the Middle East back to a time before the foundation of the State of Israel? To avert Armageddon - or bring it about? There are plenty of angry souls out there, adrift in the desert of modernity. I'm guessing. Maybe they are not at all adrift, but rather feeling that their moment has come. That they *are* modernity, just as functionaries at the temple of Karnak were once vanguard questors, the new priests on the block.

He lifted the necklace from his pocket once again, vampirically glancing across with delight at another vampire's ability to absent itself from glass. Then from a drawer he drew with care a jeweller's case, shaped like a hand-size sarcophagus, into which he laid, gently, the non-reflecting jewels. He leaned on the table, and stared at the case, as if glimpsing answers in the blankness of its lid.

- My instinct is, they're criminals, *tout court*. Successful but simple. Successful because simple.

- I don't care who they are. I'm not going to kill anyone. I don't do killing.

- You have certain contractual obligations, Felix.

-	Nowhere does it say I have to agree to commit murder…

-	You agreed to agree. With me. To do my bidding.

-	Then *you* kill the messenger.

-	I can't, not if I am to be the beneficiary of the magical properties of the amulet, the necklace, and finally the ring. Through me, of course, the organization benefits. My hands must be clean, but connected to hands that are not. That is the way this deadly garland is plaited.

-	What do we get out of this?

-	*Time*, you dear fool. How many more times. Time.

As Boxer and Manto withdrew into troubled silence, Victor Winthrope reflected on events, as an ancient tarnished jewel might reflect, not in a glass darkly, but on the company it had been forced to keep.

You didn't ask me, children, how I came by the necklace. You didn't ask what I had to pay. I *didn't* pay. Aziz sent out his minions, cast spells and scoured Cairo until he found that thief, who, begging for the life he was about lose (slowly), confessed the whereabouts of the stolen piece, which now sat, dishonoured, but reunited with its partner ring, in a jeweller's, a front for a gang of international jewel thieves. He caused the jewels to be set free. The good Doctor set out to find the necklace to make up the trio – and that was enough to make the last owner of the necklace extremely, urgently, *madly* keen to be rid of it. No one wants to tangle with Dr Aziz, particularly in his present mood.

So, Felix, I spoke the truth when I said that Aziz wants the set. I just neglected to add, now word will have reached him that Victor Winthrope has the third piece, he will, without a doubt, be on his way. Could be here as soon as tonight. And when he or his agents get here – Felix, Boxer, and the same goes for Miles – I want you to be the guard dogs that eat the poisoned meat, want you to be just what you were always meant to be, my creatures, my clowns, my clumsy stunt doubles, the ones that take the fall – to give *me* time. That is the way the garland is really plaited. If I can get those two pieces off him I can turn back time. Then I can do what I've done, do it all over again, but do it better. But if I lose? Enough, I'm *tired*.

7

Laura was awake only briefly, this time. The doctor appeared to be wearing some kind of ski-ing or diving gear, all slick and black, oiled rubber. Gloves. Muttering, chanting. His general deportment suggested the behaviour of an insane and aroused seal. This is going to have to stop, Dr Rubber-Gloves. Vegetable oils and talcum filled the air. Ugh. She caught the odd drifting word. 'Physical together-ness'. 'Underground vault'. Then she herself drifted.

8

- How, sir, do the pieces work, precisely?

Mr Boxer could sense the rising tide of danger, and their closeness as a group to a moment of energy discharged that could break the chain, forever. Felix too was white and shaking. Boxer had never seen him rattled like this before.

- The three parts of a human soul are trapped, dismem-bered like Osiris and divided between the three pieces of jewellery. If all three are worn simultaneously by a magician – or indeed by anyone – that living person will act as a conductor. The trapped soul wishes, of course, for release. It bends its energies to turning back time at someone else's behest, simply so as to be able to wind back its own time-spool to the point where it was first imprisoned by the god's son, Horus. Only then will the prisoner soul find its own liberation. The pieces can only work one more time. They brought back Osiris. After a fashion. Now, as in much magic, they will work to restore the status quo.

- Victor, I got into this line of work precisely because magic meant we could accomplish changes without killing. I'm not going to do it.

- Very well, I had thought you might take this line. There is however Miles to consider. He has the book, his damned book, but he has not made its unique powers available to us. He's running his own small ship. Surely he can do this one thing for us. He has weapons training. We may be honoured by a visit from some all-muscle, no-brain fool who doesn't know what these jewels can do, when worn together.

- And if Miles won't do it, sir?

Mr Boxer was now even paler than usual. Winthrope returned his gaze, raising one eyebrow with theatrical slowness.

<h1 style="text-align:center">9</h1>

- Professor Winthrope, *Laura*, if I may…

- Fuck off.

- I so hoped we might become better acquainted, and…

- Fuck off. Fuck off, weirdo Nazi rapist. Die, creep. Wither on the vine. Just let me out of here first.

- I'm afraid that the course of action you are recommending sits uncomfortably with your current status as a patient, sectioned under the Mental Health Act. Do you recall biting the nurse? On the hand, on your first night with us? Here, at Passing Clouds? It was not a promising indicator.

- I'll do more than bite your hand before we're through. Let me go. I'll sue.

- And what about the little disagreements with the other patients? Though, I feel bound to remark, that I personally have found your own subsequent isolation in this room as rewarding as I hope you have.

Two equal and opposite forces, doctor and patient stared at each other.

- Well, I concede it got me out of the twilight zone of tracksuit bottoms. Low self-esteem can get awfully high-decibel. I just have this old-fashioned aversion to being *drugged.* And what's with all the rubber? Are we going deep-sea diving?

- And then do you remember setting fire to the curtains in the TV room? I still haven't worked out how you accomplished that particular parlour trick.

- They wanted to watch *Supermarket Sweep.* There was a vote. We had an argument. I argued with the tracksuit bottoms. I can't stand *Supermarket Sweep! I hate Dale Winton! Let me out!*

- I can't do that. I love you.

- Oh, *God!*

At least now the pinions were gone. She ran one hand through her hair, and moved her neck back and forth, hearing unexercised gristle click. In so doing she caught sight of her leather bag, jammed, perhaps unnoticed, between the small bedside cabinet and the wall. Probably emptied. Maybe not. Was there anything heavy in there. One chance at a bull's eye, if I throw it hard enough? Can't risk it: not yet, anyway.

- Or rather, I *will* love you. Although you accuse me of a certain serious form of assault, please be assured that, save for a few essentially therapeutic interventions, it is only your soul I have penetrated. No, it is only with those, friends, who have entirely severed the cords of life that I find I can be…wholly free. Rigor mortis is an irksome feature of the first twenty four hours or so of posthumous existence, but shortly thereafter the muscles relax sufficiently to allow the most spectacular and loving configurations, which tedious pain thresholds would have prohibited in life.

Is there an alarm. Red button. Red cord. Pulling it might just tip him over the edge. But, face it Laura, this one went sailing over the edge many full moons ago. He glided towards her like an undertaker on ice skates, tears spurting unbidden.

- My own dear, late, lamented mamma! I said to her, hide yourself. Eternity, dearest eternity, I cried to her, hide with your son, remain eternal. You know, I only got to really know her, truly *know* my own mother, after I had…after her untimely death. Death is bracing, in the choices it presents. Either you are forced into silence, into the position of bystander, and this is unbearable. Or you get a grip, take hold of the life that the other has let fall into desuetude, and make of it something dignified, something stellar.

Oh no you don't, I like my own totally undignified, undead self. You go on worshipping at mummy's shrine. He gazed at her sightlessly, mouth in an O-gape of lunacy, right hand tugging his left earlobe, while with his left hand he tugged at the right. Well, there are still some gestures in the repertoire of physical movement that I'm getting to see for the first time. If he gets his way, I might see a few more - if I live that long.

- I am a doctor, by training.

He looked at her and paused, eyebrow raised, as if she might question this. Laura chose not to dissent.

- But when I am not working, my hours are devoted, as you will perhaps have anticipated, to taxidermy and a deep love of opera. Glimpses of *das reine Dauern*, glimpses in both, how they peep through the veil with the charm of dead stars. Stars that are dead but continue to shine, just for us. We, the unlikely ones, never at home to ourselves… Opera! Taxidermy! How to combine the two. This would be my holy grail. The voice of death itself! The singing heart of the glacier!

Behind him a Waterford vase sat on a trolley. In it stood carnations and gypsy grass. He caught her looking and measuring distances. Smiling, he lifted the glass up to a shelf she could never have reached, even in a situation less tense than this.

- See how the cut flower loves to drink, through the site of its own amputation. You are right, as always, once again it is this *pathos* of existence I find so unbearable. I oppose to it the *ethos* of death-in-life, preservation after the destruction of a moment, a mere moment… You will love the cooling vault of our new mortuary… *my* new mortuary. Constructed piece by piece, with my own hands. None of the other staff know about it. Those moral dwarves. Under the car park, a holy space essentially autumnal, both couch and theatre for the weary dead…

- You first. No, really.

- You should not treat me so facetiously. I have offered you nothing but devoted attention. As your doctor I have to inform you that you carry a marked strain of dissidence in an otherwise enchanting personality. That will pass, by definition, when you move to the next phase. I love your name, *Laura…*

- It means let-me-out, and we won't say anything more about it. I'll write. Promise.

- No, you are wrong. Laura means laurel – it sings of victory, honour… But once your final victory is achieved, on your journey to love, I will re-name you *Melissa*. Melissa, winged, Homeric, crossing zones of pollination, of intoxication, on diaphanous wings of desire! My desire!

Laura at this moment thought neither of etymology nor honour, but of certain practices peculiar to the ancient Egyptians. She chose not to give her thoughts vocal expression, at this stage. And I thought I was mad. You can see where the red alarm cord used to hang. He's had it taken down. Bastard.

- Well, then, that's fine. I'm going to die. And chill out in your new mortuary. Any chance of lunch, before I go? Freshly-squeezed OJ? Plastic glass of course, so I don't do anything socially irritating?

- Of course. We are not yet at the river crossing. The sacerdotal elements are not yet in alignment. And you have lost a little too much weight for my liking, *meine Schatze.…*

A stay of execution. Let joy be unconfined.

- Lunch today is poached salmon. With a watercress salad.

- My favourite. Doctor?

He turned at the door.

- You know my name. I don't know yours.

- Manfred. Manfred Klumm.

- Manfred. So romantic. The burning wreck of a demol-
  ished world.

- I'm sorry?

- Just some poet.

- Until later, Laura.

- I'll be waiting. Manfred.

She smiled. Her doctor smiled back.

10

After he left, the usual sounds returned to the forefront of her consciousness. The psycho-damaged teenager who made the incessant
machine gun noises with his mouth, but who could not speak. Probably as well. Tedious little shit. The slight squeak of passing nurses'
sneakers on the scrubbed corridor floors. Ditto. How long have I
got. It dawned on her that the volume levels were rising, suddenly.
Then she looked at the door. It was not quite closed. Why thank
you, Doctor. My state of health has improved immeasurably in the
last few seconds. Laura grabbed her bag, and waited by the door.
When sound in the vicinity dropped momentarily away, she took
a chance and moved silently into the corridor.

All the doors were temporarily malfunctioning. She was not the
only soul in custody to have taken the hint. A young woman with
prematurely grey hair peeped flirtatiously out of her door, ready

to suck to pith-dryness even a meagre five minutes of contained misrule. While two men with their backs to Laura and bits of kit hanging from their overalls messed about with a stepladder, causing sparks to shoot from an exposed corner of the corridor ceiling, machine-gun boy started ricocheting his body from one wall to the other, moving at speed, two nurses in pursuit. One was pulling on a white coat, having just emerged from a door slightly ahead on the left. Laura slipped in, to emerge almost immediately having tipped lipstick, cigarettes, lighter and hip flask from her leather bag into the pockets of a nurse's uniform. One swig of Jack Daniel's and she went off to look for the exit.

I don't have long. I'll be visible on CCTV. When are we ever not? She made it through the main entrance of the hospital and out into a mix of ambulances, taxis and parked staff cars. So far so good. She pulled her hair down around her face as much as possible. Out of the corner of her eye, a BMW was reversing to pull out of the car park. Oh God, it's him. OK, let's embrace opportunity. Even if we have to waltz with threat.

- Manfred. How lovely to see you again, and so soon. I was just taking the air before lunch…

- You are wearing a nurse's uniform. Tut, tut, Laura. You are trying to escape.

- Goodness, no! You're so wrong! Escape isn't in my nature! I always see things through!

To the bitter end. She saw his hand move to press a key on the pager he had located in his jacket. Dipping into her bag, she took a chance. Hardly in tune with current thinking on smoking cessation, but then, what price pleasure without risk. He hesitated when he saw the brand, and his life turned a corner.

- *Rameses*! My favourite. I haven't had one of those for years. Goodness. What was it the TV commercial used to say? 'I'd cross the desert for a Rameses. Rameses King-Size! The smoke of Kings!' Of course I can't say I approve…

- I'm not asking you to approve. I'm just asking you to spend a little time with me. Little man, you've had a busy day. Take five. Then *I'll* take the uniform *off*, if you see where I'm coming from…little supine, manikin, girlikin, good-as-dead me….

Laura held up her lighter as he cupped his hand. Curiously, although she certainly lit the cigarette, the flame appeared to issue from her fingernail, rather than the lighter.

That a Professor of Near Eastern Antiquity and Culture should be aware of the fact that the human jaw is hard to break when closed, but easily fractured when the mandibles are opened more loosely, as in the act of smoking, was only curious at first pass, given a knowledge of embalming procedure which she knew would come in handy one day. Summoning all the knowledge, courage and vindictiveness she could muster, Laura brought the fist holding the lighter up sharply, to immediate and impressive effect.

She slightly missed target with the next manoeuvre. Bringing Manfred's head smartly down with her left as her right hand brought up the windscreen wiper succeeded in perforating only cheek and sinus, rather than finessing the more spectacular trauma that had shimmied to the top of her improvised agenda. Oh well, any port in a storm. As the immobilised healthcare professional kept enforced and groaning watch over his own car, Laura kicked away his pager, took his keys, sat in the driver's seat, pulled it forward, took another swig of JD, lit her own Rameses, balanced paucity of time against a quantum of adrenaline-fuelled zeal, then looked around for further entertainment. Delighted to find a small toolbox in the glove compartment, she felt blessed on discovering within it not only a screwdriver, but a small hacksaw. Choices, choices – what's a girl to do? She held them up for Manfred to see, eyes Bambi-wide and letting her lower lip run beneath perfect white teeth. But, hey, *tempus fugit*. So, sadly, no. Time to go time. You'll survive, doc. The screaming sirens will be here, in two shakes of a lamb's tail.

Now speedily rifling the trunk of the car, Laura found a petty cash box containing some rolled notes – that's helpful, thank you – a sordid collection of rubber goods and extreme sports clothing, together with goggles, oils (yuck), various more macabre accoutrements, and, oh *no*! You bastard! *Photographs!* Manfred's methodical record keeping had succeeded only in reigniting her ire. Once again in the driver's seat she rammed the car without any hesitation straight into the wall. Her *coup de grâce* succeeded in glueing parts of the owner of the BMW yet more vividly and firmly to its bonnet, a sight which would arouse public consternation even in this part of London. A trifle reluctantly, Laura put on lipstick, abandoned the vehicle, and started walking away. Then she stopped. Then she cursed, and stamped. Then she spun around in a brief but vengeful pirouette with the fingers of one hand outstretched towards the car, which promptly exploded, in a gratifyingly intense ball of flame.

Always been a girl who likes leather. Rubber reeks. Where's the nearest bar, I need to clean up. *Doctors.* Uunh.

11

Either the pool was very deep, or Miles fell very slowly, for he had plenty of time as he went down to look about him, and to wonder what was going to happen next. He found he could breathe perfectly well in whatever medium it was he had now entered, here in his father's dream pool. It felt like thought. He knew at one level that he was dreaming, but had always assumed that, even in a dream, consciousness must be consciousness of something. Here in the friendly darkness, he thought only of thinking itself. It streamed. Here was a blank but warmish wave of how it felt to think, as himself, and there a matching wave of how it felt to be thought of, or to be somewhere deep in thought, but not be Miles. Sometimes himself, sometimes other, sometimes merging, at times fluttering new spores of possibility, the differences seemed not to be essential, at least not down here, falling gently and slowly through the pool.

I have travelled back in time, by looking at a photograph. This is something a lot of people do – I just take it literally. I want to know more about my past, and particularly I want to know more about the part of it that's out of reach, inside my father's mind. I think most humans want to do that, too, at some stage or another – I just take that wish more literally too – I act upon it. Am I so very different, after all? I believe in magic, yes. I believe in magic because I want to. I believe in magic because magic works. Most of all I believe in magic because the world is magic anyway. Echoes, symbols, tenuous patterns that can harden into fatedness, or lead to deeper meaning.

A windy cliff in the Kingdom of Fife. Five minutes away, and a world away. A simple powerful pull, of earth, and green, and the cleansing sea-wind, before the raven flies diagonally by, or clouds essay a question with no words. And this old house, that contains this pool, which for the time being contains me. It's all magic, whatever I promote to the status of belief, or think I know.

So thought Miles, moving in and out of thought. There is a going back, here, and there is a never going back. Letting his mind spin adrift into blossoms of light, he watched them break up as pure sentience, drifting spiral consciousness of falling, gently ever further, darkly deftly down, inside the pool.

As he continued to drift, parts of his mind broke away into lantern slides, nonsense sounds, half-thoughts that fused and split promiscuously, no mental control now, no way of turning carnage to carnation. No need. Right now, he couldn't have resolved a single anything. A single anything walks into a bar at happy hour, sits pertly and, newly scented, looks around for company. The company went bust, and scents of Spring came late this year. Too late for Uncle Jim. What they wrote in the papers is only half true, and the rest is still out there, prowling like bad weather, craving discovery, another hungry snowdrift. An unexpected something walks into the bar. Pays for a blue drink with blue dollar bills, made of sky-slides. Strikes up a conversation with the anything, while the barman calls time, but time just ran out, leaving death to take the check and pray for blankness, but flowers just kept on growing up and up between death's toes, tethering sandals to carpet. Knowing we need sunshine, if only for the vitamins, we foolishly neglect to walk abroad by night. Something and anything, walking by lunar light. Midnight and moonlight let minds grow. A journey from mulch. Mulch to mycelium. Miles kept on falling.

It seemed to him he had been falling for such a long time. Thoughts recrudescing, he tried to remember his father, sitting in his tall chair, reading. No longer had to try – he saw him clearly. And then, with a bump, he landed.

The adult Miles was now standing beside his father's chair, while Simon Proctor sat, robed and reading, one midnight by the Dream Pool, by candlelight. Miles leaned over, reading what Simon read, a medieval treatise, *On Light*, by a freewheeling prelate, Bishop Grosseteste, one of a group of thinkers calling themselves the Light Metaphysicians.

This benign philosopher argued that in the beginning, being was a flame in the darkness, itself very much like a candle. Light was the reality, spreading through the universe in an ever-unrolling carpet, the planets and cities, Jerusalem, Alexandria, persons and things, just the small bits of fluff. Charmed, Simon stared into the flame of the small candle by which he was reading, until a red after-image shaped like someone falling caused him to blink and look down into the Dream Pool. Something in the overlay of red on the blue-yellow water sent him worrying into his son's future, seeking to know in that past present how his son might come to need his future help;

and would he live sufficiently long to guarantee it. How like him
Miles already seemed.

Miles felt all this in his mind, newly washed by the waters of the
Pool, through which he had fallen, only to find himself standing
by his father, looking down at its surface. This circular journey is
impossible, he thought, and then, newly clear, this circular journey
is simply the one I just took. He blurred with his father, the two
leaning, pensive figures, an instance of over-painting, a palimpsest,
double exposure. Hopefully, both thought, Miles would not have
to live a double life, as Simon did, working by day inside a system
he abhorred but from which he dared not try to escape, for the
sake of his family. It had been made pretty clear what happened
to deserters.

As in many aspects of his work, the chosen methodology in the
United States post-war, resembled closely the ways of doing things
that certain elders in the team had built up in wartime Germany.
As in terror, so in science. But then, the move from making rockets that incinerated cities to rockets that aimed for the stars was a
fairly straightforward shift in thought. Particularly when the work
on the rockets entailed so many technological developments that
could readily be adapted for purposes of war, should the need arise.
And they were quite determined that the need would arise. And
that if it did not arise through circumstance, it could be ignited,
a flame that would spread across the atmosphere, brighter than a
thousand suns. Simon, gazing deep into the better light, hoped that
his son would escape this. All he could do was work, by night and
by candlelight, such small and countervailing bits of magic as his
lone research made feasible. Compensation, antidote; penance for
what happened by day.

Lately they had seemed kinder, in the workplace. As if to say, there
is only so much we can demand of one mind, and we admit that
we have demanded a great deal. He liked to look into the electric
blue light they had installed above his workstation. It drew the

gaze; somehow pacified. When had it appeared? He could not quite remember. He must be ageing faster than he had anticipated, when younger. There had been quite a few things, recently, he could not remember.

Miles shifted his gaze from the book to the surface of the pool, where he saw his father reflected. This doesn't feel like trespass, it doesn't feel like profanation, doesn't feel forbidden. It feels as natural as climbing inside a photograph. Amazing where things that start so simply can lead to. He caught his father's eye, as both looked down.

Miles, old boy! My goodness, you've aged! Not for the worse, though. Chip off the old block, of course. What on earth, or beyond it, are you doing here? His father rose slightly unsteadily, an old man who had been deeply absorbed in reading, now suddenly called on to play host. But no sooner had he turned around to embrace his son than he began to recede, as Miles, once more moving upwards, looked down on him. *I must be dreaming!* We both are, thought Miles, and Simon caught the thought. He thought back, *Ah. Short but very sweet. Dreaming or not, good luck, Miles. Better luck than me – I've been a very bad wizard. Take care, old chap – smart's the word and quick's the action!* as his son, shaking his head and smiling, shot vertically upwards, mind breaking surface after surface.

In mind he was briefly a boy again, wedged in a hollow tree, then hearing his mother call that it was time to come in, that the haar was stealing the light away. He climbed out, sprang to the ground, and found his red ball. Bouncing it, but thinking of other matters, the boy let the ball continue its movement unsupervised as he ran back to the house. He failed to see the bounced ball carry on bouncing, then stall in air, then fade. It hovered then passed into another world where everything is crystal, his father turning it and gazing at further worlds inside it, stepping out lightly, trapped wizard from the riven tree. Other, more companionable trees in the lane had grown into each other's grasp like giant fingers, cathedralled into thinking to say something; but the something could most likely wait. Downstairs the sea broke up rocks, and looked affectionately up at the moon, saying turn me. It's time. Behind the stage machinery, the midnight silence roared. And then dark lightning, brought alive by reading. We read with our hands, down in the graveyard of letters, making them mean, all a scrabble. Make all you can of your quicksilver life, mouthed the unseen protectors, the man to his son, or the ball to its boy; spheres of thought, fireballs of wishing, new crystals of starlit curiosity, on stage and back there in the wings of the great globe, the curving walls of time. Down in the grave, you're a long time looking at the lid.

12

A man in perfect physical condition, who had lived for several years undetected in the Great Pyramid, trained by Special Services but now working only for himself, skilled in ten martial arts, an Olympic-standard fencer and swimmer, and one moreover gifted in light and dark forms of expertise which require that mind be honed much more than muscle, a man smarting from a blow to his reputation but wholly intent on a coup without precedent, climbed silently as a spider up the wall of the antiquarian bookshop, unseen, even where white bars of moonlight fell. Doctor Aziz was wearing his latest and unique special operations suit, that could withstand sudden changes in temperature, was waxed to allow movement through impossibly narrow tunnels and apertures, wired so as to allow him to stun with an electric charge anyone who blocked his advance, and dotted with the suction cups he now so adroitly deployed as he shimmered up the wall.

This was going to be easier than he could possibly have anticipated. Expecting, at the least, poison gas, he had decided to wear his night-mask with its oxygen supply and night-vision lenses; but this old and visibly under-defended place had clearly given up the ghost. Winthrope he knew by repute, but knew too that he was getting on in years. This is going to be like picking the pocket of a sleeping man. Within minutes I will have reunited the jewels of Osiris, the eyes of my ancient nation, in an act of occult passage that will secure my premier place in the annals of Magic. The emerald ring glinted and swung slightly on the chain around his neck, bouncing light from the scarab securely pinned above it. He eased the window open silently, and dropped on all fours into the room.

His night-vision lenses glowed red, and soon led him to the drawer, to the sarcophagus case within, and finally to its precious contents. With a soft and almost erotic exhalation, he gently set the necklace on the table. Carefully, reverentially, he placed the scarab next to the necklace. The two pieces of jewellery began to glow with a green light. And then there came a humming, in the background. Adrenaline pumping, he could hardly tell what was happening, in rational terms. Moving on instinct alone, Aziz ungloved his hand, put on the ring, and waved it slowly around in the air, a rapt conductor, above the sibling jewels. The green lights glowed more intensely. The humming increased in volume, like a small swarm of bees. Then he heard a creaking, as time and space moved into a different alignment.

Humming the opening bars of the *Firebird Suite*, creaking slightly as she walked, and, as she walked, weaving just a little, Laura Winthrope entered the room. Taking one look at Aziz in his goggles and rubber suction-suit, she brought the empty bottle of Jack Daniel's crashing down on his head and, as he sank to the floor unconscious, kicked him several times, marrying anatomical knowledge and extreme prejudice. My God, what is it with these guys? Is it some kind of *cult*? Turning the inert body over for a cursory inspection, she wrinkled her nose. Ach, *rubber*, not again! She walked to the window and opened it, to let in the fresh air of London after midnight. Something tugged at the edge of her vision, and Laura turned. *Oh,* aren't you *beautiful.*

She held up the necklace in the moonlight, and placed it gently and slowly around her neck, tossing her abundant hair to lock the tiny clasp, and smoothing the green jewels down. They seemed to like her. The liking was mutual. She plucked the ring from the chain of the unconscious necromancer, and placed it, sighing, on the fourth finger of her left hand. Standing in the moonlight, she did a twirl. A little more doubtfully, she cupped the scarab in the palm of one hand, and stood, framed in the window, stroking it vaguely with her right. A faint clicking and whirring began, and had she seen herself from the street below, Laura would have been startled to see how the green lights began to flash once more an ancient code, a wheel of eyes, circling her rapt silhouette.

Never was that keen on beetles. Not really. I know the ancient Egyptians revered them, but. Even the scarabs – ugly little warriors, miniature armour-plated tanks. Anyway. Night, healing night, great London vault of secrets, I have a confession to make. I start fires. I *set* fires. That much you know. Why, or even how, is less certain to me. But my real confession? I am not, at the end of the day, when push comes to shove, when Isis comes to Osiris, much interested in ancient Egypt. Not anymore. That vast, that primitive cult of nothing but death. How to die, how not to die, how to travel to the other side, what to take with you, what to wear, how to commemorate, how to embalm: death, death, and more death for dessert. What I have really always loved – along with beautiful clothes, and jewellery (she stroked the now vibrating ring) and music, and wine and exciting company (never enough of either) – is…. looking back… how I *wish* I could turn back the clock…

Doctor Aziz groaned. Laura turned and lugged him to the sill of the open window, beneath which sat a skip, containing stained and discarded mattresses in several inches of rainwater. I wish, Laura thought, as she heaved him absent-mindedly out of the window, that I had never been caught up in this maze of mausoleums, arcane lore and, oh, doing what old Victor thought I should do – not to mention the rest of what Victor and I did. Why did I give in, time out of mind? Why did I accept that I couldn't ever be allowed to be with others, couldn't stray far from my own kind? And this endless, tedious *reincarnation.* Another Egyptian stuck-record. How I *wish now…* As the good doctor landed in the skip, Laura gazed at the moon, letting the scarab fall with him. The ring and necklace, having taken a shine to Laura, stayed with her as her outline shimmered and then vanished, free now and wholly self-forgiven, into the dreamy air of London after midnight.

For a second an old, a much older soul, also now freed, sighed, whispering thanks in a voice of dry grass and a language now lost, and was gone. Distantly, traffic honked. Eventually the dawn rose, paled and thought hard, but decided once more to occur.

13

Victor Winthrope entered the upper room. He saw the open window, and the small sarcophagus case lying on the table, denuded of its ancient lights. In the Court outside, a lorry craned and took away a skip. Oblivious to this sound and to all else, he kicked a pile of old books, sending up a cloud of votive dust, and sat heavily down at the scored and wobbly table, gnarled hands closing round the griffin on his cane. Then he laid the cane gently on the table, as a wizard might lay down his wand. He threw back his head and gazed blankly, eyes turning red.

He looked across, at length, catching sight of the forlorn and empty bottle of Tennessee whiskey on the carpet, walked to the window and peered up and down Fiddlers Court, where there was nothing remarkable to be seen. She didn't know about the jewellery. Doesn't matter, she obviously put up a fight. Always a powerful spirit, Laura. Where has he taken her? Killed her? Any attempts in that direction wouldn't end easily. But even the longest life must come to an end. Victor sat down once more, looking now significantly older, shrinking and sagging far down into himself. For hours he stayed still in the room, revolving possibilities, reaching dark conclusions. Some things were now at an end.

Books. How far can they really take you. In my case, around the globe. Around the worlds. Books moved me away from where, and from who, I was. Gave me an expanded awareness. This grew me. I suppose, too, it distracted me from reflecting on what it was that I was now becoming. And so I withdrew from the world, and in my wizard's tower I read more books, so as to become adept in transforming the outer reality from which, in the perpetual paradox of study, I had withdrawn. To study the world and understand it better, we pull back, let letters and pictures describe it for us. That old image of the world as a book that we read, just as it reads us. But now, enough of books? The ponderous folios, the black lettered quartos, the pretty little parchment-covered duodecimos. Victor fingered the pyramid of kicked and tumbled volumes, selecting a rodent-gnawed and funerary tome, bound in moss-green buckram. Some of the moss might have been real.

Turning the parchment, wavy with age, he turned over pictures both on the page and in his mind, of fire-demons, and the retribution that brings madness in its wake, before returning for the kill. Too medieval. Too elaborate. This calls for the straightforward, un-magical but ever so efficacious American bullet. Leaving the room and carefully descending the stair, he paused at the landing and knelt, stiffly, to unlock the equally old wooden chest, which held his old, but newly oiled, revolver.

- Mr Boxer.

- Sir.

- I need to see Felix Manto. And Miles Proctor. In no necessary order.

- Sir, might I…

- No. You might not.

- Is the game…?

- Up. Yes. The balloon is up. The last fair deal gone down. The game over, and the future for us, in London town at least, at zero.

- Very good, sir. With your permission then, I will begin…

- Yes. Begin it. Begin the end.

Mr Boxer stepped into another room, and with visible reluctance, searched for the key that would fit a certain lock, that would open the cupboard, that contained the shoulder holster, that would hold the gun, as together they moved to put an end to the house that Victor Winthrope had built.

14

Becky gazed at Miles, trying to read his sleeping features. Then she gasped. Not only was this the longest dream-trip he had ever undertaken, he was travelling alone. She examined his face so closely she could feel the soft wave of his breath. He was fading slightly. An ambiguous band of light, a body-halo, both emphasised his corporeal outline, and withdrew its clear boundaries. Miles was starting to fade.

Over the hills and far away, consciousness flickering inside a dream's dream, Miles was climbing the stone steps of a tower. At each full turn of the stair, he gazed out of the window to the land's horizon. Here, crazily out of synch, higgledy-piggledy, was every dream through whose doors he had travelled; the Empire State Building, rising proudly out of a Caribbean beach, shadowed by Art Deco buildings from the early phase of Hollywood: light falling through a slit in heavy curtains, onto a pyramid of books that talked amongst themselves. In his mind he heard laughter, and saw the letters *l a u g h t e r* play in green for a fugitive second in holiday skies. The sky was a tall mirror, now, in a New York hotel room, and the weather forecast said *afore ye go – storm brewing*, but was gone in two shakes of a lamb's tail before his answering and momentary shiver could complete itself. As the view to the horizon sprouted more buildings and waterways and detail, the tower itself inhaled and narrowed. Somewhere a clock tolled thirteen. Outside, the wind began to howl. The view disappeared in a wave of desert sand. His twisting tower held its own, inside a tornado. He felt he must, at last, surely, be nearing the top of his tower.

15

-   What have you done with Laura? Where have you taken her? And what do you intend to do with the jewels?

-   Now, hold on. I haven't taken Laura, or anyone, any-where, and I haven't even touched your frigging neck-lace. I don't like it. You know this. I didn't want anything to do with it. I didn't want to shoot the messenger, or anyone else.

-   You didn't want to do any work. Ever. Your contribution to the welfare of the organization stands at next to noth-ing. Close the window, Mr Boxer. You were supposed to be the action man, the do-er, the facilitator. You haven't performed. You just don't facilitate. Not one jot. It's over. It's *awl ovah.*

Mr Boxer's face was as white as a round, full moon at midnight. He stepped in front of Winthrope, who brushed him aside with a whispered 'enough'. Winthrope produced the revolver from his pocket, and shot Felix Manto in the chest.

Felix rocked on his heels, arms flailing, as blood pumped through the front of his white shirt. With a gasp that might have been the nearest a collapsed lung could summon by way of rebuke, he fell backwards into a chair and sprawled, paling and already beginning to die. Winthrope seized him by the hair, folding the convulsing upper body over the lower as much as he could, so as to muffle sound. The next shot was purposefully aimed. Felix made one last futile effort to pull himself free, far too late. One final shot. As this was going on, Mr Boxer winced and held his hands to the sides of his face. The aroma of blood and burnt flesh began to fill the room, as the erstwhile accomplice of the last two men standing began to stream and pool across the floor.

- Get that thing outa heah, then phone the contract cleaners, Boxer. Spotless Sisters, Maida Vale. And now for Master Proctor. Another work-shy fop.

And no doubt, Victor thought to himself as he began to descend the dark staircase ahead of Mr Boxer, it might have crossed your mind that it would occur to me, how you yourself might choose to finish this, by finishing me. But it will also have occurred to you, as no doubt it has so very many times before, that you don't have what it takes. You just don't have the moxie. And it was, in fact, only with the greatest regret, and a badly shaking hand, that Mr Boxer pulled his own gun from its shoulder holster and, able to hold it firmly only for a moment, pressed it to the back of Victor Winthrope's neck, closed his eyes, and fired. Winthrope slid gently over the banister like a falling raincoat. However, the loud crack as he hit the parquet on the ground floor a good three seconds later, offered adequate assurance that in bodily form at least, he was dead.

- Oh, oh, oh, oh, oh…

Mr Boxer, still holding the gun at arm's length as if it was a hot rattlesnake, and with eyes still tightly shut, stumbled down the stairs, throwing the weapon aside. It landed where his employer lay, unmoving. Nervously he stepped into the room where the camera obscura had brought intelligence of movements by the firm's employees sufficient to reassure Winthrope that his collapsing empire still remained under a modicum of control. Turning the dials, Boxer could only find an image of Becky, gazing with concern at what looked almost like a fading cartoon image of Miles Proctor. Tears came to his eyes, and he stood for a while, trembling and wringing his large white hands.

16

Miles climbed into the final room, at the top of the tower. The wind blew through open archer's windows in the stone. Ravens cawed and flew around the tower's tip, throwing brief shadows that chimed with the fitful yellow light of the surrounding storm. The storm blew leaves, the remnants of nests and webs around this space so small that Miles had to bend slightly, even at its centre. Here, on a narrow, high table, sheltered by a dome of glass, was a book. He knew, even as he carefully placed the covering dome to one side, that this was his book. Rubbing his eyes, he started to read the first page, which had changed once again.

17

Becky could no longer cope with this. She moved around the room, touching Miles' and her things, as if they or she were about to be surrendered, and never seen again. Crying, she put the raised fingers of both hands to her forehead, moved them to her single earring, then looked up and tried to compose herself. Pulling down a photograph album, she sat next to Miles, and flipped through page after page until she came across a photograph of his childhood home on the Fife coast. Gazing at it for a while, she grew pale and then slid towards sleep, her shoulder against Miles', or at least against the barely present outline of a shoulder, through which the weave of the sofa cover was now clearly visible.

But then she opened her eyes, and stared dead ahead. She couldn't do it. She couldn't travel without him.

18

The essence of Magic can be conveyed quite simply. Magic is effective action. Action of a single person, action by a group, it matters not. In one sense, it is no different from any other form of activity brought to a successful conclusion or to the next level of importance.

Consider the ships in the harbour, bringing back spices, as once they brought slaves. Consider the banks, and the clerks with their sober suits and side-whiskers, scratching with quill on parchment, seated on high stools. Think of their masters and overseers, kings of the counting-house, the cheques drawn and the sovereigns minted, and ask yourself – on what foundation does this great edifice rest? Confidence. The sober and judicious soldier ants, making their daily pilgrimage across London Bridge, are capital's agents of trust. The bankers are confidence men. The letters and numbers on the cheque, signs, swirling or straight, that so-and-so promises to pay the bearer, or may rest secure in the knowledge that such-and-such is the sum, the outcome, of other numbers and signs and activities: what is this, but an ant-heap of mutual belief? The figures and signs in themselves mean – precisely nothing. So it is with Magic.

Miles looked up. He thought about The Book, and about books, and concluded that they were the boat, or the ferryman, but not the destination. He thought that there was a paradox in books, which showed in words and pictures the larger reality from which silent reading had actually withheld the reader. He thought he had reached the top of his tower, and that it was time to go home. But, where is that place, where is home, now?

19

Felix came to, groaning. Attempting to get to his feet, he slithered in several pints of his own blood, cracking the back of his head on the bare boards. For a few minutes he remained supine, wincing regularly and trying to reassemble moments of sequential memory. He unbuttoned his wet shirt a little, and ran his finger down the skinny necktie. Damn, ruined. Eventually he managed a sitting position, legs akimbo, from which he gleaned that the loss of blood alone would have been sufficient to kill, even discounting the effects of the bullets, one of which he could feel, like grit, way down in his lung, while a second was lodged in his spine, having ploughed a fair-sized furrow, *en route*. A burning sensation deep in one shoulder suggested that the most painful of the three was also the one that had caused the least damage.

I hate being shot. Getting too old for it. Takes too long to heal – up to an hour or more, these days, just to get the volume of blood back up to optimal. And I just totally, majorly *hate* getting killed. Death really is the worst thing that can happen to a body, no two ways about it. Almost always you have to grow bits of yourself back, and you don't always know which bits, until you try some physical manoeuvre or other and find yourself suddenly leaking all over the carpet, or your lady friend. Recovery from death can be truly embarrassing. This is the last taboo, you just cannot talk about it.

Having to keeping things buttoned up sure doesn't help. A problem shared is a problem halved and all that. But who do *you* know who'd share and share alike, on this one? Personally, I am convinced there's such a thing as post-death stress disorder. Reckon I've had it twice. My problem is, I don't know enough people with comparable experience to build a statistically viable data-base. There's no big data, not on this one. Most of the dead stay that way. And just going on anecdotal evidence, I'd say over fifty per cent are content with that arrangement. No, more than fifty. Sixty five, maybe? Maybe.

Dizzy. Blood rushing back to my head. OK. Blood is good, I need more, keep it coming. Now how about the feet. No real feeling in my back paws yet.

Guess I'll lay here a little longer. No other sounds of life in London's premier bookstore.

Now there's a project. Wasn't ever much of a writer, but I could write *the* book on this one. Seems to me there are plenty of wind-filled paperbacks in the Mind, Body, Spirit section of the bookstore with titles like Coping with Bereavement. I never saw a single one called Coping with Death II – the Comeback. What was it they called our horny President? The Comeback Kid. Bet he never came the way that I just came.

I don't get what's with the tunnel, the so-called route to the beyond, not really. Why do I have to go on seeing people beckoning me on, cheering me on into the clear white light. Anyone who reads my book, I'll tell you; when you die, don't forget to pack those Ray-Bans. The clear white light is like full-on headlights, but completely filling your field of vision. It's so pure it's painful. Particularly when you've only just got used to the tunnel, which is pretty dark. Clean, though, I have to say. Every time I died the tunnel was real clean. A little slippy, but you never seem to lose your footing. And height-wise, it's manageable. A lot of problems hit you on the journey to death, but oddly enough claustrophobia isn't one of them.

Unless you're buried alive, of course. But then that's a twist in the tail, a difficulty to do with the end of life, not the beginning of death. People think Edgar Allan Poe was weird. Well he was weird, no two ways, but not about that. Plenty of folks in Poe's time, mid-nineteenth century, would ask to be buried with a little bell, on a rope. Bell above ground, end of the rope down in the coffin. So that if a serious mistake had been made, you could yank your rope, and grieving sister Agatha or a loitering sexton would, hopefully, facilitate your unexpected reprise. Rather than dancing a mazurka on your grave, shouting *I get the house! I get the inheritance! Just die – die, Ephraim, and stay dead!* But anyways, where were we. Actually, the worst outcome would be, you're down in the hole, they gave you the bell and the rope, but in the process of lowering the coffin, the end of the rope is twitched out of your hand. So you know sister Agatha's up there, weeping. You know the gravedigger is leaning on the handle of his spade, bored and ready to assist. Bobbie the new terrier is scrabbling at the earth – he knows there's a juicy bone or two down there, just doesn't know exactly how juicy. But they can't hear you. And your hand is just *this* far away from the rope. An inch away from the rope. Wouldn't that be terrible.

Well Felix, for a man who doesn't care for reading, you surely betray some of the characteristics of the literary South. Well Felix two, I do believe you're right. Always been sure there was more than one Felix. Overlaid, neatly, like cards in a pack. Some differences – dark as the Ace of Spades me, jumping Jack of Diamonds me, me the King of Hearts, Felix the Joker, the dunce – but the differences only show on the outside. In here, it's me. Again. Maybe that's why I can't die. Yet. How many cards I got left? We'll see. I'm always slightly different though, each time I come back. The same yet not the same. Last time I didn't care for reading, only music, then cocaine hit. This time feels different. Well I'll be damned. Of all the things to happen. I think I might have come back as an omnivorous reader, just as Redidivus goes under.

You haven't performed. You just don't facilitate. Man, that really hurt. More than getting shot. A year of propping that guy up. Kind of hard to facilitate, Victor, when your boss is several hundred years old, and has got to that querulous late stage of life where it's hard to share. And has totally lost the ability to hear. I knew he was on his last legs. If Boxer's had the gumption, he'll have popped him over the edge before he gets to Miles. Only thing I had in common with Mr Boxer – we both liked, both like, Miles. You have to cut the youngsters some slack. But would he? Would he have the spine? Not a fan of decisive action, Mr Boxer. And not at all keen on the sight of blood. He wouldn't like it in here, *chez Felix.* My legs are wet. Good – feeling returning. Let's try. *Oof!* OK, I'll stay a little longer. I love gazing at this ceiling.

So, yeah, the tunnel is clean. But why do I have to keep taking that journey, when all concerned know I'm only going to have to turn round and come back down again? First time, when the motor failed and I brought the chopper down, OK, I thought, you imagine that the approach to death is going to take a certain direction, look a certain way, that you'll populate it with the images from your life that you brought along with you. Personal hopes, upbringing, all that stuff. Cultural assumptions. You're brought up to imagine angels clothed in white and playing the harp, so va-va-voom, you see a blonde chick in a Holiday Inn bathrobe strumming a harp. Seen a few of those in my time. Maybe not the harp.

So, first time, tunnel and then pure white light. Fine, I read about this in magazines, so sure, this is what I'm seeing now. How I Survived my Near-Death Experience. But by the time I got caught in the fishing lines and fell in Loch Soutar? And drowned? I mean come on. I don't believe, deep down, that the tunnel and the pure white light thing is real. I think it's a funny kind of film set. Disguising the real state of affairs. Other people who haven't died, they believe there's a tunnel. I died four times so far in my life – five, counting today – and I don't think I believe in the tunnel, not any more. Irrational, on both sides. Confused? If you thought living was confusing, dying'll really blow your mind.

And then I finally get to the other end, and it's never my mother or my father – whoever he was – it's these musicians I worked with when they were alive, and they all shout *Hi Felix! It's us! Go back Fee, it ain't your time! I'd turn back if I were you. Back you go, man, no peace for the wicked…*and they're all laughing. I've had it up to here with those guys. That lousy fingerpicker from Fort Worth who electrocuted himself on stage, and took half our equipment down with him. Musicians! Jokers.

No, Boxer won't do it. I feel so…so not good about this. Let's cough the lunger up first. Then I got to get to Miles before Winthrope does.

Felix groaned his way to verticality, and after hawking until his face turned multiple hues, coughed up a bullet. Well that was a golden oldie. That gun must be straight out of Zane Grey. Now let's try a little yoga. Moving one hand down, and the other up, his back, the dead rock star turned dead magician grimaced as he tapped repeatedly on his spine, jerking his head back and forth. Another bullet fell through the circle scorched in his clothing and bounced along the floorboards. Careful, now. But not a sound could be heard, apart from the traffic in Charing Cross Road. With his right hand he attempted to probe his left shoulder. Nope. Too painful. That one might require medical attention. Felix made his way successfully down the stairs, but the bullet in his shoulder left him unable to turn his head. Consequently he missed the sight of his erstwhile employer lying stonily dead, and moved as quickly as he was able to find and warn Miles Proctor.

20

Having washed down his Friday night chicken vindaloo with the last of a six-pack, Malcolm Coates was idly watching the end of the Channel 4 News. That man's ties are enough to bring on hallucinations. Speaking of which. Humming a riff by the late great Felix Manto, Malcolm went through the pockets of his rucksack until he located the ancient tin, once receptacle of cough lozenges, now the home of his stash. What remained of it. Malcolm rolled a last fat spliff, and started flipping the zapper.

A documentary on the revival of interest in steam trains caught his attention. From the Brecon Beacons to the cathedral towns of the Home Counties, enthusiasts are banding together to resurrect the golden age of steam. Well, I can see the appeal. Here was the Flying Something, paused to take on water at Somewhere. There was the driver, waving cheerily, a rubicund and whiskery individual, appropriately Victorian. Odd. Just for a moment his face seemed to morph into a truly horrible gremlin, like a stone gargoyle, only salmon-pink. Look, there it is again. He's – it's – laughing. And *slavering.* And now he's starting the train while families and geeks with cameras are still milling around on the track and, good grief, there goes the Vicar! He's bifurcated the village ecclesiast! But now he's all whiskery and normal again and the credits are rolling, and it's goodbye from Nether Shalford and the Great South Eastern Revival Railway. Come on: how much did I put in that one? Malcolm visited the bathroom for normal purposes, but, peering into the mirror, discerned nothing stranger than reddened eyes, in somewhat acned skin. I've been working too hard on that blooming thesis.

He sat down again, and watched in a vague way a soap. Idly turning the erstwhile tin of cough lozenges in his fingers, Malcolm felt something inside the small cellophane bag inside. Strange. I thought that that had been, as the saying goes, the end of that. Fishing with finger and thumb produced a small circular chunk of black resin, with the letters Barlinnie Bazaar just visible in tiny raised lettering. Well, well. Now where did you spring from…?

Bloody hell! One hit and he was coughing as if about to expire. Barlinnie Bizarre, more like! Ow! He stubbed the joint out on the tin lid, sending sparks flying and, gasping, ransacked the kitchen area in search of Coca Cola, eventually settling for tap water, a pint of which he gargled gratefully, feeling that smoke must be coming out of his ears. Uuurrh. That's better. Kids, just say no to drugs. Panting heavily, he sat down on the sofa, where this day's episode of *Hanley Close* was winding its way towards conclusion.

Steve's daughter Tracey had run off with Lincoln Steers, the new landlord of the *Fox and Firkin,* while Steve had crashed his car and half killed himself while evading the police after ferrying stolen goods for Darren, because he owed him one, except that he didn't, because although he didn't know this, Darren and Steve's missus

Karen – Darren and Karen, how likely was that – were about to announce that they were going to Australia to start a new life, the actor Jamie Ransom who played Darren being, if the *Sun*'s allegations were true, written out of the series because of unspecified bad behaviour, though the paparazzi's unflattering shots of him lying in the gutter at 3 a.m. outside Biloxi's in Camden wreathed in sick appeared to give the first half, if not the whole game, away. So all of this was pretty much par for the course in the last ten minutes of a soap, except that Darren, Karen, Lincoln, Steve and even Mike the bodybuilder and Gemma not to mention her new baby were all now hooded, wearing robes smeared with blood in the shape of a pentagram, and gathering at the end of Hanley Close in old Mrs Manifold's back garden to worship at the altar of the Goat of Mendes.

Good grief, how can they show a goat doing *that* on prime time TV? Can goats *do* that, anyway? And now the goat's playing the flute or something, while still doing the other, don't make me laugh. Except that it did make Malcolm laugh hysterically, great floods of uncontrollable mirth that had him rolling on the floor, howling with lung-emptying convulsions, filling the room with a green miasma in which the letters *l a u g h t e r* were briefly visible, though not to Malcolm who was mentally elsewhere, so that he entirely failed to see the letters *w e a r e c o m i n g t o g e t y o u* pricked out in a green cloud, in fading gothic script. Eventually, having calmed himself sufficiently to once more assay the sofa, which now felt like climbing the side of a mountain in a high wind, Malcolm clung for support to the sofa's arm. The arm turned first into a giant hashish pipe whose brass and clay curves delineated, amid violets and leaves of vine, more goats doing more things, and then turned into a hairy, over-sized and bad-smelling portion of a real goat, after which Malcolm had to go and be unwell for a while, waking up groaning on the bathroom floor as the ceiling spun and puckered or made itself cunningly five-fold.

Taking infinite care, Malcolm crawled on hands and knees back into the living room and up the side of the mountain, which felt more accommodating this time. Indeed, the lights now dimmed subtly of their own accord, as Dr Proctor's PhD student found himself watching an old film, in point of fact *Blue Murder at St Trinian's*, in comforting black and white. Malcolm hoped for an innocuous cinematic romp from a more innocent world, all spivs and anarchy and car chases, followed by restorative sleep.

He had never realized before just how uncanny was the resemblance between the bald, heavy-eyed male actor Alastair Sim, who, wearing drag, played the Headmistress, and his near namesake, the dark magus Aleister Crowley. Curious too was the marked resemblance between the new young tutor, for whom all the pretty sixth formers had fallen hook, line and sinker, and Miles Proctor. Here, after the handsome young supply teacher had failed to engage the attention of the class, at least in ways demanded by the curriculum, he asked a pretty blonde creature with a startling resemblance to the now departed Mandy Smitten (PhD) to stay behind for an extra lesson. And what a lesson it proved to be! Not for the first time that evening, Malcolm found himself wondering how such things could be aired, not only on a Friday evening before the modern equivalent of a covered piano leg, the nine o'clock watershed, but in a film made fifty years ago for a family audience.

More alarming still was his deepening conviction that this *was* Mandy Smitten, and that the now amorous young tutor really was played by Miles Proctor, moonlighting from the academy, an outrage further compounded by the tutor's reading aloud, in tones of parody and ridicule, sections of Malcolm's own incomplete doctoral thesis, each page torn out, balled and binned, while Mandy writhed in adoration on her tutor's lap. And, oh no! Not little Heather Macmillan too! A first year undergraduate, for whom he felt a sentimental affection he hardly dared concede, let alone act on, for Malcolm the teacher was a decent and kindly soul, was now doing something that could by extrapolation have been termed kindly, but which hardly fell into what most would deem the decent category, with first Miles and then Mandy and now, oh no! with a dexterity that suggested, *inter alia*, digital manipulation unavailable to the medium of cinema in austerity Britain – both!

-   *Aye, son. Ye're shocked, I can tell. Believe me, I'm shocked, too. I'm like you. I cannae stomach demeaning behaviour like this, which reduces us sentient beings to the status of mere animals. Although an affliction of the eyes prevents me from viewing this montage of debauchery, I thank the powers that be for shielding me from such soul-soiling ordure.*

The screen was now filled by the hairless dome and spaniel gaze of Alastair the actor, or Aleister, the wickedest man in the world. Malcolm's interpretation ran intuitively to the second, though the headmaster's tones were melancholy and properly righteous. Little Heather Macmillan! How could he! Yes, here was the pensive voice of morality restored. A voice you could trust.

-   *Is it not a dreadful, dreadful thing, to so abuse the author-ity of the dominie in this callow and disgraceful way? With tender young chicks like Heather Macmillan, poor wee Heather, and the doubtless more worldly yet redeemable Dr Smitten – who, by the way, I am reliably informed, was ready to accept a proposal of matrimony from your good self, followed by an offer to willingly abandon her deluded New World fantasies, her so-called tenure-track professorship, in favour of a real job! Teaching Catering Studies, part-time, in a College of Further Education not ten minutes' walk from your present lodgings! Think of it, Malc. Your bower of bliss! 'Cottage pie tonight, Malcy? Or will it be spaghetti Bolognese?' Domestic bliss, on a plate. So to speak. Until she was dissuaded by the tempter, Proc-tor, the low-cal lounge lizard, who so derided your efforts and undermined your reputation... I can hardly bear to continue...hardly dare repeat the things he told her...your confession to him, that you have actually never…oh, Malcy Malc Malcolm…*

Malcolm was beside himself. He stared red-faced at the television, which projected powerful and shame-fuelled images on to the back of his retina, that flowed invisibly down the ganglia and other pathways of his cerebral architecture, to fester in the chambers of the heart.

- *Duty calls, Malcolm. Do it, for the sake of Higher Education in England. Do it, for wee Heather Macmillan. Kill Miles Proctor. Kill Miles Proctor! KILL MILES PROCTOR! KILL MILES PROCTOR!*

The screen was now filled with the pretty female sixth formers of St Trinians, swinging their legs back and forth, left over right, right over left, as they swarmed on to the tiered benches of a gymnasium, many of them scantily clad, as is appropriate in a vigorous sporting engagement, kohl-ringed eyes boring through the screen as they chanted the narrowed parameters of Malcolm's destiny. Not that he needed encouraging. Glassy-eyed, he stood up and moved rigidly towards the door, the words of righteous revenge still ringing in his ears. Kill Miles Proctor! Kill Miles Proctor!

- *Aye, and just one more thing, Malc. Afore ye go. Proctor has a book. An old book. It's called* Transmutations. *He stole it from me. Can you get it back? I hate to ask. But if you could just kill him and then get my old book back. Thanks a million. It has a few old recipes I want to try. Perhaps the aroma of the barbie, the sacrificial lamb, will tickle the appetite of my current Line Manager, contactable at, now where's that card, ThePrinceOfThisWorld dot com. To expedite my flight into the next. What a shame, eh. Good luck, you little shit. Good luck to both of us.*

Malcolm had departed, leaving the door unlocked, a zombie, uncaring. The TV, which was unplugged, carried on singing and raving to itself until with a green flash the colour box blew, as did the lights throughout Malcolm's flat, and in his reason.

21

Where do I get a gun on a Friday night. Town? Night clubs? Too dangerous. Town and gown friction. I know, I'll ask at the Porter's Lodge, in the College. Maybe the Head Porter has a gun he could lend me.

The zombie, his Mohawk waving slightly in the night air, was recognized by the cat who lived on scraps from the College kitchens, saved from expulsion or worse by a reputation as a mouser, which a comfortably hairy undercarriage, almost dragging on the ground, seemed at first sight to belie. The tabby cat, perhaps irrationally, thought of Malcolm, who often paused to greet and stroke, as another, taller cat. This time he walked straight past, unseeing eyes homing in on a dark future. Please yourself, thought the cat. We all get funny moods. Malcolm walked on.

In the Lodge the Night Porter was gazing into the *Sun*. Behind him, closed circuit television offered four contrasting views of life in College. In the first screen Italian summer school students were busy pouring diluted washing-up liquid down the stairs of Malcolm's Hall of Residence. In the second, two medical students retaking exams following an incident of plagiarism could be glimpsed in the bicycle sheds sharing a used needle, while a third trainee healthcare professional slid quietly down the wall and into the land of Nod. In the next screen, cars stolen by kids in town could be seen drag-racing round the statue of Jeremy Bentham not a minute's walk from the Porter's Lodge, whose occupant remained oblivious due to the high volume of his own portable television, not to mention complete lack of interest. The fourth screen showed briefly the steel-capped toe of a boot, then went blank. The Porter glanced back at the CCTV a split second after these images had cut to sunlit publicity shots of the College gardens in late Spring.

Sighing, he turned to scrutinise Malcolm, who he thought looked a little the worse for wear, and whose tonsorial demeanour grated on a man of his generation.

-      A gun. I need a gun.

-      Wotcher want a gun for? You ain't gonna shoot the Principal, are you?

-      No. I'm going to shoot my research supervisor.

The Porter relaxed visibly.

-      Right. Friday night. Let's have a think. Try Matron.

He raised one eyebrow in the general direction of the next floor up. Malcolm walked out of the lodge, posture erect and mind diamond-focussed.

He knocked on Matron's door. She bade him enter. As the first casualties of the night were unlikely to begin queuing until at least an hour after the clubs had opened, and as the new term had not yet begun, Matron was perfecting her solitaire, while decorously sipping at a pint of sherry, housed in the right hand drawer of her desk; beneath this and the left drawer her immense lower limbs were jammed.

A lightly moustachioed, obese icon of College life, who broke wind without fail on the quarter hour, Matron, who had no medical training whatsoever, divided the student population into those whose condition improved markedly under threat of physical examination, and those whose parents took one look on Induction Day and made arrangements for their offspring in the private sector. That left only the odd visitor to the College with a sprain or a fit of the vapours, and the weekend club casualties, in anticipation of whose entry Matron had made a half-hearted attempt to locate the sticking plaster, top up the Uncle Joe's Mint Balls jar with a pick'n'mix of poppers, paracetomol and pethidine, and cover, albeit in a scatter-gun way, the consulting room carpet in sheets of white kitchen roll.

- I need a gun. The Porter sent me.

Matron had always liked the look of Malcolm.

- I'll have to do a full physical. Can't have an unfit person stalking the College armed and dangerous now, can we?

- No! No! Take your hands off me! No! Stop!

Twenty minutes later, Malcolm emerged, walking a little stiffly. This was in part due to reasons best left unexplained, and partly due to the weight of the handguns bulging from his jacket pockets. Walking out into the night, he passed by the west side of the main building unremarked, save by the cat, who looked at him green-eyed and quizzically in the dark. He spotted the Principal leaving his office late and hoping to avoid human contact. Malcolm, who had never handled a firearm before, weighed the benefits of a dress rehearsal. He reached down quickly while there was still time, produced a revolver, and aiming a trifle nervously at the Principal's back view, pulled the trigger. Nothing. Malcolm peered closely down the barrel with one eye, and squeezed the trigger again, hard. Still nothing. Reluctantly, he trudged back to the first floor of the main building, and knocked on Matron's door.

- Matron! It's Malcolm! I need bullets!

- Bullets is extra.

22

Having showered, removed external traces of his old blood supply, and feeling sufficient indications of having topped up the new tank, Felix Manto sat in his car, trying to recapture what he could of Miles' home life and likely current whereabouts. All he knew for certain was that Miles had an office in Beltane College. Thither he drove.

The floodlit Victorian monstrosity bore scant resemblance to any College Felix had ever seen. It was a hive of activity this Friday evening, not all of it collegial. An improvised barbecue on the sports pitch sent infernal red flickers up the eastern wall, where, from the highest gothic pinnacle, some wag was bungee jumping and narrowly evading death at the hands of one of the joyriders from town who circled the main buildings, brakes squealing, filling the air with drum and bass. A fire alarm sounded from a distant building, though pursuant engines were nowhere to be seen. Felix shuddered, and made his way to what he took to be the Porter's Lodge. Here an old man slept, face down in a plastic tray of French fries, his snores rippling the pages of a tabloid.

Behind him a closed circuit television system haplessly replayed evidence that higher education in the south of England was defiantly alive, if not unequivocally well. The institution's Cerberus jerked into wakefulness, and swivelled his head in time to see four pleasing representations of the College taken in successive seasons, all when the student population was absent. Wildly he turned to face Felix.

- Would you have a home address for Dr Miles Proctor?

- Never 'eard of 'im.

- Miles Proctor. One of your faculty. He teaches Victorian Literature.

- No Proctors here. We're not supposed to give out home addresses. Tell you where his office is. Five pounds.

Felix pondered several options, some with dramatically physical outcomes, but given the urgency of the situation and his own still diminished resources, he produced a billfold.

- Bertrand Russell, fifth floor. He won't be there, though.

- Home address?

- We're not supposed to give out home addresses. Anyway, I ain't got it. What kind of place do you think this is.

- Directions to Bertrand Russell?

Felix raced up the stairs. Maybe there would be some indication of the home address, somewhere in Miles' office. Locked. But nobody's around. He shiggled the door open with a credit card, and entered, switching on the light.

Five minutes later, a figure in camouflage made its slow way with studied erectness up the same staircase. It had never occurred to the figure that his research supervisor had much of a home life, beyond tonight's revelations of a second life in black and white blue movies. Like most students, the figure had assumed that tutors existed mostly in their offices, or in the library. Running into your supervisor in Tesco was slightly shocking, only marginally less so than tonight's movie. The figure paused in front of Miles Proctor's office. The light was on, and movement was visible through the smoked glass set in the top half of the door. Malcolm Coates reached into his jacket, produced two revolvers, kicked the door open, and fired.

23

- I can't see!

The stone at the end of the tunnel had just been rolled back in place, sealing it and removing the final, thinning crescent of pure white light. Voices were audible, at a remove, arguing.

- It's me! Felix! Felix Manto!

- *Felix? Not again? No way, he's gone and died again? Already? Somebody get the pure white light back on, pronto. What do you mean, the generator's packed up? You let that guy from Fort Worth near it? Idiot!*

- I know you're there. I can hear you. I can't see. I'm coming up the tunnel. Ow!

- *Don't move, you might fall and break something. Stay calm, Felix. Focus on your breathing. Breathe in, breathe out. Breath out for longer than you breath in. Attaboy. We'll be right with you. Nah, it's dead as disco. Shit. Run up the emergency lighting.*

There was a humming, an unpromising crackle, and then the emergency lighting came on in the tunnel. It flickered fitfully, but offered enough illumination to cause Felix to exhale with relief, and continue his walk. Storm lanterns hung at intervals, connected by sagging wires, while green fluorescent arrows, peeling depictions of a figure running and EXIT signs pointed out, redundantly, the way. It occurred fleetingly to Felix that the signs ought perhaps to read ENTRANCE. If he ended up staying this time, he'd suggest it. So the tunnel's built of brick. Odd, never noticed that before. But then it's always been dark this end, pure white light at the other, the previous times I died. It's like the big rides at Disneyland or Universal City. The first time, it's exhilarating. So much faster and higher than when you were a kid. The second time, you start to watch how it's done, see chains and things out of the corner of your eye. Third time, you're bored. Well I'm bored with dying. Bored *of* dying, as the kids say these days. Been there, done that, got the blood-stained tee shirt. Twice in one day, this time. Man alive.

- Anybody there? Welcoming party?

Felix flicked the top of his Zippo lighter, and held it aloft. Just brick. The remains of a poster for the Wash & Brush Up Co., a torn photo of industrial cleaning equipment and a toll-free number. He called out again. With a growl, the stone was slowly rolled. The light that filtered through was light, for certain, but not especially pure, or white. A bit like daylight, in fact. Felix could hear birdsong, a lawnmower cutting in and out, distant traffic. Cool fresh air – or air-con, hard to tell – and somewhere a dog barking. The sound of an approaching ice-cream van. The long-haired guys in the entrance with their thumbs in their blue jeans looked a little sheepish.

- *Hate to do this to you, Fee, but so far, no further. You ain't even dead, this time.*

- How do you know?

- *Come on, we got CCTV, same as everywhere else. Where you been. No, you're alive, all right. But Fee, you ain't gonna like what you see, when you come round, OK? Brace yourself. Stop laughing, Ralph. This isn't funny.*

- What do you mean?

- *There's a woman the size of a grizzly bear with a moustache giving you the kiss of life. But don't be hard on her, it's working. She's a real professional. See you later. We got to stop meeting like this.*

- Look, seriously, this is a set, right? I mean, come *on*, deep breath and count to three - is there or is there not life after death? Assuming I do finally get to die… Tell me! Please! I've been here and back so many times. I have a right to know!

A muffled confabulation followed. *You tell him, you got us into this mess.* An all-thumbs guitarist from Fort Worth with a lightning streak of white in a vintage 1970s Afro was nudged abruptly to the front. He cleared his throat, put both thumbs in the pocket of his jeans, and searched for the right words.

- *Hey now. Where to begin, y'all. Course, in a basic sense there's life after death. Energy can't never die. It can move, change shape, whatever. But it can't never die. Life after *death? Well, there's a heap of different factors in play here, I mean partly it depends what kind of life y'all made – that might have a bearing on where y'all headed next. Somewhere over the rainbow, well maybe, but for other folks…somewhere else. There are some confused people, damaged goods. Down too deep where the dark things are. They don't adapt easily. Cause a deal of mayhem. Wandering, for a ver' long time. Can it Ralph, I'm losin' my train of thought… Need to start this number again, from the beginning…*

- So let me get this straight. There *is* life after death. I think that's what you're saying.

- *Well there's one crucial aspect they don't ever tell you about. You need to hear this. First thing that happens, after you die, you'll wake up looking out over a…*

At this point the lights crackled and went out, followed by the amplification. Then everything came back on again, but in fits and starts.

- *…so you take the key, not the first key but the new one, and this is the really important bit…*

- I can't hear you! The sound keeps cutting out!

- *…and you have to do this with your right hand, even if you're left-handed, or the gate that leads into the garden won't open…*

- Start again! Please. Please! You're fading…

- *…and repeat that exact phrase, three times. But then, the really totally unexpected and amazing thing is that - and it's kinda wonderful - after you've…*

But now Felix too was fading. Fading, passing out, and coming to.

As he faded out for the final time, a striding bat-eared silhouette, who had come to see how the other dead half live, trudged silent and thoughtful in his footsteps, trying to fade when he faded, coming back when he came to, hoping, wistfully, willing a real end.

In A Silent Way

1

Felix came back to consciousness, with a start. An enormous visage was gulping in air, prior to bearing down on him again.

- Thanks, but I don't think there's any need. No, really. Please!

After he had woozily found his feet, carefully felt or examined himself top to toe in the corridor bathroom and performed a quick inspection of Miles' office, Felix was reassured to find that any reports of his second demise would have been greatly exaggerated, not that he would be so ungrateful as to point this out to the visage. Of the two bullets fired by Malcolm Coates, one had grazed the side of his head, the shock of which, coming on top of his death not so long before, had been sufficient to bring on a fainting spell. The other bullet had caromed off a bust of Coleridge before hitting, sideways on, the contents of Miles' book-lined wall. There it had buried itself about two hundred pages into Stephen Hawking's *A Brief History of Time*, with a celerity denied the casual reader.

Meanwhile Malcolm was trying to bury himself in shame, hugging his knees as close to his forehead as the intervening abdominal quantum would allow, while his shoulders shook as if trying to escape. *First I set out to kill my academic hero, then I mess it up and nearly kill my musical hero. Who's dead anyway. I think. I mess everything up. I can't even tell whether other people are alive or dead, anymore. I'll never amount to anything. Miles, you were right to tear my thesis up. I ought to tear it up myself. I don't blame you for –* but then he rewound his evening to *Blue Movie at St Trinian's*, and entertained his first wholly rational thought for some hours. *When you come to think about it, there was something a bit odd going on there.*

- Matron? The guy whose office this is. Dr Proctor. His life is in danger. Much more than mine just was. We need to get to him. It's not clear where he lives, and the Porter…

- You can forget the Porter. I know where he lives, though, Miles Proctor. Seen *him* loads of times.

Matron giggled, disturbing the air circulating in the room. She continued, dreamily.

- On account of my boyfriend. He's a twitcher.

- I get restless legs at night myself. You may have to consider separate sleeping arrangements…

- No, no. A *twitcher*. A birdwatcher. So he has powerful binoculars. And things. *Things.*

She laughed more heartily, causing the door to bang shut.

- So I seen him loads. That Miles. And his bird, don't know her name…

- Address?

- Upstairs flat in one of them terraces diagonally opposite the Captain's bedroom. In Camden, obviously.

- *Camden.* OK. We're getting somewhere.

A half an hour later Matron was knuckling on the Captain's door the secret Morse Code signal that would bring her paramour to answer, knowing it was she, and not the landlord or some other agent of negativity come tapping. The door was opened by a man in full naval uniform, aged somewhere between twenty five and seventy, with a parrot on his shoulder, riding a wooden, electrically-powered scooter, which allowed him to glide silently from point to point, standing, both feet on a circular panel, hands and handles at hip height.

He beckoned them into his bedroom, where an array of telescopes and binoculars facilitated absorbing views of the night sky, and, as Felix could see with rising distaste, activities taking place within all lit and un-curtained rooms over a considerable radius. While the parrot hopped from his shoulder and perched on the windowsill, adjusting with its claw a powerful telescope the better to gaze at the stars, the Captain homed in on Miles' and Becky's apartment, where the latter could be seen through binoculars in a curious posture alone on the sofa, wearing a statuesque attitude of concern. Keen for multiple reasons to get away, Felix grabbed Malcolm, whose chin was buried in his chest, by the arm, and dragged him back to life. Lifting Matron off the ground and on to his board as if she were as light as a treasured feather, the Captain scooted gallantly to the door, bidding a cheery goodbye to Felix and Malcolm with a silent wave, as his now medically empowered companion blew good-luck kisses. This disturbed the air currents in the hallway, slamming their door firmly shut behind them.

2

- Becky, this is Malcolm Coates. Malcolm, Becky Morrell.

- I'm sorry I tried to kill Miles. He's such a great research supervisor, and I feel dreadful. I only did it after a weird man who looked like Aleister Crowley but with a Scottish accent…

Becky and Felix exchanged a significant look. There are 23,666 weird men in the world who look like Aleister Crowley and have a Scots accent, but they knew which one he meant, instantly.

- …who looked like Aleister Crowley but with a Scottish accent appeared on my television to offer consolation and some kind of hope for moral equilibrium after unsolicited pornography had undone my sense of right and wrong. Not that the dope helped. I've decided I'm going to give it up.

Becky and Felix both opted for a glance expressive of sobriety commended, and maturity recognized.

- No, I really am, I'm going to give up watching television. There's never anything good on, not really. And it'll help me get my thesis finished. Maybe, if I finish, if I get the PhD, Mandy…Mandy would…

Malcolm looked brokenly at his dead hero and his erstwhile would-be victim's girlfriend. The latter, privately of the view that Mandy, whoever she was, probably wouldn't, no, not ever, not in a million years, summoned a gesture of quasi-maternal concern. This worked only too well, causing Malcolm to sluice tears down her front at a rate of knots, while Becky's widening eyes sent up distress flares over his heaving shoulder. Eventually closing the floodgates, and after peering thoughtfully down her cleavage for signs of hope in a fallen world, Malcolm was assailed by his second rational assessment of the situation.

- You're dead, Felix.

Any element of gaucherie here was mitigated by the doe-eyed hero worship shining in Malcolm's gaze, as he looked to Felix for answers while keeping one trembling hand on Becky's bottom. She gently urged his hand elsewhere. Perhaps tautologically, he added:

- But you're here, Felix.

Becky shot a look of bafflement at the resurrected, who opened his mouth wordlessly at Malcolm, who blew his nose with more force than accuracy into the hankie Becky proffered, covertly, or so he hoped, merging the excess into the hospitably muddy green of his camouflage jacket. Everyone moved back a step.

Miles' physical presence on the sofa was now reduced to a body-shaped indentation in the corduroy. While Becky explained to Felix that Miles had gone back in time to the Dream Pool in order to resolve the mystery of his father's amnesia, Felix wondered aloud if it would be better for one of them, perhaps he as senior partner, to dive after him, and whether the combination of them both trying would bestow maximum powers of leverage in the dream world. Malcolm listened, pinching himself mentally. He was even less sure that he had completely exhaled, following his earlier inhalations, when the other two explained to him that they were going to stare in silence at some photographs of the Fife coast, which might cause one or both of them to disappear, but would, if all went well, assist in bringing Miles Proctor back to Camden. Unable to stifle the self-centred thought that if Miles didn't come back, then he, Malcolm, would be without a research supervisor, and would therefore probably never finish his thesis and so have even less of a chance with Mandy Smitten (PhD), Malcolm agreed vociferously that trying to disappear through photographs into bygone Fife in order to retrieve Miles from the mysteries of his upbringing had to be worth a go.

The two troubled savants focussed on ageing snaps. Becky, clearly unable to concentrate, kept glancing over at Felix, whose increasing pallor and insane stare were hardly reassuring.

- It's been a long day, Becky. And a very odd one. I've got a bullet in my shoulder giving me gyp…

- I thought Malcolm missed.

-    This was Winthrope.

Malcolm looked terrified. Sinking into gloom, Becky gestured silently to Felix that they needed to speak privately, in the kitchen. They left the room.

Whatever was occupying them was taking its time, Malcolm thought, idly reaching over to leaf through the album. A strange idea, yes, but strangely logical, that by focussing on a representation of a place or a person, you could transport yourself to that place, or be with that person. He used to look at the moon, sometimes, and hope that even if Mandy wasn't thinking of him at that moment, she might be looking at the same moon at the same time, somehow bringing them into sublunary contact, as a substitute for other forms of contact thus far denied him.

It was all about bringing things together – wasn't there some experiment? Chemistry? No, it was Physics. Malcolm thought himself back into Form 3B, peering up, baffled, from a lab bench, while Mr Winterbottom poured potassium of permanganate into a flask of water, or rattled on about Archimedes. The first fifteen trooped past the window, some raising a two-fingered salute behind the back of the excited scientist. That if you put two objects of equal weight and shape in a state of equilibrium and proximity, and leave them, would they eventually move even closer together? Was that it? Some such phenomenon. Even words – a word isn't exactly the same as the thing it refers to, but if you say it, or write it, it calls up that thing. Evokes it. And therefore brings you closer to it. So the staring at photographs idea has an element of sense. Becky and Felix obviously think it works. Malcolm stared hard into a photograph, the methodical researcher in him – not, admittedly, the aspect of his being most accustomed to vigorous exercise – telling him, this is mad. Barking.

Felix and Becky re-entered the lounge in time to see the photograph album fall and hit the carpet. Malcolm had vanished.

3

The storm was now at its height. It sent bars of shadow and yellow light whirling round the windswept tower. Miles looked out, eyes tightened against the wind, but could see nothing now except broken spiders of lightning smash on the greyish-pink horizon. The wind was strong enough to slip between the edge of the glass cover and the open book beneath, riffling its pages at speed. He looked down fretfully, by habit still wanting to read more, about the hidden conditions underpinning the reality he had escaped, but wanting more to be back and moving amid its real and decidedly un-hidden challenges. The rapidly alternating light and darkness of the storm made it all but impossible to read.

> *believed that it was dangerous to describe or repre-*
> *sent such actions directly*

> *the hieroglyphic nature of language, whereby to*
> *write about it, might cause it to happen again*

> *the word and the picture and the thing itself were*

> *boat to cross the dark*

> *eye*   *cold corridor, leading to real death*

In the broken, smoky light, the pages seemed intent on veiling, almost at times seemed to shed rather than adding verbal formulae.

> *linked to the perils of the journey thought to be faced*
> *by the Sun, on its voyage through the underworld of*
> *night*

The glass exploded, showering his space with tiny stars and useless miniature windows. Unharmed for this moment at least, Miles slipped the book into his pocket and, as lightning again struck the tower, crouched by instinct and made himself a glowing ball of thought. Slowly he dropped down the dead centre of the twisting and now disintegrating tower, as, in a related dream, a small boy looked puzzled as the ball he had been bouncing started to glow, then stilled itself in air, then moved into a world he could not see, solar disc heralding the safe arrival, boat up from the underworld, raw emotion up from inside hiding, Miles himself now shot through time past to re-inhabit, for a second, his younger self (to whom he kindly returned his shadow) before, with a deep breath, filling out the contours of his adult body, he found himself splayed on the rock where once again an enraged seabird, oblivious to his blindness, would once again be about to turn, and bear savagely down.

4

- *Doctor* Proctor, for a thin man, you are one heavy man!

Malcolm Coates shoved his sizeable arms under those of his mentor and, legs braced on the cliff edge from the land side, pulled him up to safety. The gull screamed and wheeled herself high in the sky, as small rocks pattered and whispered down gullies to the sand and to the white waves, far below.

- Not a bad place to grow up. Nice place to bring up kids.
  A bit fresh.

Malcolm sniffed the sea breeze, and looked around at Miles' past. Miles himself remained speechless.

- Come on Frodo, back to Middle Earth.

Still no reaction. More gently, Malcolm asked:

- Did you find your father?

- Yes. It was him all right. I mean, I was him, some of the time, so I could see. How it all happened. How everything happened.

Miles wheeled around, so the sea breeze lifted his hair, but the wind against which he tightened his eyes was not that of Fife, and the stormy light moving in shards across his facial planes reflected the force of a tornado raging elsewhere.

- In the beginning, in any beginning, there's light, and it rolls out in waves, which means time, like the flame of a lit candle spreading. Then things, whether they're planets or people, animals, events, are the fluff on the rolling carpet of light. And every single thing is unique, and because this is happening in time, every moment is unique, which means every single thing or moment has a potential to be cherished or important. But they're not the light, we're not the light, we're the bits caught up in the light, so nothing works one hundred per cent. Nothing can be perfected. You can say no, but look, it flies! It works! But really it's all held together with rubber bands and spittle and goodwill. Some rough magic keeps the show on the road. And people don't work properly, not for very long. They fall to bits eventually, or get themselves stuck down some rabbit hole. Then again, you can't help but…

While Miles' mind drifted, rationality not quite returned, Malcolm's eyes filled. I dedicate myself, he thought absently. I'm not sure to what, quite yet, but I dedicate myself. I now know I have that capacity. He prompted Miles.

- Can't help but love them for it?

Let me be your prompter.

- Oh, can't help but love. Of course. Can't help but…

He shivered, and wholly re-entered the moment.

- No. Yes. You *can* help.

He smiled knowingly. Malcolm thought for a moment.

-   Right. Just one question, boss. How do we get out of here?

5

-   Don't take this personally, but. Actually do, do take it personally. You don't look great, Felix. You look as if you're at death's door.

-   Tell me about it. I'm pouring sweat. It's this damned bullet Winthrope gave me as a parting gift. He's probably cruising the neighbourhood right now, looking to take us all out. There are bits of myself I just can't reach into properly. I need a doctor. But I'd surely hate to leave you all alone with my former employer on the prowl, plus, from what Malcolm was saying, our Scottish friend, and with Miles….

They both looked forlorn and at the indentation left by the departed.

-   Miles so…not here. Then there's Malcolm, though. Who would have thought it. Perhaps we could encourage a little professional development? Might be a useful addition – start a new team?

Mutinously silent, Becky looked doubtful beyond dubiety. If there still is a team, Felix sighed to himself, and stepped out into the bathroom, where he took off his jacket, loosened the new skinny tie he put on after his death, and threw water over his face. Ugh, I look rough. If I don't get this fixed my temperature will go through the roof and into hyperspace, and I'll have to die again. I really don't want that. I've seen enough of those guys today.

-   *Me too, Mister Manto. And I can't even see. I can hear the long hair of the dead, rustling on their shoulders. Hear a lot of things. I've had years of practice. Hear the worms wriggling towards you in the earth, the sweet pop as a worm or a beetle makes a start on your freshly interred eyeball, or some equally toothsome organ. Partial to pancreas? Speaking for myself, I thrive on spleen. But where were we? Ah yes, beneath the veiling sod, such a hive of gay activity. The tickling under the ribs, as the frisky wee rat starts his scrabbling. Scream for mercy as he dines on heart and lung. Your heart, your lung. Because you're buried, but you're not properly dead. That's your fear, isn't it Felix? And how often fears have a habit of coming true...*

Felix blinked hard into the bathroom mirror, but there was no shifting the superimposed bald cranium, the unseeing eyes. And those *ears*. How can he see with them, as well as hear?

-    *Stop staring at my ears. That is unconscionably rude!*

An electric shock ran through his neck, and ran down to where the bullet maintained its hot lodging. The bullet jumped. Felix screamed and fell to the floor, his head wrenched up by invisible hands to maintain his enforced gazing at the face in the mirror.

-    *Poor white trailer-park trash. Not your fault you were schooled by alligators, brought up on, what is it? – forgive my terrible imitation of your even more revolting accent - collarrrd greens and blee-ack-eyed peas? Not to mention black-eyed Susan. I said don't mention her! I plucked her eyes out, wore them all that Sunday. Dropped them in my collard greens and can't find my way home. And she, she wandered all the length of Main Street seeing nothing, nothing but darkness. There's nothing but the dark, Felix. Believe me, I've tried to get back here. I've joined the queue for Over There and tried to get my hand stamped at the night club. But mah name's no on the Gezzie List. Can – you – imagine – that!*

With every spaced word a bolt of lightning turned and heated further the bullet in Felix's shoulder girdle. What powers can I summon. It feels like it's moving. This could mean the end, again.

- *The tunnel's a stage set. The white light's a con trick. Your friends, they deceased musicians. They are the hollow men, the stuffed men. Not the happy, grateful dead. The hacked-off stinking dead. Nowhere to go, nowhere to hide, in the nowhere that's now here, nothing to eat but the charnel house air, all the dead words, and each other.*

The round mad face grew pensive.

- *I cannae tolerate rock music. Too loud, too crude. It derives from the blues, and I dinnae like that, either. So repetitive. Bit of an intellectual stretch for watermelon boy, though, I grant you that. Probably his greatest historic achievement, apart from learning how to run around in circles to win prizes. No, leave me my Gilbert and Sullivan. 'Three little maids from school' has to be a personal favourite. Aye, how unlikely it seemed to the homecoming trio, skipping along the suburban pavement, that the limo with the blacked out windows just slowing to open its maw would prove such an Aladdin's Cave of frolics for the next, their final, day on earth. Prior to eternal night. 'Eternal Night', is that no a Gilbert and Sullivan? Alban Berg? Some other berg – Iceberg, Schoenberg? Afore he went atonal? 'Atonal Night', aye that's a good one. Must remember that one. Always loathed the Darmstadt crowd. Pretentious shite. 'Three little M-A-I-D-S…. frrrrom school!'*

The sung, the screamed, rolled 'rs' caused the room to vibrate and shudder, along with Felix's ear drums and the agonising bullet. Can't Becky hear? Why isn't she doing something?

- *Becky's tied up right now. However, notwithstanding my entrenched aversion to the molasses sentimentality of negro spirituals, the nugatory plink-plunk of African-derived popular idiocies and the solipsistic cacophony of jazz, I must confess to a wee soft spot for hip-hop. I find the rappers' lyrics refreshing, often piquant, in their representation of the female psyche, and the reiterated interest in firearms I find almost arousing. That Slim Shady! What a wag. I'd love to spank him. And Dr Dre! That elasticated bass-to-treble spectrum! I'm lovin' it!*

There followed a spirited karaoke rendition of 'Brain Damage', followed in short order by 'Kill You', and then for an encore, a version of Dre's 'Darkside/ Gone', remarkable not least for the fact that the original track would not be released until 2015. Although Felix was not yet dying, he was beginning to feel that every cloud had a silver lining.

6

-   Well. We could start by consulting the manual.

Miles produced the book. His mother stood watching through binoculars by the hall telephone, wondering if it would be advisable to phone the police station down in St Andrews. She didn't like the look of that tubby green-haired paratrooper, not one bit. The other character seemed a bit distracted, unlikely to do harm. And in silhouette, so curiously like Simon. She sighed, put down the binoculars, and turned back towards the interior of the house, Sam clattering lightly in her wake. Her little boy Miles would be away in his own head, somewhere nearby, playing.

-   How very odd. Or perhaps not.

Miles smiled pensively, and put the book away.

-   Right, Malcolm old sport. Looks like we're going to have to think our way home.

- Think. Our way. Home.

Having felt that he'd done pretty well so far, got the hang of this time travel lark, Malcolm suddenly felt profoundly at a loss. He missed his own time-zone. Stifling an urge to weep which had brought unexpected dividends in Miles' lounge but which would not advance their fortunes in the current situation, he tried thinking about thinking. This proved circular and unsuccessful, as far as he could tell.

- I think you'll need to tell me what and how to think.

This proved to be a slightly unfortunate choice of formulation. Miles cleared his throat, put his hands behind his back, and, reinvigorated, began as if addressing a hall filled with freshers.

- It all comes down to the relationship between words and things. Words can describe, outline, shadow, haunt or otherwise follow the thing in question, but words can never actually *be* those things…

Get on with it, Miles. I'm not one of your bloody students. Oh hang on, yes I am.

- Except that they can.

Make your mind up, Professor of Applied Thinkology.

- In exceptional circumstances. Words can, if skilfully directed, *conjure* the things to which they refer. This direction of travel you can see latent in the Chinese ideogram, which is a verbal picturing of the thing in itself, or numerous ancient languages. Not to mention our own proven ability – and by the way, congratulations, you have just joined an elite and tiny group – proven ability to bring picture and place together by thinking. I've had one or two experiences with words becoming literally true that I won't bore you with now.

Red carnations danced briefly in his mind, and a memory of a card in a phone booth silvered and shivered into dust. Words, memories; conflate them, catch them, put them in your pocket. Never let them fade away.

- So what we need to think, Malc, is where we want to be. And if we think with sufficient persistence, we're there. Or I hope we'll be there. Remember the layout of my flat? View from the window, rough dimensions, all that. Let's see if you can remember the colour of the sofa. Build up a picture. Cotton-covered, or leather? Corduroy, maybe?

Malcolm closed his eyes, thought back, and thought hard. All he could so treacherously see in his mind's eye at this moment was the hint of paradise in Becky's cleavage.

- Leather, definitely. Red leather.

Miles sighed.

7

The Librarian of Beltane College was a patient man. He was also a very tired man, having lugged heavy glass cases hither and yon, phoned Estates Management for assistance with fitting lights and placing furniture, waited in vain, done the job himself, gone to the Porter's Lodge in hopes of a taller ladder, wondered at the Porter's absence, then glimpsed such terrifying scenes on the CCTV as to understand that absence, and fearing for the safety of the College's significant trove of Victoriana, hurried back to his office to locate the numerical combination to the recently installed security keypad. Having done this, he had disbelieved the late hour visible on his desk clock, looked in a mirror and passed beyond disbelief, and checked his email before departing for bed only to find one more ludicrous and procrastinating message from young Dr Proctor, sent a day or so previously.

Right, that's it. Enough. He wrote a sharply-worded note with his fountain pen, underlining several words so brutally as to verge on tearing the paper, changed his mind, balled the paper and threw it in the bin, swore aloud, retrieved Miles' home address from the Library's encrypted User Data, and set off for Camden. On the way to the car park he thought for a second he saw one of Proctor's students level a firearm at the Principal. Tired, he thought. Too tired for this malarkey. Seeing things. He hesitated by his car, and sighed. Then he got in and drove off towards Camden. Taking a wrong turn through lack of familiarity with North London, he was soon lost.

8

- Let's try again. What colour are the walls of the lounge painted? Against which wall is the sofa located? And what kind and colour of covering does the sofa have? Your starters for ten. If we don't get this right, Malcolm, you could soon be catching or even frying fish for a living, in Anstruther. Enster, to the locals. You'll need elocution lessons. They'll throw you in the harbour, first. That's the traditional East Neuk welcome to incomers. Now *think*.

- White. The walls are white. But the ceiling…

- Yes?

- Is blue.

- Bingo. Now against which…?

- The far wall, as you come in through the door. The door is unpainted. Brass handle. Ball-shaped.

- You're on a roll, Malc. Now for tonight's jackpot, a journey in time, all expenses paid for, what is the material and what is the colour of the cover on the sofa?

Malc thought, hard. Suddenly, he was remembering watching that bizarre dream-film, and feeling resentful at Miles' behaviour, even though he now accepted that the movie was unreal, and that the shared dream in which he was currently standing was the real world, or part of it.

-    Corduroy. White corduroy. Well, off-white. Cream?

Miles sighed again. So far, neither of them had noticed the 1950s television in a walnut cabinet, moving of its own volition at about five miles per hour towards them across the fields of maize, carving out a straight unswerving furrow, wire and plug trailing in its wake.

-    I don't like the look of that. Not one bit.

Matron was standing in the dark of the Captain's flat, peering through binoculars in hopes not so much of titillation, at least on this occasion, as a simple reassurance that everything was as it should be with Miles Proctor. Instead she could see Becky, seemingly bound to a chair. Though no rope was visible, Matron winced as she saw her tipping the chair from side to side, trying to escape. And who wouldn't want to escape, stuck in a room with him. Huge bald bloke with ears like a bat. Horrible.

-    He's taunting her. I really don't like the look of this, at all.

-    Pretty Polly!

The parrot moved the angle of the telescope, and gazed at the same spot.

-    Grub up! Fuck me blind, what a carry on! Pretty Polly!

-    What's he up to now? Polly, can you tell? A right one, he is.

-    Pretty Polly! Grub up! He's talking to the telly! Winds of

change! You've never had it so good! What a carve-up!
They think it's all over! It is, now.

The parrot flew round the room, apparently deranged for the nonce
by what it had seen, then settled on the Captain's shoulder, humped
and thoughtful.

-    Nevermore! Pretty Polly. Nevermore.

-    Right, that's it. I'm going in. Keep watch, Captain.

Aye-aye, Matron, the Captain mouthed silently. Polly amiably
rubbed her chartreuse head against the visor of his braided cap,
to scratch an itch, then kept it there. Matron put on her coat, and
went to choose her weapons.

9

-    OK Malcolm. The sofa cover is corduroy. Blue, to match
     the ceiling.

-    Got it. Yeah, you're right.

-    I know I'm right, I live there. But you got the rest of the
     space nailed down, pretty much. So. Let's join hands and
     try to contact the living.

As the two young men held hands, closed their eyes and bowed
their heads in silence, the walnut television set made its way towards
them, pausing a few feet away. The cabinet doors opened of their
own volition, and, an absence of power notwithstanding, the Test
Card came on, in late 1950s black-and-white. Then the scene cut
to a filler, a five minute silent of a potter's wheel in action, which
the BBC, in those pioneering days of only a single channel, used
to screen in order to bridge the gap before the news. Having failed
once more to travel through space and time, Miles and Malcolm
opened their eyes and let their hands drop. Miles motioned to

him silently, and Malcolm, eyes widening in amazement, turned to observe the television cabinet.

Both were drawn to the mildly hypnotic film of an amphora emerging vertically from the spinning clay. Though both looked puzzled, neither spoke. The elegant hands of the potter, seemingly female, continued in their quest to nudge and whirl practical design from rotating mud. Abruptly the hands were not female, and the tower of mud had been flung through the screen, where it now lay, bubbling ordure, around the feet of the dreaming pair, who stepped back sharpish. Behind the potter's wheel, all still in black-and-white, could now be seen the interior of Miles' flat, and Becky tied to a chair with invisible cords.

> - *An old trick, I grant you, Commander Bond, but it might just work. As the nuclear device is primed to explode in under five minutes, and as my personal submarine awaits, I see no harm in your knowing the details of my plan. Actually I lied – isn't that awful? Wholly uncharacteristic behaviour. I do apologize. I dinnae have a submarine. And there is no nuclear device. Not unless your amnesiac banjo-crazed warlock of a father left one ticking away in the attic. Unlikely. How to make a crystal radio from two jam jars was more his level. I do have a plan, though. Gentlemen, without a net, and with only these shears at my disposal…*

The camera moved to a close-up of poultry-shears, purloined from the kitchen. Miles cursed his love of winged game, inwardly vowing a conversion to vegetarianism should they escape from all this. Meanwhile Malcolm was getting terrible déjà-vu.

> - *…and only this delightful young lady to dispose of. Forgive me, I'm ending sentences with prepositions, I'm so overcome with excitement at. The possibility of. Slicing and dicing her with. Ooh, missis, what a conjunction! Reducing*

her comely form to! THIS!

He lunged. Becky screamed. Miles sprang instinctively towards the television screen. The man with the shears sprang back into view.

- *Just my wee joke. I have to have my joke. I need the book, Miles. The Great Little Joke Book. "Our Laughing Cosmos". Mummy, mummy why am I walking round in circles? Can it Damian or I'll nail your other foot to the floor. Mummy there's a man at the door with a bill. Don't be stupid, darling boy, it's a duck with a hat on. Mummy, mummy, quite contrary, lie in a sarcophagus coma for thousands of years then wake in this vile world and wish that you'd stayed dead. There's a man at the door with the head of a jackal. That's our new lodger, Mister Anubis. There's a man at the door with the Head of Security. He turned the corpse of Osiris into the first mummy, ringed by spells of Thoth. Is that an apotropaic wand, or are you just pleased to see me? I'll be pleased to let the young lady go, Miles, if you let me get my hands on the book. It's my passport to a quiet grave. Or the start of a new career. A new grave, a quiet career. Perm again Whittington, no one has a job for life in this recombinant mash-up, not anymore. Take a little walk with me, under the moon of love, into the Valley of the Shadow of Death. Now. Where is it? The Time Out Guide to the Valley of the Shadow of Death. Part Two, the After-Life. I've searched your bijou hidey-hole. Found some interesting flotsam but as the bishop said to the transvestite, I still haven't found what I'm looking for. It's not here. Where. Is. It.*

- Here. It followed me.

Miles calmly withdrew the book, *Transmutations*, from his pocket, and dangled it tantalisingly close to the screen. Without turning to look, the man with the shears idly flicked them backwards, drawing blood beneath Becky's ear. She screamed, and then swore copiously.

- *I cannae see too clearly. That's terrible reception you have, up there in Fife. Wrong coast. I can hear perfectly well, though, and see with my ears, so turn the dial down Rebecca, you little fool, it's the first Mrs De Winter here. Last night I dreamt I went to Manderley again. To tell the truth I did no such thing, I dreamt happily for hours about the Massacre of the Innocents. Rebecca, describe the cover to me, or you'll be joining them, one piece at a time. Maxim just isn't your type. Nor am I, darlin'. Now exercise those antiquarian skills.*

In a shaky voice, Becky described the cover.

- *Throw it into the screen. A bottle in time's ocean. I need to scry its messages.*

- You can have it. But it won't go without me. Look.

Very gently, he tossed the book from a distance of a few inches. Loyally, it played dumb, landing in slow motion and safely in the grass. Miles tried not to look at Becky for a moment, and contrived somehow to keep his voice level.

- I think we have a stand-off, Kenny. Either you come here, and take the book, or we come back to you – with the book. But even if I give it you, it won't stay with you. The book wants me, not you. Forget the Valley of the Shadow of Death for a minute, and think about Death Valley. Not your habitual gothic comfort-zone. A real place. You couldn't even bear to be in the vicinity of it. It hurt you, physically. The book hates you. Can't bear you. Of course you *do* bear a striking resemblance to Aleister Crowley. So, sure, come and get it. Try your hardest. But let Becky go.

> - *Let the queen go? Put myself in check? Don't play the silly laddie.*

Miles shrugged. He held the book open at the final page, and made as if to start to tear it. At this, both Miles and Malcolm felt a powerful magnetic pull, emanating, it seemed, not so much from the book as from the screen.

> - Go with the flow, Malc. We weren't getting far on our own. The TV's just one more portal. Doors to manual…

Pocketing his book as he crouched and ran forward, Miles flew in soft monochrome waves through the screen of the old television. The soles of his shoes were visible for a moment to Malcolm, then he was gone. The cabinet doors closed with a firm click.

> - Oh no! Don't leave me here! I'm coming with you…

The cabinet obliged, and the walnut doors flew open. Malcolm's green Mohawk dipped flat on his pink head like a dowser's wand, as he knelt, took a deep breath, and threw himself into the screen. An otherwise smooth and flowing motion was stalled momentarily as his abdomen jammed the cabinet, then Malcolm too was on his way elsewhere.

> - *Where are they? What happened? That wasnae me did that. Jings. They seemed to leave the ground and float a wee bit then hit the screen and then. I just don't know. Was this your doing?*

> - Of course not, you pest, I'm tied here to this blasted chair with invisible ropes, what could I possibly do?

> - *You could pipe down a wee bit, darlin', my hearing's awful sensitive.*

Becky let out an ear-splitting, protracted scream.

- *Will ye no do that! I cannae bear it!*

She did it again. Louder, with feeling. And held the note, *con molto furioso.*

10

In a post-existential and profoundly hypothetical quarter of the next phase of things where dead musicians like to congregate, Charley Patton was shuffling the deck, Rabbit Brown was pouring a drink, Robert Johnson was staring into space at a point beyond it, and Thelonious Monk was playing the piano from a point beyond that. Monk stopped in mid phrase.

- Hear that?

- Couldn't really miss it.

- If we can hear it, it's a friend in need.

Patton fanned the deck of cards in an S-shaped swirl across the table. They heard Becky's scream for help again.

- Bust my buttons! Can she scream.

It was the Jack of Hearts who had spoken, fluttering on the table. Monk looked across, and turned his piano stool round. The quartet leaned forward, focussed on the articulate deck.

- So who is it?

- I don't know for sure. I'm only a playing card. Any views, Ace?

It was the Ace of Spades who spoke next, vibrating slightly on the table as he did so.

- I'm only a playing card, too. I mean, that goes without

saying – but anyway, you did ask me, so here goes. I've never met the lady, and I wouldn't know for sure, but people have been using packs of cards to tell the future or to see into the hidden life of things for many hundreds of years now, correct? As with tea leaves, and in the time of the Roman Empire, haruspication using the entrails of horses, right?

Mumbles of general assent.

- So, as I say I don't know much, having spent the day if not most of the year getting completely shuffled and hanging out with you fellows…

- Cut to the chase, Ace.

This from the Queen of Diamonds, a feisty looking individual in a serious snood.

- …but I think, and this is just intuition, born as I say of the minimal prerogative bestowed by the fortune-telling tradition, I think it's possibly Harry Smith's passing acquaintance Simon Proctor's son Miles' girlfriend Becky, trapped in their apartment by a dead Scotsman who looks like Aleister Crowley…

- Well, she's not the first and she won't be the last. Twenty three thousand six hundred and sixty six weird men with a Scots accent who look like Aleister Crowley are roaming around up there, or is it down, I can never remember…and that's just the living ones…if you throw in the dead ones too, well…

- Up or down, Thelonious, dead or alive, that's an arresting demographic.

- It's just a cosmic fact, Mr Johnson.

But is she going to be OK? asked Rabbit Brown quietly and anxiously of the assembled company. At this point there came a protracted roar, from so deep a point on the bass spectrum that the floorboards shook, followed by a series of thumps. The cards shuffled nervously and squared themselves into a neat deck. Watch out, He's coming. Lights flashed on and off. Thelonious Monk put his head in his hands. Robert Johnson's saucer eyes radiated a degree of amusement, cut with apprehension as he put a shading hand to his brow, and pulled the brim of his hat down.

- She is now. I guess the noise woke Him.

Nobody moved an inch as a dead musician approaching seven feet in height, weighing a good three hundred pounds, walked in noisily through one door, stamped to the end of the room and was gone through the other.

- He's riled. Takes a lot, but.

- Heaven help that half-dead Scotsman. If heaven thinks he deserves it.

They all shuddered, momentarily. Charley Patton cut, and dealt.

11

Miles and Malcolm were on a transparent helter-skelter, travelling down. The speed and camber were more pleasant than not, which gave Miles an opportunity to ponder the whys and wherefores of this latest episode. From time to time he looked back at Malcolm. He tried yelling *I think we've left Kansas, Toto!* by way of reassurance, but his student either couldn't hear for the loud sluicing and whooshing of time and space flying by them, or was currently oblivious to allusion. Malcolm looks happy enough, anyway. Somewhere in his own seventh heaven, eyes glazed, watching time fly. The helter-skelter meant nothing one way or the other, in itself. All these tunnels and TVs, Miles thought, these mirrors and trap doors and stage props; the panel by the portrait in the haunted house which suddenly swings open, revealing a torch-lit winding stairwell to the cellar; the phantom coaches on the moonlit moor, the cigar-shaped silver transporters from another galaxy, even books, and pictures, all representations, the whole round world itself, were variable portals, and portals only. Leading where? Generally speaking, to more portals.

Just sometimes, or with someone, there was a significant pause in the journey, a stopping to take stock, and this was – what would you call it? – a station, a temporary stopping-point, to take on under-standing, like steam trains took on water. The word 'station', even as Miles brought it to mind, resonated somewhere in his thinking as more than itself, or rather, as completely and literally itself, for the first time.

Let's daydream a little. There's time. Let's conjure a station. A real, made-up station.

When he got off his train of thought, Miles was alone. Standing, stationary. The locomotive pulled out of the country halt, whistling loudly in his imagination and obscuring for several seconds, with clouds of smoke and steam, the landscape beyond the platform. Birds sang, the heavy magnolia nodding their grey and pink candles in the breeze. Miles put his bag down on the platform with a thump, and wondered what would happen next. Nothing. The sun shone brightly and blankly on the white picket fence, where the faces of sunflowers watched him, as if to say, this is your call. Miles cleared his throat, and began to test his theory.

> -   Porter!

In a trice, the small and rubicund figure was hurrying towards him, complete with peaked cap, and a tight waistcoat from which the chain of a fob watch swung, as did the whistle on a lanyard around his substantial and perspiring neck.

- Terribly sorry sir, I was just…

- Think nothing of it. I'm getting the hang of this. Now, giraffe!

Instantly a giraffe was stepping gracefully along the platform, stretching its neck to nibble at the topmost leaves by the picket fence. So this was the way forward. Better do a quick double-check, then back to London.

- Grand piano! Lights, camera, action!

The grand piano landed with a dissonant clatter of strings on the railway line, and started to play itself merrily, as Kleig lights and mounted cameras zoomed and veered around each other. No crew, of course, no gaffer or best boy, because I didn't ask for those. Asked for? Commandeered? Got it. *Named.* Now, back to the helter-skelter, and London. Miles cleared his throat.

- Destination London!

Ah, but which of the many Londons. And when. And then he was back on the dreamlike slalom ride, eyes and images and fragments of colour, time and space flying past as they carried on down. He remembered standing outside Redidivus Books, haplessly trying to gain entrance, and seeing in faded script some words beside the door, from the late Victorian period. Subsequently there had been plenty of time in which to work out what they said. Now it was time to put that discovery to good use. He turned his head as far as he could safely do so, and hoped his student would hear.

- Malc, Malcolm! We need to do a little preparatory work before we go back to the flat, OK with you?

- Just say the word.

- Precisely. *Mr Machen's Magic Shop.* With the opportunity for a short walk en route. Make that Trafalgar Square!

12

They were standing in the southwest corner of Trafalgar Square, having stepped out of a brougham-landaulet, which is what the helter-skelter had instantly become. The driver on the box seat tipped his cap, made a click-click with tongue on teeth, and his horses obediently cantered away. The curious little structure where they had alighted, resembling some form of early telephone box, was in fact the smallest police station in the world, with enough room to contain a single policeman, who of course occupied it for purposes of surveillance. But surveillance was not uppermost in their minds, as the two walked past gas-lit arcades and up the cobbled streets towards Charing Cross Road.

- This is fantastic, Miles. I could get used to travelling in time.

- You've been doing it all your life, you should be used to it by now.

- Yes but you know what I mean. Anyway, speaking of time, do we have enough of it? That was a pretty desperate situation we saw on the television. Every time I've watched a television lately the situation's been fairly desperate. I mean, should we be savouring the delights of late Victorian London, when there are such heinous things going on back at your place, in approaching-the-millennium Camden?

- I sense that hardly any time has passed, there. A few seconds. Our dream time here is stretching to accommodate what will be necessary to resolving the situation there. Magic aims to rebalance, essentially. Plus we need to choose our weapons – perhaps just one – with extreme care. Hence this visit to *Mr Machen's Magic Shop*.

- Far to go?

-   No. Fiddlers Court.

-   You obviously know this place.

-   You could say that.

Miles cast back in his mind to the day, some weeks or an eternity ago, when Becky had almost thrown him through the doorway of the building they were about to visit. Under Victor Winthrope's capricious and self-serving regime, it had been allowed to fall into a state of disrepair. Winthrope. On his way out, but people can cause a lot of damage as they dither on the threshold. Time to think about him later. One thing at a time. And his amazing daughter, if that is in truth the right word. I hope Laura's on the mend. Miles pictured her in a cottage hospital, a Victorian heroine getting her strength back, sipping broth proffered by a Florence Nightingale figure with hair in a bun and one of those watch chains. (In a parallel universe, Matron was sharpening the end of a stout umbrella, having also loaded and pocketed a Saturday night special.) You're drifting, Miles. Something's happened to Laura. Later. It can wait.

They passed beggars, crossing sweepers, and two young-old women in a doorway called to them softly. Malcolm blushed, and gazed straight ahead. Then they turned into Fiddlers Court, and walked up to the building on the left where Redidivus Books would one day be, but where *Mr Machen's Magic Shop* was the sole emporium open for business at this late hour, the wavering light of tall candles behind mullion windows spilling out across the cobbles. Miles reached instinctively for the bell pull he knew would be there, but even before he could move to pull it, the door was opened by a familiar figure.

-   Get these invisible ropes off me! *Now!* I'm warning you, I'll scream again!

Kenneth McLeod was holding his ears, and crashing in to walls and chairs as he tried to get the lingering echoes and vibrations of horror out of his head. Reluctantly, and steadying himself, he cut the invisible ropes with the real poultry shears, which Becky then seized from his grasp and jabbed up towards his jaw.

- Sofa! *Now!* The far end. And stay there! Keep your hands folded between your legs. *Do it! I'll scream again!*

- *I'm awful sorry...*

- No you're not! You're not sorry! You're not sorry at all! What you are is *nearly extinct!*

- Hi. Sorry I was gone so long. The bullet.... *You bastard!*

Felix was still pale, and wore a blood-stained towel around his neck, but the steaming bullet he dropped in a waste bin before proceeding to wallop the sofa-bound figure hard around the head was indication enough that he had once again cheated death, this time without even dying. Suddenly there came, all out of sync with this domestic drama, a sighing like the patter of autumn leaves, drifting along a cobbled Victorian street. All three looked over to the indentation in the sofa, which had started to shimmer a little. Somewhere in the far distance, enchanting and then gone, a hurdy-gurdy played. The aroma of hot chestnuts was there for a moment, then that vanished too.

13

- Mr Boxer!

- Toby Machen. At your service, sir. And you, sir?

- Malcolm. Malcolm Coates.

- Mr Coates. Welcome to my Magic Shop.

Toby Machen, purveyor of curios, who would in a different future become a Mr Boxer, led the bemused visitors past dolls in white crinoline whose faces seemed almost human. Miles was sure a bonneted head turned slightly to peer at him as they moved into the interior, lit only fitfully by the wavering flare of church candles, and occasional gaslights on the wall that hissed, and cast a warmer glow within encroaching shadows. Malcolm's eye was caught by a doll's house, where for a second he thought he discerned not only tiny furnishings, wardrobes and bathrooms and dining rooms, but tiny figures who seemed to be moving from room to room, cooking, eating, giving the baby a bath, gesticulating. Living. Malcolm whispered to Miles.

- You called him Mr Boxer.

- It's a long story. Evidently our companion has had a longer life than I assumed. I have to say that in my – later? Anyway my other life – Mr Boxer always struck me as stationing himself on the side of the angels.

- Indeed, sir.

Toby Machen smiled and pointed out a statue of a seated angel, hand to pensive forehead, reading, fashioned out of white marble. The statue looked up, and the visitors jumped a little as the stone reader's eyes glowed like hot green coals inside the semi-darkness.

- Good evening, Mr Machen. Gentlemen.

- Still reading, Gabriel?

- It's what I am cut out to do. Lord Tennyson.

- Ah. Modern poetry. Though a good deal more mellifluous than the Spasmodics, and less pallid than the Rhymer's Club. Not that I am averse to the Celtic Revival, in itself. We'll leave you to your book.

As the statue smiled thinly, lowered its gaze and withdrew into poetry and stone, the trio moved further, into a room which Miles recognized, and where he had not so very long ago been interviewed by his current guide. They reached a space enclosed by tall cabinets, cases and grandfather clocks, which whirred and chimed gently and at intervals as they spoke, sitting in three high-backed Victorian chairs which Machen drew together. Miles described the urgency of the situation back in present time, where Becky had been kidnapped and an armed Victor Winthrope was allegedly on the loose. Toby Machen gently interrupted him.

- I know. Some things, at any rate. My longevity, of which you have just been made aware, is matched by my powers of recollection, which stretch into the other roles I have occupied, or will occupy. First, you no longer need concern yourself regarding Victor Winthrope.

- Is he…?

- Let us say that, like many of the more curious volumes in his possession, he is now definitively *hors de commerce*. The details are not gratifying, and should wait for a subsequent occasion. And I am aware of Miss Becky's plight. In fact it was I who pulled you through the veletision.

- The…?

- The veletision. The screen arrangement, in the Logie Baird box. The demonic Scot sent it, but I intercepted the…wavelength? Honestly, these portmanteau terms. Reality is recombinant, as you have lately come to understand, but as for the linguistic consequences as one travels through time, well…

- Don't apologize. We're just grateful you pulled us out.

- Any time, Dr Proctor. *Any* time. One time's much like another. But, to cut to the heart of the matter. You need a weapon, appropriate to the powers of the entity with whom you are in conflict. And he is, as we know, a profoundly violent and exceedingly determined individual.

In a parallel version of the multiverse, Matron was now bursting through the door of Miles' flat with a shout of 'Charge!' – aiming for the dazed and confused figure at the end of the sofa, the bayonet of her sharpened umbrella pointed straight at his chest. Back in a different *fin-de-siècle,* Machen pondered further.

> - The weapon employed needs to be one that does not merely oppose, and indeed terminate the activities of this disagreeable individual, but one which succeeds in the end, by having caught him out in the beginning. He is fascinated by magic, is he not, though of an order better suited to the music hall turn than to our own endeavours? I think I have the very thing.

He rummaged in the drawers of a cabinet, and then presented Miles with a wooden box, about a foot in length.

> - The contents are self-explanatory. It will only work once. Choose your moment with care. Activate that part of your now very powerful mind that links things and words. It is essentially the infant stage of understanding, infinitely more sophisticated than anything, you must forgive me, to which the academy can lay claim. We all possess at least one magical gift, some more complex than others. To take just one example, Mr Coates here is clearly a time traveller of some considerable intrepidity, and adroitness.

Malcolm puffed out his chest, and blushed.

> - In your own time, Felix Manto, though he does not yet know I know this…

Yet, thought Miles to himself. Interesting.

- …has the invaluable, though not entirely enviable, gift of immortality. He has not yet been immortal for long enough to have fully experienced and understood either the positive or the negative aspects. Ah well. Everything in its own time.

- And you, Mr Machen? What is your gift?

- I too am pretty long-lived, Mr Coates. I long ago made myself useful in time and space, so I estimate that I am probably a permanent fixture. I believe I have won my spurs. For the most part, I enable and encourage the magic powers of others. As with you, my visitors today. That is my happiest gift. But now I will bid you goodbye, and wish you luck. Miles. Malcolm.

Again Miles looked at him carefully. They shook hands.

- Getting back shouldn't prove too difficult, not from here. Just go back the way you came.

14

Before Malcolm's jaw had had time to drop, he was moving backwards at cartoon speed through the shop, legs flying to Trafalgar Square, and into first, a backward-moving brougham, thence to an upwardly rocketing helter-skelter working in reverse, through a television screen into a field in the East Neuk of Fife, thence to a cliff-edge, and, finally, with a whump, into a chair in Miles' flat.

Here he found himself gazing at the immense rear view of Matron, effectively obscuring at least for now the identity of the figure who cowered in terror in the face of her umbrella, firearms, dimensions and general deportment. Felix Manto looked, in a manner of speaking, as if he had died and gone to heaven. Becky was leaning against a wall rubbing a reddened arm, and looked as if she'd had enough of all of them. For a moment everyone stared at the sofa. The shimmering outline grew features, and, the distant whistle of a steam locomotive fading in the air, Miles Proctor was back.

Becky leapt on him, delighted beyond words. Malcolm looked at the sofa, and blinked in annoyance.

- That sofa! The corduroy isn't blue, it's *cream*, Miles, cream! *You* held us up, in that field. Miles, *you got it wrong!*

Felix Manto, Kenneth McLeod and Matron stared at him in bafflement. Miles shrugged, petulant.

- You can't expect me to remember everything.

Malcolm mouthed 'yes I can', then got a full view of Kenneth, yelled, ran at him and was pulled off by Matron, who shouted that she'd got there first.

- Squatter's rights, Malcolm Coates! He's mine, mine I tell you!

Matron squatting on Kenneth caused him to emit a howl of anguish. Miles cupped his hands and tried to gain their attention, over the din:

- All of you! Please! How did everyone get hold of my home address?

All looked at each other, and began to talk at once.

There came a knock at the door. The group froze in silence. The Librarian of Beltane College burst through the door, glared wildly around, and demanded to be given the book, right now. Kenneth shouted that it was his and his alone, by the power invested in him by Set and Horus, at which Spendrift, showing an unprecedented level of bottle, jumped on him and attempted to fight Matron off. As mayhem supervened, Miles put his face in his hands and groaned. Becky massaged his neck and shoulders. Everyone who isn't dead and some who are, are here, he thought, in my flat. There's no place like home. Victor Winthrope won't be coming, that's one less thing to worry about. Laura will still be in recovery somewhere.

In the general uproar, nobody heard a demure hiccup. Weaving slightly, a beautiful woman in her middle years entered, took in something of the scene before her magnificent eyes, and shrugged. Then her gaze located Miles, and her eyes lit up.

- I got bored. Miles. Bored. But, *Miles*. You'll be so… pleased. With me. I've been out for a while. And I've been *practising*. And, Miles, I'm free now. Free of him. The past is…gone. Wiped clean. It never happened.

Becky looked at Miles looking at Laura, and frowned. Laura showed Becky her perfect teeth, in what would have passed for a smile, in the jungle. Laura then took one look at Kenneth, shivered in revulsion, and set him on fire with a single flick from her finger-tip. John Spendrift, Malcolm and Matron sprang free, the first two falling on the third, Becky yelling, *The sofa! It's made in Thailand, it doesn't have any flame retardant!*, while Miles glared at Laura and demanded to know where she had found his home address. Laura raised slowly one louche eyebrow, and ran her still-hot finger lingeringly down the front of his shirt, failing to stop when she reached the belt.

- Conflagration, Miles. That's my unlisted address. Hang out with me, in carmine conflagration. Those hot little slivers of destruction, how they…tingle….

Becky went for her full-tilt, not that it had much impact. Felix threw the tulips out of a jug of water, poured the water over the smoking sofa and pondered his next career move.

15

When the smoke cleared, however, they could hardly fail to notice the absence of Kenneth McLeod. His boots lay smoking on the carpet, but the rest of him was nowhere to be seen.

Then someone looked at the ceiling.

-   There!

What had been the recognizably if repugnantly human form of the man calling himself Kenneth McLeod, was now transmuted into a contorted, writhing figure, an animate horror from a region beyond space and time, an unholy cross between giant bat and spider. The modern London apartment suddenly reeked of the charnel house, as if no air had been let in or out for centuries. The hairy, bony-kneed legs clung to Miles' ceiling, questing one by one the foetid air, maintaining their purchase only by the exudation of a gummy, yellowish ichor, which dripped down and left acid craters sizzling in the carpet. The bald head rotated insanely on the neck, its fixed grin a death's head leer, the yellow-grey incisors grown now to full length, matching the bat-like ears. The thing chattered and squealed idiotically, its nails-down-a-blackboard screeches alternating with a horrible cooing. The distended belly rippled from inside with the tiny faces of its erstwhile prey, many human; trapped, pleading or warning.

Miles stood, and put forth his hand with ritual severity, the middle nail over the index finger, and called out, his voice harbouring a new note of command.

-   Demon!

Nobody was in any way minded to contradict this assessment. Then Malcolm sprang to his feet and joined in, fingers pointed at the ceiling, thinking that this must be how these things are done.

- Demon!

After looking for confirmation from each other, the whole group leapt up and pointed accusingly at the arachnid, cosmic horror, whose legs continued to wave menacingly, its bloated body dripping pus, its degenerate head weaving and turning in eldritch circles as its eyes grew wider with hatred then narrowed to vengeful slits, while its vile and spotted tongue licked hungrily at the air. Miles led the group in a call-and-response that left no doubt as to his intentions.

- Out, demon, out!

- *Out, demon, out!*

- Begone, creature of the night!

- *Begone, creature of the night!*

- Demon, return to the waste and desolate place whence you have come to plague us!

- *Demon, return to the waste and... Malc what was the last bit again?*

- Out, demon, out!

- *Out, demon, out!*

- Begone, vile entity!

- *Begone, vile entity!*

- Demon, confess your true name!

- *Demon, confess your true name!*

- Demon that called itself Kenneth McLeod, I command you, tell us your true name!

- *Demon that called itself Kenneth McLeod, I - I mean we,*

command you, tell us your true name!

The creature slavered and howled balefully, tongue smacking and dribbling, eyes glowing with a venomous and cornered hatred, but blurred now, at bay. Rotating, in contrary directions, both head and body in a final *danse macabre*, whirling its legs as if speared, the hideous thing convulsed, vomiting bile and a foul black smoke, redolent of the cemetery. Then it sighed, and gave answer.

> - *OK. I give in. The name's McKellar. Kenneth McKellar.*

This was met with silence and furrowed brows. The thing tried again.

> - *I didnae want to get confused with the singer. You know - the singer, Kenneth McKellar. Paisley's finest. The greatest tenor that ever walked the stage of the Glasgow Alhambra….I didnae think I was in that league.*

Matron was the first to risk a rejoinder.

> - Never 'eard of 'im.

> - *What! Is nothing sacred? The greatest of Scottish singers, star of Decca records, Kenneth McKellar. Evidently before your time, lassie. 'Just a Song at Twilight'? 'It's All Just a Longing for my Ain Folk'? 'The Auld Hoose'? Not even 'The Auld Hoose'. Aw, come on. Gis a break. Can ye no manage one chorus?*

The thing called McKellar tried a few bars, hopefully. Everyone winced a little, less at the sight of the creature than at the octave jumps, then shook his or her head.

> - *Och, what's the point. Standards have crumbled to an historic low. The reference points are dust and ashes. That's it. My day is done…*

With great difficulty and more than a few sticky moments, the creature made its way falteringly down the wall, then hesitated for a moment over the settee, one hairy leg testing the air, gently and slowly, in all ways but the visual a snowbound Victorian orphan left out on the moor, tapping softly on the cottage door at midnight, fearing never again to be admitted by genteel company. It continued to wait, tentatively stroking the air with a mournful tenderness. Nobody moved. All looked elsewhere except Laura, who feigned sleep. The thing slowly let its skull drop onto its chest. Silently, it began to cry.

Eventually Matron weakened and shuffled along the sofa. The creature sat down next to her carefully, keeping all squeaks and pus-exudations to the bare minimum and trying not to draw attention to itself. It attempted to fold its legs demurely, but with evident discomfort. First one and then another hairy limb proved surplus to requirements and draped awkwardly over the arm of the sofa, or was held in the air like an unheeded question mark. On the far side of Matron, Laura continued to recline, her eyes closed. Malcolm and Miles were both staring at her pneumatically animated contours, at least until Becky abruptly reoriented Miles' attentions.

- *I cannae go on like this. My life has fallen into the sere and yellow leaf. My little race is run.*

This was met with silence. Then Becky, who had had more than enough, erupted.

- Kill him off, Miles. Despatch him, whatever. Get the scimitar. Just so long as he goes. I can't allow him back in the flat. Either kill him, or force him to get a life, and look after himself. Either way, he can't ever be allowed back here. He's banned. Look what he's done to the carpet.

Miles pondered. He scrutinised Kenneth, in the manner of a social services professional, evidently trying to put all he knew behind him in order to essay an impartial assessment. Then he put his fingertips together, and asked the group for their views, in turn.

- John?

The Librarian cleared his throat, weighing alternatives, then offered the group his considered opinion.

- Miles, I may be flying a kite here, but there's a lot of interest just now in oral history. This…man's…circumstances are sufficiently unusual to make it worthwhile to interview him and tape the results. I'm afraid I can't offer help, personally. Sadly my audio grant has been cut. Plus…well, I have to be honest.

- Please. I think honesty is what's required, all round.

- There's a secondary agenda, with oral history. It's supposed to be illustrative of a time with which we might otherwise lose contact, and there I think he's probably got quite a lot to offer. But oral histories are also, tacitly, supposed to be uplifting, in terms of an implied social agenda. I don't think, on the basis of what I've seen this evening, that he really meets the criteria. Sorry, Mr McLeod.

- *The name's McKellar.*

- Mr McKenna.

As a fresh emanation of acidic pus sizzled on the carpet, the creature strove to cover it with one arachnid foot, a move accomplished with more pathos than dignity.

- Matron?

- Well, I've been thinking while the Librarian here was saying his piece. Fair's fair, you know what I mean, and I do think we live in a society that puts too high a premium on good looks, glamour and all that. Some of them supermodels just look half-starved, to me. There's got to be room for, well, people who are *different.*

The creature slowly turned its skull towards her as, for the first time, a flicker of hope dawned in the rheumy, bloodshot eyes. Matron scrutinised him objectively.

- But, nah. He's not English. He's not from round here, he's from Scotland or Liverpool or one of them places up there. Kill him.

- Thank you, Matron. Laura?

Laura was half way to pointing an inflammatory fingernail at the creature when Becky slapped her hand down. She sighed, producing and then lighting a cigarette, which Becky smartly removed from her lips. Laura stared darkly into space for a moment, then slowly turned her heavy, jaded eyes towards Becky, in silent anticipation of the moment that would surely come, and the pleasurable ways in which she would fill it. The creature stared hopelessly at the carpet.

- Malcolm?

The latter furrowed his brow, pursed his lips, placed his fingers in a church steeple formation, peered up at the still slightly messy ceiling, and attempted to impress his research supervisor.

- His problem is essentially linguistic. It's the old word-thing dichotomy. There's a gap, for Kenneth, between words and the things to which they refer. Of course, that's true for everyone – words can depict, sketch, signal, but never *be* the thing to which they refer. Except in the case of magic, whose spells and formulae conjure the thing into existence, conflating sign and referent, closing the gap.

It occurred to Miles that if Malc ever finished his PhD, they'd better block out a whole day for the oral defence.

-   Kenneth's habitual discourse, *per se*, is unusually broad-spectrum – in terms of vocab, say, or cultural allusion – not that anyone here is old enough to get the allusions…

Kenneth winced. The others were growing restive. Miles tried to remember where the box from *Mr Machen's Magic Shop* had got to, while Matron quietly broke wind and John Spendrift began casting around for the book.

-   …but he's words, he's a creature of words. Not things.

Malcolm looked puzzled, having lost himself as well as the group. It was Kenneth who broke the silence.

-   *Polish me off. I've had enough. I ask of you just one single, final favour.*

Becky looked at him with the deepest suspicion, but Miles indicated that the group should hear him out. The creature McKellar had become almost sheepish in tone.

-   *The book. Could I possibly just hold it, for a second? It can't matter, not now. If it burns me, if it spurns me: so be it.*

Miles pondered for a moment.

-   Yes. I don't see what harm it can do.

He walked across the room and then approached Kenneth McKellar, the box under one arm, and the book in the hand he extended.

-   Here.

The creature hesitated, first putting out a hairy hand then letting it fall again. Suddenly he snatched the book and held it triumphantly aloft, then slowly brought it down and handed it, with reluctance, to Becky.

- *Could you… Would you mind, darlin', what with my disability…*

Becky sighed, took it from him and opened the book at random. Staring in growing disbelief, she turned page after page, and gasped.

- Miles? Miles! There's nothing in it! The pages are all blank.

- Mmm.

John Spendrift, unconscious of his open mouth, took the book from her, looked, and groaned.

- It's a printer's dummy. Look, someone's pencilled the word *essai* on the flyleaf. It's a mock-up, made prior to printing. Printers used to do it to check whether the design of the cover was perfectly straight, or might need to be cropped.

- Yes. A test pressing, as my father used to say of some of his vinyl acquisitions. Not even that, really.

Given all that had occurred, Miles seemed curiously unbothered, certainly much less troubled than Kenneth, Becky and John Spendrift, who all exclaimed different things at once. All Miles heard was a mondegreen, to the tune of what does it matter, now. He shrugged, and tried to explain.

- It was a good book. It took me somewhere. It was there, when I needed it. What else could a reader want of a book? Even if, come to think of it, the reader in this case was the writer. *May* have been the writer. But maybe I've got it wrong. You say it's a printer's dummy now. Well maybe there never was anything in it. To tell the truth, I'm no longer sure. I used to know reams of it off by heart. But did I, really? The words kept changing…

They looked at him in stunned silence.

- Anyway, whatever, I don't need it anymore. Beautiful cover though, don't you think?

Yes, John Spendrift thought, with a certain melancholy, it's a fine period piece. It will still look the part. Under glass. Beneath the sightless gaze of Queen Victoria.

- *I just want to go, now. I want it to end.*

- Words and things. Goodbye, Kenneth. Safe journey.

While their attention was all on the book entitled, so aptly, *Transmutations*, they had failed to see Miles produce the oversized silver duelling pistol from its box. Then they moved aside instinctively, and tightened eyes in anticipation of the bang. It never came, yet it did come, as Miles pulled the trigger and, as word became thing, the small flag unfurled that read in outsized letters, *Bang! You're Dead!*

Just then, the door opened. Something about the face of the woman who entered caused everyone to avert his or her gaze. Meg was pushing a hospital gurney. With gentleness but also with uncommon, in fact supernatural strength, she carefully lifted the body of her brother, who in death had now reverted to his human appearance, and set him down on the white coverlet. Gently, she patted it into place, then kept her palms for a moment on his cheeks, and bent to kiss, solemnly, his forehead.

- *What a shame, eh. Never mind, you're going home, now. The party's over. The children all have to go home too, do they not? Here's your palanquin, Ken. Kenneth, my love. My big brother. My dear dead king.*

She looked once at the assembled company, without rancour. It was over. Slowly and with head bowed, Meg drew the gurney back into a corridor to elsewhere, cold astral light lifting them both from human view, cold flames seemingly flickering from the corridor to where they were headed, an icily choral note fading in dead air. The door closed softly, of its own accord.

Matron was the first to rise.

- If you'll excuse me. The Captain will be wondering what's become of me.

John Spendrift slipped the book into his pocket, as Laura looked for a moment at Becky, then pursed her lips, and rose to go. Malcolm also looked at Becky, who moved a single eyebrow with sufficient force to lift him at once to his feet.

- The door's stuck. It's jammed.

Matron yanked hard with both hands, but the door would not give. Miles frowned and went to try it, unsuccessfully. Then the lights flickered on and off. Moments later, the only light in the room came from the television, as a familiar voice delivered its parting gift, the huge dome of a head filling the screen.

- *You can all relax, folks. I'm dead. Honest Injun. This is one I made earlier. My parting gift is a novel twist on a new concept. Actually it's a shameless rip-off of someone else's idea, but in the place I hope I'll be occupying by the time you see this, I don't think the laws of copyright apply. Welcome to The House. Welcome to the first, and very possibly the last episode of BIG DADDY!*

The bathroom door flew open. This time the voice came from the bathroom mirror.

- *How long before Laura takes out Miles' bitch? What's to become of Matron's ample dimensions, after weeks pass, with no nourishment other than tap water? Or will cannibal activity have shed its taboo by that point? What does a Librarian taste like? Who cares? You will, after days in each other's company, smelling each other's smells, sick of each other's whining voices, desperate to escape your sealed vault. Your communal sarcophagus.*

The logo of a giant solar eye filled the television screen.

- *Let's fast forward a little. And remember, it's good to talk. Any time you feel like a wee moan, remember Big Daddy is only as far away as the bathroom mirror. Any ideas you want to run by me – anything eating away at you – sorry, my phrasing is so inept, we're all descended from Neander- thals on the Celtic fringe - but aye, sexual transgression, going for your friends with a knife or fork just for jolly, not even as mains or an* hors d'oeuvre, *that kind of bright idea, I'm around. I'm not going anywhere. More to the point, neither are you. Now, just a few housekeeping rules. If a fire alarm sounds, it's not a test. It's for real, and you'll all burn to death. If Laura hasn't flipped and done a piece of work on you by that point. And, to add piquancy and alleviate the boredom, one of you will be voted off. Each week. Right off. Habits, accents, all become tedious after a while. In the dark. But there will be music…which will come on automatically every time someone falls asleep.*

Hip-hop, played at ear-splitting volume, drowned out their screams.

16

They were experiencing some difficulty in finessing the list of invitees to the wedding. The relatives not seen for many years, but who could still take offence if not invited. The transatlantic airfares neither they nor the invitees could easily afford; the ex-workmates, ex-partners, everything newly aligned. Laura Winthrope's name was, by telepathic agreement, never raised. The final hour of that dreadful evening still lingered in the memory. The sixty minute opening episode of *Big Daddy* still caused Becky and Miles to wake up screaming. It had terminated only when an even bulkier and even more unlikely *deus ex machina*, the three hundred pound ghost of blues legend Howlin' Wolf, had trampled down the door and liberated the captives.

Malcolm Coates could no longer even glance at a television. He was spending much of his time half-listening to the radio, while staying up far into the night to finish his thesis. Mind you, some of the messages I've begun to receive from this thing are on the strange side, he thought, twiddling the Bakelite knob to find his new favourite radio show, 'The Witching Hour'.

- The Hurlingham Club? Don't they do wedding receptions?

- I doubt we can afford it.

- Won't know unless we ask. They're bound to have a website. I'll check.

Miles moved away from her, and walked through the open doorway to his study, where she saw him in part-profile, opening the lid of his laptop. Out of the corner of her vision Becky caught the magnesium flare of light across the screen, and for a split-second thought she glimpsed on it a cartoon figure of a coyote, or perhaps a jackal.

- Ow! What was that? Ow!

- You OK, Miles?

- My eye hurts a bit. Some kind of screen malfunction. Maybe the battery expired.

- Miles, are you sure you're OK?

- Not sure. I think so. Bit dizzy.

- Shall I just go and phone the Hurlingham Club?

- The What Club?

- You know, we were just talking about the reception…

- We were?

- *Miles!*

Becky stared in terror at the gangling and amiable figure standing in the doorway, who took off his scholarly glasses, and blinked at her, shyly, all assertiveness gone.

- Sorry, Becky. No. I don't remember.

17

Over the intervening days before their wedding, Becky's own memory of recent events shifted into a form of rewind as she searched for an explanation of what had really happened. The book, the famous book, that they had staggered through the heat of Death Valley to bring back to London, turned out to have nothing in it. Quite literally, there were no words left to say what she and Miles had been through, and for what. That absence of words on the page started to pull the rug of credibility from under so much of what had preoccupied them, which now seemed to belong to a fantasy life, lived by someone Becky knew terribly well, but who was no longer quite her.

They had spent so much time together on this sofa, looking at photographs of places both wanted to visit, places to soak up and explore together, stepping out into the sunshine of some magical city of new light. But magic had lost its savour; it smacked of untrustworthy fantasy, and on the verge of the most serious practical step in her life thus far, Becky wanted to be sure that the boards on which she would take that next step would stay real. She remembered, or thought to herself now that she half-remembered, travelling through a photograph into a walk through New York City with Miles. She remembered that while everything around and in front of them seemed perfectly solid, when she looked behind there was – nothing. It all melted into air. Now she couldn't shake off an uncomfortable sensation that she too had been like a character in a movie or story, only real for that time, and then, well, she thought, if that's Magic – I'm not sure I want it.

But perhaps there was magic at work, after all; magic with a small 'm'. We can't be the only people who've wrapped ourselves round each other on a sofa like this one, pulled out a book of photos or a Rough Guide, and thought, wouldn't it be great to go there. See the Big Apple. And pluck when time and tides are done, the silver apples of the moon, the golden apples of the sun. Who was it wrote that? I forget.

She heard Miles put his key in the door, enter the apartment, and close it. When he stepped into the room she took him in at a glance, remembered all over again in a flash of love the pepper and salt hair, the clothes, always a lot of stylish black, the hirsute wrists, the elegant hands, the slow smile and the somehow, these days, faintly empty eyes. He suddenly looked very like his father Simon, on the basis of the photos she had seen. Had almost been him, at some level that she couldn't fathom and probably now would never need to. Something had happened to him too. The dates never quite fitted, the decades, and destinations; clearly something had been done to him, but many people seem to tire of the work they do, feeling that it was somehow done to them, that it used them up – particularly that generation. Home from the War. They didn't want to talk. Didn't want to remember.

Miles threw himself down on the sofa next to Becky, kissed her and idly pulled a volume of photos of Manhattan from a teetering ziggurat of books on this and that. His attention was held by the Chrysler Building, seen from the West Forties near Fifth Avenue, its cloud-capped tower only faintly visible in a rainy mist.

- Be great to actually go there, Becky, don't you think? What a sheltered life your husband-to-be has lived. The academy. Then that strange bookstore, off Tottenham Court Road. Nearly thirty and never been to New York!

A little of the rainy mist seemed to have travelled to the corner of Becky's vision, but she brushed it aside, took Miles' hand in hers, and smiled brightly.

18

One of the curious aspects of a wedding day is that the bride and groom get to see everyone, but talk properly to no one, including each other. Everyone of significance in the lives of both who is physically capable of travel is brought to the same spot, on the same day, and at considerable expense, so that a new distance from all those people can be established. In this sense the day is perhaps symbolic of the married state, into which small world the couple retreat, in a way silent henceforth, or at least possessed of a new opacity, sometimes a mystery, to the outside. Ancillary mysteries always come to light on the day itself or during its preparation, as when Maya, who Becky had asked to be bridesmaid, had to ask in turn who would look after her daughter, who then duly became second bridesmaid. The little girl would bring as a wedding gift a spherical paperweight, a bride and groom standing in a snowstorm, but decide on impulse not to give it, playing with it thoughtfully instead amid the forest of smartly dressed knees, beneath the main table.

Mysterious also is the capacity of a wedding, which has as its focus two people only, to trigger massive changes in the lives of the applauding onlookers. Unbeknownst to bride or groom, three couples would subsequently date the beginning of their break-up to that bright day, as would one individual his coming out, following an unanticipated but exciting encounter behind the tent. In a sense, the celebration of new union ages everyone. The immensity of it weighs quietly but heavily. In any case, Miles appeared to have less and less to say. He seemed gentled by time or by something that had happened, or so thought some of the old crowd; that spark, that something magical Miles once had, seemed to have gone. Perhaps he feels the same way about us. While she mourned inwardly, Becky had little time to dwell on anything but the wedding. She felt sure that getting married was the right thing to do. She loved him. Would love him. And Miles would make a great father.

And so violets and leaves of vine curved round the pillars in the tent, on a beautiful September day in Chelsea. Some of the hats rivalled in tiered magnificence the cake, which proved resistant to cutting. Having agonised over possibilities ranging from a fulsome meringue to a dark suit, Becky had opted in the end for classical whiteness, long gloves, and a necklace of moonstones belonging to her great grandmother, which, although of modest origins, had by day's end been up-scaled by rumour into a priceless heirloom.

Frank, the bride's father, seemed a touch overwhelmed, most of all to himself, though he could not have articulated precisely why. His angular frame somewhat confined by a new and rather tight suit, he slightly mangled a speech written for the most part by his wife Suse, but charmed all present, if only because to British eyes he was one of the recognizable and reassuring kinds of American. Everyone would remember his piercing blue eyes, which of course were as brown as his daughter's, and as he spoke, many of a certain age thought amiably, 'James Stewart', while Suse thought how lined, and Becky how handsome he looked. The bride was less enamoured of the best man's speech. Philip rose to his feet, resplendent in cummerbund, floral bow-tie, blinding gold Rolex and other accoutrements aimed consciously or otherwise at upstaging the groom. He succeeded in proving yet again to Miles how little his brother knew him, baffled the assembled company with a risqué anecdote from which he decided to excise the punch-line at the last moment, and, congenitally unable to speak for any length of time without reverting to his own career, closed with a mandarin and overly technical assessment of the importance of complex derivatives to the new world order. Becky clapped with visible delight, thinking him a complete idiot, while Miles' feelings of detachment and introversion, with which he had begun his day, became lost for a moment in the effects of champagne, and the reassuring sensation of suppressed rage that his brother had been effortlessly able to induce the whole length of their lives.

Post-trifle, he did the rounds, thinking to mix and mingle while the elderly were still just about awake, and the children still cheerfully rowdy, not yet tearful. A pinstripe suited figure emerging from the shadows was an unexpected, if welcome sight.

- Mr Boxer! You made it! I'm so pleased. We wanted to invite you, but of course we didn't know where to send....

- The name is *Fleet,* Miles. Actually it's John Jarvis-Fleet, but that's a bit of a mouthful, so I generally shorten it. For many decades with the Hong Kong police, then private detective, in essence. Retired. We're playing down the Redidivus days. Probably for the best, all round. But – here's my card – always interested in a little part-time work. Any work, any time. *Any* time.

Mr Fleet-Boxer-Machen patted the groom's elbow fondly, but Miles wanted, suddenly, completely, not to be here, indeed not to be anywhere. Not to have a past, not to have obligations; neither to owe, nor be owed; not to have done, or contemplate doing, one single thing of significance. With part of his being he wished simply to sleepwalk through the rest of his life, though another part of him abruptly missed his mother and father, who he suddenly wanted by him.

The moment froze. The two figures, one holding a business card, one frowning and not taking it, stood immobile for a moment in time as if in the act of being photographed by an invisible third party. A young but rumpled individual with hair like iron filings, who looked as if he had stepped out of a different narrative, did in fact watch them intently for a moment, but was soon obscured by the crowd. Then Miles himself turned abruptly, and stalked off. Nothing in his expression was legible. Still proffering his card to empty air, Mr Fleet-Boxer-Machen watched his back, smiling at something, as patient as ever, and perfectly unperturbed.

Completely out of sorts, Miles realized that he had walked in a complete circle back to the place where he had left Mr Boxer, without saying a thing to a living soul. He caught sight of Becky, who he felt had been taken away from him by her wedding. In an instant he knew that he wanted all this to end, wanted everyone to leave, and, most of all, wanted to be alone with her. He opened his mouth to call, but could not speak or see for a long moment. Claustrophobia threatened, until he had wiped the snow of confetti from his lips. He thought he might have swallowed some. Maya and her daughter giggled, and threw some more.

- I think Zeke has something to say.

Zeke cleared his throat, and looked around before speaking. Nearby a beaming young man in a hoodie was busy chatting up a passing waitress while his companion lifted drinks from her tray. Hearing a slight commotion, Becky, who had joined the circle, glanced back to the main table, where her younger sister Ellen had clearly just slapped the face of a slightly older version of Miles in a banker's suit, cummerbund and floral bow.

- Come on, Zeke. We told you what to say.

- Miles, on behalf of the group…

- What group?

Miles looked at them severely.

- *The* group. We – well, first off, congratulations, and have a great honeymoon in New York…

- How did you know that? It's supposed to be a secret. I hadn't even told Becky…

Zeke blushed and stammered an apology, while Maya and Becky looked innocently up at the sky.

- Well, anyway – I'm really sorry about that – but anyway, when you're back, you know, from your honeymoon, in wherever, well we're ready. Any time.

- But ready for what, Zeke?

- Ready to help, Miles. Can help. Ready for work.

Maya had the last word, as Becky looked at them all adoringly, and the groom gazed through them all inscrutably, miles ahead.

- We're just saying we're here, if something comes up.

Maya waited, then shot him a tart look – for the time being at least, disappointed.

- *If* you decide to get your memory back, that is. If not, be happy. Your call. Just say the word. Miles.

Miles ran his hand through his hair. He needed fresh air. And a little time to myself. Am I being rude? Can't I be rude, at my own wedding? He shot a glance back at the group, but they had forgotten him now, were wholly the bride's people, busy fawning on Becky and exclaiming at the novelty of a white dress at a wedding as loudly as if she'd been wearing a tiger skin.

19

That's odd, I never clocked that. There's another tent. I thought we only paid for the one? Well, one's mind has certainly been on other things. Maybe this other tent isn't anything to do with our wedding. The river looks so beautiful today. Turning away from the dark opening, he looked towards the almost-Autumn sun, and the silver and gold discs and rings of light flung lavishly on this placid confluence of the River Thames. Miles walked a little further, along the green edge, and then, feeling more composed but a little thirsty, passed into the tent. Becky's busy with her own people. Five minutes won't matter.

The grass still smelled newly mowed, under the candy-striped awning. His eyes took a while to adjust to the darkness, as a coloured after-image flickered in his retina. There was seemingly no one inside, save for a cocktail lounge pianist playing chords softly to himself, ruminating, and the barman, an unusually tall and bulky man, face in shadow. The small tent fronted a trio of mirrors, in which Miles could see himself advancing, a trifle self-conscious in his morning suit.

- Congratulations, sir. What can I get you?

- Thank you. I think I'll have…

He smiled, as the bearded pianist, of whom he could see little but his hat and silhouette, stayed with the chords he was exploring, but morphed them into a BeBop jazz anthem – now, what was the name. Miles smiled. Zeke used to love that one. He played it to me so many times, I remember hearing it once in a dream. Funny what you remember and what you don't. Miles looked absently out to the Thames, where in the play of light he noticed a cyclist on a distant towpath, a couple walking hand in hand with a toddler. On the water a rowing boat was briefly visible, but then gone, beneath a weeping willow. The chords had morphed yet again, as he turned to place his order with the barman.

- Sorry. I think I'll have a…

- A large Kentucky Bourbon on the rocks. Certainly, sir.

The barman, who was already moving away, gestured downward to the drink that had already materialised on the bar. Curious, thought Miles. Well, sure, bourbon. And on the rocks, why ever not? He raised the glass to his lips.

- The groom, I believe. All the best, man.

As the barman turned his back to dry some glasses, Miles, puzzled, looked into the mirror in front of him, and saw in its somewhat smoky light three men in straw boaters smiling and raising their glasses, behind his shoulder. Those old-fashioned suits! Zoot suits, was that the phrase. The youngest had eyes that bounced light off the tall glass and somehow spun it. It was his turn to speak.

- To the bride and groom. Here's to the future. And while we're on that subject, Miles…

Whatever he said next was drowned out by the third man's coughing. As the three men laughed, two patting the third on the back, Miles caught their mood and held it. Must remember to get them a round of drinks before I leave the tent. And I don't even know them, at least I don't think I do. Do I? He turned round to look at them face to face. In the space of that split second they had gone. But now the pianist too had moved on, and was playing that most moving tune, Irving Berlin's *Remember,* as only Monk could play it. So Miles did.

Author's Notes

You're Not Dead was begun in Los Angeles in 2009, and completed in London and Cambridge in 2015.

For the idea of linking the memory theatre and metaphysical philosophy of Robert Fludd to the work of Harry Smith, I am indebted to Robert Cantwell's book on the Folk Revival, *When We Were Good* (Harvard UP, 1996). Further information on Smith can be found in Perchuk and Singh, eds., *Harry Smith: The Avant-Garde in the American Vernacular* (Getty Research Institute, 2010).

The studio conditions in which Charley Patton made his 1929 recordings are described in the booklet accompanying *The Definitive Charley Patton* (Catfish Records, 2001), and are used suggestively in an essay, 'Objectivist Blues: Scoring Speech in Second Wave Modernist Poetry and Lyrics' by Charles Bernstein, in *Attack of the Difficult Poems* (Chicago UP, 2011). To the best of my knowledge the various recordings mentioned in the novel are all available, with the exception of the songs of Felix Manto, though a boxed set is thought to be in preparation.

GW
2015